"I WAS HOPING TO SEE YOU AGAIN."

Seven words that made Daisy's heart skip a beat and stirred a slow heat in the pit of her stomach that quickly ignited an answering fire in her loins. Flushed with anticipation, her handbag clutched tightly in one hand, she turned, ever so slowly, to face him.

He was just as handsome as she remembered. His eyes were just as dark, his smile just as devastating. Tonight he wore a thigh-length black leather coat over a dark green shirt and khaki pants.

Canting his head to one side, he held out his hand. "I think they're playing our song."

She hadn't even realized the band was playing, or that it was the same tune they had performed the night before. With no thought to refuse, Daisy dropped her handbag on a recently vacated table, then stepped into Erik's embrace as if she had been doing it all her life.

Other titles available by Amanda Ashley

Published by Kensington Publishing Corporation

EVERLASTING KISS

Amanda Ashley

ZEBRA BOOKS
Kensington Publishing Corp.
http://www.kensingtonbooks.com

ZEBRA BOOKS are published by

Kensington Publishing Corp.
119 West 40th Street
New York, NY 10018

All Kensington titles, imprints and distributed lines are available at special quantity discounts for bulk purchases for sales promotion, premiums, fund-raising, educational or institutional use.

Special book excerpts or customized printings can also be created to fit specific needs. For details, write or phone the office of the Kensington Special Sales Manager: Attn. Special Sales Department. Kensington Publishing Corp., 119 West 40th Street, New York, NY 10018. Phone: 1-800-221-2647.

Zebra and the Z logo Reg. U.S. Pat. & TM Off.

ISBN-13: 978-1-4201-0443-1
ISBN-10: 1-4201-0443-8

First Printing: February 2010

10 9 8 7 6 5 4 3 2 1

Printed in the United States of America

For Wade
and
Jessica

His voice
slides over me
like black velvet
warm
and soft

making me think
of long
dark nights
and hot
desire.

I lean into him
wanting more
wanting to feel
his breath
on my face

hear his voice
whisper
that he loves
only
me.

Take me . . .
take me now.
The words rise up
like a plea
a prayer.

Wrapped in
his warm embrace
I am his
only his
and he is mine.

Together
we soar upward.
Together
we die the little death
that is love.

Chapter 1

Daisy O'Donnell's compass wasn't much good for finding north or south; but then, she wasn't lost or trying to navigate her way around the world. She was hunting vampires, and her little silver compass with its bright golden needle worked perfectly fine for that. Although it wasn't really a compass. More like a GPS for locating the resting places of the Undead. All she had to do was drive down the street and follow the needle, which turned bright red when she was within a few feet of an occupied lair.

There was no dearth of locations for vampires to hide in the greater Los Angeles area these days. She had found lairs inside shallow caves up in the hills, in dusty attics and cobwebby basements, in ancient cemeteries, abandoned buildings, and foreclosed tract homes.

Daisy felt a rush of satisfaction as the needle shimmered and quivered, telling her she was getting close to the daytime resting place of one of the Undead. The vampire she was currently hunting had made its lair inside an old wine cellar in an abandoned restaurant in downtown LA.

Daisy paused outside the lair, her nose wrinkling with

distaste as she sprayed herself with Scent-B-Gone, a concoction guaranteed to mask her distinctive scent from all but the most powerful vampires. The spray itself evaporated within an hour or two, leaving nothing behind.

The door to the wine cellar creaked like something out of an old Vincent Price movie as Daisy pried it open with a crowbar. Leaving the crowbar outside, she stepped through the doorway, turned on her trusty four-cell flashlight, and cautiously made her way down the rickety wooden stairs. She swept the beam from right to left, uttered a soft sound of satisfaction as the light disclosed a pale pink casket in the far corner.

Her feet made hardly a sound as she walked across the dusty cement floor and raised the lid. The vampire, a young female, slept inside. Her name was Tina. Daisy recalled a well-known maxim that claimed old age and treachery would overcome youth and skill. She didn't know if that was true among mortals, but it definitely applied to vampires. They got stronger and meaner as they grew older. And unlike their young counterparts, really old vampires weren't completely helpless or unaware of what went on around them during the day, which made hunting the old ones doubly dangerous.

Although Daisy had done this sort of thing many times before, it always startled her to look at one of the Undead at rest, because they looked very dead indeed. The vampire lay on her back, her arms folded over her breasts. Her hair was dark brown; her skin beyond pale. Had Daisy been a bounty hunter who destroyed the Undead instead of a Blood Thief, she would have had to obtain proof of her kill, either a sample of blood, or—grisly thought—a hand or a finger. Of course, if the destroyed vampire was very old, the hunter had to gather its ashes, since that was all that was left after the ancient ones were dispatched.

After tucking the flashlight under her arm, Daisy pulled

a large syringe out of one of the deep pockets of her jacket, several small plastic bottles out of another, and got to work. There were vampire hunters who drained the Undead of their blood for fun and profit and then took their heads, and other hunters who destroyed vampires simply because of what they were.

Daisy didn't have the stomach for bounty hunting. Taking a head or driving a stake through the heart of an unconscious vampire was a nasty, messy business, and she couldn't forget that, no matter how horrid she thought vampires were, they had once been human. Still, there was good money to be made as a Blood Thief. She had earned a tidy fortune by selling vampire blood on the Internet. Do you have an injury that refuses to heal? Rub a little vamp blood on it. Got a cold that simply won't go away? Take two aspirins and a spoonful of blood mixed with the drink of your choice. Want a high that lasts all night? Vampire blood will do the trick with no ugly aftereffects, as long as you don't imbibe too much. An ounce enhances all the senses. Anything over that, and you probably won't wake up in the morning.

Daisy herself had never indulged. The mere idea of drinking blood, even if it was mixed with something more palatable, like a glass of fine red wine, was totally repugnant.

Daisy took a pint or so from a vein in the vampire's left arm, enough to fill her current orders, and tiptoed out of the cellar with the sleeping vampire being none the wiser. When Tina woke that night, she would know someone had siphoned some of her blood, but Daisy would be long gone by then.

After retrieving her crowbar from outside the cellar door, Daisy returned to her car. She stowed the bottles in the ice chest in the backseat, slid behind the wheel, and headed home. She didn't feel the least bit of guilt for what she had done. Why should she? Selling vampire blood wasn't against the law, and since vampires had no human rights and no legal recourse, there was nothing the Undead could do about it.

Unless they caught you.

And then all the laws and ordinances in the world weren't worth the paper they were written on.

Chapter 2

Tina usually roused with the setting of the sun, her mind and body alert. Tonight, she was overcome with a feeling of lethargy. Had she been mortal, she would have blamed it on not getting enough sleep, but she was a young vampire, compelled by a force beyond her control to rest from sunrise to sundown.

There could only be one answer to the overwhelming sense of weakness that engulfed her. The Blood Thief had preyed on her while she slept. A glance at the partially open door at the top of the cellar stairs confirmed her suspicion that her lair had been violated. She would have to find a new resting place. Craig had been pestering her to move in with him. Maybe it was time she did. He would protect her during the day.

Rising, she sniffed the air, hoping to catch the scent of the mortal who had dared enter her resting place uninvited, but there was no hint of anything out of the ordinary, no trace of soap or cologne, no human scent at all.

Feeling defiled, Tina left the wine cellar and went to visit her current mortal lover.

Craig didn't seem the least bit concerned when she told him what she thought had happened.

"You probably just imagined it," he said with a shrug. "After all, we went at it pretty hard before you left last night." He grinned at her. "I expect even a vampire would be a little tired after that."

"Maybe. But that doesn't explain the door. Someone forced it open. I didn't imagine that."

"If you're all that worried, why not mention it to Rhys?"

Tina nodded. Rhys Costain was her sire. He had brought her across two years ago. Her feelings toward him were somewhat ambivalent these days. The only reason she had asked for the Dark Gift was because she had fancied herself in love with Rhys, and because she had believed he loved her, too. She knew better now. Rhys had never loved her. He didn't love anyone but himself. But he was still her sire, sworn to protect her with his life, if necessary. And even though she hated to admit it, she still harbored feelings for him. How could she not? Of course, being a little older and a little wiser now, she realized that what she really felt for Rhys was lust, not love. Even though he was an old vampire, you couldn't tell it by looking at him. He had been turned a week shy of his twenty-first birthday. Tall and slim, well muscled without being bulky, he had short, spiked blond hair and dark brown eyes, eyes that never let you know what he was thinking or feeling.

Tina nodded again. "Maybe I will."

"You can talk to him later," Craig said, dragging her into his arms. "We've got better things to do now."

Tina smiled as Craig bared his throat. She would drink from him, and then he would drink from her. And after that . . . she closed her eyes as her fangs pierced his flesh. After that, they would make love all night long.

Chapter 3

The Crimson Crypt was the most popular Goth club in the greater Los Angeles area, especially on a Friday night. In addition to the ever-growing Goth crowd and LA's dwindling Undead population, the Crypt had become a popular hangout for up-and-coming Hollywood starlets, producers, musicians, and fans of the same.

Erik Delacourt grimaced as he made his way toward the bar, which was unique in its circular design. Made of polished black onyx, it stood in the center of the floor ringed by black leather bar stools. Three bartenders, all clad in black muscle shirts and tight black leather pants, waited on the customers at the bar; a handful of waitresses wearing black tank tops and short black leather skirts took orders from those sitting at the booths that lined two of the walls. A small square dance floor took up space on one side of the club; half a dozen pool tables were scattered near the back wall. Subdued lighting offered a measure of privacy to the rich and famous who sought anonymity in the club's dark corners.

Erik found an empty seat at the bar and ordered the house special. Glancing around the room, he spotted several celebrities holding court, as well as the drummer from a popular Irish band. Unlike Erik, the drummer, who was known only as Cougar to his fans, made no attempt to hide the fact that he was a vampire. Instead, he used the inherent charisma of their kind to his advantage. Many mortals, females especially, were drawn to the air of mystery and danger that clung to members of the Undead community.

Erik sipped his drink. It satisfied his physical thirst, but he found no pleasure in it. It was like hungering for milk and being given water, though in reality, he had no taste for either.

He had just ordered a second glass when a woman entered the club. A pretty woman in her midtwenties, with lightly tanned skin and heavily lashed green eyes. Her hair, a deep reddish brown, fell halfway down her back. She wore flat-heeled white boots, blue jeans, and a long white leather jacket over a white shirt. His nostrils flared as she passed by him on her way to a vacant stool not far from his.

Erik frowned. She was human, but she smelled of vampire. No doubt she was one of the dozens of human females who frequented the club, getting their kicks from rubbing elbows with the soon-to-be famous and the infamous. Or maybe she got off on letting vampires feed off her. Drinking vampire blood was all the rage now, though only the very rich could afford it. The thought of her feeding off him stirred his desire; the thought of him feeding off her aroused his hunger. He ran his tongue over the tips of his fangs, imagined himself bending over her neck, licking her skin, tasting her life's essence.

As if sensing his thoughts, she whirled around to face him.

She was lovely, young, ripe. Erik put aside the glass in his hand, no longer interested in its watered-down contents. Not when there was a possibility he could score something better. Something hot and fresh, directly from the source.

Daisy stared at the man sitting at the bar, felt a rush of heat engulf her from head to foot when his gaze met hers with such intensity, it was almost physical. Dressed all in black, he was long legged and broad shouldered, with thick black hair and the kind of rugged countenance that made a girl look twice. But it was his eyes that captured her attention. Deep, dark eyes that seemed capable of penetrating her innermost thoughts, of probing the depths not only of her heart, but her very soul.

Shaking off her fanciful thoughts, she took a seat at the bar and ordered a strawberry daiquiri. Even though she was no longer looking at the dark-haired man, she could feel the weight of his gaze resting on her. Without moving her head, she slid a sideways glance in his direction, felt a jolt of desire sweep through her when her gaze again met his. Never in all her life had she felt such a strong attraction to a complete stranger.

Her stomach knotted as he rose smoothly to his feet and walked toward her, although *walked* didn't really describe the way he moved. More like a jungle cat stalking its prey. The thought made her mouth dry and her palms damp. Her gaze darted toward the exit, but it was too late to escape. He was already standing in front of her. He was tall, she thought, looking up. Very tall.

"I'm Erik."

His voice, as deep as ten feet down, raised goose bumps on her arms.

He gestured at her glass. "May I buy you another drink?"

"No, thank you." Was that pitiful whimper her voice?

"Are you sure?"

Daisy nodded. What was wrong with her? She was behaving like some teenager who had just met her favorite rock star.

His gaze moved over her face, warming every place it touched. When he smiled, her heartbeat kicked up a notch.

Pull yourself together, Daisy, she chided. *It's not like you've never talked to a handsome man before.* So why did this one have her tongue tied in knots?

"I suppose a dance is out of the question?"

She felt her cheeks grow hotter as she imagined being in his arms. She was about to decline when she heard herself say, "I'd like that."

He looked as surprised as she was.

And then there was no more time for thought. He held out one large, well-manicured hand. After a moment's hesitation, she placed her hand in his. A shiver of awareness coiled in the pit of her stomach as his fingers closed over hers, and then he was leading her toward the small dance floor, drawing her into his arms. Long arms. Strong arms that made her feel protected and endangered at the same time.

She had watched numerous scenes in movies where couples danced and everything else faded away—Kathleen Turner and Michael Douglas in *Romancing the Stone*, Michael J. Fox and Julie Warner in *Doc Hollywood*, Amy Adams and Patrick Dempsey in *Enchanted*. As much as she had loved those scenes, she had always found them hard to believe. Until now. She wasn't aware of the music or the other couples on the floor; she wasn't aware of anything but the man holding her close. Too close, she thought, but feeling his body brush against hers felt so good, she had no inclination to object. He was tall and dark and decidedly masculine. Being in his embrace made her achingly aware of her femininity, of the delightful differences between male and female, of the way their bodies had been created to fit together, complementing each other.

Her only regret was that the music ended too soon. Or maybe just in time, she thought, because as sure as she knew her name, she knew what was coming next. He was going to ask her to go to his place, and she didn't think she was strong enough to refuse. Just thinking about being alone with him made her ache in places no man had ever touched.

Murmuring, "Thank you for the dance," she pulled her hand from his and all but ran out of the Crypt. She knew it was only her imagination, but she could have sworn she heard the sound of his amused laughter following her all the way home.

Daisy thought about Erik all the next day. In the shower. In the kitchen. At her computer. At the post office. His beguiling image seemed branded in her mind. The sound of his voice, low and sensual, played over and over in her head, as relentless as the theme from "It's a Small World" at Disneyland, although there had been nothing childish or fanciful in the way Erik's decidedly deep masculine voice had caressed her. Just thinking about him made butterflies dance in the pit of her stomach and brought a flush to her cheeks.

Admit it, Daisy thought, *you're as giddy as a high school girl with her first serious crush.*

She wished her best friend and confidante, Jennifer, still lived in LA, because she definitely needed someone to talk to about Erik, but Jennifer had married the love of her life last month, and after an extended honeymoon in Europe, would be moving to France with her new husband.

Daisy found herself daydreaming about a honeymoon with Erik while she did her laundry. She imagined the two of them in a romantic villa in Italy, walking along the canals, riding in a gondola, being serenaded by a handsome gondolier.

Later, she went outside to water the yard. What would Erik think of her home? It wasn't a very big place, certainly not very grand, but it was hers, a small two-story house painted white with bright yellow trim. In the spring and summer and sometimes into the fall, fat yellow roses bloomed on either side of the walkway. She didn't have much luck with other flowers, but her roses made her proud.

She thought about Erik while she ate dinner, and while putting her dishes in the dishwasher. Drat the man; no matter how hard she tried, she couldn't get him, or the sensual allure of his voice, out of her head. She tried to tell herself he couldn't be as gorgeous as she remembered, that his voice hadn't been *that* deep, that his touch hadn't been any different from any other man's. But to no avail.

Irritated with herself because she couldn't concentrate on anything else, she decided the only solution was to see him again and prove to herself that she had exaggerated the comeliness of both his appearance and his appeal. With that thought in mind, she changed into a pair of navy slacks and a white sweater and headed for the Crypt.

The nightclub was even more crowded tonight than it had been on Friday. Every booth was taken; the dance floor was jam packed; it was standing room only at the bar.

Daisy walked around the edge of the club, her gaze sweeping the sea of humanity, when her good sense returned. What on earth was she doing here, looking for some man she knew nothing about? And what if he was as drop-dead gorgeous as she remembered? She had met lots of good-looking men. Even dated a few. If there was one thing she had learned, it was that a handsome visage didn't always guarantee a pleasing personality.

With a shake of her head, Daisy started toward the exit. For months, her mother had been trying to set her up with "a nice young man." Irene O'Donnell had met Kevin O'Reilly at the local pub last Saint Patrick's Day and was convinced that Kevin was the perfect man for her only daughter.

Daisy sighed. Maybe her mother was right. Maybe it was

time to leave LA, go back to Boston, meet Mr. Perfect, settle down, and give her parents grandchildren.

And maybe not.

She was almost at the door when a deep male voice sounded from behind her.

"I was hoping to see you again."

Seven words that made Daisy's heart skip a beat and stirred a slow heat in the pit of her stomach that quickly ignited an answering fire in her loins. Flushed with anticipation, her handbag clutched tightly in one hand, she turned, ever so slowly, to face him.

He was just as handsome as she remembered. His eyes were just as dark, his smile just as devastating. Tonight he wore a thigh-length black leather coat over a dark green shirt and khaki pants.

Canting his head to one side, he held out his hand. "I think they're playing our song."

She hadn't even realized the band was playing, or that it was the same tune they had performed the night before. With no thought to refuse, Daisy dropped her handbag on a recently vacated table, then stepped into Erik's embrace as if she had been doing it all her life. The music was slow, with a deeply sensual beat that made her think of sweat-slick flesh and satin sheets.

Erik's gaze warmed her cheeks, and when he drew her body against his, every rational thought fled her mind. As she had the night before, Daisy followed his lead as if they had danced together a hundred times instead of only two. He was remarkably light on his feet for such a big man. Once, she glanced down to make sure his feet were touching the floor.

Daisy searched her mind for something witty to say to break the taut silence between them, but to no avail. She couldn't think coherently, not when he was holding her so close. He smelled of sandalwood and leather, two scents she knew she would forever associate with him in the future.

The song ended and another began.

His arm tightened around her waist, drawing her closer. "You never told me your name."

"What? Oh, it's Daisy."

A slow smile spread over his lips. "Daisy," he murmured with a nod. "A fair flower indeed."

His compliment as much as his smile brought a warm flush to her cheeks. His hand moved lightly up and down her spine, eliciting tiny sparks of excitement.

When the music ended, he led her off the dance floor. After retrieving her handbag, he led her toward the back of the club, obviously in search of an empty booth. There were none. Holding Daisy's hand, Erik stopped beside a booth occupied by two middle-aged men in business suits. No words were exchanged, but the men took one look at Erik and practically tripped over their feet as they vacated the booth and hurried away.

Daisy looked at Erik, wondering if she had missed something.

"After you," he said, gesturing for her to take a seat.

"I really can't stay," Daisy remarked as she scooted into the booth.

"Sure you can." His dark eyes glowed with amusement as he slid in beside her. "After all, you came here looking for me, didn't you?"

Heat bloomed in her cheeks. "Of course not!"

He lifted one expressive black brow. "No?"

"No."

"All right, little flower. Have it your way."

"You didn't come here looking for me, did you?"

"As a matter of fact, I did."

Flustered by his answer, she could only stare at him. She

didn't have a lot of experience with men. Because she was their only daughter, her parents had always been overly protective of her. The boys had been able to do pretty much whatever they wanted, but not Daisy. They had refused to let her date until she was sixteen, and then only once a week. Daisy had always believed it was due to the escapades of her two brothers that her parents insisted on meeting the young men she went out with. Not only did they insist the guys she dated call for her at the house, but they insisted they pick her up at the door. No honking the horn, or waiting in the car. Not only that, but her parents had given her a stringent midnight curfew. Daisy had argued that whatever she could do after midnight, she could do before midnight, but that hadn't swayed her mom and dad in the least. They had enforced the curfew until she turned eighteen. She had only had two serious relationships since then. The first had come to a screeching halt when she went to Stan's apartment and found him in bed with another woman; the second had ended when Blake refused to take no for an answer. Daisy's adamant refusal to go to bed with him had surprised them both. The night she had gone to Blake's condo, she had been certain she was ready to bid farewell to her virginity, certain that she wanted Blake to be the one to show her what all the fuss was about, but when the time came, she just couldn't do it. And it was all her mother's fault. *If a man really loves you,* her mother had said, *he will never ask you to surrender your virtue outside of marriage. Remember, once the deed is done, it can't be undone.*

After taking a deep breath, Daisy admitted, "I was looking for you, too."

"I'm glad we got that cleared up. Perhaps the next step would be a real date, where I pick you up at your house."

"Not until I know you better," she said primly.

"What do you want to know?"

"Your last name. Your age." He didn't look much older than her own twenty-four years, yet he seemed older, wiser. "What you do for a living."

"Delacourt. Thirty. Nothing." Nothing wasn't exactly the truth. Because he had lived a long time, and the nights could be lonely, he had pursued a number of hobbies before discovering he had a talent for painting. He had even sold a number of canvases through the years, which was why he didn't have to work. Currently, some of his paintings were on consignment at one of the city's finest galleries. He kept the rest of his canvases, and there were dozens, in one of the empty rooms in his house.

"Nothing?" she repeated. "What are you, a millionaire?"

"Not quite, just reasonably well off."

"You're not married, are you?"

"Would I be here with you if I were?"

She shrugged. "I don't know. Lots of men cheat on their wives."

"Lots of men aren't lucky enough to meet a girl like you."

Daisy's heart skipped a beat. The man definitely knew what to say, and when to say it.

The rest of the evening passed like something out of a romantic movie. They danced several times, talked about the music they liked and movies they had seen, and danced again.

Before she knew it, the club was closing and Erik was walking her to her car. She fumbled in her handbag for her keys, wondering if he would kiss her good night. When she pulled the keys from her bag, he took them from her hand, then drew her into his arms. "You didn't think I'd let you get away so quickly, did you?"

Daisy stared up at him, her heart pounding with anticipation as he backed her up against the car door, his body pressing lightly against hers. Her eyelids fluttered down as he bent his head toward her. He kissed her gently at first, the pressure of his lips gradually increasing as he deepened the kiss, his tongue sweeping over her lips before delving inside. She twined her arms around his neck, certain that if she didn't hold on tight, she would simply dissolve into a puddle of need at his feet.

When he took his mouth from hers, she felt a little light-headed, as if she'd had too much champagne to drink.

Brushing his knuckles across her cheek, he asked, "Will I see you tomorrow night?"

"I don't know." It was tempting, so tempting, yet there was something about him, something she couldn't quite put her finger on. Something . . . dangerous. Had those men in the booth sensed it, too? One look at his face and they had fled the scene.

"I'll be here at nine," he said, opening the car door for her.

Murmuring, "Good night," Daisy slid behind the wheel, then looked up at him as he closed the door.

She glanced in the rearview mirror as she pulled out of the club's parking lot. Erik stood in the driveway, his hands shoved into his pants pockets as he stared after her. And then, as if he had been swallowed up in the darkness, he was gone from her sight.

Daisy had no intention of going back to the Crypt on Sunday night. Instinctively, she knew that Erik was away the heck and gone out of her league. He was worldly wise in ways she wasn't. True, she was twenty-four years old, she lived alone, and she hunted vampires for their blood, but that didn't mean she knew how to handle a man like Erik Dela-court. She was willing to bet her new Manolos that he had been around the block more than once. Womanlike, she couldn't help wondering what he saw in her. She was pretty enough, but she wasn't beautiful. She had a nice figure, good hair and skin, but men didn't stop and stare when she walked by. Mostly, she was just average.

She found herself watching the clock all day long. At eight thirty, she hurried upstairs, changed her clothes, combed her hair, freshened her make-up, brushed her teeth, and practically ran out of the house.

She made it to the Crypt at nine fifteen.

Heart pounding, she stepped into the nightclub and glanced around the room, disappointment tugging at her heart when she didn't see him.

With a sigh, she made her way to the bar. Maybe he was late, too. Thinking she might as well have a drink while she waited, Daisy ordered a margarita. She nursed it for over half an hour; then, telling herself it was just as well that he hadn't shown up, she left the Crypt and headed for home.

It wasn't until she was getting ready for bed that the tears came. Daisy told herself she wasn't crying because Erik had stood her up. She was just depressed because she was missing her best friend. And even though she was happy for Jennifer and wished her all the best, she knew their friendship could never be the same, now that Jen was married.

Padding barefooted into the kitchen, Daisy fixed herself a cup of hot chocolate liberally sprinkled with marshmallows and told herself there was nothing to cry about.

But the tears kept coming just the same.

Chapter 4

Erik shifted restlessly in his chair. His internal clock told him he had missed his date with Daisy, but it couldn't be helped. Rhys had called a meeting of the Vampire Council and Erik had no choice but to attend. Rhys wasn't just his friend, he was the current Master of the West Coast vampires, a fact that Rhys never let Erik forget, just as he never let Erik forget that he, Rhys, was older, wiser, and stronger.

Erik glanced around. The house itself was just an empty shell. There were no carpets on the floors, no lights. Except for three large tan leather sofas and a couple of chairs, there was no furniture in the place. No pictures on the walls. A medieval sword sheathed in a leather scabbard hung over the fireplace. It wasn't merely for decoration. Rhys had used it on more than one occasion.

Rhys used the house as a meeting place to conduct vampire business; on occasion, he took his rest in the walk-in pantry that had been converted to serve his purpose.

Vampires rarely let anyone know the location of their lairs. As far as Erik knew, Rhys was the only one who knew where all of the others took their rest.

Besides himself and Rhys, there were seven other vampires gathered in the living room—five males and two females. Erik was acquainted with all of them to one degree or another. He trusted none of them, including Rhys, even though Rhys had been his closest friend for over two hundred years.

". . . time to do something," Damon was saying.

Damon had been a vampire less than ten years. Blond and blue eyed, he had been turned by his lover, Mariah, when he was seventeen. She had found Damon bruised and bloody, lying facedown in a culvert, a casualty in the war between rival gangs. Erik couldn't imagine what Mariah saw in the kid. He reminded Erik of a weasel.

As for Mariah, she had been Nosferatu longer than Erik though not as long as Rhys. She should have been stronger than Erik. Unfortunately, she had been turned by a young vampire, whereas Erik had been turned by one of the old ones. His sire's ancient blood gave Erik a distinct advantage in that he was stronger and more powerful than Mariah, even though she was older. She hated him for that. Erik grinned inwardly. Now that he thought about it, Mariah hated just about everyone.

"We've let this kind of thing go on for too long," Nicholas said, glancing around the room. Nicholas was a tall, angular vampire with wispy gray hair and blue eyes. He had been turned five years ago, when he was in his late seventies. Rumor had it that Nick had paid a vampire ten thousand dollars in gold to help him cheat death.

"Damon's right," Mariah agreed. She ran a well-manicured hand through her pale blond hair. "We should have put a stop to this as soon as it started."

Rupert, a handsome vampire who looked like a 1930s matinee idol, nodded. "Thanks to the Blood Thief and others like him, the Internet market for our blood is growing."

"Better they take your blood than your head," Erik re-

marked. They had been talking about the Blood Thief and
what to do about him for hours. Solutions were few and far
between, with the major consensus being to set a trap of some
kind. "I think we're worrying too much about this Blood
Thief. So he takes a pint or two. If you want to get a vendetta
going, why not go after the hunters?"

"Delacourt has a point," Saul agreed.

With his bright red hair, pencil-thin mustache, and flamboyant clothing, Saul looked less like one of the Undead than
any vampire Erik had ever met.

"Maybe so," Rhys said, "but the Blood Thief has tagged one
of mine." He glanced at Tina and smiled. "And I've promised
to avenge her."

Erik grunted softly. "If she'd made a more secure lair, it
wouldn't be necessary."

"She's young," Rhys retorted.

"Another mistake like that, and she won't get any older,"
Erik retorted.

"Enough, you two!" Mariah said impatiently. "This isn't getting us anywhere. The demand for our blood is spreading. I've
heard there are others like the Blood Thief in Chicago, New
Orleans, and St. Louis, and who knows where else. They're in-
vading our lairs, taking our blood, and in some cases, heads."

"We need to retaliate!" Damon said, his voice rising with
excitement. "Take out a few hunters."

"I agree, let's shed some blood!" Julius spoke up for the first
time. "We haven't had a good rumble in years." He pumped his
arm in the air, displaying the red and black snake tattoo that
seemed to slither down his left arm.

That was Julius's answer to everything, Erik thought, but
then, it wasn't surprising. A former drug dealer, Julius Romano
had been turned when he was twenty-three. With his short
brown hair and mild brown eyes, he had often passed himself

off as a high school kid when looking for new customers. Now that he was a vampire, he still preyed on the young and the innocent—the younger the better.

Rhys snorted. "Taking hunters out is sometimes easier said than done. And from what Tina told me, the Blood Thief didn't leave so much as a footprint behind. No scent, nothing."

Rupert shrugged. "Maybe Tina imagined the whole thing."

"I did not!" Tina exclaimed hotly.

Erik crossed his arms over his chest. It was almost eleven. If Daisy had gone to the Crypt, she had surely left by now. "This isn't getting us anywhere," he muttered. "I'm going home."

"Erik . . ." Rhys spoke mildly, but the warning was there, just the same.

But Erik wasn't listening. Moving with preternatural speed, he left Costain's house. Impatience, anger, and disappointment intensified his hunger and he preyed on the first lone mortal he encountered.

Later, strolling toward home, he told himself it was just as well that there had been a council meeting that night. The last thing he needed was to get involved with a mortal female like Daisy O'Donnell.

Chapter 5

Daisy went hunting the next afternoon. Driving through the city, she tried not to think about Erik, but the more she tried to put him out of her mind, the more firmly entrenched he became. She couldn't help wondering why he hadn't showed up. He didn't have a job, so he hadn't been working late. Maybe he had just decided she wasn't his cup of tea. Maybe he had arrived at the Crypt before nine and found someone he found more appealing. Or maybe he had lied about being married and his wife wouldn't let him out of the house.

She spent two hours driving up one street and down another, and at the end of that time, she had nothing to show for it. She glanced at the compass again. The needle remained gold, unmoving. Muttering, "Oh, well, you can't win them all," she turned the car around and drove into town. After picking up her mail at the post office, she had a quick lunch at the coffee shop, and then, on impulse, she decided to treat herself to a manicure and a facial before going home.

She felt better, inside and out, when she left the salon. There was nothing like a little pampering to chase away the blues.

Later, at home, she couldn't seem to settle down. She

wandered through the house, her thoughts constantly turning toward Erik. Every time she closed her eyes, she saw his face. Like it or not, his image seemed indelibly imprinted on her mind. Where was he now? Why hadn't he shown up?

"Stop it," she muttered. "You're not the first woman in this century to be stood up, and you won't be the last." But it hurt just the same.

She ate dinner, then turned on the TV and flipped through the channels. It must have been down-with-love night, because every movie channel featured ill-fated lovers, from Dracula and Mina to Heathcliff and Cathy.

With a wordless cry of frustration, Daisy tossed the remote on the coffee table. Drumming her fingers on the arm of the sofa, she glanced at her watch. It was almost ten o'clock. Was he at the Crypt, hoping she would show up? Maybe he had a good explanation for last night. Maybe he would have called if she had given him her number.

Chiding herself for being a hopeless fool, she grabbed her handbag and her keys and headed out the door.

The Crypt didn't do much business on a Monday night. Daisy sat at a table in the back of the room, an untouched margarita in one hand. There were perhaps a dozen people at the bar. The dance floor was empty. Three young men were shooting pool. Two women shared a table near Daisy's. The younger of the two was pouring out her heart to her friend. From what Daisy could overhear, the younger woman had just discovered her husband was being unfaithful.

Maybe Mr. Right didn't exist for anyone. Well, except for Jennifer, who was off on her honeymoon and, according to her last letter, having the time of her life with the love of her life. But who knew how long that would last? These days, some marriages were over almost before they began. Daisy sighed. If there was a Mr. Right in her future, she certainly wasn't going to find him in a place like this.

She glanced at her drink, still untouched, and decided she didn't need it. What she needed was to go to Boston and visit her family. Her parents had their differences and their disagreements, but they had managed to survive thirty-five years of married life without killing each other. Maybe that was the best you could hope for. Maybe she would take her mom's advice and go out with Kevin O'Reilly. And maybe she wouldn't.

And maybe it was time to call it a night. It was almost eleven.

She was reaching for her handbag when there was a subtle change in the atmosphere in the room. Even before she saw him walking toward her, Daisy knew Erik had entered the Crypt.

She clutched her handbag. Seeing him, she felt suddenly foolish. Why had she come here? He would know she had come here looking for him. How pathetic was that? Why hadn't she stayed home where she belonged, and let him come to her, if he had a mind to?

She would have fled, but there was nowhere to go, nowhere to hide. And then it was too late.

"Daisy."

Just her name, but hearing it on his lips made her stomach curl with pleasure. "Erik." She pressed her handbag to her chest. "I was just leaving."

"So soon?"

She shrugged. "It's late."

"Not really." His gaze moved over her, warming every place it rested. "At least give me one dance."

"There's no music." The band didn't play on Monday or Tuesday nights.

"There's always music when you're around," he murmured.

Daisy frowned as a slow ballad emanated from the jukebox.

How had that happened? No one had put any money in the machine.

"One dance?" Erik coaxed.

She knew it was a mistake, but she couldn't resist the thought of being in his arms again. "All right, maybe just one." She dropped her handbag on the table, then let him lead her onto the empty dance floor.

"I'm sorry about last night," he murmured as he took her into his arms.

With a sigh, Daisy melted into his embrace. Later, she would demand to know why he had stood her up, but not now. Now all she wanted was to forget everything else and enjoy being close to him. But a little nagging voice in the back of her mind had other ideas.

"Where were you last night?" The words slipped past her lips before she could call them back.

"At a business meeting."

"Really?" she said, her voice frosty. "I didn't know men who didn't work had meetings."

"It wasn't work related. Simply a meeting of an . . . an organization I'm heavily involved in."

"What kind of organization?"

"I could tell you, but then I'd have to kill you."

She frowned at him. "Very funny." Irritated, she tried to pull away, but his arm tightened around her waist. "Let me go."

"No. I'd tell you if I could, but I really can't talk about it. I'm sorry about last night. Believe me, I'd much rather have been here, with you. Forgive me?"

She wanted to hang on to her anger, but how could she when he was looking at her like that? He had the most expressive eyes, deep and black, with thick lashes that any woman would envy.

He smiled a slow, sexy smile. "I knew you couldn't stay

mad at me." The music ended, but he didn't let her go. She felt a little silly standing there in the middle of the dance floor, swaying back and forth when the music had stopped.

"How about that date?" he asked, "now that you know me better?"

"I don't know."

"Still a little angry about last night?"

"Maybe."

He blew out a sigh. "Will you meet me here tomorrow night?"

"I don't know. Will you show up this time?"

"I promise." Bending down, he kissed the tip of her nose. "I didn't promise last time."

"All right. I'll give you one more chance."

"What time will you be here?"

"Eight thirty."

He nodded. "Eight thirty. Tomorrow night," he said with a grin. "It's a date."

Daisy woke Tuesday morning with a smile on her face. She told herself not to get too excited. Just because he had promised to show up didn't mean he would. But she couldn't stop smiling.

She showered and dressed, made her bed, ate a quick breakfast, read her e-mail, and left the house, her mind filled with thoughts of Erik.

Daisy had been driving around the north side for almost an hour when she realized that the only lairs her compass was leading her to were houses or hideouts she had already visited. The same held true for the east side. Since she hated to visit the same lair more than two or three times, she decided it was time to widen her net. Up until now, she had avoided the slums on the south side, and the upscale west side, but that was about to change. She had orders to fill.

Making a sharp U-turn, she drove south. She seemed to recall her father telling her that one of the New Orleans vamps had recently taken up residence in this part of the city. If anyone would know, it was her dad. He had been a vampire hunter most of his adult life.

Daisy had only gone a couple of blocks when the needle on her compass changed colors. Muttering, "thanks, Dad," Daisy made a quick left turn.

The lair was located in a run-down motel that, by the looks of it, had gone out of business quite some time ago. The windows were boarded up. The grass was dead. The pool was empty. Several sun-faded signs warned against trespassing.

Daisy parked out of sight behind the motel. After spraying herself with Scent-B-Gone, she grabbed the tools of her trade and followed the compass. It led her into the motel office. Following the now bright-red needle, she went through the office door and down a narrow hallway that led into a small room that held nothing but an old-fashioned, beat-up, boxlike freezer.

Frowning, Daisy stared at the needle and then at the freezer. She tapped the compass lightly, but the needle continued to point at the freezer. Daisy grunted softly. The vampires on the popular TV show *Moonlight* had slept in freezers. She had never heard of real-life vampires doing such a thing and thought it rather odd, but, hey, the whole vampire thing was odd.

Shrugging, she reached for the lid, only it wouldn't open. Locked from the inside, perhaps. Time for the crowbar.

It took several tries, but she finally managed to pry the lid open. A shiny black coffin rested inside the freezer.

With a shake of her head, Daisy put the crowbar aside and lifted the lid of the coffin. The vampire inside wore a flamboyant red dressing gown embroidered with silver dragons and green pagodas. His bright red hair made a sharp contrast to the white satin lining.

Daisy was reaching for her syringe when the vampire's eyelids flew open. His eyes, a pale brown, quickly turned a hellish red as his hand—his cold, dead hand—snaked out and grabbed her by the wrist. His grip was like iron.

For a taut moment, they stared at each other. Then, with a shriek, Daisy yanked a wooden stake from her jacket pocket, only then realizing that, with only one free hand, she couldn't hold the stake and use the mallet at the same time. In a panic, she raised the stake and drove it into the vampire's heart.

She had never staked a vampire before and she was surprised at how easily the wood pierced its flesh, and how quickly the body turned to ash, until all that remained was the gaudy dressing gown looking like a splash of fresh blood on the white satin, and her stake.

Daisy pressed a hand to her chest as her legs went out from under her and she slid down to the floor.

She had destroyed a vampire, killed something that had once been human. The idea filled her with horror and revulsion. She had taken a life.

Turning her head to the side, she was quietly sick to her stomach.

Erik drummed his fingers on the bar top. Either Daisy was late, or she wasn't coming. Was this her way of getting back at him for standing her up the other night? Or had something happened to her? Perhaps she was sick, or injured. Humans were such fragile creatures. The thought of her in pain distressed him more than it should have. He hardly knew the woman, although that was something he hoped to remedy as quickly as possible.

By ten thirty, he accepted the fact that she wasn't going to show. He couldn't remember the last time he had felt such keen disappointment.

He was about to leave the club when Rhys appeared at his side. Vampires were notorious for keeping their emotions well hidden, but one look at Rhys's face and Erik knew something was wrong.

"It's Saul." Costain's words, though quietly spoken, were edged with steel. "He's been destroyed."

After taking a long, hot bubble bath, Daisy put on her favorite pj's and her fluffy white robe and curled up in a corner of the sofa. She couldn't stop shaking, couldn't get the image of the vampire's hell-red eyes out of her head. She hadn't wanted to destroy him. All she had wanted was a little of his blood. Was that so bad? Strange that there had been no blood when she drove the stake into his heart. Maybe he wasn't really dead. Maybe he had just disappeared. Worked a little vampire voodoo and vanished. Wishful thinking, that.

She told herself it had been self-defense. She had seen her death in the vampire's hellish gaze and her instinct for self-preservation had kicked in. She'd had no choice. It had been him or her. And he was already dead.

Drawing her robe tighter around her, she went into the kitchen for a cup of hot tea heavily laced with honey, hoping it would calm her nerves.

It didn't. Maybe she should have added a shot of brandy, only she didn't keep anything stronger than root beer in the house.

Knowing she was never going to be able to sleep, she turned on the TV and skipped through the channels until she found an old comedy she hadn't seen in a while. But even Gene Wilder couldn't chase the memory of what she had done from her mind.

She glanced at the clock, hit Mute on the remote, then picked up the phone. She knew her dad was in bed at this time of the night, but she needed someone to talk to.

The sound of his sleepy hello made her feel a hundred percent better.

"Daisy?" His voice sharpened. "Is something wrong, honey?"

"I . . . I destroyed a vampire tonight."

"Are you all right?" he asked, his voice sharp with concern.

"Yes. Did you hear what I said?"

"I heard. What happened?"

She told him, as quickly and succinctly as she could, what she had done.

"It was you or him, honey, you did the right thing. I'm just glad you're okay. Do you need us to come out there?"

"No." Now that she was feeling a little better, she was ashamed of herself for calling home. But then, it had been calling home that made her feel better. As far back as she could remember, her father had been her bulwark. He had never made light of her fears, never chided her for being afraid. Instead, he had helped her face her fears, whether it was her dislike of spiders, or her irrational fear of the dark.

"Do you know which vamp you destroyed?"

"No. But I think he must have been an old one, otherwise he wouldn't have turned to ash. I don't know if it was the one you told me about or not."

"An older-looking vamp with gray hair?"

"No, this one had red hair. Bright red."

"Ah, Saul."

"Saul." Knowing his name made it worse somehow.

"Daisy?"

"I'm all right, Dad. Sorry I woke you."

"No problem, honey. Mom wants to say hi."

Daisy assured her mother she was fine, then spent the next ten minutes listening while Irene O'Donnell extolled Kevin O'Reilly's many virtues.

"Yes, Mom, I'm sure he's wonderful," Daisy said, hoping to cut the conversation short by agreeing with her mother. "He sounds like a cross between Brad Pitt and Johnny Depp. Yes, Mom, I love you, too. Good night."

Tossing the cell phone on the table, Daisy grabbed one of the sofa pillows and clutched it to her chest as images of a vampire moved across the silent TV screen. With an aggrieved sigh, she switched off the set, only then remembering that she had missed her first real date with Erik.

Chapter 6

Irene O'Donnell sat up, a worried expression on her face. "You should have told Daisy to come home," she said, folding her arms over her chest. "She would have listened to you."

"She's a big girl," Noah O'Donnell replied. "Sure and she'll be all right."

Irene shook her head. "Dealing in vampire blood is no fit occupation for a young woman. It's bad enough that our sons followed in your footsteps."

"Darlin'," Noah said patiently, "we've been through this before."

"And we're going through it again. Daisy is a beautiful girl. She should be out looking for a husband, not vampires."

"Oh, Lord, don't start with Kevin O'Reilly again," Noah said, groaning. "The man's a first-class idiot."

"He is not!" Irene said hotly. "He's a perfectly fine young man with a wonderful future."

"He's an insurance salesman."

"And what's wrong with that? It's a nice, safe line of work. Steady income. Fixed hours. Good retirement. "

"Safe!" Noah scoffed.

"What's wrong with safe?"

"He's boring. Daisy would never be happy with him in a million years. Our girl needs a man who's strong enough to stand beside her and hold his own, not some namby-pamby insurance salesman who'd run for cover at the first sign of danger."

"Oh, you, you . . ." She slapped one hand on the mattress in frustration. "You are the most infuriating man I've ever known!"

"That may be, but at least you're never bored when I'm around."

She glared at him. Damn and blast, he was the most handsome, annoying man she had ever met, and she loved him more than life itself.

Noah laughed softly. "Irene, would you be happy married to Kevin O'Reilly?"

With a sigh, Irene scooted closer to her husband. "No," she admitted. "Not in a million years."

"Don't worry about our Daisy," Noah said as he turned off the light and drew his sweet wife into his arms. "The right man will come along soon enough."

Chapter 7

The Vampire Council met in the wee small hours of the morning. Anger and a need to avenge one of their own filled the air like thick smoke as each vampire spoke in turn.

Erik stood against the wall, his arms folded over his chest. He didn't know who the Blood Thief was, but the man's fate had been sealed when he destroyed Saul. All that remained now was to find the thief, and execute him.

Easier said than done, Erik thought. Whoever the man was, he was smart enough to eradicate any trace of his presence.

"Perhaps we could set a trap," Mariah suggested.

Rhys nodded. "Perhaps."

"A couple of us could set up new lairs," Damon said. "Make them easier to find, easier to breach."

"Who's going to protect you while you're vulnerable?" Erik asked, not bothering to mask the disdain in his tone.

Damon shrugged. "Rhys?" Of those present, Rhys was the only one who was old enough and powerful enough to venture outside his lair during the day, even if it was only for a short time.

"He can't be in more than one place at a time," Erik pointed out.

"Yeah, I didn't think about that," Damon admitted, looking sheepish.

"A trap is still a good idea," Mariah insisted. She fixed Erik with a hard look. "You can be awake during the day. You can be the bait. Rhys can back you up."

"We don't need to set any traps," Erik said. "The Blood Thief isn't having any trouble finding us."

"What's the matter, Erik?" Mariah asked, her brown eyes narrowed with contempt. "Don't tell me you're afraid?"

"Why don't you worry about your own head," he retorted, "and let me worry about mine?"

"That's enough," Rhys said, glancing from one to the other. "Erik's right. The Blood Thief isn't having any trouble finding us. He found Tina. He found Saul. And even if we set a trap, there's no guarantee that the thief will fall for it. And while I'm guarding the trap, there's nothing to stop the thief from attacking someone else."

"Perhaps a different kind of trap," Erik suggested.

Rupert leaned forward in his chair. "What kind of trap?"

"Cameras. If we each set up a motion camera in our lair, we can catch the thief on tape."

"That might work," Nicholas remarked.

"I agree," Rupert said. "The thief is using modern technology to mask his presence. I say we use it to catch him."

"We're in agreement, then," Rhys said. "I expect you all to have cameras in place by tomorrow night." He thumped Erik on the back. "Good thinking, buddy. Let's go out and get a drink to celebrate!"

Chapter 8

With a low groan, Daisy opened her eyes and checked the time, twice. It was almost two o'clock in the afternoon. Little wonder she had slept so late. She didn't think she had gotten more than a few minutes of sleep last night. Every time she had closed her eyes, the image of the red-haired vampire had risen, sharp and clear, across the canvas of her mind. She could still feel the stake in her hand, the way it had slid into his flesh, like a knife through butter. See the look of astonishment on his face as it pierced his heart, see his body disintegrate into a pile of gray ash. The crimson robe, like a splash of bright blood, against the white satin.

Gagging, she scrambled out of bed and into the bathroom. Dropping to her knees, she leaned over the toilet, grateful that she had very little in her stomach.

Rising, she rinsed her mouth, then stripped off her pj's and stepped into the shower.

She stood there, her forehead pressed against the glass, until the water grew cool. Washing quickly, she stepped out of the stall and wrapped a towel around her middle, then padded downstairs. Coffee. She needed coffee. And chocolate. The world and all of its problems always looked better after a quick jolt of caffeine.

Minutes later, she sat at the table with a cup of coffee in one hand and a chocolate buttermilk doughnut in the other. For the first time, she found no comfort in caffeine or chocolate, but it didn't stop her from drinking the coffee or eating the doughnut.

With a sigh, she went upstairs to dress. She couldn't sit in the house and mope all day. She couldn't stay in here and hide from her fears. She had to get out on the street again.

But not today.

Today, she was taking a vacation.

She spent the early part of the afternoon sitting outside working on her tan. She took a nap. She read a book. She drove into town and treated herself to a full-body massage. She went to dinner at a nice restaurant. And then, feeling the need to be around a lot of people, she changed clothes, checked her make-up, and drove to the Crypt.

She sensed Erik's presence the minute she stepped into the club. He must have been looking for her, she thought, because he was at her side before the door closed behind her.

"I was worried when you didn't show up last night," he said, his gaze moving over her face. "Is everything all right?"

"It is now," she said, and meant it. Just the sound of his voice, and suddenly all was right with the world again. *Oh, Daisy,* she thought, *you've got it really bad.*

Curling his fingers around hers, Erik led her to a secluded booth in the back and slid in beside her. Little frissons of heat raced across her skin when his thigh brushed hers.

"I'm sorry I didn't make it last night," she said. "Something unexpected came up." *Or woke up,* she thought, suppressing a shudder.

"I was afraid you were still angry because I stood you up the other night."

"No."

"We don't seem to have much luck arranging dates." He took her hand in his again, raised it to his lips, and brushed his lips across her palm. "But we're together now. How about a late movie?"

Her heartbeat kicked up a notch at the thought of sitting beside him in a dark theater. "All right."

They left the club hand in hand. Erik paused at the curb. "We can take my car," he said. "Or we can walk."

"It's such a beautiful night," Daisy said. "Why don't we walk?"

"As you wish."

His gaze rested lightly on her face, his expression clearly saying exactly what she was thinking—that she didn't feel comfortable getting into a car with a man she hardly knew. And yet it seemed right to be walking down the street by his side.

"Do you have family here in town?" They were stopped at a corner, waiting for the light to change.

"No." *Or anywhere else on earth,* he thought.

"Have you lived in California very long?"

"Three or four years."

"Where did you live before that?"

Erik chuckled. Technically, he hadn't "lived" anywhere for over three hundred years. "I move around a lot. I've lived in New York, Chicago, New Orleans, Atlanta, Nashville." And Rome, Paris, Transylvania, and just about every other city in the world.

She looked up at him as they crossed the street. "Got itchy feet, do you?"

"You could say that." It didn't pay for a vampire to stay in one place too long. People got curious, and then suspicious, about neighbors who were never seen during the day, and who never got any older. "What about you?" he asked. "Are you a California girl?"

"I am now, but I was born in Oregon. We lived there until I was six, and then we moved to Boston."

"Why did you leave home?"

"I like the West Coast. And I wanted to be on my own."

They were at the theater now. Erik bought two tickets and they went inside.

"Do you want anything to eat?" he asked as they neared the snack bar.

"Just a Coke."

They entered the theater just as the lights went down. Moments later, they were sitting side by side in the dark while movie trailers flashed across the screen. Daisy knew a little thrill of excitement when Erik reached for her hand. Just a simple touch, his fingers curling lightly around hers, and yet it made her feel safe, protected. Which was odd, she thought, since she wasn't in any danger.

She glanced at Erik. His profile was sharp and clean. He was easily the most handsome man she had ever met. And the sexiest. Just looking at him aroused a longing deep within her. A longing to feel his body against hers, to run her hands over his shoulders, to wrap her fingers around his biceps, to run her tongue over his skin, to touch him and taste him . . . all of him.

A rush of heat warmed her cheeks when she realized he was watching her. Thank goodness he couldn't read her mind!

Dragging her gaze from his, she turned her attention to the screen, surprised to see that the movie had started. How much had she missed? How long had she been staring at Erik like some lovesick calf?

Leaning toward her, he whispered, "I like the way you look, too."

Startled, Daisy drew back. Lordy, maybe he *could* read her mind.

She met Erik at the Crypt the following night. As always, just seeing him made her heart skip a beat. Tonight, he wore a pair of snug black jeans that hugged his long legs, a navy blue striped shirt unbuttoned over a white tee, and a pair of scuffed black boots. Just looking at him made her mouth water. If she had created him, he couldn't have been more perfect.

He smiled when he saw her. "You're early."

Daisy glanced at her watch. "So are you."

He closed the distance between them. She could see the heat in his eyes now, feel it as his gaze moved over her. Her stomach quivered in response. "I guess I was anxious to see you again." His voice poured over her like honey.

"You guess?" She had intended to sound flippant and worldly wise; instead, her voice came out in a breathy whisper.

"All right, I admit it. I couldn't wait. So, what would you like to do this evening?"

"I don't know." His nearness, the warmth in his eyes, made it hard to think of anything but her yearning to be in his arms. "Anything you want to do is fine with me."

He smiled, as if he knew exactly what she was thinking. "How about a moonlight swim?"

"I didn't bring a bathing suit."

"It's dark." His gaze moved over her from head to foot. "No one will know."

The words "but me" hovered in the air between them.

For once in her life, she decided to be daring, spontaneous. Foolish, maybe. Throwing caution to the wind, she said, "Let's go!"

"That's my girl." Taking her by the hand, Erik led her outside to his car.

He drove a sleek black Trans Am convertible with black leather interior. Daisy grinned inwardly as she settled into the front seat. Everything about the man was dark and sexy, including his car.

She watched him slide behind the wheel. He moved with a grace and economy of motion she had rarely seen in a man of his size.

He slid the key into the ignition and the engine turned over, purring like a contented cat. "Ready?"

"Ready."

Daisy's heart skipped a beat as he peeled away from the curb. Minutes later, they were on the 101 freeway headed toward the beach. Daisy stared out the window as Van Morrison crooned "Someone Like You." It was one of her favorite songs.

She slid a sideways glance at Erik. Why had she agreed to this? Last night, she had been reluctant to get in a car with him; tonight, she had done it without a qualm.

She was trying to figure out what had changed since last night when he said, "You're very quiet."

"Just listening to the music. It's one of my favorites."

"Yeah, Morrison's got a great sound."

Daisy nodded. What was she doing, driving off to the beach at night with a man she hardly knew? What was it about him that made her good sense fly right out the window whenever he was around? If she told him she had changed her mind, would he take her back to the club?

Her stomach was in knots when Erik pulled off the freeway forty minutes later. There were no other cars parked off the road, and no other people on the beach, as far as Daisy could see. Once again, she asked herself what she was doing there.

She looked up when Erik opened her door and there, in his

eyes, she saw the answer to her question. Right or wrong, for better or worse, for reasons she didn't pretend to understand, she knew her fate was somehow tied to his.

Daisy took off her sandals; Erik removed his boots and socks, and they walked hand in hand along the shore, the damp sand squishing between their toes.

It was a beautiful night. Millions of stars twinkled brightly overhead, reflecting their light on the gently rolling waves that kissed the shore. A bright yellow moon smiled down on them.

"So, how about that swim?" Erik asked.

"I don't think so. I'm not into skinny-dipping on public beaches."

"No? Then how about a quick dip in your underwear? It probably covers as much as today's swimwear."

Daisy weighed the pros and cons for a moment, but in the end, it was the cool water lapping at her ankles that made the decision. At least that's what she told herself. And it was partly true. But mainly, it was her desire to see Erik in the buff that made her agree.

She turned her back to him while she undressed. This was so stupid. If a shark ate her, she would have no one to blame but herself.

"Ready?"

She turned at the sound of his voice. Clothed, he was gorgeous. Clad in nothing but a pair of black briefs, he was a Greek god come to life. His body was muscular without being bulky. His legs were long and firm, his shoulders broad. His abs looked rock hard; his biceps tempted her touch.

He grinned under her blatant regard. "Like what you see?"

She nodded. What was there not to like?

"Good. I like what I see, too." He took a step toward her. "You're beautiful, Daisy." His fingertips glided down her cheek, along her neck, across her collarbone to settle in the hollow of her throat. "Truly beautiful."

A blush warmed her cheeks, more from the admiration in his eyes than his words. "Thank you."

"Come on," he said, and taking her hand in his, he turned and ran toward the water.

Daisy shrieked as she followed Erik into the waves. The water had felt cool on her bare feet; it felt downright cold when it reached her knees, and higher.

She was thinking of turning around and swimming back to shore as fast as she could when Erik grabbed her hand. Floating on his back, he lifted her onto his chest so that her body covered his.

"What are you doing?" she exclaimed, certain they would both go under, amazed when they didn't. It was like surfing on a human surfboard.

"You okay?" he asked, a hint of amusement in his voice.

"Yes, but . . ."

"Relax, I won't let you drown."

He floated out past the waves to where the water was as smooth as black glass.

"Still okay?" he asked.

She glanced to the right and to the left. No fins that she could see. "I guess so."

"Are you afraid of the ocean?"

"Ever since I saw *Jaws*."

Erik grinned at her. "There's nothing to be afraid of." Animals avoided him, especially those that hunted for their food. Something about one predator recognizing another, he supposed.

Nothing to be afraid of, Daisy thought, *except drowning or being stung by a jellyfish, or attacked by a shark.*

It was oddly exhilarating, and a little frightening, floating there, just the two of them, alone in the vast ocean at night.

Gradually, Daisy relaxed enough to rest her cheek on Erik's chest. Lying there, she noticed the reflection of the moon on the water, the way the moonlight glistened on the waves.

For all that it was exciting to drift on the sea with Erik, she was relieved when, at last, he made for the shore.

It was good to feel solid ground beneath her feet, Daisy thought when they reached the edge of the water. Dropping down on the sand, she gazed up at Erik. He was truly a remarkable human being, she mused, and certainly stronger than any man she had ever known. She would have bet her house and everything in it that Erik couldn't float and carry her at the same time.

He sat down beside her, his thigh brushing intimately against hers. The touch of his damp flesh sent a shiver down her spine, a shiver that had nothing to do with his cool skin and everything to do with his nearness, and the look in his dark eyes.

He's going to kiss me.

The thought had no sooner crossed her mind than he was leaning toward her, his hand curling around her nape as his mouth covered hers. The touch of his lips, though cool and slightly salty, ignited a fire deep within her.

She moaned softly as he eased back on the sand, carrying her with him, so that her body lay sprawled across his, their legs entwined.

Erik slid his hand up into the thick fall of her hair, his fingers tangling in the damp strands. A deep breath carried the scent of strawberry shampoo and warm, womanly flesh with an underlying scent of musk that told him she was as aroused as he.

He kissed her again, his hands sliding restlessly over her bare back, her shoulders, skimming the curve of her breasts. She moaned low in her throat, a primal sound that aroused his senses. All of them. The hunger stirred within him. She was here. She was his for the taking. He could steal a taste, or take it all. When his fangs brushed his tongue, he turned his head away.

"Don't stop," she murmured, her voice low, breathy with desire.

He gazed up at her, momentarily at a loss as to what to do next. He hadn't let himself care deeply for a mortal woman in centuries, not since Celestine DuBois. His affair with her had ended badly, as such things usually did, and he had vowed he would never again get emotionally involved with a mortal female. They were too fragile, too easily wounded. Too easily broken.

But Daisy . . . ah, his fair flower. Her very being spoke to something deep within him, something he had thought dead long ago, along with his humanity. What was he to do with her?

A streak of decency he had forgotten he possessed pushed its way through the hunger. Rising, he took her hands in his and pulled her gently to her feet.

"We should go," he said, brushing a bit of sand from her hair.

She blinked up at him, her eyes wide, her lips slightly parted.

He brushed a kiss across her cheek. "It's late."

Stunned by the abrupt turn of events, Daisy slipped her clothes on over her damp bra and panties. Carrying her sandals in one hand, she followed Erik. Barefooted, they trudged up the beach to where he had parked the car.

She glanced at him from time to time on the ride home. Had she done something wrong? One minute, they were going at it hot and heavy and the next he was telling her it was late.

With a shake of her head, she stared out the window. It was probably just as well that he had called a halt to their lovemaking. If he had kept kissing her like that, there was no telling what might have happened.

When they reached the Crypt's parking lot, Daisy stepped into her sandals. Erik opened the door for her, then walked her to her car. Feeling somewhat confused, Daisy reached into her handbag for her keys. Would he kiss her good night? Or good-bye?

Not quite meeting his eyes, she murmured, "Good night."

"Dammit!"

Startled, she looked up at him.

He raked a hand through his hair. "The night shouldn't end like this. Let's go inside and have a drink."

"You said it was late."

"It's not that late." He smiled down at her. In spite of his vow to avoid mortal females, he was involved with Daisy O'Donnell, for better or worse. "What do you say?"

"I don't think so. I need to shower and wash my hair."

"You look fine to me."

"I doubt that. But I'd be happy to meet you here tomorrow night for that drink."

"I don't think I can wait that long."

Daisy shook her head. No way was she going inside looking the way she did.

"How about if I meet you back here in half an hour?" he coaxed.

"You don't give up, do you?"

"Not when I see something I want," he replied, stunned by the realization that all his good intentions in the world weren't going to keep him from pursuing this woman. "Say yes."

"All right." What the heck, she didn't have to get up early in the morning. "But you'd better make it forty-five minutes."

Daisy drove home, took a shower, and washed and dried her hair in record time, her stomach fluttering all the while. In spite of what had happened on the beach, he wanted her. After pulling on a gauzy white skirt and a pale pink tank top, she stepped into her sandals, grabbed her handbag and her keys, and drove back to the Crypt. Erik's car was already in the parking lot when she arrived. After locking her handbag in the car, she pocketed her keys and hurried into the club.

He was waiting for her at the bar, looking gorgeous in a black turtleneck sweater and black jeans. His welcoming smile warmed her right down to her toes.

"Hi," she murmured, taking the seat to his right.

"Hi, yourself." His gaze moved over her. "You look terrific."

"So do you. Black is definitely your color."

Erik grunted softly. It wasn't really a fashion statement. Most vampires tended to dress in dark colors. It made it easier to blend in with the shadows, to stalk and catch their prey unawares.

When the bartender came to take their order, Daisy asked for a margarita. Erik ordered the house special.

"I'll have to try one of those sometime," Daisy remarked when the bartender served their drinks.

"I doubt if you'd like it." He wasn't crazy about it himself.

"Why not?"

He shrugged. "It's an acquired taste. A margarita suits you."

"How so?"

"Margarita means *Daisy* in Spanish."

"Really? I didn't know that."

When the band struck up "Someone Like You," Erik reached for her hand and led the way to the dance floor.

Daisy listened to the words of the song, thinking that if they were a couple, this would be their song.

"Daisy?"

"Hmm?"

"What would you say if I asked you to come home with me?"

She stared up at him, sorely tempted to accept in spite of the warning bells that went off in her mind. One night, she thought, what could it hurt? She contemplated it briefly. He would drive her home, take her into his house, into his bed, where they would share a night of unbridled sexual pleasure. . . . At this point, her imagination took over, since she had never experienced a night of sexual pleasure, unbridled or otherwise. True, she had been tempted with other men, even come close a time or two, and been called a tease when her good sense reasserted itself at the last minute.

Daisy felt a prickle of unease as Erik gazed deeply into her eyes, almost as if he was trying to hypnotize her. The first time she had seen him, she'd had the feeling he could see into her heart and mind, her very soul.

Taking a deep breath, she drew her hand from his. "I don't think so." In spite of her overwhelming attraction for him, it was way too soon. Even though she sometimes felt as if she had known him forever, it had been less than a week.

He smiled wryly, as if he had anticipated her reply.

Silence stretched between them. Daisy cast about for something to say, some safe topic they could discuss. She frowned a moment, then said, "You must have a lot of spare time, since you don't work. What do you do to pass the time?"

He shrugged. "Whatever pleases me at the moment." He drew her closer, his breath fanning her cheek when he murmured, "Right now, you please me."

The words, combined with the silky tone of his voice, sent a shiver of pleasure through her.

His gaze moved over her face. "I would like to please you, in return. Change your mind. Come home with me, pretty flower. Let's go exploring together."

It was the most intriguing offer, and the scariest, she had ever received. For a moment, she could only stare at him, all the while fighting the urge to take a walk on the wild side with Erik Delacourt, but try as she might, she simply couldn't go home with him. She could stake a vampire, but she couldn't muster the courage to surrender to the look in this man's eyes, a look that promised pleasure unlike anything she had ever known, if she could just summon the nerve. But she couldn't, at least not at the moment.

He read the answer in her eyes before she spoke her refusal aloud.

"Perhaps another night," he said, "when you're feeling braver."

Daisy frowned. How did he know what she was feeling, thinking? Maybe those deep dark eyes really could see into her heart and soul. Heaven knew this wasn't the first time he had voiced what she had been thinking.

There was a brief silence as the song ended, and then the strains of a slow ballad filled the air. Daisy had thought they would return to the bar, but Erik didn't let her go. Content to be in his arms, she rested her head against his shoulder. She had never danced with anyone so light on his feet. He moved like liquid silk, every movement smooth, unruffled, unhurried. The look in his eyes made her feel beautiful, the intensity of his gaze made her feel like she was the most important thing in his life. What would it be like to go home with him, to run her hands over his broad chest and flat belly, to feel his hands moving in her hair, caressing her bare flesh . . .

His voice, soft and sultry, sounded in her ear. "Are you sure you won't change your mind and come home with me?"

"Quite sure." Lifting her head, she took a deep breath. "I think I'd better go."

"Let me walk you to your car."

She didn't think that was a good idea. She needed to put some distance between them, but it seemed rude to refuse.

She was acutely aware of him as he followed her around the edge of the dance floor toward the exit. He was tall and broad, but it was more than his imposing stature that she was aware of. Erik Delacourt radiated power and authority. Men with his confidence and self-assurance were usually CEOs of large companies who were accustomed to making decisions and giving orders. But Erik wasn't a businessman or a tycoon. By his own account, he was a man who spent his time doing what pleased him.

And she pleased him.

She slowed her steps as some inner sense of self-preservation warned her not to let him think she was afraid of him. Afraid of him? Where had that thought come from? She wasn't afraid of him. Was she?

In the parking lot, she pulled her keys from her skirt pocket and unlocked her car door, slid behind the wheel, and rolled down the window. "Good night."

"What?" He lifted one brow. "No good-night kiss?"

The prospect of having his mouth on hers sent a frisson of heat straight to the pit of her stomach. Before she could refuse, he leaned down and claimed her lips with his. She had thought his kisses on the beach were the ultimate aphrodisiac, but this kiss was deeper, hotter, more persuasive. It was like Christmas morning and Fourth of July skyrockets all rolled into one. She moaned softly when his hand caressed her nape, then slid up to cup the back of her head as his tongue plundered the depths of her mouth. It made her toes curl inside her shoes.

She felt hot all over when he took his mouth from hers.

"Good night, little flower," he said, his lips curved in a knowing grin. "Sweet dreams."

Sweet dreams, indeed, she thought as she drove home. She could only imagine what kind of dreams his kisses would inspire. Something sexy and X-rated, no doubt. *Lordy, the man's kisses should come with warning labels.* Just thinking about being alone with him made her skin feel tight and her heart pound with anticipation. Where had he learned to kiss like that? She had been kissed lots of times. It was a pleasurable experience, but no other man had ever made her feel the way Erik did. His kisses urged her to throw caution to the wind and the consequences be damned. She fanned herself with her hand. No doubt about it. Erik Delacourt and his kisses were a volatile combination, dangerous in the extreme.

At home, she took a long, cold shower, brushed her teeth, slipped into her favorite Snoopy sleep shirt, and climbed into bed, only to lie there, wide-awake, her fingertips pressed to her lips.

If she went to the club tomorrow night, would he kiss her like that again?

Would she still be able to deny him what they both wanted if he did?

Chapter 9

Friday morning, Daisy decided she had avoided doing her job long enough. It took considerable effort, but she pushed all thought of Erik Delacourt and his sizzling kisses out of her mind. She ate a quick breakfast, made her bed, and then read her e-mail.

Humming "Someone Like You," she shut down her computer. The morning mail had brought her a dozen new orders. It was time to put her fears behind her and get back on the street. She had bills to pay, after all.

After dressing in a pair of jeans, a long-sleeved T-shirt, her favorite jacket with the roomy pockets, and comfortable shoes, she grabbed her handbag, her keys, and her compass and left the house. Surprisingly, she didn't feel the least bit of anxiety at going out on the streets again. She had destroyed a vampire and in so doing, she had proved she could handle herself when the going got tough.

Smiling with new confidence, she slid behind the wheel. She drove with one eye on the road and the other on the needle of the compass, which jumped and quivered when she turned down a cul-de-sac in a very old, very elegant part of town.

There were only three houses on the street, each separated from the other by large yards and tall fences. The needle turned red when she neared the house on the left. It was set well back from the street. The windows carried a dark tint, no doubt to block the sun's light. For all that it looked abandoned, the house itself was in good repair. There was no grass in the front yard, only a variety of cactus plants that needed little watering.

If it hadn't been for the blinking red needle on her compass, she would have sworn the house was empty. She wasn't sure why she felt that way, and then grinned. Technically, no one "lived" there, unless the vampire had a human companion. Daisy shook her head. She knew there were people who served the needs of the Undead and counted it a privilege to do so. She had never understood the attraction.

After making sure she had everything she needed, Daisy stepped out of the car and walked up the narrow walkway to the front porch. She rang the doorbell, heard it echo inside the house. When there was no answer, she knocked. And when there was still no answer, she got out her handy-dandy lock pick and went to work.

Minutes later, she stood just inside the doorway, her head cocked as she listened to the house, and heard nothing. A quick glance showed a large living room with a corner fireplace, leather furniture, and mahogany tables. Thick, floor-length drapes kept the sun at bay.

The compass guided her through the living room and down a narrow hallway, which led to a stairway. Moving cautiously, she tiptoed down the stairs, which ended at a large steel door. She assumed the door led down to the cellar. A common vampire resting place. She glanced at the compass in her hand. In the dim light of the stairwell, the needle glowed bright red, assuring her that she was in the right place.

Tucking the compass away, she pulled a syringe from a

pocket of her jacket and then regarded the door, wondering if she should have brought her crowbar with her. Only one way to find out.

She was reaching for the handle when the door swung open to reveal a tall man clad in a pair of sweatpants and nothing else. Several candles burned in the room behind him. The light cast dancing shadows on the walls and gilded his thick black hair with silver highlights.

Daisy's heart jumped into her throat, and then plummeted to her toes. "You!"

A slow smile spread over Erik Delacourt's handsome face. "Does this visit mean you've decided to go exploring with me?" he asked, a wicked gleam in his dark eyes.

"Hardly." *Vampire. Vampire!* The word screamed inside her mind. He was a vampire. Now that she knew, she couldn't believe she hadn't realized it sooner. Lordy, not only was he a vampire, but she had let him kiss her. Not once, but several times. She had even considered going to bed with him. The memory should have disgusted her, but it didn't. Why didn't it? She would have to examine her feelings about that later. Right now, she had to get out of there before he . . . no! She wouldn't think about that. And yet she couldn't stop herself from imagining him bending over her neck, his fangs at her throat as he drained her dry. Or worse, made her what he was.

"So, you didn't come to go exploring the dark side with me." Erik folded his arms across his chest. "Why are you here?" He glanced at the syringe clutched in her hand. "Don't tell me, you're working for the Red Cross. I didn't know they were going door to door collecting blood these days."

She forced a smile. "Very funny." She took a step backward, wondering what the odds were that she could outrun him.

She jumped when the door at the top of the stairs slammed

shut. She was well and truly caught, she thought. Like a rabbit in a trap.

He grinned at her, and his eyes glowed as red as the needle on her compass. "Welcome to my parlor, said the spider to the fly."

"What do you think you're doing?" she exclaimed.

"Isn't it obvious? You were about to leave. And I want you to stay."

"Why?" She slid her hand into her pocket, her fingers curling around the wooden stake inside. Yet even as she contemplated driving it into his heart, she knew she couldn't do it. It was one thing to destroy a vampire you had never met; quite another when you had kissed him.

"Come now, my little flower," he chided softly. "You must know why."

She took another step backward and tripped on the bottom step.

His hand shot out, catching her before she fell. "Careful."

Daisy shook off his hand, and even as she did so, she knew it was only because he let her. He had a grip like iron. "Let me go! You have no right to keep me here."

"And you have no right to take our blood."

"I can do whatever I like," she retorted. "It's you and your kind who have no rights."

He regarded her curiously for a moment. "You're the one they call the Blood Thief, aren't you?"

"Of course not!" Even as she denied it, fear coiled like a snake in the pit of her stomach as her newfound courage deserted her. It was one thing to face a vampire when he was lying helpless in his coffin, quite another when he was wide-awake and towering over you.

He gestured at the syringe in her hand. "Then why are you here, with that?"

Thinking quickly, she said, "I indulge, from time to time."

"Is that so?"

"What if it is?" she asked with a nonchalant shrug. "It's perfectly legal."

"Is that how you get your kicks? Stealing our blood?"

"I don't have to steal it. You can buy it online."

"Let me get this straight. You can buy it online, but you decided to cut out the middle man by breaking into my house. What were you going to do? Siphon some of my blood and drink it on the premises?"

"Yes. No. I mean . . ."

"Why drink from a bottle when you can enjoy it fresh and warm from the source? I'm told you get a better high that way."

At the thought, Daisy felt all the color drain from her face. She couldn't think of anything more repulsive than drinking vampire blood. She had never understood how her clients could drink it, or why they wanted to.

Lifting his left arm to his mouth, he bit into his wrist, then offered it to her. "Please, help yourself."

She stared at the dark red blood welling from the shallow wound and thought she might be sick to her stomach. She had taken some first aid classes, worked at a hospital as an aide one summer. What better way to learn about drawing blood? She had seen injured people and bloody wounds. None of that had made her stomach churn like this.

She looked up at the vampire, her heart pounding. He knew, she thought. Knew she was lying.

He offered her his arm again. "Go on, help yourself."

"Will you let me go if I do?"

"Sure."

She didn't believe him, but what other choice did she have? With hands that trembled, she took hold of his arm and ran her tongue over the bloody wound. Lifting her head, she stared up at him in confusion. She had expected to find it repulsive. Instead, she had the craziest impulse to taste him again.

He smiled at her, as if he knew exactly what she was thinking. Without taking his gaze from hers, he licked the wound.

It was too much. Her legs suddenly refused to hold her, and with a faint cry, she pitched forward as everything went black.

Chapter 10

Erik caught the girl before she hit the ground. Plucking the syringe from her hand, he tossed it into a wastebasket, then cradled her in his arms. She was feather-light as he carried her up the stairs and down the hall to one of the unused bedrooms.

He had bought the house back in 2007. Real estate in LA had taken a sharp nosedive back then. Unable to pay their mortgages, people had walked away from their homes. He had bought this place for three hundred thousand dollars, a third of what it would have sold for a year earlier. He figured the former owners must have moved out in the middle of the night, since they hadn't taken anything with them except their clothing. They'd left their furniture, the appliances in the kitchen, the sheets on the beds. It was a well-built place, with three good-sized bedrooms upstairs, and one guest bedroom on the first floor. He had no use for the large, family kitchen, or for any of the other rooms, save for the master bedroom where he kept his clothes, and the adjoining bathroom. The rest of the rooms he kept closed.

He had chosen this particular house for three reasons: it sat on a quiet street well separated from its neighbors, there were no houses behind it, and it had a large downstairs family room, which now served as his lair. He had made the necessary adjustments to ensure his security, which had included installing a three-inch-thick iron door to keep the world at bay while he rested.

Save for the alterations to the family room, he had done little to the house other than change the paint in the living room from a hideous yellow to a more restful shade of pale sage green, and to repaint the master bedroom and bathroom, both of which had been a virulent shade of pink, but were now an inoffensive off-white.

He tucked the girl into bed, then stood at the foot, gazing down at her. She looked as delicate as the flower whose name she bore. Hard to believe anyone so young and lovely could be the Blood Thief. He grunted softly. How the hell had she found him? And, more importantly, had she been looking for vampires in general, or for him in particular? And if she had been looking for him, why?

Sitting on the edge of the bed, he slid his arm beneath her shoulders, brushed her hair from the side of her neck. Closing his eyes, he breathed in her scent. She smelled of strawberry shampoo, soap, and woman. And blood, of course. He could smell it, hear it moving through her veins.

Erik scrubbed one hand across his jaw. She had come seeking his blood, he thought as he bent over her neck. What was the old saying? Turnabout was fair play. As his fangs pierced the tender skin of her throat, he wondered if she would agree.

Daisy woke slowly. Feeling groggy, she pressed her hands to her temples. Why did she feel so strange? Had she gotten drunk last night?

Opening her eyes to mere slits, she sat up. Groaned. And then bolted off the bed. Where was she? Not her own bedroom, that was for certain. This room was painted a bright lilac. A purple carpet covered the floor. Purple curtains hung at the windows; a matching spread covered the twin bed. Hand-drawn pictures of Care Bears were painted on the walls.

Feeling light-headed, she hurried out of the room. She remembered where she was now. The vampire's house. She had fainted. She shook her head, disgusted with herself. She had staked a vampire and yet she had fainted dead away when Erik licked his own blood. Where was the sense in that? And where was he? And what had he been doing awake in the middle of the afternoon?

She slowed her steps, suddenly cautious. What time was it? Was he awake? There was no sign of him as she made her way to the front door. Perhaps he had returned to his lair. Grateful for her good luck, she curled her hand around the knob and gave it a twist. And nothing happened. The knob didn't turn. The door didn't open. She tugged on the handle. It didn't budge.

Aware of time passing, she turned on her heel and went looking for another way out. She found a back door in the kitchen but it, too, refused to open. She stared at it in confusion. It wasn't locked. Why couldn't she open the darn thing?

A window, then. She dragged a chair over to the sink, climbed up on the counter, and tried to open the window. Only it refused to cooperate.

Fear clogged her throat. Was she dreaming?

Feeling like Alice lost in Wonderland, she climbed off the counter, picked up the chair, and threw it at the window. The chair bounced off the glass, almost hitting her in the face. But it didn't break the window.

She had to be dreaming.

She was fighting a burgeoning rush of hysteria when she realized she was no longer alone. He was there, behind her. She could feel his presence. Hands clenched at her sides, she slowly turned to face him. "You said you'd let me go if I . . . I drank your blood."

"All in good time. How do you feel?"

She blinked at him a moment, and then her eyes narrowed with accusation. "You drank my blood, didn't you? Took it while I was unconscious? That's why I feel so funny." Although funny didn't really describe it. She felt . . . how did she feel? She shook her head. She had never felt this way before, and she didn't like it. Was this how vampires felt after she siphoned their blood?

He shrugged. "You came here to take my blood. You have no right to complain if I take yours." He wondered if she knew there was now an unbreakable bond between them, formed by their exchange of blood. If he let his guard down, she would be able to read his thoughts, just as he could now read hers.

Eyes wide, she lifted a hand to her throat. "Am I . . . did you . . . ?"

"No." He made a dismissive gesture with his hand. "I just took a little taste. You're a very healthy A-negative female, by the way. Maybe a little iron deficient."

She glared at him. "You said I could go. Let me out of here!"

"No."

"Why won't the doors open?"

"Because I don't want them to."

"What does that mean?" she asked, frowning.

"It means I put an enchantment on all the doors and windows. Usually a lock is sufficient to keep unwanted visitors out." He reached into his pocket and withdrew the case that held her lock picks. "Stealing my blood may not be against the law, but I'm pretty sure the cops still frown on breaking and entering."

Her eyes shot sparks at him. "Who are you to talk to me about the law? You're a . . . a . . ."

"Monster? Vampire? Warlock?"

"Warlock?" she murmured.

He nodded. "Dark magick. Very dark. My mother was the head of a large coven. A very dark, very nasty coven. I inherited some of her supernatural powers, powers that grew stronger when I was sired."

Daisy shook her head. A vampire that practiced dark magick. Now that was a scary combination. "What do you want with me?" She shivered as images of black-clad crones performing human sacrifice under a full moon flashed through her mind.

"Why were you looking for me?"

"I wasn't. I didn't know you lived here."

"How did you know a vampire lived here?"

Lips pursed, she slipped her hand into the pocket of her jacket.

Erik frowned. While she'd been unconscious, he had relieved her of the small leather case that contained her lock picks, as well as a couple of empty glass vials and a pretty blue bottle of holy water. He had also found what he had thought was a silver compact. He grunted softly, thinking he probably should have taken that, too. Or at least opened it to see what it was. "Give it to me."

"I don't have anything."

He held out his hand and murmured a few words in a language she didn't understand. And the next thing she knew, her compass was in his palm. He opened it, then looked at her. "What does it do?"

She shrugged. "It's a compass."

If it was, it was like none he had ever seen before. "What does it do?" he repeated, his voice tinged with impatience. "You know I can make you tell me."

"It finds vampires."

"Indeed? How does it work?"

"I don't know, it just does."

"Where did you get it?"

"From a witch." A faint smile played over her lips. "A white witch."

"You're a witch?"

"No." She folded her arms under her breasts. "I wish I was."

"Wouldn't do you any good."

"Why not? Everyone knows good is stronger than evil."

"And I'm evil?"

She shrugged. "You said it."

He grunted softly, and then he frowned. "I never thought of myself as evil."

"Well, you are. Everyone knows vampires are horrible creatures . . ." Her voice trailed off. What was she saying? She shouldn't be telling him what a monster he was. She should be reminding him that he had once been human, that killing was wrong.

"Go on," he said, a trace of amusement in his tone.

She shook her head.

He folded his arms over his chest. "I'll finish for you. Vampires are horrible creatures. They hide in the shadows. They exist on human blood. They kill indiscriminately. They have no conscience." He took a step toward her. "They prey on the young and the innocent."

"I'm not young!" she said quickly. "Or innocent!"

"No?" He took another step toward her, his eyes narrowing, his nostrils flaring.

He was crowding her, but she refused to back up, refused to let him know how scared she was.

"I'd say you were right around twenty-four years old," he drawled. "And as innocent as the day you were born."

Daisy stared up at him. How could he possibly know that?

"Am I wrong?"

"Yes. I'm thirty-five, and I've slept with dozens of men. Hundreds."

"Liar."

She glared at him. "It doesn't matter what you think. Just let me go."

"Are you hungry?"

She hadn't realized it before, but she was. She hadn't had anything to eat since breakfast and it was now . . . she glanced at her watch. Almost five o'clock.

"I'll order you something," he said, pulling a cell phone from his back pocket. "What would you like?"

"I'd like to go home."

"Pizza? Hamburger?"

"Pizza, heavy on the garlic."

"Garlic doesn't repel vampires," he said, laughing softly. But it was a remarkably offensive odor to one with a keen sense of smell. Still chuckling, he called information for the phone number of the nearest pizza place.

As inconspicuously as she could, Daisy searched her pockets for her cell phone, only then realizing that the phone he was using was hers.

Filled with fear and frustration, she stomped out of the kitchen into the living room. She paced the floor, her thoughts racing. She had to get out of here. The pizza man! Of course, when the pizza arrived, she would yell for help.

She was sitting on the sofa when the vampire entered the room.

"Your pizza will be here in twenty minutes. I also ordered you a salad and a Coke."

"Thank you," she said, and then wondered why she was being so polite. He was keeping her here against her will. He had promised to let her go, and now he had reneged on that promise.

He took a seat on the other end of the sofa. "Relax, Daisy. I'm not going to hurt you."

She snorted softly. "Uh-huh. Everyone who believes that, raise your hand."

Erik shook his head. "You're right, I'm up to no good. I only ordered the pizza to fatten you up for later."

He swore as her heartbeat slammed into overdrive. "I'm kidding. Dammit, I'm not going to hurt you." He took a deep breath. "So, what's the going rate for vampire blood these days?"

"Two hundred dollars an ounce if it's from a young vampire. Three hundred if the vampire is over a hundred years old." She canted her head to the side. "How old are you?"

"Old enough that you could probably get five or six hundred."

"Really? It doesn't matter, though. I only hunt the young ones. Less dangerous that way, you know. But still lucrative."

"How do you know how old they are?"

Daisy folded her hands in her lap. Her father had a list of the names and descriptions of all known vampires and their last known lair. It helped her to avoid the old ones, but she couldn't tell Erik that. The list was a family secret. She wondered why he wasn't on it.

"I'll have to remember to hunt the old ones if I'm ever strapped for cash," he muttered dryly. "On the other hand, I guess vampires could start selling their own blood and put your kind out of business. How'd you get into your line of work? It really doesn't seem like the kind of thing a pretty young girl would find fulfilling."

"It runs in the family. My father works out of New Orleans. There are a lot of young vampires there." Her brothers were hunters, too. Brandon trafficked in blood; Alex preferred to take heads, but that, too, was information Erik didn't need to know.

Erik snorted softly. And they called his kind monsters. Sure, he preyed on mortals, but for survival, not profit.

Daisy clasped her hands in her lap. She hadn't intended to tell him anything about her family, so why had she? Had he worked some sort of vampire magic on her? She was no closer to the answer when the doorbell rang.

The vampire rose fluidly to his feet. "Not a word," he warned. "Or I won't be responsible for what happens to the young man outside."

Daisy bit down on her lower lip as Erik opened the door and paid for the pizza. It was all she could do not to cry out for help, but the thought of being responsible for the delivery boy's death kept her mute.

Erik put the pizza box, the soda, and the salad container on the coffee table. "Might as well dig in. It's the only food in the house."

"Are you just going to stand there and watch me?"

He shrugged, then wrinkled his nose against the strong smell of garlic, pepperoni, and tomato sauce. Although garlic didn't repel him, he found the odor decidedly unpleasant.

"I'll take a walk while you eat," he muttered. "Enjoy your meal."

Daisy watched him leave the house. She waited a few minutes, then went to try the front door, hoping against hope that whatever magick he had used to secure the door had lapsed when he opened it. But luck was against her. The damn door refused to open.

With a wordless cry of frustration, she picked up the pizza box and hurled it against the door. It made a satisfying *smack* as it struck the wood. The lid flew open, raining cheese-filled crust, pepperoni, and tomato sauce over the carpet in a gooey mess.

She stared at it in horror for a minute, then shrugged. If he wanted to keep her here as his prisoner, then he could just clean up after her.

Sitting on the sofa, she nibbled at the salad, drank half the Coke, then threw the remains of the salad and the drink against the door. The green lettuce made a nice contrast to the red sauce and yellow cheese.

Fear rose in the midst of defiance as she stared at the mess she had made on the floor. And then she stiffened her spine. No matter what Erik said to the contrary, she knew he was going to kill her. Better to go down fighting back than just sit there like some sacrificial lamb and wait for him to drain her dry.

She glanced around the room. She needed a weapon, she thought. Something. Anything. But there was nothing to be found in the parlor. She searched the rest of the house, giving vent to her rising frustration as she moved from room to room.

Returning to the living room, she tried the front door again, then perched on the edge of the sofa, her foot tapping impatiently as she tried to think of a way out. She didn't know how much longer the vampire would be gone, but after what she had done, she didn't want to be there when he returned.

Erik moved quickly through the shadows. He preyed upon the first human he found, took what he needed, and moved on. Deciding to keep the girl had been one of the stupidest decisions he had ever made. Thinking about it now, he wasn't sure what had possessed him to do such an idiotic thing. He couldn't keep her indefinitely. And now that she knew where he lived, he would have to move on. He hadn't lived as long as he had by being careless, or by trusting others. Until now, no one, save Rhys, knew the location of his lair.

Erik cursed softly. He had three choices. He could wipe his memory from Daisy's mind, though that might be difficult now that they had exchanged blood. He could kill her. Or he could let her go, pack up his few possessions, and search out a new lair. To his chagrin, he wasn't inclined to do any of them. His lair suited him. He had no desire to take Daisy's life, and, somewhat surprisingly, he didn't want her to forget him. One thing for certain, he knew he would never forget her.

Eager to see her again, curious to see if he could coax her into his bed, he quickly returned home.

A wave of his hand opened the front door. As he crossed the threshold, his eagerness to see Daisy was dampened by the sight that met his eyes. His living room, sparsely furnished to be sure, was a shambles. The carpet was splattered with tomato sauce, melted cheese, pepperoni, and lettuce, as well as a dark stain that turned out to be Coke. A Tiffany lamp lay in pieces. Sofa pillows were strewn across the floor.

Daisy O'Donnell sat on a chair in the middle of the living room, her arms folded over her chest, a defiant expression on her face.

Wordlessly, he moved past her. A quick inspection of the downstairs showed that Hurricane Daisy had blown through every room. The kitchen had escaped her wrath, but then, there was nothing in the drawers or cupboards for her to savage.

Tamping down his temper, he went upstairs and looked in the master bedroom. His bedding was piled on the floor; the pillows, too. She had emptied his dresser drawers and added the contents to the pile on the floor, along with his shoes and the clothes from his closet.

She had emptied the medicine cabinet and poured his specially blended, one-hundred-dollar-a-bottle of cologne down the sink. His comb and his toothbrush were in the toilet; she had written *I hate you* on the sink top with toothpaste, and *vampires suck* on the mirror.

She had trashed the other bedrooms as well, although the damage was minimal.

He was reluctant to open the door to his studio. He frowned as his gaze swept the room. He took a quick look in the other rooms, then took a deep breath in hopes of quieting his anger.

He let it out in a long, slow sigh, and then returned to the living room. Standing in front of the fireplace, he crossed his arms over his chest. "Do you feel better now that you've destroyed my home?"

"Yes, thank you," she said, even though it was a lie. Trashing his house had been a stupid, childish display of temper, although she had to admit it had made her feel better at the time. Now she just felt guilty, and ashamed.

He took a place in front of her chair, his arms folded across his chest. "You do realize that I can compel you to do whatever I want?"

A shadow of what might have been fear passed behind her eyes. She quickly blinked it away, her lips thinning.

"You don't believe me?"

"No."

He summoned his power, watched her expression change from defiance to wariness as preternatural power filled the room.

Daisy stared at him as his power swept over her. It lifted the fine hairs on her arms, sent a shiver of awareness trembling down her spine.

Speaking to her mind, Erik commanded her to rise, to wrap her arms around his waist, to press her lips to his.

His hands bracketed her hips, drawing her body tight

against his as he kissed her deeply. And as he did so, he let her know that she was completely at his mercy. When she understood that she was powerless to resist him, he released her from his hold and took a step backward.

"Exactly," he said. "Anything I wish. Perhaps you should contemplate what that means while you're cleaning up the mess you've made."

Cheeks burning with humiliation, she spun away from him, her movements as jerky as a robot's as she cleaned up the mess on the floor and put the living room to rights, then marched down the hallway toward the guest room.

Erik dropped down onto the sofa, one arm draped along the back, silently berating himself for his strong-arm tactics. What did he hope to gain by keeping her there against her will? And what was he going to do with her now?

Chapter 11

Daisy fumed silently as she stood in the middle of his bedroom, wondering where to start. Muttering an oath that would have made her father blush, she began hanging up Erik's clothes and putting them back in the closet. She couldn't help noticing that he only bought the best, whether it was shirts, slacks, or sweaters. His scent tickled her nostrils as she hung up a long black cloak reminiscent of the type Dracula always wore in movies. It was a compelling scent.

She folded his underwear and put it away, then put the sheets on the bed, only then wondering what need he had for a bed when he slept in a casket in the basement.

Going into the bathroom, she washed the toothpaste from the sink top and the mirror. Could he see himself in a mirror? In the movies, Dracula had no reflection. She wasn't sure why. One supposed authority on the subject said it was because a vampire had no soul, but Daisy didn't think that was possible. How could anyone live without a soul? And if they didn't have a soul, did it leave the body when the vampire was turned? And if it did, where did it go? Of course, since vampires weren't truly alive, but Undead, maybe a soul was just so much excess baggage.

With a shake of her head, she dropped his comb and his toothbrush into the wastebasket. Funny, she had never thought about vampires brushing their teeth. Did they have coffin breath when they woke in the morning?

Reluctant to return to Erik's presence, she plopped down in the middle of his bed and contemplated her immediate future. What was he going to do with her, or to her? Whatever he had in mind, she was certain she wouldn't like it the least little bit. She liked his kisses, though.

The thought brought a rush of heat to her cheeks. His kisses should have been repellant, disgusting, so why weren't they? Or maybe they were. Maybe he had used his vampire mojo to mess with her mind so she only thought they were pleasant.

She shuddered with the memory of his thoughts controlling hers. It had been a horrible experience. She had felt him inside her head, heard his commands, and been helpless to refuse.

I can compel you to do anything I want.

Now that was a scary thought. Of course, she hadn't believed him when he said it. She wouldn't make that mistake again. When she got out of there—*if* she got out of there— she would consult her grandmother. Nonnie O'Donnell was a white witch of the highest order. If anyone could conjure a spell to keep Erik out of Daisy's mind, it was Nonnie.

Daisy bolted off the bed when Erik appeared in the doorway. His gaze swept the room.

"I hope it's done to your satisfaction, *master*," she said with as much sarcasm as she could muster.

His gaze moved over her, ever so slowly, lingering on her lips, the swell of her breasts, the curve of her hip. "I'd like the bed better if you were in it."

"I'll bet you would!"

"You might like it, too," he said with a wicked grin.

His words made her heart race. Had that been a threat? Would he force her to submit to him?

Erik swore softly. He hadn't meant to frighten her, but he had. She stared at him, wide-eyed, like a deer caught in a bright light. He could hear her heart pounding, smell the fear on her skin.

Blowing out a breath, he shook his head. "I'm not going to hurt you." How many times had he said that? "You must know that I can't let you go."

"Why not?"

"Because you know where I rest." He spoke to her as if she were a child who must be made to understand. "No one living knows that." He stressed the word *living*.

Her face paled. "I won't tell anyone, I promise."

"Of course. That's what they all say."

Daisy stared at him. How many others had he killed? Would she become one more casualty in a long line of men and women he had silenced? The thought made her knees go weak.

Erik muttered an oath as all the color drained from her face. Fearing that she would faint again, he swept her into his arms, then sat on the edge of the bed, holding her close to his chest.

"Daisy, Daisy," he murmured, his voice low, husky with desire. "What am I to do with you?"

She stared at him through the thick veil of her lashes. Her eyes were wide and very green in her pale face, her lips slightly parted.

It was an invitation he couldn't resist. Lowering his head, he claimed her mouth with his, his tongue sweeping across her lips, demanding entrance, boldly exploring.

Daisy gasped as his tongue dueled with hers. Heat, like lightning, exploded through her, sizzling through every nerve and fiber of her being. Her hands curled over his shoulders, holding on for dear life.

Breathless, she closed her eyes as the world swam out of focus. There was a roaring in her ears, a sense of loss as he took his mouth from hers.

Bereft, she looked up at him. A small cry of panic escaped her throat when she saw the faint red glow in his eyes.

Vampire! The word screamed in her mind as he lowered his head to her throat.

Her whole body went still when she felt his fangs against her skin, but the pain she expected didn't come. Instead, a sweet warmth crept into her limbs, stealing her strength, stilling the protest she knew she should be making.

What was he doing to her? If only he would stop. If only he would never stop. Her eyelids fluttered down as she gave herself into his keeping. She was dying. The thought hovered at the edge of her consciousness, but it no longer seemed important.

Aware that he had almost taken too much, Erik drew back. Daisy lay limp in his embrace, her eyes closed, a faint smile on her lips.

Cursing himself for his lack of restraint, he ran his tongue over the small wounds in her neck, sealing them with his saliva. Gazing down at her, he shook his head. What was he to do with her? He couldn't keep her there indefinitely, he thought with no small degree of regret, and then he grunted softly. He was Erik, a vampire without equal. If he wanted to keep her in his house for a week or a year, who was going to stop him?

Whistling softly, he tucked her into bed, then left the house. She would need food and drink and a change of clothes when she woke.

* * *

Daisy snuggled under the covers, reluctant to wake. She had been having a most unusual dream, one in which she had been a princess being kept prisoner in a castle by a fierce dragon . . .

Bolting upright, she glanced around the room. She wasn't home. She wasn't in her own bed. She was being kept a prisoner, not in a castle, but a house. Not by a dragon, but by a monster just the same.

She lifted a hand to her neck. He had seduced her with kisses last night, and then taken her blood. And she had reveled in it. How disgusting was that? He must have hypnotized her or worked some sort of evil magic on her, to make her think she had enjoyed it. How could anyone enjoy being a vampire's dinner? Oh, Lord, was that why he was keeping her here? To feed on?

Her fingertips lingered on her throat as vivid images painted themselves across her mind, images of Erik's eyes as he bent over her, the erotic seduction of his unholy kisses, the feel of his arms around her, the husky timbre of his voice, the taste of his lips, his tongue . . .

Heat pooled in the pit of her belly. Monster he might be, but he knew how to arouse a woman. And she hated him for it.

Rising, she went into the bathroom to rinse her mouth, only then realizing that there were no dishes or glasses in the house.

And no food, she thought as her stomach growled, reminding her that all she'd had to eat since breakfast the day before was a few bites of salad.

She could call and order something, only Erik had her cell phone. Besides, there was no way to get past the wards on the house. She needed a bath, only she didn't relish the idea of bathing and then putting on her dirty underwear, or, worse yet, having Erik enter the bathroom while she was in the tub.

Returning to the bedroom, she noticed several packages piled on the dresser. They hadn't been there the night before.

Frowning, she poked into the largest one, a soft sigh of surprise rising in her throat when she pulled out a pair of sweatpants and a matching velour jacket, several pairs of socks, and a pair of fluffy pink slippers. The other bags yielded three pairs of jeans and six T-shirts in assorted colors, a pair of sandals, a comb and brush, a blow-dryer, hair spray, toothpaste, a pink toothbrush. And several sets of underwear in rainbow colors. How had he known her size? She shuddered to think!

After taking a quick shower, she pulled on the sweats and went downstairs, where another surprise awaited her. The kitchen, once barren, had been fully stocked with food. Boxes, cans, and dishes were neatly stacked in the cupboards. Milk, juice, eggs, cheese, and butter filled the refrigerator, along with a number of fresh fruits and vegetables. She spied a set of stainless steel cookware on the floor near the stove, along with a state-of-the-art coffeemaker.

Standing there, she didn't know whether to laugh or cry. On the one hand, she was touched that he had been thoughtful enough to provide for her needs. On the other hand, she was filled with apprehension, since it was obvious he had no intention of letting her go anytime soon. Of course, since he intended to feed and clothe her, she supposed that meant he didn't intend to drink her dry, at least not right away.

On that happy note, she decided to have breakfast and worry about her future after she'd had her morning coffee.

Consciousness returned with the setting of the sun. Sitting up, Erik opened his senses, nearly gagging as the scent of cooked meat stung his nostrils. He had no one to blame but himself. He had gone grocery shopping for the woman the night before. Not knowing what she liked and not being particularly familiar with the food of the day, he had bought a little of everything.

Erik shook his head. The odors coming from the kitchen were almost enough to convince him to let her go, but the memory of holding her in his arms, of sampling her sweet lips and her sweeter blood, quickly dispelled that notion. His mouth watered at the thought of holding her again, tasting her again.

Rising, he pulled on a pair of well-worn jeans and a long-sleeved gray T-shirt. Late last night, he had brought some of his clothing down to his lair, partly for convenience's sake now that he had a houseguest, and partly to keep her from slicing his entire wardrobe to ribbons should Hurricane Daisy go on the rampage again.

Enthused at the thought of spending the evening with her, Erik unlocked the door to his lair and padded silently up the stairs.

Daisy was eating dinner in the living room when she felt a peculiar tingling along her nape. Startled, she glanced around the room. One minute she was alone, the next Erik was standing in the doorway.

"You!" She pressed a hand to her heart, startled by the realization that his presence had caused that odd tingling sensation. Frowning, she lifted a hand to her neck. She had tasted his blood; he had taken hers. Was that why she was suddenly so in tune to his presence?

He jerked his chin toward the plate in her lap. "Your dinner is getting cold."

"What? Oh." Trapped by his gaze, she had completely forgotten her meal.

She couldn't stop watching him as he moved into the room.

Though he was dressed in ordinary jeans and a dark gray T-shirt, there was nothing ordinary about Erik Delacourt. Not the way he looked, not the way he moved. She was aware of him in ways she never had been before. She frowned. Was that another side effect of his drinking from her? Or her drinking from him? She didn't understand why she hadn't been repulsed by the taste of his blood. But one thing she knew for sure, it was never going to happen again.

She glanced at her dinner, but seemed to have lost her appetite.

Taking a seat at the other end of the sofa, he regarded her through narrowed eyes. "Something wrong?"

"How long are you going to keep me here?"

His gaze slid over her from head to heel. "As long as it pleases me."

"Well, it doesn't please me," she retorted. "I want to go home. Now!"

He nodded, then blew out a sigh. "Very well."

"Just like that?" she asked, suddenly suspicious.

"More or less."

"What does *that* mean?"

"It means you can stay here, or I can wipe my memory and this place from your mind and let you go."

She liked the idea of going home. Surprisingly, she didn't like the idea of forgetting him. "Are you afraid of me?"

Soft laughter filled the room. "Of you? No."

"Then why do you want to wipe your memory from my mind?"

"Because you're the Blood Thief. Because you probably know other hunters who take more than blood. Because I haven't lived this long by trusting mortals. Because . . ."

Daisy held up her hand. "Enough. I get your drift."

"So, what will it be?"

"Isn't there a third choice?"

He didn't say anything, but he didn't have to. She saw the answer in the depths of his unblinking black eyes.

"You'd kill me? Just because I know where you live?"

Again, he didn't answer. He simply looked at her, waiting for her decision.

"But I . . . you . . ." She blew out a sigh of exasperation. How did one argue with a vampire, anyway?

He crossed his arms over his chest. "Go on."

Refusing to let him know she was afraid, determined not to back down, Daisy squared her shoulders and lifted her chin. "I don't like any of those options."

"No?"

She glared at him, annoyed by the amusement evident in his tone. "No."

Erik stifled the urge to laugh. He knew she was scared. He could hear the rapid beat of her heart, smell the fear on her skin. It teased his hunger even as it raised his admiration for her courage. "What do you suggest?"

"That I promise not to tell anyone where you live, and you let me go home, and we get to know each other better before there's any bloodshed on either side."

"And you expect me to take your word that you won't come hunting me again, or worse, send someone to take my head?"

"Are you suggesting that I can't be trusted?" she exclaimed.

"I think that's been proved."

"What do you mean?"

"You're the Blood Thief. You took Tina's blood. You came here to steal mine. Now that you know where I live, what's to stop you from trying again?"

"How do you know about that?" she blurted, then bit down on her lower lip. *Stupid move, Daisy,* she thought angrily. *Now he knows you're guilty.*

"It's hard to keep a secret in my world."

"You know her?"

"Yes, but that's not the problem."

"No?"

"No. The problem is the vampire who sired her," Erik said quietly. "And he's looking for you."

Chapter 12

Daisy stared at Erik, her eyes wide. She didn't try to mask her fear this time. "I don't believe you."

Erik shrugged. "I may have exaggerated, but Rhys . . ."

"Rhys!" Daisy exclaimed in horror. "Rhys Costain?"

"You know him?"

"I know of him." Fear shot through Daisy. The hunters had an online network. They shared information such as the names and physical descriptions of vampires, their approximate age, their last known resting places. Rhys Costain was known throughout the vampire-hunting world.

And he was after her.

"Are you all right?" Erik asked. "You look a little pale."

"I'm fine. You were saying?"

Erik studied her a moment, wondering if she was going to faint again. "Rhys isn't looking for you in particular, at least not yet. But he'll sniff you out, sooner or later."

Rhys Costain. The name alone was enough to strike terror in the heart of the strongest hunter. Though he wasn't the most ancient vampire in existence, Costain was believed to be the oldest, most dangerous vampire in North America. No one knew for sure just how old he was. It was said that very old vampires required less blood to survive, that they could even endure the sun's light for brief periods of time. Their strength was phenomenal; their preternatural senses without equal.

Daisy swallowed past the lump of fear in her throat. "Just how old is he?"

"Five hundred and twelve, give or take a decade or two."

Five hundred and twelve. Few vampires had the will or the stamina to survive that long. If she ever got home again, she would have to share what she had learned with the other hunters.

She wrapped her arms around her middle. What chance would she have against a vampire that old? "Are you going to hand me over to him? Is that why you're keeping me here?"

"No, but you do present a problem."

Daisy shuddered. How did vampires handle a "human problem"? And did she really want to know? "What are you going to do with me?"

"Beats the hell out of me." Erik wasn't sure what Rhys and the Council would do if they discovered he was harboring the notorious Blood Thief. Looking at her, with her guileless green eyes and petite figure, it was hard to imagine her searching out vampires and stealing their blood.

Erik swore softly. If he had just followed his own advice, he wouldn't have gotten mixed up with Miss Daisy O'Donnell in the first place. Mortal females were nothing but trouble. You'd think that, after 325 years, he would have absorbed that fact.

He grunted softly as a new thought occurred to him. "You destroyed Saul, too, didn't you? You don't have to answer. I can see the truth in your eyes. Dammit!"

"It was self-defense!" Daisy exclaimed. "What was I supposed to do, let him kill me?"

"You should have stayed the hell away from him." Erik

shook his head. What the devil was wrong with Daisy's parents, to let their daughter engage in such a dangerous business? Sure, most vampires were helpless during the day, but not all. Any vampire over a hundred was capable of sensing danger and defending himself if necessary.

He swore again. It was bad enough that she trafficked in vampire blood. He might have been able to talk Rhys out of taking revenge for that, but no way in hell could he protect Daisy from Rhys once Rhys knew she had destroyed one of their own.

She was shivering now. "I guess I'm in big trouble, aren't I?"

"Oh, yeah," he muttered as he took her in his arms. *And so am I.*

Erik left the house later that night, after Daisy had fallen asleep. What was he going to do with her? The question repeated itself in his mind over and over again. He couldn't let her go home. If Rhys learned Daisy was the one who had taken Tina's blood and staked Saul . . . Erik shook his head. He didn't even want to think about what Rhys would do to her. Rhys was pretty easygoing most of the time, but cross him or someone under his protection, and he could be downright vicious, even by vampire standards.

So. He couldn't let her go, but he couldn't keep her in his house indefinitely, either. He wasn't sure he could rest comfortably knowing the Blood Thief was under the same roof. Destroying Saul had proven she was a hunter to be reckoned with. And Erik didn't intend to be her next victim.

He was about to return home when Rhys materialized beside him.

"Hey, buddy, you in the mood for a little midnight snack?"

"I was just heading home."

"No way. It's early and I smell fresh blood."

Deciding a refusal might stir Rhys's suspicion, Erik followed him across town to Santa Monica where they found two old derelicts sitting at the end of the pier huddled over a bottle of cheap wine.

"I'll take the one on the left," Rhys remarked.

"You always take the best for yourself," Erik muttered.

Rhys shrugged. "That's because I'm older and—"

"Wiser and stronger," Erik finished for him. "Yeah, I know."

With a smug grin, Rhys dragged the man on the left into his embrace. A moment later, the scent of blood filled the salty air.

Erik grimaced as he wrapped his arm around the other man's shoulders. The wino smelled of booze and urine and too many days without a bath. Muttering an oath, Erik released his hold on the drunk, who staggered backward, then turned and ran down the pier as fast as his unsteady legs could carry him.

Lifting his head from the wino's neck, Rhys smirked at Erik. "You always were a picky eater."

"And you were always a pig."

"Yes, but an older, wiser pig."

"Older and wiser, my ass," Erik retorted. Rhys had been turned a few months short of his twenty-first birthday; Erik had been thirty. But Rhys had been a vampire longer. Perhaps that made him wiser, but sometimes he acted like an arrogant teenager. As for stronger, Erik couldn't argue with that. Vampires grew stronger as they grew older.

With a bark of laughter, Rhys lowered his head to his prey's neck and drank.

Moving to the rail, Erik stared out over the dark water, his thoughts drifting toward Daisy. What was he doing here when he could be home with her? He turned when Rhys slapped him on the back.

"Shall we go find something more to your liking?" Costain asked good-naturedly.

Erik shook his head. Rhys never let him forget the differences in their upbringing and background. Erik had been the oldest son of a wealthy landowner. When he came of age, he had inherited property and a title. Rhys had been the bastard son of a prostitute, forced to steal food and beg for money to survive. Erik thought it an odd twist of fate that the two of them had met and become friends.

"Something perfumed and refined," Rhys suggested with a faint leer, "as befitting a man of your station."

"Enough!" Erik said curtly.

"Never enough," his companion drawled.

"Here we go," Erik muttered as they walked down the pier toward the beach. Rhys might be one of the oldest and strongest of their kind, but he had a melancholy streak a mile wide.

"Never enough." Rhys waved a hand in the air. "In five hundred and twelve years, I've never had enough. Not like you. You had it all."

"It was a long time ago."

"But you still had it," his companion said, his voice turning bitter. "A wife, children . . ."

"Rhys, don't go there."

"You're right! You're right! The past is over and done, but we've got an hour or two before sunrise, and I'm still thirsty. Come on, let's finish off the night with something that's young and smells good."

Like a wounded animal seeking shelter, Daisy snuggled deeper under the covers. She was usually eager to be up and about, but not today. Why not today, she wondered. The reason hit her like a splash of cold water. Rhys Costain was hunting for her and, according to Erik, he wouldn't stop until he found her.

"So, what are you going to do about it?" she muttered. "Just lie here and wait for him to find you?"

Flinging the covers aside, she went downstairs. Coffee. She needed coffee. And something to write with. A search in her handbag turned up a pen and an old envelope.

Sitting on the sofa, a cup of coffee close at hand, she began to write down everything she knew about vampires. Her father had always said knowledge was power, so what did she know about the Undead? Garlic didn't faze them. Old ones weren't entirely helpless during the day. Grimacing, she remembered that she hadn't needed a mallet to drive a stake through Saul's heart. Erik was able to place wards on his house that kept her from leaving. Was that vampire magic, or warlock magick? According to her father, holy water and crosses didn't provide much protection. As for mirrors, only the very young ones cast no reflection. Daisy had always puzzled over that.

She sat up straight as a new thought occurred to her. Why wasn't Erik's name listed on the vampire hunters' networking site? Of course, he could have changed his name. Vampires did that from time to time, but sooner or later, one hunter or another always ferreted out any new alias, as well as the location of a new lair, if the vampire moved when it changed its name. She thought about asking Erik why he wasn't listed, but she was pretty sure he wouldn't tell her. It was just as well, because she wasn't supposed to talk about her father's list or the networking site.

After finishing her coffee, Daisy returned to the kitchen. Since she wasn't really hungry, she settled on buttered toast and orange juice for breakfast and then, because she was curious, she made her way down to Erik's lair.

She paused at the door, suddenly reluctant to see him at rest.

"Suck it up, Daisy," she muttered. "You destroyed a vampire a couple of days ago. If you could do that, you can look at Erik while he's asleep, or resting, or dead, or whatever the heck he is."

And so saying, she reached for the knob, somewhat surprised that the door wasn't locked. Of course, why should he bother? He had nothing to fear from her since he had taken her weapons, her syringe, and her cell phone.

Taking a deep breath, Daisy stepped inside. She hadn't had time to look around the last time she had been in his lair. Now she saw that it wasn't a cellar at all, but a large, finished room. Most likely it had been a family room, she thought, or maybe a bonus room. An eight-branch candelabra on a thick black chain hung from the ceiling. Two floor-to-ceiling bookcases stood on either side of a brick fireplace. Other than the bookcases, there was no furniture in the room. There was no light in the room, either, save for the illumination that spilled down the stairway, making it hard to see details from the doorway.

But there was no mistaking the shape of a shiny black coffin, even in the dim light. Staring at it, Daisy felt her courage desert her. Erik was inside. He was a vampire. She had danced with him. She had let him kiss her. She had kissed him in return.

Giving her courage a swift kick, she tiptoed across the floor.

The lid was open. And Erik Delacourt lay inside. Clad in a faded gray T-shirt and a pair of black sweatpants, he looked like he was just taking a nap.

All the vampires she had seen looked indisputably dead. Why didn't he? His skin didn't look pale and waxy. If she touched him, would he feel it? Was his skin cold? Did his heart beat when he was asleep? She frowned. Did it beat when he was awake?

And even as those questions chased themselves across her

mind, his nostrils flared and then his eyelids opened and she found herself gazing into his eyes. Dark eyes instantly filled with awareness and concern.

As if by magic, the candles overhead sprang to life, illuminating the room in a soft, golden glow.

"Daisy, is something wrong?"

She shook her head, too discomfited to speak. He sounded so . . . so normal.

He leaned up on one elbow, worry creasing his brow. "What are you doing down here?"

"I was . . ." She lifted one shoulder and let it fall. "Just curious, I guess."

"Curious?"

"I . . ." She worried her lower lip, then decided, what the hell, why not tell him the truth? "I was curious to see how you looked when you were . . ." She gestured at the coffin.

"Ah," he murmured. "You wanted to see me while I was at rest?"

She nodded.

And his frown deepened. "Why?"

"I'm not sure."

"Feminine curiosity, perhaps, like Alice, wandering in Wonderland."

"I guess so."

"Being a Blood Thief, I'd think you would have seen a number of vampires at rest."

She nodded absently. "How did you know I was here?"

"I smelled you."

"Do I stink?" Daisy asked, embarrassed by the thought.

"Not at all," he said with a wry grin. "You smell quite delectable."

She didn't think that was a good thing, not when he was a predator and she was prey.

"As entertaining as this is," he said, smothering a yawn, "I need my rest."

"Of course, I'm sorry. I shouldn't have . . ."

He made a vague gesture of dismissal with his hand. The candles flickered out as he sank into the depths of the casket, his eyes closing as he succumbed to the Dark Sleep.

". . . disturbed you," she murmured. She watched him for a few moments; then, with a sigh, she left the lair. She closed the heavy iron door as quietly as she could before making her way up the stairs.

Vampire or not, he was still the most intriguing man she had ever met.

Daisy passed several hours reading and watching TV. She fixed lunch, watched another movie, and when she grew bored with that, she found a crossword puzzle book. Vampires doing crossword puzzles. Who'd a thunk it? Opening the book, she noticed that several of the puzzles had been completed. In ink.

She fixed an early dinner, partly because she was hungry, and partly because cooking and cleaning up afterward gave her something to do. Time had never passed this slowly at home.

She had just started another crossword puzzle when Erik appeared. One minute she was alone in the living room, the next he was there.

The book fell to the floor as she pressed one hand to her heart. "How do you do that?"

He shrugged. "Mind over matter, I guess."

Daisy retrieved the book and laid it on the table beside the sofa.

Erik sat beside her. "I didn't mean to startle you."

"Well, I think you startled me out of a year's growth," she

muttered irritably. "Can all vampires materialize out of thin air like that?"

"As far as I know."

Daisy frowned. For a girl who came from a family of hunters, it occurred to her that she didn't really know a whole heck of a lot about vampires, and that some of the things she thought she knew were false. She supposed she should have paid more attention when her father had explained things to her, but she had been young and a little cocky at the time. Looking back over the last few years, she realized she was lucky to be alive. How much longer would her luck hold out, she wondered, now that she was being hunted by a 512-year-old vampire?

Curious, she canted her head to the side. "How old are you?"

Coming out of nowhere, she supposed she couldn't blame him for looking surprised. For a moment, she didn't think he was going to answer.

"I've been a vampire for a little over three hundred and twenty-five years."

Ah. That explained how he had been able to be awake when she arrived the other afternoon. Maybe it also explained why he didn't look dead when he was at rest. No doubt his blood would bring a high price, just as he had said.

One thing she did know about vampires was that they were considered young for the first hundred years; anything that survived over five centuries was viewed as ancient. Of course, you could never tell how old vampires were just by looking at them, or how long they had been undead, since they stopped aging once they were turned.

"When were you turned?" She had heard of one female vampire who had worked the Dark Trick on a five-year-old child because she was lonely and wanted a little girl for company. It was said that the little girl aged emotionally, but her body never matured. A cruel fate, Daisy thought, to have an adult mind trapped in a child's body.

Erik draped one arm along the back of the sofa. "You're full of questions tonight, my little flower. Any particular reason?"

"Not really." Sitting back, she folded her arms under her breasts. "Just curious."

He regarded her through narrowed eyes, as if trying to judge her sincerity, and then he shrugged. "I was turned on my thirtieth birthday." Beyond doubt, it had been a night he would never forget, nor forgive.

"Not a very nice present," Daisy remarked.

"True enough, although it lasted far longer than any of the other gifts I received that night."

Daisy frowned, surprised that he could make jokes about something that had surely turned his whole life upside down. "How did it happen?"

"My wife . . ."

"You were married?"

"Of course. I was a healthy male in my prime."

"Did you have children?"

"Yes." He looked past her, his voice almost a whisper. "A boy and a girl."

"I'm sorry, I didn't mean to bring up unhappy memories."

"It was a long time ago." And yet, even all these years later, he could see their faces clearly in his mind, hear the sound of his wife's voice, the laughter of his children.

"But it still hurts," Daisy said quietly.

"Yes."

"Did your wife know you were a warlock?"

"Of course. I couldn't keep a thing like that a secret."

"And she didn't mind?"

"I wasn't a practicing warlock then, hadn't been for years." He had forsaken his magic completely when he married. His mother had never forgiven him for turning his back on his heritage. There were those who practiced the art of magic, and those, like Erik and his mother, who were born to it.

"Go on," Daisy coaxed. "You said you were turned when you were thirty."

"Yes. Abigail, my wife, had given me a surprise party. I think she must have invited everyone in London . . ."

"You're from England, then?"

"Yes, originally." He had been a wealthy man back then, landed gentry, with a large estate and a dozen servants to do his bidding.

"You don't sound English."

"I lost my accent years ago."

She tried to imagine what Erik would have been like back then. In her mind's eye, she tried to imagine him wearing the clothing of the period, overseeing a large estate, presiding at the dinner table, but she couldn't. It was even more difficult to picture him with a wife and children.

"As I was saying, Abigail had given me a party. I was mingling with our guests in the ballroom after dinner when I saw a woman I didn't recognize. I supposed her to be a friend of Abigail's. I went over to introduce myself . . ."

He paused a moment, his thoughts turned inward. "Needless to say, she wasn't Abigail's friend, or anyone else's. She persuaded me to take her outside, saying she wanted to see the gardens in the moonlight. Once we were alone . . ."

He paused again. A muscle throbbed in his cheek. "Once we were alone, she mesmerized me, and then, while I was still in her thrall, she let me see what she really was. I fought her as best I could, but to no avail. Small and petite though she was, she had the strength of twenty grown men. She held me down and drained me to the point of death, and then offered me a choice. I could die, or I could become what she was."

Rising, he began to pace the floor in front of her. "At the time, I didn't fully realize what it meant to be a vampire. I thought all it entailed was drinking a little blood to survive, and I was willing to do that, to do anything, to stay with my family." He laughed, a cold, bitter laugh. "How incredibly foolish I was! I didn't return to the party. I spent the rest of the night trying to come to terms with what had happened. I convinced myself that everything would be all right, that I'd be able to hide what I was from Abigail and my children. I spent the next day buried under a pile of straw in the stables. When I woke that night, I was ravenous."

Daisy stared up at him, afraid to hear the rest.

He stopped in front of the hearth, his hands resting on the mantel. "I could hear the beating of the hearts of those in the house. Servants. Guests who had spent the night. Abigail. My children. I climbed down from the hayloft, my only thought to feed."

"You didn't . . . ?" She imagined him bursting into the house, mad with need, fangs bared, attacking his wife and his children.

Slowly, he turned to face her. "No, but I would have. Instead, I attacked one of the grooms who had come in to feed the horses. The thirst . . . it was more powerful, more painful, than anything I had expected. He didn't survive. When I came to myself, when I saw what I'd done, I knew I could never face Abigail, never trust myself to be with her or our children. I saddled a horse and left the estate. I never went back."

"Never?"

Erik shook his head. "I sent her a letter, told her I was going to America, that I was sorry . . ." It had been the hardest thing he had ever done. His only solace had been knowing that he was leaving her and his children well off financially, and that she wasn't entirely alone. Her parents had lived close by, as had his. He knew they would look after his family.

"So, you never saw them again?"

"They never saw me again. I didn't go to America. I couldn't leave them. I stayed out of sight, but I was never far away. I watched my children grow and marry and have children of their own. And when my great-grandchildren were grown and doing well, I left the country." Unwilling to return to his homeland and resurrect unhappy memories, he had never gone back.

"What happened to the vampire who made you?"

"I destroyed her." As though exhausted by the tale, Erik dropped onto a corner of the sofa. It had taken him fifty years to find Iliana. His only regret was that her suffering had been quickly over, while his heartache remained to this day. "I'm curious about something," he said after a time.

"What?"

Afraid he was opening a topic of conversation he didn't want to pursue, yet driven by a burst of uncharacteristic curiosity, he found himself asking, "Why didn't you trash the paintings when you trashed the rest of the house?"

Chapter 13

Daisy frowned, wondering why he had waited so long to ask, and then she shrugged. "I thought about it," she confessed, "but I couldn't do it. They're wonderful!" She made a broad gesture, encompassing the room's blank walls. "Why don't you hang a few in here where you can see them? It seems a shame to keep such masterpieces in a room where no one can see them."

She had never seen such beautiful artwork. Most of the paintings had been dark in nature—storm-tossed seas, sinking ships, winter-starved wolves skulking beneath barren trees, a mounted knight battling a fire-breathing dragon. Her favorite had been of a lonely-looking castle on a windswept promontory.

"Who's the artist?" Daisy asked. "I'm no expert, but they looked like they were all painted by the same hand."

"Indeed, they were," he admitted, pleased that she had seen his work and admired it. He had often thought of hanging a few of his paintings, but it seemed like the height of vanity to cover the walls with his own work.

"I'd love to have one, but I'm sure I couldn't afford to buy . . ." She stared at Erik a moment, and then she knew. "They're yours, aren't they? You're the artist."

He lifted one shoulder in a casual shrug. "Guilty as charged."

Daisy could only stare at him. Whoever heard of a vampire having such an amazing talent? Of course, he'd had 325 years to perfect his craft.

A dozen questions chased themselves through Daisy's mind, but before she could ask any of them, someone knocked at the door.

Hope fluttered in Daisy's heart. Perhaps she could find a way to pass a message to whoever had come to call.

Erik stood abruptly. "Daisy, go upstairs. Now."

"I don't want to."

"Yes, you do." He held up a hand to stay the protest he saw rising in her eyes. "It's Rhys."

Rhys! The very name struck terror in Daisy's heart. Rhys was the vampire who was looking for her. Without another word, she ran out of the room and up the stairs.

Erik waited until he heard the bedroom door close before he invited the Master of the City into the house.

"I've been out checking lairs," Rhys remarked as he crossed the threshold. "Checking cameras." He glanced around the room, his eyes narrowed, his nostrils flared. "Have you got company?"

Erik smiled affably. "A dinner guest, you might say. I was just about to dine."

"Ah." Rhys smiled, showing a hint of fang. "Any chance there's enough for two?"

"Not tonight."

Rhys nodded. "Did you install a camera?"

"Not yet."

"It was to have been done by tonight."

"The night is still young." Erik glanced toward the staircase. "And my dinner awaits."

Rhys lifted his head, his nostrils twitching like a cat's at a mouse hole. "She smells young and unspoiled."

"Nothing gets by you," Erik remarked dryly. It took considerable effort to keep his expression passive, to keep from putting himself between Rhys and the stairway, but any move on his part now might arouse Rhys's suspicion or, worse, his innate need to hunt.

"Bon appetit, mon ami."

"Yeah, you, too," Erik replied. "But not here."

Rhys threw up his hands in a gesture of surrender. "Okay, okay, I'm going. Meet me at La Morte Rouge later. I've got a taste for French food all of a sudden."

Erik nodded. Rhys had opened La Morte Rouge—the Red Death—ten years ago. It was located along a deserted stretch of highway and catered to an elite clientele. Only vampires, and mortals who got their kicks from nourishing the Undead, were allowed entrance.

After seeing Rhys out and locking the door behind him, Erik made his way to the bottom of the stairs. He stood there a long moment, looking up, his thoughts troubled. He had sworn allegiance to Rhys and the West Coast vampires. Sworn to protect them against all enemies, as they had sworn to protect him. And he had done as promised, until now.

He muttered an oath as Daisy appeared at the top of the stairs. What the devil was he doing, harboring the Blood Thief under his roof? Protecting the one who had taken Tina's blood and destroyed Saul would surely be considered treason of the highest order. If Rhys and the others found out, retribution would be swift, and final.

As much as he liked this house and enjoyed the climate in Southern California, maybe it was time to give some serious thought to finding a new lair, preferably a city on the other side of the country, or perhaps the other side of the world.

Daisy looked down at him, her brows drawn together. "Is it safe?"

"He's gone."

Erik admired the sway of her hips as he watched her walk down the stairs. She was young, beautiful, desirable. Easily worth the risk of keeping her there.

"He scares me," she said when she reached the foot of the stairs.

"And rightly so," Erik remarked. Rhys was a vampire's vampire—cold and calculating. There was little in the human world that Rhys Costain gave a damn about. To Rhys, mortals were useful for one thing, and one thing only. Beyond that, he had little regard for them, perhaps because he had once been betrayed by a mortal female. Only a few people knew that Rhys had been enamored of a noblewoman in the distant past. When he found Josette in bed with another man, he had flown into a rage and killed them both. Erik knew nothing of the affair beyond the bare facts of what had happened. It was something Rhys refused to discuss in detail.

Erik followed Daisy into the living room, beguiled by the scent of her hair, her skin, her blood. He wanted her, all of her, now, tonight. Wanted her in his arms, in his bed. Wanted to taste the warmth of her lips, feel the heat of her skin, savor the sweetness of her life's essence. He could hear it flowing through her veins—the rich, red elixir of life.

As though sensing his thoughts, she whirled around to face him.

Erik paused when he saw the wary expression on her face and knew, in that moment, that what he was thinking, feeling, must be evident in his eyes. A vampire in the throes of the hunger was never a pretty sight.

Muttering an oath, he turned away, his hands clenched at

his sides. He was confident he could keep her safe from Rhys. He was less certain he could keep her safe from himself.

Daisy stared at Erik's back, chilled by the predatory gleam she had seen in his eyes. He had looked like a wild animal ready to attack its prey. Fear coiled deep within her, sending an icy chill to every extremity. Just as she had feared, he was obviously keeping her here for only one reason.

A frantic glance around the room showed there was no place to run, nothing she could use for a weapon. She had only her wits and her bare hands, neither of which would repel him. Resigned, she closed her eyes and waited.

Erik scrubbed his hands up and down his thighs, annoyed that he had frightened her. Did she really think he was keeping her here as some kind of midnight snack?

Dammit, he was trying to protect her from a vicious killer. Even as the thought crossed his mind, he heard the voice of his conscience, laughing. Rhys wasn't the only vicious killer. As a young vampire, Erik had committed acts he now regretted, done things he was bitterly ashamed of.

Taking a deep breath, he turned to face her. "Daisy? Daisy, look at me."

She opened her eyes ever so slowly. Their vivid green accentuated her pale face.

"I'm not going to hurt you."

"I'd like to believe that," she said. "I really would, but . . . just now . . . your eyes . . ."

"Yes, I know, they turn red when . . ." He made a vague gesture with his hand.

"When you're hungry? Thirsty?"

"Either one will do." He took a step toward the sofa, but stopped when she recoiled. "I'm sorry I frightened you, but you're a very desirable woman in more ways than one."

She blinked up at him, certain that, as prey, she shouldn't

be flattered by his words. After all, she was pretty sure that zebras weren't flattered when stalked by hungry lions.

Erik blew out a sigh. Affairs with female vampires weren't nearly as difficult, which was why he had avoided emotional entanglements with human females for the last three hundred years.

Crossing his arms over his chest, he asked, "How can I convince you that I'm not going to hurt you?"

"You can let me go home."

"Is that what you really want?"

"Yes, of course." But even as she spoke the words, Daisy found herself having second thoughts. A vampire as old as Rhys could probably be out and about both day and night. If Erik truly meant her no harm, she was probably safer here, with him, than at home, alone. Unless she could get Nonnie to come and stay with her. She was pretty sure Nonnie would be able to protect her. But was she sure enough to bet her life, or her grandmother's, on it?

Erik remained silent as he watched Daisy wage a silent war with herself, trying to decide who presented more danger to her survival, himself or Rhys. In the long run, it didn't matter what she decided, because she was staying whether she liked it or not.

"Will it ever be safe for me to go home?" she asked with a sigh of resignation.

"I don't know."

"I could go stay with Nonnie." She voiced the suggestion aloud, curious to see Erik's reaction.

"Who's that?"

"My grandmother. She's the one who made my compass. Since she magicked a way for me to locate vampires, I'm sure she could conjure something to protect me from Rhys."

"And from me?"

Her gaze slid away from his.

It was all the answer he needed. "Where does she live?"

"In Boca Raton. She has a gift shop there."

"Is she a hunter, too?"

"No. She sells handmade jewelry and seashells. And an occasional charm or two."

"And you think she can protect you from Rhys?"

Daisy nodded, although she wasn't sure at all.

"I'll think about it," Erik said. "Right now, I've got to meet Rhys."

"You won't tell him I'm here?"

"What do you think?"

"I'm sorry, it was a silly question."

"I'll be back soon," he said, caressing her cheek with his knuckles. "Behave yourself while I'm gone."

Stifling the urge to stick her tongue out at him, she watched him leave the house, although *leave* wasn't exactly the right word. He didn't go out the door, he merely dissolved into a mist of sparkling dove gray motes and vanished from her sight.

Daisy stared at the place where he had stood only moments before, then shook her head.

"If I could do that," she muttered, "I wouldn't have to worry about Rhys or anyone else."

When Erik arrived at La Morte Rouge, Rhys was waiting for him at the bar.

"So, you're here. Are you ready for dessert?" Rhys asked with a good-natured grin.

Erik shrugged. "Sure, I could use a bite or two." Or three or four, he thought, his hunger rising as his nostrils filled with the mingled scents of warm blood and desire that filled the air.

He glanced around the club, noting the usual Sunday night crowd was in full swing. The human females wore provocative clothing, mostly black, that bared their throats and a good deal of cleavage. Of course, none of them used their real names. Instead, they wore delicate brooches inscribed with the French names they were known by in the club—Monique, Babette, Fifi. The males wore vests and slacks, again, mostly black, and had names like Henri, Etienne, and Jacques.

"I've reserved two rooms," Rhys remarked, slapping Erik on the shoulder. "Monique is already waiting for you in number three. I'll meet you back here later."

Erik nodded. He watched Rhys stride across the floor toward room six where his choice of the night awaited. Rhys didn't have a favorite at the club. His usual requirement was that his companion for the evening be young, female, and blonde.

Wondering why he felt a sudden twinge of guilt, Erik went into room three. The rooms at the club were all decorated with Louis XV furniture and artwork. The bed linen was changed after each visit. A small bathroom provided a place to wash up after each encounter, if necessary.

Monique was waiting for him on the bed, a smile of welcome on her face. She was a beautiful woman in her mid-forties, with a toned body and tanned skin. Long red hair framed an oval face. He had been visiting her regularly ever since he moved to California. Some nights he wanted only to feed, some nights he satisfied his other hungers.

"Good evening," she purred. "What are you in the mood for tonight, *mon chevalier foncé*?"

Erik snorted softly. Her dark knight, indeed. Sitting on the edge of the bed, he brushed the hair away from her neck, then bent to drop kisses along the smooth curve of her throat.

With a sigh, she surrendered to him, willing to give whatever he asked.

Erik fed quickly, wishing all the while that it was Daisy in his arms. After closing the wounds in Monique's neck, he kissed her cheek, then gained his feet. "Till next time, *cherie.*"

"I was hoping you'd stay till morning," Monique said, pouting prettily. "It's been a long time since we shared a night together."

He forced a smile. "Another time. Rhys is waiting for me."

The smile faded from her lips. Monique and Rhys had a long-standing dislike for one another. Erik wondered from time to time what had caused the rift, but neither of them would discuss it.

"Until next time," he said and left the room, relieved, for the first time since he had met Monique, that he had an excuse to leave.

Rhys joined him at the bar a short time later.

"So," Erik asked, "what's going on?"

"That's what I wanted to ask you."

"What do you mean?"

"You've been a little distant the last few days."

Erik shrugged. "So I wanted a little alone time. Anything wrong with that?"

Rhys rested his elbow on the bar. "It's Mariah. She thinks you're up to something."

"Yeah? Like what?"

"Beats the hell out of me. You know Mariah," Rhys said with a grin. "She's always out for blood of one kind or another. She doesn't think you're taking the whole Blood Thief thing seriously enough, that maybe you're hiding something."

"She's right," Erik said. "I'm hiding the Thief in my back pocket."

"Look, I know Mariah's not your favorite person, but cut her a little slack. She's worried."

"Aren't we all?" Erik muttered.

Rhys punched Erik in the arm. "So I told her I'd have a talk with you, and now we've had it."

"Maybe I should be asking you what's going on," Erik said. "Since when do you worry about what anyone else—especially a woman—thinks?"

"Mellowing in my old age, I guess. Hell, I'm just trying to keep the peace. Oh, one more thing and then I'll be on my way," Rhys remarked, all humor gone from his eyes. "The Blood Thief has struck again."

In an effort to buy a little time, Erik sipped his drink. He didn't know which Blood Thief had struck again, but it couldn't be the one living under his roof. Could it? He shook the thought from his mind. Such a thing was impossible. Daisy hadn't been out of his house in days. Still . . . "How do you know?"

"I just got a phone call from Mariah. She was supposed to meet Tina at Craig's place tonight. When she got there, they were both dead."

"I'm sorry to hear that." Though Erik had harbored no real affection for either Tina or her mortal lover, senseless death was always unfortunate. "What makes you think . . . ?"

Erik swore softly. He had almost asked Rhys what made him think there was another thief in town.

"What makes me think what?" Rhys asked.

"What makes you think it's the work of the Blood Thief and not some other hunter?"

Rhys looked at Erik, his eyes narrowed. "What makes you think it isn't?"

Erik shrugged. "Maybe Tina and Craig had a fight and killed each other." It was a slim possibility, but in his world, stranger things had happened.

"I guess Craig and Tina could have committed suicide, too," Rhys remarked, his voice dripping with sarcasm, "but Craig had a ten-inch knife in his back and Tina had been drained dry and staked. Doesn't sound like a double suicide to me."

"Okay, okay," Erik muttered. "Have it your way."

Rhys nodded. "I always do."

Erik grunted softly. If there was one thing about the Master of the City that annoyed Erik more than anything else, it was that, right or wrong, Rhys always managed to get things done the way he wanted.

"The Blood Thief's never killed a mortal before." Erik drummed his fingertips on the bar top. "Besides, if he wanted to destroy Tina, why didn't he do it the first time he attacked her? Why take her blood and not her head?" Erik didn't know who had killed Tina and Craig, but he knew it hadn't been Daisy.

"Beats the hell out of me."

"Doesn't make much sense."

"A lot of things in this old world don't make sense," Rhys muttered dryly.

Erik nodded. He couldn't argue with that.

"Maybe somebody scared him off the first time," Rhys said, thinking aloud. "But that's neither here nor there. He's as good as got."

"Yeah?"

"Yeah." Rhys smiled, a predatory gleam in his eyes. "I forgot to tell you the best part."

"Oh? What's that?"

"The Blood Thief left his scent behind this time."

Chapter 14

Erik went suddenly still, and then relaxed. It couldn't be Daisy, but another hunter in the city was bad news for all of them. "Was it anyone you recognize?"

"No," Rhys said, "but now we have something to go on."

"You didn't follow his scent?"

"I lost it on the freeway. If the murder had taken place at Tina's, we'd have it on video."

Erik grunted softly.

"I want a camera in your place by tomorrow."

"No."

"Why the hell not?"

"I don't like the idea."

"It was your idea!"

Erik shrugged. He couldn't install a camera as long as Daisy was in the house.

"I don't give a damn whether you like it or not. We all agreed it was the thing to do."

Erik cocked his head to the side. "Is there a camera in *your* lair?" he asked, deciding to take the offensive.

Rhys cleared his throat before muttering, "No, not yet."

"Well, there you go. When you get one, I will."

Muttering an oath, Rhys pushed away from the bar and stalked across the room.

"Damn." Erik finished his drink, then stared into his empty glass. If there really was another hunter in town, it would take the heat off Daisy. None of the vampires were aware of her or knew she was the one who had taken Tina's blood, or that she had destroyed Saul. She hadn't left her scent at either place. That being the case, she was probably safe from Rhys and the others. He could probably let her go home. He should have been relieved at the thought of having his house to himself again. He should have been, but he wasn't.

Rhys returned to the bar a few minutes later, one arm draped around the shoulders of a leggy blonde. "We'll talk more about our problem some other time," he said. "Right now, I have some urgent business to take care of with the delectable Jean Marie."

Jean Marie looked up at Rhys. Her face was extremely pale, her expression rapt with anticipation. Erik wondered how many other vampires had fed off her that night. There were deaths at the club from time to time, mostly accidents that happened when a mortal got so caught up in the thrill of consorting with a vampire that they let too many take too much. Such deaths were quickly hushed up. The victims were disposed of, their bodies never found.

Erik watched Rhys and the woman disappear into one of the rooms. He sat there a moment, thinking how complicated his life had suddenly become, and then, smiling inwardly, he hurried home, eager to see the woman who was the cause of it all.

Daisy was stretched out on the sofa, drifting toward sleep when she sensed Erik's presence in the house. Bolting upright, she glanced around the room, fearful that Rhys might have come home with him.

"It's just me," Erik said.

"What did he want? Does he know who I am?"

"No. Apparently there's another hunter in town. Rhys got a whiff of him at Tina's boyfriend's house."

Daisy wrapped her arms around her body, relieved that Rhys didn't know who she was. "Is Tina . . . did the hunter destroy her?"

"Yeah, she's dead for good this time, and her boyfriend, too."

"Was he a vampire?"

"No, just a kid in the wrong place at the wrong time."

Daisy bit down on her lower lip. She was sorry to hear about the deaths, but at the moment, the only thing that mattered was that Rhys didn't know who she was.

"I can go home now, can't I?" she said, thinking aloud.

"I suppose so." He dropped into the chair across from the sofa. She was so beautiful. How could he let her go? He had known her little more than a week, but it seemed like she had always been there, a part of his life. He was going to miss her company and her conversation, the scent of her shampoo, the sound of her laughter, the sexual awareness that flowed between them.

Daisy stared at Erik, wondering why she suddenly felt so depressed. She should have been thrilled that she was out of danger, delighted at the thought of going home and sleeping in her own bed, living in her own house. Why wasn't she?

"I can take you tonight, if that's what you want," Erik remarked.

"Well, I need to pack, and . . . and it's late. I can go tomorrow, if it's all right with you."

He nodded. "Sure. Anything you want."

"Thank you for looking after me. For protecting me. I . . . I appreciate it."

"No problem."

"You're not going to leave town, are you? I promise not to tell anyone where you live, or come here again."

Leaning back in the chair, Erik crossed his arms over his chest. Leaving LA would be the smart thing to do. He knew Rhys wouldn't like it, but it wasn't Rhys's decision to make.

"Erik . . . please don't go."

"Why? I'm evil, remember? You said so yourself. Vampires are horrible monsters."

Daisy felt her cheeks grow hot as he parroted the words she had said. "I was wrong about that, at least where you're concerned. You're not a monster."

"Oh? What am I?"

There was no way to answer that without making a fool of herself, she thought frantically. She knew he was a vampire, a creature who existed on the blood of others, but it no longer seemed to matter. She had grown inordinately fond of him in the last few days, so much so that she couldn't imagine her life without him. But she couldn't say that, because no matter how much she cared for him, how attracted she was to him, they were worlds apart. They had no future together, yet she couldn't abide the thought of his leaving town.

"What am I, Daisy?"

"You're . . . you're my friend, and I don't have many of those and I'd hate to lose one." She blurted the words in a rush, then lowered her gaze, afraid he might laugh at her.

"Daisy, look at me."

Slowly, she lifted her gaze to his.

"I don't have any friends."

"What about Rhys?"

"I guess he qualifies, in a way, but I don't trust him, not the way I trust you."

"Then you'll stay?" she asked hopefully.

"Yeah." He would have stayed whether she wanted him to or not, Erik thought, because there was no way on earth that he could leave the city as long as Daisy was in it. "I'll take you home tomorrow night."

For Daisy, the next day passed slowly, and yet all too quickly. She wandered through the house, then went upstairs to Erik's studio. It was a large room, unfurnished save for a long wooden table that held palettes and tubes of paint, brushes and palette knives, cans of gesso and linseed oil, paint-stained rags, an easel. A stack of blank canvases stood in one corner. She paused to admire the painting of the castle that she liked so much. Was it a real place, she wondered, one that held some special significance for Erik?

Later, she went into the bedroom to fold her clothes, only then realizing she had no suitcase in which to put them. She took a shower and washed her hair, spent a pleasant two hours watching a love story on TV, and then went into the kitchen to make lunch. It was while she was making a sandwich that it hit her—she was going home. Tonight, she would fix dinner in her own kitchen. It had been days since she had been outside. Perhaps tonight she would go out to eat.

After fixing a tall glass of iced tea laced with lemon and sugar, Daisy sat at the kitchen table to eat lunch and contemplate her future. She had always thought of vampires as evil creatures, monsters beyond redemption. She had never felt the least bit of guilt at taking their blood; she had always been proud of her brother Alex. While she and Brandon collected vampire blood, Alex took heads. He was one of the best hunters in the States, maybe the world.

Daisy put her half-eaten sandwich aside. Since meeting Erik, she no longer thought of all vampires as evil. How could she? True, he had tasted her blood, but that was what vampires did. Might as well hate cats for hunting birds, or lions for hunting gazelles. It was the nature of the beast. Erik had kept her there against her will, but it was only to protect her from Rhys.

"Erik . . ." She whispered his name, jumped when he appeared before her as if she had wished him there. And perhaps she had. "You're up early."

"You're leaving tonight. I wanted to spend as much time with you as possible."

"I'll miss you, too." She was tempted to ask him if she could stay a little longer, but what was the point. The longer she stayed, the harder it would be to go. Instead, she reminded herself that they were worlds apart. She was the Blood Thief. He was a vampire. She sold the blood of the Undead; he drank human blood to survive.

Looking at him, she wondered how any female in her right mind could ever think of leaving. Every time she saw him, she was struck anew by the chiseled masculine beauty of his face and form. Maybe what she felt wasn't affection. Maybe it was just plain, old-fashioned lust. After all, no woman over the age of twelve could look at Erik Delacourt and not want to run her hands over his arms, or feel those arms around her. Just thinking about being in his embrace brought a rush of heat to her cheeks.

Giving herself a mental shake, she watched him stride across the room. Pulling a chair out from the table, he spun it around, then straddled the seat.

"You okay?" he asked. "You look a little flushed."

"I'm fine."

Grunting softly, he reached into his jacket pocket, withdrew her cell phone and her tool kit, and slid them across the table. Reaching into another pocket, he ran his fingers over her compass. He was reluctant to return it to her even though there was no point in keeping it. If she was determined to hunt vampires, all she had to do was ask her grandmother the witch to make her another one.

"Any chance you've decided to stop being the Blood Thief?"

"No."

"Just because Rhys doesn't know who you are now doesn't mean he won't find out. You've been lucky up until now."

She lifted her chin in a gesture he was becoming all too familiar with.

"I can't talk you out of this, can I?"

Daisy shook her head.

"I didn't think so." Pulling her compass out of his pocket, he tossed it on the table. "You might need that."

"Thank you." She rubbed her hand over the compass, remembering the day Nonnie had given it to her . . .

"Are you sure you want to follow in your father's footsteps?" Nonnie asked. They were sitting in her screened-in porch. Below, the waves made their endless journey to the shore and back to the sea. A gull floated in the air; a dolphin surfaced in the distance.

"Yes," Daisy had said confidently. "It's what we O'Donnells do."

"It is a course fraught with danger and very little reward," Nonnie remarked.

Daisy shrugged. "Dad's been preparing me for this since I was a little girl. It's the only thing I ever wanted to do. The only thing I know how to do."

"Now, Daisy, child," Nonnie said, giving her a skeptical

look, "I know that's not true." Nonnie picked up the compass and rubbed her gnarled hands over it. "This will guide you, but it cannot protect you."

"I understand."

"If you follow it, it may guide you in paths you never thought to follow."

Daisy frowned at her grandmother. "What does that mean? Are you having one of your visions?"

"You will know, in time."

Daisy looked at Erik. Was he the path she never thought to follow? She shook her head. As much as she had come to care for Erik, their lives were miles apart. If she was smart, she would keep it that way. She had heard stories through the years of mortals who had fallen in love with vampires. None of them had ended happily; most of the time, the mortals ended up dead by the hand of their lover, sometimes on purpose, sometimes by accident. Dating a vampire was like bringing a wild animal into your house. You just never knew when it was going to turn on you.

Erik rested his folded arms on the back of the chair. "So, are you in a hurry to go home, or can I persuade you to go dancing at the club?"

"I'd like that." One last night together, she thought glumly, before they said good-bye.

"Are you packed?"

"Sort of. I don't have a suitcase."

"Come on. I've got a couple you can have."

She followed him up the stairs to the bedroom she had been using. Going to the closet, he pulled down a large navy blue suitcase and another, smaller one.

She had expected him to leave, but he stood in the doorway, watching while she packed, putting her clothing into the larger case and her toiletries and make-up in the smaller one.

"I guess you'll be glad to be rid of me," Daisy remarked as she closed the large suitcase. "Glad to have your house all to yourself again."

"I thought I would be, but now . . . I think I'm going to miss you." Picking up both suitcases, he walked down the hall to the room where he kept his paintings. "Take whichever one you want."

"Oh, I couldn't . . . I mean, they're so . . . do you mean it?"

He nodded. "Consider it a peace offering for keeping you here against your will."

"That one," she said, gesturing at the painting of the castle. "It's my favorite."

"Mine, too," he said, smiling. "Go on, take it."

Unable to believe he was actually giving her one of his works of art, Daisy picked up the painting and carried it down the stairs and out of the house.

Outside, Erik stowed her suitcases in the backseat of his car, then opened the trunk so Daisy could place the painting inside. She looked at it a minute, thinking again that she had never seen or owned anything so beautiful.

"Do you want to stop somewhere and get something to eat?" Erik asked.

"No, I'm not hungry. Are you?" she asked, then felt her cheeks grow hot.

"Are you offering?" he asked with a good-natured leer.

"No, sorry."

Laughing, he held the door for her, then walked around to the driver's side and slid behind the wheel. He was still grinning when he pulled out of the driveway.

It was early and a Monday. The club was practically empty,

which suited Daisy just fine. Erik ordered drinks, a margarita for her, the house special for himself.

Daisy stared at his glass when the drinks arrived. "What is that anyway?"

"Are you sure you want to know?"

"I think so."

"It's very expensive Madeira laced with a little blood."

Was he kidding? She hoped so, but there was no humor in his expression. And then he lifted one brow. "Want a taste?"

"No, thank you!"

"Want to dance?"

As had happened once before, the jukebox came on when he took her hand in his and led her onto the empty dance floor. As had happened before, she forgot everything else when he took her into his arms and held her close. She wasn't sure swaying back and forth, their bodies so close you couldn't have put a piece of paper between them, qualified as dancing, but she didn't care. She loved being this close to him. Loved the smell of his cologne, the way his hands dwarfed her own, the sense of power that clung to him, the touch of his lips in her hair. Closing her eyes, she lost herself in his nearness, in the bittersweet lyrics of A Fine Frenzy singing about someone who was an "Almost Lover."

Oh, yes, she had it bad!

Time ceased to exist as they danced. As if in a dream, he whispered in her ear, his words warm and soft, relaxing her completely, so that when she felt the touch of his fangs at her throat, it seemed like the most natural thing in the world.

Erik knew a brief moment of guilt as he closed the tiny wounds in her neck. Had he been less honest, he could have lied to himself, told himself it wasn't his fault. She was beautiful, irresistible, and he was only doing what came naturally.

And it was partially true. She was beautiful. And he had done what came naturally because he had no desire to resist.

When the song ended, he willed another to start. The rest of the world drifted away and there was just the two of them, slow dancing to Fleetwood Mac singing "Beautiful Child." Erik smiled inwardly. His Daisy was certainly a beautiful child, so young when compared to the centuries he had lived.

Later, he ordered her another drink, and then they danced again, this time to Fauxliage singing "Let It Go." The lyrics seemed made for the two of them. Did Daisy want him as badly as he wanted her?

They stayed until closing time, and then he drove her home. After carrying her bags to the front door, he went back to retrieve the painting. After propping it beside her luggage, he drew Daisy into his arms.

"So, my little flower," he murmured, "where do we go from here?" He could have forced her to surrender to him, to be his slave in any and every way he demanded, but he didn't want to compel her to care for him. He wanted her affection, freely given.

"What do you mean?" Daisy asked, though she knew exactly what he meant.

"Even though I know it's not a good move for either one of us, I'd like to see you again, get to know you better."

"You're right. It isn't a good idea."

"Is that a no?"

She lifted one shoulder and let it fall. "Why ask for trouble? I know you're attracted to me, and I have to admit, I'm attracted to you, too, but what's the point? There's no future for us. You must know that."

"There could be."

It was tempting. He was tempting, with his silky black hair and smoldering ebony eyes. She felt herself weakening, wanting. Wanting to sit on his lap and feel his arms around her. Wanting to taste his mouth devouring hers, wanting to touch him, to kiss and taste and explore every masculine inch.

"Why don't you give us a chance?" he asked in that soft, honeyed voice that sent shivers of delight down her spine. "What have you got to lose?"

What did she have to lose? Her life, for starters.

"I'm not a young vampire," Erik said quietly. "I won't hurt you. The scent of your blood doesn't enflame my senses beyond control. I won't take anything you don't want to give." He gazed deeply into her eyes. "I think I'm in love with you."

Of all the things he might have said, that was the last thing Daisy had expected to hear. "But . . . that's impossible. I mean, we hardly know each other." She stared up into his eyes. "Haven't you forgotten something? I'm the Blood Thief . . ."

"And I'm a vampire," he said.

And that said it all.

"So you see," Daisy said, blinking back the sting of tears. "There's just no way it will work."

"You're sure?"

She gazed up at him, mute. She couldn't be in love with a vampire. In her family, it simply wasn't done. She was an O'Donnell. They hunted vampires. Her father and her brother Alex destroyed vampires for a living. Her younger brother, Brandon, didn't have the stomach for killing, so he earned his living the same way she did, by selling the blood of the Undead at two hundred bucks a pop. And since you only needed a very small amount for the desired high, a pint or two of vampire blood went a very long way.

"Daisy?"

He was waiting for her answer, but she had no answer to give as cold logic warred with her growing desire.

She jumped when the front door opened behind her.

"Hey, Daisy Mae, it's about time you got home."

"Alex!" Daisy stared at her brother in disbelief. "What are you doing here?"

"Hey, can't a guy come to see his little sister once in a while?" Alex's gaze settled on Erik, an unspoken question in his eyes.

"Alex, this is Erik Delacourt. Erik, this is my older brother, Alex."

The two men eyed each other warily for a moment; then, at a look from Daisy, Alex stuck out his hand. "Pleased to meet you."

Erik nodded as he shook the other man's hand.

Daisy glanced from Erik to her brother and back again, her heart beating wildly as vampire and vampire hunter continued to size each other up. Inviting Erik inside was the polite thing to do, but all things considered, it really didn't seem like a good idea.

Erik took the dilemma out of her hands. "I'll say good night, Daisy. I'm sure you and your brother have a lot of catching up to do." He kissed her on the cheek. "I'll see you around."

Speechless, she watched him get into his car and drive away.

"So, who's that guy?" Alex asked.

"Just a friend."

"Uh-huh."

"Bring my bags in, will you?" Without waiting for an answer, she went out onto the porch and picked up her painting, and then swept past him.

Returning to the living room, Daisy propped the painting on the mantel. She admired it for several moments, hardly able to believe it was really hers, and then turned to face her brother.

Alex dropped her bags beside the sofa, then jerked his chin toward the picture. "Where'd you get that?"

"From Erik. Do you like it?"

"Yeah, I guess it's all right, if you like that kind of thing."

"I do. Erik painted it."

"You're kidding. He doesn't look like an artist to me."

"Well, he is. What are you really doing here?"

Alex shrugged as he glanced around the room. "Dad was worried about you."

Daisy groaned softly. She never should have called home after destroying Saul.

"Mom, too," Alex said. "She wants you to come home—"

"And meet Mr. Right. Yes, I know."

Alex dropped onto the sofa and picked up the remote. "Well, I don't know about that, but I know she wants you to move back home. Permanently. She thinks it's too dangerous for you to be out here alone. And after seeing that guy . . . that *artist* you're hanging out with, I think she's right."

Sitting on the sofa, Daisy crossed her arms over her chest and counted to ten. "What's wrong with him?"

Alex fixed her with a hard look. "Well, if I didn't know better, I'd say he was a vampire."

"Don't be ridiculous!"

"Where'd you meet him?"

"At a nightclub, not that it's any of your business."

"How long have you been dating?"

"We're not 'dating.'"

"No?" Alex glanced pointedly at her luggage. "Then what are you doing?"

"Get your mind out of the gutter. And what I'm 'doing' is no concern of yours."

"I'd like to argue with you some more," Alex said, smothering a yawn, "but I'm beat. I made myself at home in the guest room. Hope you don't mind."

"A little late to be asking, don't you think?"

He grinned at her. "That's why I didn't ask."

"Alex . . . ?"

"Yeah?"

"Did you destroy a vampire and her mortal lover here in LA?"

"Yeah, how'd you know about it?"

She shrugged. "That kind of news travels fast, you know that. You were careful, weren't you?"

"I'm always careful," he said with a wink. "See you in the morning, little sister. Oh, and I'd like eggs, bacon, and French toast for breakfast."

"Have whatever you want. The frying pan is in the drawer under the stove."

"Very funny." Whistling softly, he headed down the hall toward the guest room.

Daisy stared after him. Her domineering big brother was one complication she definitely didn't need in her life right now. She chewed on her thumbnail. She should have warned Alex that Rhys had his scent, but then Alex would start asking questions she didn't want to answer. Questions she couldn't answer unless she wanted Alex to know that Erik was indeed a vampire, just as he suspected.

Yawning, she grabbed the smaller of her two suitcases and carried it up to her bedroom. Maybe things would look better in the morning, she thought as she unpacked her nightgown and got ready for bed.

And maybe not.

Chapter 15

Rhys prowled the dark underbelly of the city. Though he no longer needed to feed as often as he once had, he was addicted to the chase. Life didn't hold much excitement for a man who had lived as long as he had, but hunting . . . ah, that never grew old. He chose a different kind of prey for each hunt—one week he might decide to stalk only blondes, the next week, only brunettes. Another week he might prey on nothing but young males, then on females. He could be as discriminating as he chose.

Tonight, he was hunting only women between the ages of twenty and thirty who had black hair and blue eyes and who were exactly five feet tall. Thus far, he hadn't had much luck.

He was thinking he would have to redefine his search when Erik appeared beside him.

"What brings you here?" Rhys asked, unable to completely mask his surprise. All of the West Coast vampires had their own hunting grounds. Trespassing on another's territory was forbidden and had, on occasion, led to bloodshed.

"I felt the need of some company," Erik said, falling into step beside the other vampire. "What's on the menu tonight?"

"Black-haired females with blue eyes."

Erik grunted softly. "Any luck?"

"Not yet." Rhys lifted his head, his nostrils flaring as he caught the scent of prey. "But I think my luck's about to change."

"She's blond," Erik said. "A streetwalker. And very young."

"And how would you know that?" Rhys asked, his eyes sparking red with anticipation.

"I passed her on my way here."

Muttering, "All cats are gray in the dark," Rhys moved quickly down the street.

With a shake of his head, Erik followed him, though at a slower pace. Coming here had seemed like a good idea at the time, but now . . . he swore softly, thinking that Daisy's brother couldn't have shown up at a worse time.

His hunger stirred as the scent of blood drifted on the wind. Up ahead, he could see Rhys standing in the shadows, his head bent over the neck of the blond hooker. Apparently the Master of the City wasn't averse to altering the cuisine he had chosen for the night.

Rhys looked up as Erik approached. A vampire caught in the midst of feeding was rarely a pretty sight, and Rhys was no exception. Blood dripped from his fangs; his eyes burned red. He growled softly, warning Erik to stay away.

Erik took a step backward. Folding his arms across his chest, he watched Rhys drink his fill and in so doing, Erik understood why he was there. It was to remind himself of what he was, what he was capable of.

While watching Rhys feed, Erik knew Daisy had been right. There could be no future for the two of them.

Chapter 16

Daisy awoke on Monday morning to the deliciously mingled aromas of fresh-brewed coffee and frying bacon. She frowned, momentarily disoriented. This wasn't her bedroom at Erik's, she thought groggily, and then remembered that she was home and that it had to be Alex, cooking in the kitchen.

Muttering under her breath, she headed for the shower, wondering how long Alex intended to stay, and how she could persuade him to leave sooner if he was planning to stay more than a day or two.

After pulling on a pair of faded jeans and a blue Mickey Mouse sweatshirt, she padded barefoot to the kitchen door. Pausing a moment, she took a deep breath, pasted a smile on her face, and entered the room.

"Hey, good morning, sleepyhead," Alex greeted her cheerfully as she stepped into the room. "I wasn't sure what you were in the mood for, so . . ." He gestured toward the stove. "I made a little of everything. You take what you want, and I'll eat the rest."

Daisy glanced at the counter and shook her head. He had made a little of everything, all right. There were plates of bacon, sausage, scrambled eggs, pancakes, waffles, buttered toast, and a ham and cheese quiche.

"Alex, there's enough food here to feed a family of six."

"Well, I don't know about you, but I'm famished. Do you want coffee, milk, tea, juice, or hot chocolate?"

Realizing there was no point in arguing, Daisy sat at the table. "Juice and coffee will be fine."

Alex carried all the plates to the table, then slid onto the chair across from hers. "Dig in, sis."

Daisy helped herself to a couple of pancakes, two strips of bacon, and a helping of scrambled eggs. "You really are a good cook," she remarked. "If you ever get tired of taking heads, you could probably open a restaurant."

Alex snorted softly. "Where's the fun in that?"

"Where's the fun in taking heads?"

"It's not in the *taking*," Alex said, speaking around a mouthful of eggs. "It's in the *hunting*. You know how it is, the way your mouth goes dry and your heart beats with excitement . . ."

"With fear, you mean."

"Fear, excitement, whatever it is, it makes you know you're alive."

"So, you've never thought of doing anything else?"

"No," Alex said, looking surprised. "Why? Have you?"

Daisy shrugged. She had considered finding another line of work from time to time. Since destroying Saul, she'd been thinking of it even more, but she was reluctant to admit it, especially to her gung-ho brother.

"It's because of that vampire you killed, isn't it?"

"In a way. It made me feel good, knowing I could defend myself if I had to, but . . ." She pushed her plate away, her appetite suddenly gone. "I killed a man . . ."

"He wasn't a man," Alex said curtly. "He was a vampire."

"Well, he was a man once," Daisy insisted. "If it wasn't for me, he'd still be alive or undead, or . . ." She threw up her hands. "The point is, I killed him."

"Listen, Daisy, vampires aren't human any longer. You know that. And you can't kill them. They're already dead, remember? The only reason they aren't fish-belly white and six feet under is because they exist on our blood."

"And I sell theirs!"

Sitting back in his chair, Alex crossed his arms over his chest. "All right, Daisy Mae, what's this all about?"

Daisy glared at him. Even though it was a long-standing joke between them, she hated it when he called her Daisy Mae. Usually, she reciprocated by calling him Little Abner, but this morning, she wasn't in the mood for levity.

"Daisy?"

She couldn't tell him the truth, of course; she couldn't tell her brother that it was her feelings for Erik that were making her doubt her chosen line of work.

"Does this have anything to do with that guy that was here last night? That artist?"

"Of course not." Using her fork, she pushed the eggs around on her plate, careful not to meet her brother's eyes. "Why would it?"

"I don't know." Alex leaned forward, his arms folded on the table, his brow furrowed. "You tell me."

"I'm not like you," Daisy said. "I can't kill someone, destroy someone, and tell myself it doesn't matter. Taking their blood . . ." She shrugged. "It seemed like a bizarre game at first, finding their lairs, sneaking in, stealing their blood, leaving without a trace. But now . . . now it just seems wrong."

"They kill us, Daisy," Alex said quietly. "They don't just take our blood. They take the lives of innocent men, women, and children. We aren't people to them, we're prey. They're all monsters, and the worst of them lives right here, in LA."

Daisy's heart skipped a beat. "What do you mean?" she asked, praying he wasn't talking about Erik.

"The Master of the City," Alex said. "Rhys Costain."

Relief washed over Daisy. "Is he the reason you're here?" she asked, careful to keep her voice and her expression impassive.

"No, I came because Mom and Dad were worried about you. It's just a coincidence that the vampire I'm hunting lives in the same city you do."

"Why are you hunting him? Don't tell me you've run out of vampires in Boston?"

"I wish," Alex said with a grin, and then he turned sober again. "A private citizen put a hefty price on Costain's head."

"You're kidding." She had never heard of anyone doing such a thing. "Who is it?"

"I don't have a clue. I don't care. They're offering two hundred grand for his head, he's supposed to be here, in the city, and that's all I need to know."

"Wow, someone must want him out of the way really bad to offer a reward like that. And you don't have any idea who it is?"

"Nope, but I'm the someone who's gonna take his head and collect the reward."

"Every hunter in the country is probably out looking for him," Daisy remarked. "What makes you think you'll find him?"

Sitting back, Alex puffed out his chest. "'Cause I'm the best of the best."

"And the most conceited," Daisy muttered, suddenly uncomfortable with the turn of the conversation. She came from a family of hunters. By all rights, she should tell Alex where to find Erik, because Erik could lead Alex to the Master of the City.

Instead, she changed the subject. "So, how's Brandon doing?"

"Same as always. He sends his love." Alex grinned. "I take it you haven't talked to him lately."

"No. I've been meaning to call, but . . ." *But I was being held prisoner by a vampire,* she thought, choking back a wave of hysterical laughter. "Why, has something happened to him?"

"You could say that. He's in love, but it's a secret."

"Brandon?" It was hard to think of her little brother taking an interest in girls. Brandon had always preferred pets to people and computers to conversation. When he wasn't hunting, he was usually online, lost in a world of his own.

"Yeah. Funny, isn't it? The geek found a gal."

"Where did he meet her? What's her name? Is it serious?"

"Pretty serious. He's been seeing Paula for over a month. Kevin introduced them . . ."

"My Kevin?" Daisy exclaimed. "I mean, the Kevin that Mom's been trying to set me up with?"

"The very same. Paula's his younger sister."

Oh, Lordy, Daisy thought. Her mother would be trying harder than ever to get her and Kevin together. She could just hear her mom now—*Wouldn't it be nice if you and Kevin got married? Think how nice it would be if you moved back home. We could have Thanksgiving and Christmas with the O'Reillys. . . .*

Daisy shook her head. *Sorry, Mom,* she thought, *but it's never going to happen.*

"Well," Alex said, slapping his palms on the table, "I've got work to do." Rising, he gave her shoulder a gentle shake. "Since I fixed breakfast, dinner's on you."

"Where are you going?"

"Where do you think?" he asked with a wink.

"Be careful."

"Always. You don't have any idea where I should start looking, do you?"

"No, I'm afraid not." She felt like a traitor for not telling her brother about Erik. Alex was family, after all, but how could she betray Erik?

"Okay," Alex said cheerfully. "I'll see you tonight. Steak sounds good for chow. Don't forget to call Mom and Dad."

"Right."

"Oh, hey, do you have an extra can of Scent-B-Gone? I didn't bring any with me."

Daisy shook her head. "Always careful," she muttered. "There's a can in the closet by the front door. Top shelf."

"Thanks. I won't be late."

Daisy stared after her brother. Brandon was dating Kevin's sister. Alex was hunting Rhys. She had late Internet orders to fill, a ton of dirty dishes to wash, a house to clean, clothes to launder, and groceries to buy, but all she could do was sit there and think about Erik and her brother, and what would happen if Alex discovered Erik's true nature. She offered a fervent prayer, hoping that would never happen, certain if it did, only one of them would survive.

Daisy found herself watching the clock all day long, her concern growing with each passing hour. Alex was always uppermost in her thoughts. Had he found Rhys? Was Erik safe? Would she ever see him again?

She made a quick call to her folks to assure them that she was fine and that Alex was taking good care of her.

After telling her mom good-bye, Daisy went in search of a hammer and a nail, then dragged a chair over to the fireplace and hung the painting Erik had given her. She shook her head as she imagined him painting it, and wondered how long it had taken him, and wondered again if it was a real castle. A place in his past, maybe. Try as she might, she just couldn't wrap her mind around the fact that her vampire was an artist.

Her vampire. The thought made her sigh with regret. Why was it, the first man she had ever truly fallen head over heels in love with wasn't a man at all?

Climbing down from the chair, she admired the painting for several minutes before returning the chair to the kitchen and the hammer to the drawer where it belonged.

She found herself going into the living room from time to time to stare at the painting. What had he been thinking when he painted it? Was it a place he had visited? A house he had owned in days gone by? Or was it just something he had drawn from his own imagination?

For the rest of the day, whether she was answering her e-mail, taking new orders, or mopping the kitchen floor, Erik was never far from her thoughts. And that was just wrong. Erik was no longer human. No matter that he was the handsomest, sexiest man she had ever seen, her brother was right. Erik wasn't really a man, but a monster, one who preyed on humankind to survive. One who had tasted her blood . . .

She lifted a hand to her neck, wondering why the thought of Erik drinking from her wasn't more repugnant. She should be horrified, shocked, disgusted. So why wasn't she?

It was the fact that she wasn't horrified, shocked, or disgusted that worried her. Had he worked some kind of vampire voodoo on her, or was she some kind of abnormal freak? She knew there were men and women who got their kicks from letting vampires drink from them. She had never understood the attraction. Of course, she didn't know why any normal person would want to get high on vampire blood, either, but somehow, drinking a tiny bit mixed with the beverage of your choice didn't seem as revolting as offering yourself to one of the Undead for an evening snack.

Which reminded her that she needed to call Nonnie. Going into the living room, she sat on the sofa, one leg curled beneath her, and called her grandmother.

"Daisy, how good of you to call, dear. Is everything all right?"

"Of course. Why do you ask?"

"I saw something unusual, something . . . I'm not quite sure what it was."

"I need your help."

"Anything, dear, you know that."

"You can't tell anyone one about this," Daisy said. "Do you understand? This has to be just between the two of us."

"All right, if that's how it must be."

"Is there any spell or charm or . . . or potion, that will shield my thoughts from a vampire?"

"I believe so, as long as there's been no exchange of blood. Daisy? Daisy, are you there?"

"Yes."

"Oh, my dear, tell me how it happened."

"It doesn't matter how it happened. I think everything will be all right. I was just curious."

"Is there anything else I can do? Anything else you need?"

"No." Daisy sighed. Nonnie had been her only hope.

"Daisy, you didn't . . . you haven't . . . tell me you haven't been turned."

"Of course not!"

"You're not thinking about it?"

"No way. It wasn't a big exchange. It was just a taste. I'm fine, honest."

"Except that there's a bond between you and this vampire now, one that can never be broken."

A bond. Good heavens, she hadn't even thought about that!

"Daisy? Are you still there?"

"Yes."

"I'm sorry I couldn't be of more help."

"It's all right," Daisy murmured. "I love you, Nonnie."

"I love you, too, dear. Please, be careful. And come and see me when you can."

"I will. Bye, Grams."

Daisy sat there a minute, her thoughts in turmoil. Her life just kept getting weirder and weirder, Daisy thought as she went into the kitchen to start dinner, although, with her mind filled with thoughts of vampires, she wasn't sure she was going to have any appetite.

Alex arrived shortly after dusk, a disgruntled expression on his face.

"I take it you didn't have any luck in finding Rhys," Daisy remarked as she pulled two steaks from the refrigerator. Removing them from the package, she seasoned them and placed them on the broiler pan.

"You take it right. I looked everywhere I could think of. Guess I should have asked Nonnie to make me one of those magic compasses."

"I guess so," Daisy agreed. She would have suggested Alex take hers, only it wouldn't work for anyone else. "I'm sorry your day was so unproductive."

"I didn't say that. I dispatched two fledglings."

Daisy's heart skipped a beat. She told herself there was nothing to worry about. Erik wasn't a fledgling. "Where did you find them?"

"They were holed up in an abandoned movie theater just outside of San Diego. Young and stupid," Alex said disdainfully. "They never knew what hit 'em. Just like that other couple."

"What other couple?"

"I don't know who they were. The ones I took out the night I got here."

Ah, Daisy thought. Tina and her mortal lover. Knowing what her father and brother did had never bothered her before, so why did the thought of what Alex had done bother her now? What if the vampires Alex had destroyed had been turned against their will, like Erik? What right did her family have to decide who lived and who died?

"Hey, Daisy Mae, you look a little green around the gills. You okay?"

"What? Oh, nothing. I'm fine."

"So, how about cookin' up those steaks while I take a shower?"

Daisy nodded.

"Don't forget, I like mine rare."

"Right." She hoped Alex was hungry enough to eat both steaks, because there was no way she was going to be able to keep anything down while watching her brother devour a filet mignon that was still blood-red inside.

Chapter 17

Erik wasn't in the best of moods when he arrived at Costain's house at nine o'clock that night.

"Another meeting?" he asked irritably, glancing at the other vampires gathered in the living room. "We haven't met this often in the last fifty years."

"And we wouldn't be meeting tonight if it wasn't necessary," Rhys said. "Sit down."

"I prefer to stand."

Rhys glared at him a moment, then shrugged. "Do whatever the hell you please. We're still waiting for Julius."

Erik grunted softly. "He's probably out preying on some helpless infant."

"Whether he is or isn't is none of your business," Rhys said. It was an unwritten law among vampires that you didn't judge or interfere with another's choice of prey.

"The man gives vampires a bad name," Erik said flatly. "Why don't you get rid of him?"

"What's the matter, Erik?" Mariah asked, a sneer in her voice. "Are you going all goody-goody on us?"

Erik glanced at Damon, who sat beside Mariah. "I'm not

surprised you don't see anything wrong with Julius's choice of prey," he said, "considering you like little boys."

Mariah sprang to her feet, her eyes blazing red, her fangs extended.

"Enough!" Rhys's voice cut through the tension between them. "We have more important matters to settle here."

"I say let 'em fight it out," Julius said, materializing beside Rhys.

"Don't we have enough people out to get us without turning on each other?" Rhys asked.

Julius shrugged.

"Mariah, sit down!" Rhys said impatiently. "Erik, you, too."

Erik glared at Rhys and remained standing.

"So, why are we here?" Julius asked.

"I had a call from a friend of mine in San Diego. Two fledglings were destroyed earlier today. I was at the scene a little while ago."

"Any idea who the hunter is?" Damon asked.

"No. If it was the same bastard who destroyed Tina and killed Craig, he didn't leave any scent behind this time."

"We need to find out what he's using to mask his scent," Rupert said.

"Yeah," Julius agreed. "Then find the guy who's making it and put him out of business."

Damon pumped his fist in the air. "Sounds good to me!"

"You young ones," Nicholas remarked with a wry grin. "Always ready for a fight."

"This isn't getting us anywhere," Rhys said. "I want each of you to take a part of the state and see if you can find this guy before he finds us."

"I'll take the coast," Mariah said.

"I'll head up north," Rupert decided. "I always liked it up there."

Erik glanced around the room. "I'm staying here, if no one objects."

"I do," Damon said. "I want to stay in LA."

Erik let his eyes go red. "You want to fight me for it?" he asked, displaying a hint of fang.

Damon shook his head. "No, I guess not. I'll go down south."

Rhys met Erik's gaze and grinned. The kid didn't have the guts for a fight and they both knew it. They had a bet going as to how much longer Damon would survive. Rhys gave the kid another five years; Erik had doubts he would last another two.

While the other vampires picked their areas, Erik's thoughts turned to Daisy. He needed to see her, to assure himself that she was all right. Last night, she had as much as said there was no chance for them. He could live with that if he had to. What he couldn't live with was not seeing her again. Going to her house probably wasn't the wisest thing to do for two reasons— one, she might slam the door in his face. Two, her brother, the hunter, was there, but what the hell? A man had to take a risk now and then.

Daisy glanced at her watch when someone knocked at the door. It was a quarter to eleven. She frowned, wondering who would come calling at such an hour.

Alex glanced at Daisy over the magazine he was reading. "A little late for visitors, isn't it?"

"A little."

"Want me to get it?"

"I think I can handle it," she said, rising. "I've been answering the door by myself for years now."

Muttering, "Smart-ass," Alex turned the page.

Daisy's heart skipped a beat when she opened the door and

saw Erik standing on the porch. What was he doing there? Hadn't they decided not to see each other again?

"Hi," he said. "I know it's late, well, for you, but . . . I just came by to say hello."

"Hello." She took a step back. "Come on in."

"Why don't you come out?"

Daisy glanced over her shoulder to find Alex watching her intently. "I think that's a good idea. Alex," she called, raising her voice, "I'm going out."

"Now?"

"Yes, now. Don't wait up." She closed the door before he could object. "So, where do you want to go?"

"Anywhere you want. To the Crypt. For a walk. To my place."

"I think I've spent enough time at your place, thank you very much."

Erik laughed softly as he pulled her behind a tree and drew her into his arms. She could be charmingly prim, even naïve, at times. It fascinated him almost as much as her innate sexiness. She seemed totally unaware that she was a beautiful, desirable woman.

"I've missed you," he murmured huskily, and claimed her lips with his.

Pleasure flowed through Daisy, warm and sweet, tantalizing her senses. She pressed her body against his, reveling in his touch, loving the way their bodies fit together, her softness to his strength.

He kissed her again, and yet again, his tongue dueling with hers in a primal dance of mating and seduction. His hands skimmed up and down the length of her back, moved to tease the curve of her breast, then slid down over her buttocks to pull her closer.

Daisy moaned softly. She savored his kiss for another moment, then pushed him away, afraid that if he kissed her again, she might drag him down on the grass and do it right there.

"I think we should go for a walk and cool off," she said, somewhat breathlessly. "What do you think?"

"I don't think you want to know what I'm thinking," he muttered dryly.

"Erik . . ."

"Yeah, yeah," he said, taking her by the hand. "Come on." They walked in silence for a few moments before he said, "So, how's your brother?"

"He's fine. He's looking for Rhys."

"Is he?" Erik grunted softly. "You'd better hope he doesn't find him."

"What do you mean?"

"Rhys will kill him," Erik said flatly. "Your brother won't be the first one to try to take Rhys out. And he'll fail, just like all the rest."

Daisy's heart went cold at his words. "Has he killed a lot of hunters?"

"Oh, yeah. Right around twenty that I know of, and that's just in the last three or four years. If you're smart, you'll tell your brother to pack up and go home."

"As if he'd listen." She hesitated a moment and then, shoving her guilt way down deep, she said, "Did you know someone has put out a hit on Rhys?"

"Yeah, we know about that."

"What am I going to do? Alex is determined to collect that reward. He's like a pit bull when he sets his mind to something. He sinks his teeth in and doesn't let go."

Erik squeezed her hand. "Sounds like your brother and Rhys have a lot in common."

"I can't let him kill my brother!" Alex had always been Daisy's favorite. He was the one she had run to for comfort when she was in kindergarten and Bobby Thomson called her names, the one who had showed her how to blow a bubble with bubblegum, the one who had taught her how to roller-skate. As a teenager, it had been Alex she confided in, Alex who had stood up for her.

"Honey, if your brother finds Rhys, Rhys will kill him, and there's nothing you can do to stop it."

Coming to a halt, Daisy looked up at Erik, her gaze searching his. "Can you?"

"I don't know," Erik said after a moment. He had wondered, from time to time, if he could whip Rhys in a fight. Realistically, he hoped he would never have to find out. "He means a lot to you?"

"Alex? Of course. He's my brother."

"Of course." Sometimes it was hard to remember how strongly woven familial ties could be. He had loved his wife and children, but that had been centuries ago. In the first few years after he had been turned, he had sometimes spied on other families, torturing himself with what he had lost. He had stood on the outside, watching mothers and fathers gather their children around the hearth at Christmastime, carving pumpkins for Halloween, coloring eggs at Easter. He had ached inside as he observed mothers rocking their babies to sleep, watching fathers tuck their sons into bed at night.

Daisy started walking again and he fell into step beside her, shortening his stride to match hers.

"Did you have brothers or sisters?" Daisy asked after a while.

"No. My mother used to tell me I was all she needed. I always thought she didn't want any more kids because I was such a horrible child."

"Were you? A horrible child?" It was hard to imagine Erik as young and vulnerable. He was so self-assured, so invincible.

It was easier to picture him as a young Greek god than as a mortal child.

"Yes," he said, smiling. "I suppose I was. I burned down the stable while trying to master the art of conjuring fire. I killed a chicken when I tried to turn it into a duck . . ."

"Are those the kind of things that young warlocks do?"

"I don't know, but it's what I did." Eventually, he had mastered fire, among other things, but on the day he married Abigail, he had put his magick behind him. And then he had been turned and found he possessed supernatural powers he had never dreamed of, inherent vampire magic that didn't require magical spells or enchantments.

"Here you are, safely home again," Erik remarked when they reached her house.

Daisy nodded. Always her protector, Alex was waiting for her on the front porch. "About time you got back," he said gruffly.

"Alex, I'm a big girl now. You don't have to wait up for me."

"Uh-huh." Alex glared at Erik for a long moment, then turned on his heel and went inside.

"Big brothers," Daisy said fondly. "They can be a pain in the butt sometimes."

"If you say so. Can I see you tomorrow night?"

"Erik . . ."

"I know all the reasons why we shouldn't," he said, drawing her into his arms. "But right now they don't seem to matter."

Happiness bubbled up inside her at the prospect of being with him again. "What time?" It wasn't the smart answer, it wasn't the safe answer, but it felt like the right one.

"Whatever's good for you," he said with a wink. "I've got all night."

"Eight o'clock?" She could have Alex fed and settled down by then.

"Shall I pick you up?"

"No, I'll meet you somewhere."

"At the Crypt?"

"All right." She gazed up at him, her heart pounding with anticipation as he lowered his head to claim her lips with his. She would see him again tomorrow night. She was already counting the hours.

"Sweet dreams, my little flower," Alex murmured as he kissed her lightly on the forehead; then, mindful that her brother was watching his every move from the living room window, Erik walked slowly to his car, unlocked the door with the key instead of his preternatural power, and slid behind the wheel.

After starting the car, Erik blew a kiss to Daisy, who was still standing on the front porch. And then he waved to her brother, who glared at him from the window.

Grinning, Erik pulled away from the curb.

Chapter 18

"Hey, sis," Alex called. "Are you ready to go yet?"

"I'm coming." Daisy checked her pockets and her handbag, making sure she had everything she needed, including her keys. "What's the rush?"

"I don't want somebody else to beat me to that two hundred grand. Here," he said, thrusting a can of Scent-B-Gone into her hand, "spray me, will ya?"

Daisy sprayed her brother from head to foot, then held her nose while he returned the favor.

Alex grinned at her. "Sure stinks until it dries, doesn't it?"

With a nod, Daisy followed Alex out to his car. She had spent the wee small hours of last night and all of this morning trying to talk her brother out of going after Rhys, but to no avail. The two-hundred-thousand-dollar reward drew him like a magnet.

"I need to be home early," she said, fastening her seat belt. "I have a date."

Alex shook his head as he backed out of the driveway. "I really don't like that guy."

Daisy rolled her eyes. "Are you still harping on that?" It was all she'd heard since Erik had brought her home last night.

She'd had no intention of going with Alex to look for Rhys, but Alex had asked her to tag along in hopes that her compass would lead him to the vampire he sought.

"I don't trust him. If he's an artist, I'll eat my Harley."

A sound of impatience rose in Daisy's throat. "He is an artist, you idiot. I have a painting to prove it."

"Yeah? Did you see him paint it?"

"Alex, you're impossible. Turn right at the next corner." She stared out the window, watching as the houses grew farther apart. They were in an older neighborhood now, one that looked like it had once been a pricey part of town. The homes were large, but mostly run-down, the lawns unkempt, the paint faded.

"Okay, he's an artist," Alex said. "What do you say we ask him to do a family portrait?"

"Sure, next time we're all in Boston. I'm sure Erik's got nothing better to do. Turn left at the corner."

"Afraid to put him to the test?"

"Don't be an idiot."

"Hey, there's something about him." Alex shook his head. "I don't know what it is, but something ain't right."

Muttering, "Oh, give it up," Daisy glanced at her compass. "Stop here!"

The needle on her compass shimmered a bright red when Alex braked in front of the last house on the block. There were bars on the windows, a security screen door, and a ferocious-looking mastiff standing stiff-legged behind a wrought-iron fence.

"Whoever lives here doesn't want any company, that's for sure," Alex muttered, peering through the windshield. "Wait here, I'm going in."

"It's too hot to sit in the car."

"I'll leave the engine running. I won't be long." Getting out of the car, Alex slung his kit over his shoulder, then opened the small ice chest stowed on the backseat. Reaching inside, he pulled a large chunk of fresh hamburger out of a plastic bag. "Pays to be prepared," he said with a wink and a grin.

Daisy grinned back at him. It was an old trick, doctoring hamburger with a sedative. She watched Alex toss the meat over the fence. The dog gobbled it down in one swallow; less than a minute later, the animal was out cold.

Alex gave her the high sign, vaulted over the fence, and loped up to the front porch. Quick work with a lock pick, and he was inside the house.

Daisy leaned back against the headrest and closed her eyes. What was Erik doing now? She knew he could be awake when the sun was up, though he preferred to take his rest then. She wondered what happened if vampires didn't sleep during the day. Did they just get cranky? Was it only the very young who were compelled to rest, or was it something they all did? What was it like, to sleep by day and be active only after the sun went down? Did it seem normal to vampires after a time?

Lifting her head, she stared at the house, then glanced at her watch. How long had Alex been inside? Why hadn't she paid attention to the time? He should have been back by now.

Grabbing a stake and a bottle of holy water from her bag, she switched off the engine, slipped the holy water and the keys into her pocket, and got out of the car.

She sent a nervous glance at the dog as she opened the gate. It was the biggest mastiff she had ever seen. More like a small horse than a dog. After making sure it was still sleeping deeply, she made her way to the front porch and opened the door.

The inside of the house was dark. Heavy drapes covered the windows. There were three sofas and several chairs in the living room. The floors were polished hardwood. An ancient-looking leather scabbard hung over a marble fireplace.

She paused a moment, listening, but heard only silence. Taking a deep breath, she counted to ten and then called Alex's name. When there was no reply, she tiptoed across the floor.

A shiver of unease skittered down her spine as she moved deeper into the house. Most lairs were in basements or, occasionally, in a dusty attic. Vampires didn't seem to be bothered by dirt, dust, or spiderwebs.

Her footsteps echoed on the hardwood floors as she peered into one room after another. All were empty.

She froze when a muffled cry reached her ears. Alex! Another cry, harsher than the first, set her heart to pounding. Alex was in trouble. All thought for her own safety fled as Daisy pulled the bottle of holy water from her pocket and followed the sound of her brother's voice.

The vampire's lair was located in what had once been a walk-in pantry that was big enough to have made a fair-sized bedroom. A shiny black coffin sat in the middle of the floor.

Daisy came to an abrupt halt just inside the doorway, her mind barely able to comprehend what she was seeing. Alex was on the floor. Covered in blood, he was trying to fight off the vampire hovering over him.

Galvanized by fear that the vampire would drain her brother dry, or worse, turn him, Daisy uncorked the bottle of holy water and flung it at the back of the vampire's head. The scent of scorched hair and preternatural flesh immediately stung her nostrils.

Howling in fury, the vampire spun around to face her, his narrowed eyes as red as hell's own flames, his fangs dripping with blood. Alex's blood.

With a cry of horror, Daisy grabbed the stake from her pocket, charged forward, and plunged it into the vampire's chest. Snarling, he took several steps backward, his hands curling around the stake as his curses filled the air.

"Alex!" Sobbing his name, spurred by the need to get the two of them out of there as fast as possible, she dragged her brother to his feet. Sagging under his weight, she somehow managed to get him out of the house and into the passenger seat of the car.

By the time she got behind the wheel, her hands were shaking so badly, it took three tries to get the key into the ignition. Shoving the gearshift into drive, she slammed her foot down on the gas pedal. The car lurched crazily before she got it under control.

She didn't dare look back, afraid if she did, she would see the vampire coming after them. But that was impossible. She had killed him. Hadn't she? But if she had destroyed him, why hadn't he dissolved into dust? Oh, Lord, what if she had missed his heart?

She drove like a maniac, her mind whirling as she headed for the freeway. She glanced at her brother. He was unconscious. She had to get him to a hospital, and soon. Blood leaked from dozens of deep bites on his arms, legs, chest, and neck from where the vampire had savaged him. More blood bubbled from a wound in his stomach, a wound she dared not examine too closely for fear she would lose control of the car.

He needed help, she thought anxiously. And he needed it now.

Help he couldn't get from a hospital. She knew instinctively that a doctor couldn't save him.

Erik, she thought. She needed Erik.

Giving the wheel a hard twist, she sped past the freeway on-ramp and headed for the one man who might be able to help her.

The sound of someone knocking on the front door roused Erik from his daytime slumber. A deep breath brought a familiar scent to his nostrils, and a smile to his lips. Daisy was there.

And then he frowned. What was she doing here in the middle of the day?

Rising, he hurried to the front door.

"Erik!" Daisy stared up at him, her eyes wild. "I need help!"

"Sure, honey, come on in."

"It's not for me." She waved a frantic hand toward the car parked at the curb. "It's Alex!"

Erik swore softly as he glanced at the stretch of sun-dappled sidewalk between his house and the car. "Wait a minute."

Turning, he grabbed a long leather coat from the rack just inside the door. Pulling it over his head and shoulders, he moved with supernatural speed toward the car. One look at Daisy's brother and he feared the man was beyond help. He was bleeding from numerous wounds; his face was deathly pale, his lips were turning blue.

Erik muttered an oath as the sun's light warmed his back. Any further examination would have to be done inside. His skin tingled uncomfortably as he pulled the unconscious man out of the car.

Draping Daisy's brother over his shoulder, he transported himself back into the house.

Shouting, "Close the damn door!" he carried Alex up the stairs and into the bedroom adjacent to the one Daisy had used not so long ago.

Daisy was right behind him. She pulled back the covers, then hovered beside Erik as he lowered Alex to the bed. Blood immediately soaked into the Spider-man sheets.

"What the hell happened?" Erik asked. "He looks like he's been through a meat grinder."

"We were hunting vampires . . . hunting Rhys."

Erik leaned over Alex, his nostrils flaring. "And you found him," he muttered, disbelief evident in his tone. "How the hell did you do that?"

"Just by chance," Daisy answered. They had found Rhys and lived to tell the tale. She swayed on her feet, feeling suddenly light-headed.

Erik's gaze swept over her. "Are you okay?"

"Yes, don't worry about me."

Erik shook his head. He had once warned Rhys that he needed more security for their meeting place, but Rhys had shrugged it off. He had always been arrogant to the point of carelessness. There had been times when Erik wondered if Rhys kept such an easily breached establishment because he was tired of his existence.

Daisy tugged on Erik's arm, drawing his attention back to the matter at hand. "Please, do something."

Erik studied Daisy's brother. Alex's heartbeat was slow and erratic, barely discernable. The scent of his blood teased Erik's nostrils, tempting him to take what little blood the man had left.

"Erik?"

"I warned you to stay away from Rhys."

"You can lecture me later," she said, choking back her tears. "Right now, Alex is dying. But you can save him! I know you can!"

"You want me to save a vampire hunter?" Erik exclaimed. "Dammit, Daisy, if he had come here alone, he might have taken my head."

"He's my brother. Please, Erik, I'll do anything you want!" Tears welled in her eyes and dripped down her cheeks. "Please! You can't just let him die!"

Erik waged a silent war with himself. It went against the grain to save the life of a hunter, yet what else could he do, with Daisy standing there, tears streaming down her face?

"Get him out of those clothes."

She didn't argue, didn't ask for help, but Erik gave it

anyway. Moments later, Alex lay on the blood-soaked sheets, stripped to his briefs.

"You might not want to watch this," Erik warned.

"I'm staying."

"He's pretty far gone. There's no guarantee my blood will save him. If it doesn't . . . ?" He left the question hanging in the air between them.

"Don't ask me that," she said, her eyes wide. "I can't make a decision like that for him."

With a curt nod, Erik bit into the deep blue vein in his left wrist. Dark red blood oozed from the two shallow wounds. Using his fingers, he smeared his blood over Alex's injuries.

Daisy watched in fascinated horror as the gashes on her brother's body began to heal, all but the one in his stomach. She looked up at Erik.

"Lift his head a little."

"You're not going to turn him?" she asked, horrified by the idea.

"No. I'll just give him a little drink, to strengthen him."

Swallowing the urge to vomit, Daisy folded one of the bed pillows in half and put it under Alex's head. She looked away when Erik held his bleeding wrist to her brother's lips, only to glance back as some shred of morbid curiosity got the better of her. A small trickle of blood flowed from Erik's wrist into Alex's mouth, and then, incredibly, Alex took hold of Erik's arm, suckling as though it were mother's milk. Within moments, color returned to her brother's waxen cheeks.

She glanced at the wound in Alex's stomach, her eyes widening with amazement as the ugly wound began to knit together. She had known vampire blood had miraculous qualities. Didn't it say so on her Web site? But she had never actually seen what it could do, never really believed a few drops of Undead blood could work miracles.

She was a believer now, and even as the thought crossed her mind, the room began to spin out of focus. "Erik . . ."

"Steady, girl."

His voice curled around her like loving arms, holding the dizziness at bay.

A moment later, he lifted his arm and licked the bloody wound in his wrist.

Revulsion swirled in the pit of Daisy's stomach, and then the world went black.

Erik caught Daisy in his arms and carried her into the room she had occupied before. What the hell had Alex been thinking, to take his sister with him when he went to hunt the most dangerous vampire on the West Coast? And what had Daisy been thinking when she agreed to go with him? And how the devil was Rhys? Had Daisy and her brother destroyed him?

Dammit!

He removed Daisy's shoes, then tucked her under the covers. He gazed down at her a moment, thinking how right it felt to have her under his roof again. Too right.

Muttering under his breath, he returned to her brother, who was still unconscious. Lifting the man with one hand, Erik stripped the ruined sheets from the bed, noting that the mattress was ruined, too. He dropped the bloody sheets on the bathroom floor, along with Alex's navy blue briefs, and turned on the shower.

Fully clad, Erik stepped into the stall with Daisy's brother cradled in his arms. Erik shook his head. If anyone in the vampire community discovered what he had done, he would have no defense. In the world of the Undead, it was vampire against mortal. There was no neutral ground.

Erik glanced at Alex. Even the cold water had failed to revive him. Perhaps his efforts to save the man had come too late.

Once the blood had been rinsed away, Erik turned off the water and stepped out of the shower. After wrapping Alex in a towel, he carried him down the stairs to the guest room. He hesitated a moment before opening the door, then chuckled softly as he imagined Alex's reaction if he regained consciousness. Erik had wondered, on more than one occasion, what kind of people had owned the house previously, and if they had been color-blind. Three of the walls in this room were painted a virulent shade of orange; the fourth wall was decorated with pink, yellow, and magenta flowered wallpaper.

Pulling back the matching spread on the twin bed, Erik tucked Alex under the covers, then left the room. What the hell was he doing keeping a hunter and a Blood Thief under his roof? Dammit, there was no way he was going to get any rest with the two of them in his house. And no way he could explain their presence to the Master of the City.

And what about Rhys?

He cursed softly. Another two hours until sunset. There were times, like now, when he hated the weakness that kept him trapped inside until sundown.

After changing into a dry T-shirt and jeans, Erik found his cell phone and dialed the number of the vampire who had been his best friend for the last two hundred years.

He feared the worst when there was no answer.

Chapter 19

Daisy woke with a start, surprised to find herself in Erik's house. What was she doing here? And then, all too vividly, she remembered going hunting with Alex, finding Rhys, although they hadn't known it was Rhys at the time. She would never forget the sight of Rhys hovering over her brother, never forget how she had doused the vampire with holy water before driving a stake into his chest. And missing his heart, she thought bitterly.

Swinging her legs over the edge of the bed, Daisy hurried out of the room. Alex. She had to find Alex.

Her heart seemed to stop beating when she opened the door to the room where he had been. Last night, she hadn't paid any attention to the room's décor. Now she wondered how she could have missed the garish green paint and jungle wallpaper.

She moved toward the bed, only then noticing that it was empty. The sheets had been stripped from the mattress; the mattress was stained with blood. She peeked into the bathroom, but it, too, was empty.

Where was Alex?

And where was Erik?

She stared at the door at the end of the hall. If she opened it, would she find Alex or Erik inside?

She stood in the hallway, listening to the house. It sounded as dead as its owner. As dead as her brother? No! She couldn't think that. Alex had been alive when she saw him last, alive and drinking Erik's blood.

"Your brother owes me a new mattress and a set of sheets."

Daisy whirled around, her hand at her throat, at the sound of Erik's voice. "Where is he? Where's my brother? What have you done to him?"

"I haven't done anything to him. He's downstairs, still unconscious. I don't imagine he'll be waking up anytime soon."

Daisy stared at Erik, hurt and confused, trembling now. She hated him because he was a vampire, because one of his kind had almost killed Alex and yet, if it wasn't for Erik's vampire blood, Alex would be dead now.

"I'm . . . I'm sorry," she stammered. "I should be thanking you."

"He'll be all right. That was quick thinking on your part, bringing him here."

"I was going to take him home. I've got some . . . some blood there, but it isn't fresh, and he looked so pale . . . and you were closer."

"I doubt that any of your old blood would have worked on that belly wound."

"Thank you for saving him."

"As I recall, you said you'd do anything I asked."

Her gaze flew to his face. "Yes. I . . . I did."

"Did you mean it?"

She nodded, unable to speak past the growing lump in her throat.

"Come here, then."

She stared at him, her heart racing. She willed herself to

move forward but her feet seemed rooted to the spot. *Not like this,* she thought. *Please, not like this.*

When she didn't move, he closed the short distance between them. As though spellbound, Daisy stood motionless while he drew her body against his, then pushed her hair behind her ear.

His fingers traced the curve of her throat. "Sweet," he murmured. "So sweet."

His tongue skimmed over her skin, hotter than any flame. Why hadn't she realized he would rather have her blood than her flesh? And why was that thought so disappointing?

Placing one finger beneath her chin, he tilted her head back, then claimed her lips with his.

As always when he kissed her, Daisy's mind seemed to shut down. His lips were firm on hers, cool at first, then slowly warming. His tongue teased hers as his hands cupped her buttocks, drawing her against the unmistakable evidence of his desire. And in that moment, she would have given him anything he asked.

She felt bereft when he took his mouth from hers. She blinked up at him, her eyes filled with desire and confusion. "I thought . . ."

"Did you really think I'd take advantage of you?" he asked.

Still confused, she lifted her chin defiantly. "Don't you want me? I said I'd do anything."

"Oh, I want you all right, more than you can imagine. But when you come to my bed, it'll be your idea, because you want it, not because you think you owe me a favor." He raked a hand through his hair. "You'd better go check on your brother. He's waking up."

Before she could ask how he knew that, Erik vanished from her sight.

Daisy stared at the place where he had stood only moments

before, thinking how incredible it was that he could just disappear into thin air like that. What was she going to do about Erik? She knew he wanted her in the most primal way, but he wanted more than that. He wanted her body and her blood, her heart and her soul. How could she surrender herself to him? How could she not, when she wanted him as much as he wanted her? Ever since the night she had met him, he had been in her mind, in her heart. It didn't matter how often she told herself it was foolish to even think of having a relationship with him, the thought was always there, like an itch she couldn't scratch.

"It's impossible," she muttered. "The whole thing is impossible. He's a vampire, you're a Blood Thief. Your father and Alex are hunters."

Daisy scrubbed her hands up and down her arms. How could she and Erik ever find any common ground between them, besides the insatiable desire that flared between them whenever he was in the room? Her parents would never accept him. And what about her friends? Her best friend's little sister had been killed by a vampire. Jennifer would never, ever understand how Daisy could be friends with one of the Undead, let alone be in love with one . . .

In love. For the first time, Daisy admitted she felt more for Erik than just affection, more than an undeniable attraction. She was deeply, hopelessly, in love with him. She didn't know when it had happened, didn't know if what she felt was real or if he had worked some sort of supernatural vampire mojo on her, but it felt right. It felt real.

In love with a vampire, Daisy thought. How could that be? She had been taught since childhood that they were no longer human, that it wasn't a crime to destroy them or to sell their blood. Hunting vampires, marketing their blood online, those were considered laudable occupations.

Oh, Lord, what was she going to do now? How could she explain her feelings to her family, to her best friend, to herself?

Try as she might, she couldn't find an answer. Feeling the mother of all headaches coming on, she pushed the tumultuous thoughts from her mind. Alex was waking up. Dealing with her brother was something she could handle.

Taking a deep breath, she went downstairs to the guest room. She paused a moment, then opened the door and stepped inside.

Alex was sitting up, his back against the headboard. He glanced around the room. "Daisy, what the hell's going on? Where am I?"

Pasting a reassuring smile on her face, she sat on the edge of the bed. "Don't you remember what happened?"

"Happened?" Alex blinked at her, and then he frowned. "Oh, yeah, we went looking for Rhys."

Daisy nodded.

"Yeah, I remember now. We found a lair." Alex looked at her, his face as pale as the pillowcase behind his head. "I found his resting place . . . I was going to stake him when he sprang at me . . ." His eyes narrowed. "I don't remember much of anything after that."

"I went in looking for you," Daisy said, forcing a smile. "Just in the nick of time."

"Was it him? Was it Costain?"

Daisy nodded.

"And you killed him?" Astonishment swept over her brother's face. "Hot damn, the reward's ours!"

Daisy shook her head. "I don't think I destroyed him. I staked him, but I think I might have missed his heart."

"You didn't make sure? You didn't take his head?"

"At the time, I was more interested in getting you out of there." For the moment, she decided not to tell her brother that he had been half dead, or that Erik had given him his blood and saved his life, both facts she was certain Alex wouldn't appreciate, at least not at the moment.

Alex's gaze moved around the unfamiliar room. "So where are we?"

"A friend's house," she said with a shrug. "It didn't seem smart to go home."

"Yeah, you're probably right," Alex agreed somewhat dubiously. And then suspicion flared behind his eyes. "What friend?"

Daisy worried her lower lip with her teeth. There was no point in lying. Sooner or later, Erik would appear and Alex would know where they were.

She was about to answer when Alex said, "This is *his* house, isn't it? The artist's?"

"Yes, it was closer than ours and I . . . I didn't know where else to go."

Alex snorted. "You think *an artist* can protect us from the likes of Rhys Costain?"

"I don't know," Daisy said quietly. "I hope so."

Erik propelled himself across the city to Rhys's main lair; when he found it empty, he went to check on the house where the Vampire Council met.

A harsh command silenced Lucifer as Erik vaulted over the fence and landed on the front porch. A glance at the lock showed it had been picked. Dreading what he might find, Erik pushed the door open and stepped inside. The scent of fresh blood was unmistakable.

Expecting the worst, he was relieved to see Rhys sitting on the sofa, his fangs buried in the neck of a leggy blond Erik recognized as one of the girls from La Morte Rouge.

Rhys lifted his gaze when Erik entered the room.

"Sorry," Erik muttered. "I didn't mean to interrupt your dinner."

Snarling softly, Rhys pushed the girl aside and licked the blood from his lips. "What the hell are you doing here?"

Damn! Why hadn't he anticipated that question? He rarely showed up on Rhys's doorstep without an invitation or a darn good reason. Unfortunately, he didn't have an invitation, and he couldn't very well tell Rhys that he had just stopped by to see if he had survived Daisy's attack.

"Well?" Rhys muttered impatiently.

Stalling for time, Erik cleared his throat. What possible excuse could he give? "I was in the neighborhood," he said, keeping his voice carefully casual. "Thought I'd stop by and see if you were in the mood to go hunting down by the docks." He gestured at the blonde sprawled on the sofa. Her eyes were closed; a drop of bright red blood glistened like a ruby on her slender throat. "I didn't know you were ordering in."

Rhys glanced at the girl, as if he had forgotten she was there. "You want to go hunting? What's the occasion?"

"Nothing special," Erik said with a shrug. "Just thought I'd like some company for a change."

Rhys grunted softly. "I'm glad you're here." Giving the girl a nudge, he gestured for her to leave the room.

Rising, her legs none too steady, the blonde left the house.

With a wave of his hand, Rhys closed the front door. "I was attacked today."

"Attacked?" Erik repeated. "By who?"

"I don't know. He didn't leave his smell behind, but I've tasted his blood. I'll know him when I find him."

Erik swore under his breath. If Rhys found Alex, he would find Daisy. And if he found the O'Donnells at Erik's house . . . damn! Erik didn't want to think about what that would mean. "Are you all right?"

"What do you think?" Rhys draped his arm over the back of the sofa. "It was a near thing, though."

With a casualness he was far from feeling, Erik dropped into the chair across from Rhys. It took every ounce of his self-control to keep his face impassive, his manner relaxed.

"He wasn't alone."

Erik went still as he waited for Rhys to go on.

"He had a girl with him. A tasty-looking little morsel with auburn hair and green eyes. When I find her . . ." He licked his lips. "For all that she was a fragile-looking thing, she had spunk." Lifting one hand, he rubbed his chest. "Drove a stake through me, she did. An inch or two to the left and it would have been all over."

He'd seen her, Erik thought, his hands clenching into tight fists. Rhys had seen Daisy.

"You okay, buddy?" Rhys asked.

"Yeah, sure. Sounds like a close call."

"Too damn close!"

"I always said you needed better security around here. A baby could break into this place."

"How did they know where to find me?" Rhys asked, his voice sharp. "That's what I want to know."

"You think I sent them?" Erik asked, his tone equally sharp.

"I don't know." Rhys stared at him, his eyes narrowed with suspicion. "You're the only one who knows I rest here from time to time."

"It wouldn't take a genius to figure it out. Anyway, I'm probably the only one on the West Coast who *doesn't* want you dead. The rest of them would be fighting to take your place before your ashes were cold."

Rhys grunted softly, and then chuckled. "Come on," he said, his good nature restored. "Let's go find you some dinner, and then we'll have dessert."

Chapter 20

"Daisy! Dammit, Daisy, where are you?"

"I'm up here. What's wrong?" She peered over the banister, startled to see Erik moving swiftly toward the foot of the stairs, so swiftly he was little more than a blur.

"Get your things together. We're leaving."

"Leaving? Why? Where are we going?"

"Rhys knows what you look like. He's tasted your brother's blood. How long do you think it will take him to track the two of you down?"

"So he's still alive," she murmured.

"Very much so."

Daisy felt the blood drain from her face. All too clearly she recalled the fury blazing in the vampire's hell-red eyes when he had whirled around to face her. She had seen death in those eyes. Her death.

"We need to go, Daisy. Now."

"You're right, of course. Alex . . ."

"What about him?"

"We can't tell him that you've talked to Rhys."

"Right."

Daisy chewed on her lower lip thoughtfully. "I'll just tell him that I think we need to get out of LA, that I've got a bad feeling about staying here any longer since I'm not sure that I destroyed Rhys."

"Will he buy that?"

"I think so."

"Tell him whatever you need to, but do it now."

While Daisy went to talk to Alex, Erik went upstairs to his room. He threw a change of clothes and a long, black hooded cloak into a suitcase, packed his laptop, and shoved a pair of sunglasses into his pocket. As an afterthought, he grabbed a T-shirt and a pair of gray sweatpants for Alex and headed downstairs to the guest room, wondering, as he did so, how he had gotten so tangled up in the affairs of the O'Donnell family. Of course, he knew the answer, and her name was Daisy.

Alex was sitting up in bed when Erik entered the room. Daisy glanced at him over her shoulder, her expression telling him that she had explained things to her brother.

Erik tossed the T-shirt and sweats on the bed. "Are you strong enough to get dressed on your own?"

"Damn right!"

"Then do it. We're leaving in five minutes." With another glance at Daisy, Erik left the room.

She followed him into the living room.

"Have you got everything?" Erik asked.

She nodded. She hadn't had anything with her other than her handbag, her cell phone, and her kit when they arrived. "You don't think we waited too long, do you? You don't think he's out there?"

"No, but we need to put some miles behind us before sunrise."

Daisy glanced at her watch. It would be light in a few hours. "Does Rhys . . . can he be out during the day?"

"Not in direct sunlight." He looked past Daisy as Alex entered the room. "Are we ready?"

"I think so," Daisy said. "Let's go."

"We'll take my car," Erik said.

"Hey, what about my Lexus?" Alex asked.

"Leave it," Erik said. "You're in no condition to drive."

As they left the relative safety of Erik's house, Daisy felt a rush of anxiety. What if Erik was wrong? What if Rhys was outside, waiting for them? If he attacked, could the three of them fight him off? Alex looked better, but she could tell by the fine lines around his mouth that he hadn't yet regained his full strength. As for herself, she was out of holy water and the last time she had seen her hawthorn stake, it had been sticking out of Rhys Costain's chest.

She glanced at Erik, who was helping Alex, none too gently, into the backseat of his car. Erik was their only hope.

She climbed into the front seat, thinking it was a bit ironic that she had spent her adult life hunting vampires, and now the oldest vampire in the city was hunting her.

"What?" She glanced at Erik, realizing he had asked her a question.

"I asked if there's anywhere in particular you want to go?"

"Home," she said. "I want to go home to Boston."

"Do you think that's a good idea?" Erik asked.

"I don't know. I don't care. I just want to go home." She glanced over her shoulder. "Alex?"

"We should go home," he agreed. "Safety in numbers and all that."

Erik grunted softly, wondering if he had made a mistake in letting Daisy decide where she wanted to go. Under the circumstances, returning the brother and sister to their vampire-hunting parents didn't seem like the wisest thing for him to do.

They drove in silence for the next hour or so.

Daisy sighed as she stared out the window at the passing scenery. Alex had fallen asleep. Erik appeared to be deep in thoughts he didn't seem inclined to share. It was probably just as well. She had caused him nothing but trouble. He was probably regretting the fact that he had ever met her. Well, there was nothing she could do about that now. He would probably take her home and drop her off and she would never see him again. Sadly, she knew that was probably for the best.

As the miles slipped by, Daisy found herself constantly looking behind them, expecting to see Rhys right on their tail, his eyes glowing like twin coals from the pit of hell.

Daisy woke when the car came to a stop. She hadn't meant to fall asleep. Sitting up, she saw that they were parked behind the Big Top Motel. The sky was growing light in the east.

"Stay here," Erik said. "I'm going to get a couple of rooms."

She nodded, her gaze following him as he got out of the car and walked around the building. Two rooms, she thought, and wondered who was sleeping with whom.

Erik returned a short time later. Opening her car door, he handed her a room key. "You and Alex are in twelve," he said. "I'm right next door."

After getting out of the car, Daisy shook her brother's shoulder. "Alex?"

He muttered something unintelligible, but didn't wake up.

"What's wrong with him?" Daisy asked.

"Nothing. He's still healing. I'll carry him inside. He'll be fine when he wakes up."

With a nod, Daisy stepped out of the car and opened the back door. Erik lifted Alex as if he weighed no more than a child, carried him into the room, and settled him on one of the twin beds.

"I guess I don't have to tell you to keep the window closed and the door locked," Erik said, turning to face her.

"Will you be all right?" Daisy asked. "Wouldn't it be better if we all stayed together?"

"Probably, but I think I'll live longer if your brother goes on thinking I'm an artist."

"Probably," Daisy said, grinning. "Although he's going to wonder why we're spending the day here."

"Just tell him I drove all night and I needed the rest."

"All right." She looked up at him, wishing he would take her in his arms. Right or wrong, she felt safe in his embrace.

Her stomach tingled with anticipation when his gaze moved over her face, lingering on her lips. He was going to kiss her.

Murmuring her name, he pulled her roughly into his arms. "What am I going to do with you, Daisy, darlin'?"

She looked up at him, drowning in the depths of his deep black eyes. He could do anything he wanted with her, she thought. Didn't he know that?

Her eyelids fluttered down as his mouth covered hers. She pressed against him, wanting to be closer, wanting to feel his skin against hers, his hands on her flesh. In his arms, she could face anything, be anything. She wanted to be a part of him, to give him everything she was, everything she would ever be.

She moaned softly as his hand moved restlessly up and down her spine, his touch somehow erotic, even through her clothing. She wanted to touch him, needed to feel his skin beneath her hand. Tugging his shirt from his jeans, she pressed her palms to his back. His skin was smooth and cool.

"My turn," he whispered.

She gasped his name when his hands slid under her sweater. He walked her backward until she was against the wall, and then he leaned into her, letting her feel his desire. She writhed against him, aching and needy, willing, at that moment, to do anything he wanted if he would satisfy the ache building deep inside.

She might have surrendered to him then and there if Alex hadn't cleared his throat. "Do you guys think I could get some breakfast before you devour each other?"

Erik drew back, his eyes hot. He stared at Daisy a moment, then pressed his car keys and a handful of cash into her hand. "Get him something to eat," he said, his voice ragged. "But have it delivered. I'll see you tonight."

Before Daisy could say ah, yes, or no, Erik was gone.

Daisy glared at her brother. Couldn't he have stayed asleep for another hour or two?

"Maybe you two had better get a room of your own," Alex said dryly.

"Oh, shut up!" Daisy said irritably.

Muttering under his breath, Erik darted from Daisy's room to his own. The rising sun burned his eyes, but it was nothing to the fire burning in his loins. Damn her brother's untimely interference!

Slamming the door, Erik stood with his back against it for a moment, cursing his bad luck. Another five minutes and he would have had Daisy in his arms, in his bed.

After locking the door, he drew the curtains over the windows, then surveyed the room that would be his tomb until sunset. It was remarkably unremarkable, with dark furniture and nondescript carpeting. He grunted softly as he glanced at the insipid painting on the wall over the dresser. A monkey could have done better.

Throwing back the covers on the bed, he stretched out on the mattress and closed his eyes. Daisy's image quickly came to mind, her hair like a cloud of russet-colored silk, her skin smooth and clear and warm. And her eyes . . . they sparkled like green fire. He had often heard it said that the eyes were windows to the soul. If that was true, then Daisy O'Donnell had the soul of an angel.

He laughed softly. An angelic Blood Thief. That was something you didn't run into every day.

Daisy. Her image lingered in his mind as his body relaxed, slowly succumbing to the lethargy that drained his strength and his consciousness.

Daisy paced the floor of the motel room. She and Alex had finished breakfast hours ago and now Alex's soft snores told her he was asleep again. She sighed with frustration. Her brother could sleep anytime, anywhere.

She glanced at her watch, dismayed to see that it wasn't even noon yet. She switched on the air conditioner to drown out the sound of her brother sleeping. If only she had a book to read.

Sitting on the foot of her bed, she switched on the TV and flipped through the stations. Game shows and soap operas, soap operas and game shows. In this so-called age of enlightenment, you'd think programmers could come up with something more original and interesting.

Switching off the set, she pulled her phone from her handbag and called home.

Her mother answered on the second ring. "Daisy, is something wrong?"

"No, Mom, why would you think that?"

"Well, we haven't heard from you much lately. Your dad's been trying to get in touch with Alex, but he doesn't answer his phone. Have you talked to him?"

"Alex is fine, Mom. He's with me. We're on our way home."

"There is something wrong," Irene O'Donnell said. "Are you hurt?"

"We're both fine."

"Your dad wants to know if Alex found Rhys."

"We found him," Daisy said, and quickly told her mother what had happened, omitting the part that Erik had played in saving Alex's life.

"But you're both all right?"

"Yes." Daisy took a deep breath. "And so is Rhys."

"I'll let your father know. How soon will you be home?"

"A couple of days, I guess. I'm bringing a guest."

"Oh?" There was a wealth of unasked questions in that simple word.

"Yes, Mom, a man. A very special man."

"That's wonderful, dear. You're sure you're all right?"

"Yes, Mom, stop worrying."

"I can't help it. That's what mothers are for. Have you talked to Brandon lately?"

"No, why?"

"He's in love."

"Really?" Daisy asked, feigning surprise. "Who's the girl?"

"Kevin's sister, Paula, can you believe it? He just told us about it last night. It sounds serious."

"How long have they been dating?"

"Only a few weeks, but he's very much in love."

"So soon?" Daisy asked, and then wondered why she was so surprised. There had been a time when she didn't believe in love at first sight, but that was before she met Erik.

"I think he's planning to propose. He told us he was out looking at engagement rings last night."

"That's wonderful, Mom, I'm happy for him. Listen, I've got to go, my battery's almost out of juice. I'll see you soon."

"About that," Irene said. "Your aunt Judy and I are leaving for New Zealand in the morning. We'll be gone for two weeks."

Aunt Judy had never married. She had been a schoolteacher for twenty years. She had taken a vacation every year since she retired, and she always dragged Daisy's mother along with her. Daisy had mixed feelings about her mother being gone. On the one hand, she would miss seeing her, sure. But on the other hand, it meant her mother wouldn't be bugging her about Kevin O'Reilly, although she probably wouldn't say anything as long as Erik was there.

"That's okay, Mom."

"I wish I'd known sooner that you were coming, but it's too late to cancel the trip now."

"Don't worry about it. Have a wonderful time. I'll see you when you get home."

"All right, dear. I love you."

"Love you, too."

Daisy ended the call, then sat there staring at the phone. So, her little brother was in love and thinking about getting married. It was always the quiet ones, she thought, grinning. Brandon had been shy and introverted for as long as she could remember, yet it sounded like he was going to beat both of his siblings to the altar.

Marriage. Did vampires marry? She had never heard of such a union. When people married, they could expect to spend fifty or sixty years together. But vampires, Lordy, they could be married for centuries. People always talked about being in love forever, but could any two people really expect to stay together that long? She grinned inwardly. Maybe, if one of them was Erik. What was he doing now? Was he sleeping the sleep of the Undead, or was he sitting next door, thinking about her the way she was thinking about him?

Would she have stopped him earlier, if Alex hadn't interfered? What would it be like, to make love to Erik? Did vampires make love like normal people? Heat flooded her cheeks and pooled in her very center as she imagined the two of them locked in each other's arms.

Shaking off the image, she fanned herself with her hand. Would this day never end?

Daisy had hoped her brother would sleep until sundown. After all, he had been badly hurt, and even though Erik's blood had saved his life, Erik had told her Alex was still healing. And there was nothing like sleep to help a body recuperate.

She glanced at the wall that separated their room from Erik's. Was he sleeping? Would he wake up if she knocked on the door? Would he invite her inside and take up where they had left off when Alex interrupted them? Lord, what was she thinking? She tried to banish the image of herself and Erik wrapped in an embrace, but it was no use. She wanted his arms around her waist, his mouth on hers, his tongue teasing her lips. She wanted to touch him and taste him, and even though the idea excited her, there was a little part of her mind that kept asking if she knew what she was doing.

Right or wrong, she was thinking of going next door when Alex sat up. Yawning, he stretched his arms over his head.

"I'm hungry," he said, glancing at Daisy.

Daisy shook her head. No matter what time he woke up, he was always hungry.

"So," he said, "how about you?"

She shrugged. "I could eat something."

"Good, I hate to eat alone." A search of the bedside table turned up a phone book. After finding the phone number for the nearest pizza place, Alex ordered a couple of pizzas and two sodas, then looked at Daisy. "Should I order something for your friend?"

"I don't think so."

Alex completed the call, then went into the bathroom to take a shower.

He emerged twenty minutes later, shirtless, his hair still wet. "I can't believe they don't have a blow-dryer in this place. I don't suppose you've got one in that handbag of yours?"

"No, sorry."

Muttering under his breath, he went back into the bathroom.

They were watching a pay-per-view movie when the pizza arrived. Alex tossed one of the boxes on Daisy's bed. "Ham and pineapple for you."

"Thanks."

"What do you suppose your friend is doing?"

Daisy shrugged. "He's probably still asleep. He drove all night, you know."

Alex grunted softly.

They ate in silence for a few minutes. Daisy licked a bit of sauce from her fingers. She didn't know if the pizza was really good or if she was just really hungry, but she couldn't remember when anything had tasted so wonderful.

"So, what do you say we hit the road? I don't know about you, but I'm going stir-crazy in here."

"Erik might still be sleeping."

"Wake him up," Alex said, speaking around a mouthful of pepperoni.

"Later. I want to take a shower, too, you know." She sipped her drink. It was three hours until sundown. She wondered what distraction she could come up with if Alex insisted on going next door to wake Erik.

She was still trying to think of something when Alex said, "There's a mall across the street. Since you don't want to disturb Sleeping Beauty, what do you say we do a little shopping after you get cleaned up? I could use a change of clothes."

"Good idea," Daisy said. Her brother loved to shop almost as much as she did. With any luck, they could spend an hour or two at the mall, she thought, and then sent a wary glance at the door. Maybe leaving the motel wasn't such a great idea. What if Rhys had followed them last night? What if he was out there, waiting for them? It was said that vampires couldn't enter a dwelling without an invitation, but what if that only applied to homes, not motels? What if it was just a myth? "Maybe we should just stay inside."

"Why?"

"Rhys knows who we are. What if he followed us?"

"Bring him on!"

"Are you crazy? He almost killed you."

"Come on, Daisy Mae, you're exaggerating. Do I look like someone who almost died?"

It was on the tip of her tongue to tell him that he would be dead now if it wasn't for Erik, but of course, she couldn't say that, couldn't tell her brother that his savior was a vampire.

"It was a close call," she said. "Too close."

"I can handle myself."

"Oh, sure. You proved that the other day."

"Dammit, Daisy . . ."

"We've never hunted a vampire as old as he is," she said, her trepidation growing with each passing minute. "We don't know what he's capable of, what powers he possesses."

"Fine. Stay here if you're afraid," Alex said, a note of scorn in his voice. "I'm going out."

Daisy drew in a deep breath and let it out in a long, slow sigh. "And I'm going with you."

"Thought you were afraid of the great and powerful Rhys?"

"Maybe I am," Daisy retorted. "Maybe that makes me smarter than you."

Alex snorted. "You wish."

Daisy couldn't help it. She grinned because this argument sounded just like the hundreds of others she and Alex had had through the years. She finished her pizza, drank the last of her soda, and stood up. Her father had always said the only way to overcome your fears was to face them head-on.

Grabbing her handbag, she headed for the door. "Let's go."

"I thought you wanted to shower first?"

"I'll take one when we get back. Put your shirt on, big brother. Maybe we can find some holy water along the way."

Erik stirred with the setting of the sun. Like all vampires, he woke fully rested and aware of his surroundings.

Rising, he cocked his head to the side, muttered an oath when his preternatural senses told him that the room where Daisy and her brother should have been holed up was empty.

Damn fool kids. Where the hell had they gone?

Moving to the window, he drew back the curtain, squinting against the last rays of the setting sun. Where was she?

Stealing himself for the pain to come, he unlocked the motel door and stepped outside. His skin tingled as he navigated the short distance from his motel room to his car. Unlocking the trunk, he opened his suitcase, pulled out his cloak, and quickly wrapped it around him, flipping the hood in place with a flick of his wrist. The cloak's heavy black cloth blocked the sun's rays as he hurried toward Daisy's room. Closing his eyes, he took a deep breath, then followed her scent into the single-story, L-shaped mall located across the street.

After a five-minute search, he found Daisy and Alex at the cash register inside a men's store.

"What do you think you're doing?" he asked, his voice low but harsh.

"I needed a change of clothes," Alex retorted. "You got a problem with that?"

Erik glared at him. "I don't give a rat's ass what *you* do, but if you put Daisy's life in danger again, you'll answer to me."

Whatever retort had been in Alex's mind died, unspoken, at the look of fury in the other man's eyes.

Erik looked at Daisy, his expression softening. "Do you want to die? Why did you leave the motel? What the hell were you thinking?"

She met his gaze defiantly. "We needed something to wear."

"I see. You want to be well dressed when Rhys finds you, is that it?"

"Don't be absurd," Daisy retorted.

Fighting back his anger, Erik took Daisy by the arm and led her away from her brother. "Have you forgotten that Rhys isn't bothered by the sun?" he asked, keeping one eye on Alex. "Rhys doesn't have to stay indoors as long as he's out of direct sunlight, nor is he compelled to rest during the day." Erik captured her gaze with his. "He could be here now and you wouldn't know it until it was too late."

His words had the desired effect. Daisy's eyes widened as she quickly looked around.

"We need to go. Now," Erik said.

"Well, look who's in a hurry all of a sudden," Alex said,

coming up behind them. "We'd have been on the road a long time ago if you'd dragged your sorry butt out of bed before sundown . . ." Alex's eyes narrowed thoughtfully as his voice trailed off.

"Let's go!" Daisy grabbed Erik by the arm and hustled him toward the exit, hoping to get out of the store and back on the road before her brother put two and two together and got vampire. "Come on, Alex," she called over her shoulder. "We're wasting time!"

Chapter 21

It took only a few minutes to throw their stuff together and check out of the motel. As much as Daisy had wanted a shower, she decided to forgo it for two reasons. Firstly, because Rhys was after them, but, more importantly, she didn't want to leave Alex and Erik alone together for any length of time for fear that Alex might ask Erik questions that Erik would be reluctant to answer.

They had been on the road for over an hour now, and thus far, no one had said much of anything. Alex sat in the backseat, his arms crossed over his chest, his expression pensive. Daisy could almost hear the wheels turning. How much longer before her brother concluded that Erik was a vampire? She could only imagine the dust-up that would follow.

Erik's attention appeared to be on the road. Daisy glanced at him from time to time, wishing she knew what he was thinking. She hadn't had a chance to talk to him alone since they left the motel. She needed to explain her reasons for agreeing to go to the mall with Alex. Maybe it hadn't been the smartest thing to do, but it had seemed like the best way to keep Alex from discovering Erik's secret.

With a sigh, she stared out the window. Taking a vampire home with her probably wasn't a very smart thing to do, either.

But there was another, more pressing matter to be considered. She waited until Alex dozed off to mention it to Erik.

"What are we going to do tomorrow?"

"What do you mean?"

"Alex won't want to spend the whole day in a motel again. He's going to wonder why we don't travel during the day."

"Yeah, I've been thinking about that, too. I think we'll drive straight through to Boston."

"Are you kidding? It's still two days away."

"I know. I'll drive until sunup, and then you and Alex can take over until nightfall."

"But . . . the sun . . . you can't . . ."

"Haven't you noticed the dark tint on the windows? I'll be fine as long as you keep the windows up."

Daisy mulled that over for a few minutes. "What if Alex wants to stop at a motel again?"

"If it's at night, no problem. If it's during the day, just tell him you don't think it's a good idea, not with Rhys looking for the two of you."

Daisy's stomach did a funny flip-flop at the mention of the vampire's name. "It probably wasn't smart of us to stop last night," she muttered.

"Probably not. Will your family be able to protect you?"

"Aren't you going to stay?"

"Sure, if you want me to." He had no intention of leaving her as long as Rhys was a threat. "But I can't be at your place during the day."

"No," she said with a faint grin. "I guess not." Her parents were pretty easygoing about most things, but not about vampires. Her father hunted them relentlessly, like his grandfather and his great-grandfather before him. Irene O'Donnell had given up hunting when she married Daisy's dad, but she could still swing a wicked mallet, if necessary. "You don't think Rhys will find us, do you?"

"I don't know. He's pretty big on revenge, but he's easily distracted. Your best hope is that someone else ticks him off."

"Will he think it strange that you left town without telling him?"

"I doubt it. I've done it before. I'll call him in a day or two and tell him I needed a change of scene."

"I'm sorry I got you involved in all of this."

Erik slid a glance in her direction. He could see her clearly in the darkness. Her hair fell loose over her shoulders, a fall of dark silk that tempted his touch. Her brow was furrowed, her eyes shadowed with worry, not only for herself, but for her brothers and her parents.

"I won't let him hurt you, or your family," Erik said quietly.

"Erik . . ."

"What?"

"Nothing."

He smiled at her, pleased that she was worried about him, too. It had been a long time since anyone cared whether he lived or died. Sometimes, he hadn't much cared either. But that was before he met Daisy O'Donnell. She had revived his flagging spirits, made him glad to be alive.

With a sigh, Daisy lowered the back of her seat and closed her eyes.

Erik watched her from the corner of his eye. It took only a few moments for her to fall asleep. His hands tightened on the steering wheel as he listened to the slow, steady beat of her heart. Her scent filled his nostrils. For a brief moment, he imagined pulling off the freeway, finding a dark, secluded place, taking Daisy in his arms to still his hunger and ease his desire. There was just one problem, and it was snoring softly in the backseat.

With a sigh of exasperation, Erik rolled down the window. It wasn't easy, being in such a confined space with two mortals, especially when one of them was as tempting and tasty as the woman sleeping only inches away. Everything about her called to him—her beauty, her humor, her laughter. The way she looked at him, always a little wary, yet unafraid. The way her body molded itself to his, the intoxicating taste of her lips, the womanly scent of her skin, and yes, her blood, warm and sweet, unlike anything he had ever had before. Since that first small taste, he had hungered for more, knowing he would never again be satisfied with the blood of another.

He glanced at her again. She was so young, so beautiful. Even now, after knowing her, it was difficult to imagine her as the Blood Thief. Harder still to imagine that they could have any kind of future together. And yet, how could he let her go? Only now did he realize how empty, how meaningless, his existence had been. He had accepted being a vampire centuries ago. He had put the past behind him, made the necessary adjustments. Told himself he was happy. Lies, he thought. All lies to make the emptiness of his life bearable. But now, with Daisy, his life was no longer empty.

Which led to another problem. He wanted her. She wanted him. Finding a way to make their relationship work might be a problem. Finding a way to coexist with her family would be an even bigger obstacle. And then there was her brother, Alex, who was already suspicious. Erik wondered how much longer it would take for Alex to figure things out. Not long, since he was already suspicious. And then there was the other brother to consider.

Erik raked a hand through his hair. He hadn't made many

mistakes in his life, but falling in love with Daisy O'Donnell could prove to be fatal.

Alex woke an hour or so later, demanding to be fed. Erik exited the freeway and pulled into the first hamburger place they came to. He opted to stay in the car while Daisy and her brother went inside.

After a few minutes, he got out of the car to stretch his legs. He was hungry, too, he mused, but not for a cheeseburger and fries. He wanted something warm and fresh. The thought had no sooner crossed his mind than a couple of teenagers approached, heading for the restaurant. It took only moments to hypnotize the two of them and lead them into the shadows.

Erik fed quickly, released them from his spell, and was back in the car before Daisy and her brother returned.

"I bought you a burger and a Coke," Daisy said, thrusting a brown paper sack into his hand.

Erik looked at her, one brow arched in amusement as he muttered his thanks, then pulled out of the parking lot.

"You'd think we could stop long enough to eat inside," Alex said. "I don't know about you two, but I could use a break."

"Forget it," Daisy said, unwrapping her cheeseburger. "I want to put as much distance between us and Rhys as possible."

"Smart girl," Erik murmured.

"What do you know about it?" Alex asked brusquely.

"Just what Daisy told me," Erik replied mildly.

"Yeah?" Alex said, frowning. "Just what did she tell you?"

"Just that some pervert named Costain is after her, and that she's afraid of him."

"That's all she said?"

Erik shrugged. "Pretty much. The guy sounds like some kind of psycho to me, and that makes him dangerous."

"I can look after her."

"Yeah," Erik said, unable to keep the sneer out of his

voice. "I saw how well you did that the last time you and Costain tangled. I don't want the same thing happening to Daisy."

Daisy glanced over her shoulder. Alex's jaw was so tight she thought it might crack.

When the silence got unbearable, Daisy turned on the radio, then scanned the stations until she found one playing soft rock, hoping it would ease the tension in the car.

It didn't, but try as she might, she couldn't think of anything to say. Some time later, Erik pulled into a gas station. Daisy and Alex got out of the car to use the restroom and pick up some snacks, leaving Erik to fill the tank. While they were gone, Erik tossed the hamburger and Coke Daisy had bought him into the trash.

The tank was full and he was standing by the driver's side door when Daisy and her brother emerged from the mini-mart. He felt a twinge of jealousy as he watched them talking and laughing together. He had never had any brothers or sisters. His parents, his wife, and his children were long dead. He had lived alone so long, he could scarcely remember what it was like to be part of a family, to share a house with people you loved, people who loved and cared about you in return.

"Are you sure you don't want anything?" Daisy asked as she climbed into the passenger seat.

"I'm sure."

"You don't eat much, do you?" Alex asked, settling himself in the backseat.

"I eat when I'm hungry," Erik replied. Sliding behind the wheel, he started the car and pulled onto the street.

Moments later, they were back on the highway.

* * *

It was near dawn when Erik pulled off the freeway onto a side road. "One of you will have to drive for a while," he said. "I need to get some rest."

"Suits me," Alex said. Climbing out of the backseat, he stretched his back and shoulders. "I was getting claustrophobic back there."

Erik sent Daisy a meaningful glance as he took Alex's place in the backseat. She nodded, silently letting him know that she would make sure the windows stayed up.

He winked at her, then reached for the blanket on the floor. Drawing it up over his shoulders and head, Erik closed his eyes and felt himself falling into nothingness.

Alex jerked a thumb over his shoulder. "He's kind of strange, don't you think?"

Daisy's heart skipped a beat, afraid that they were about to have a conversation she definitely didn't want any part of. "Strange? No, I don't think so. Why?"

"Well, let's see. He sleeps all day. I've never seen him eat. He wears a lot of black." Alex shrugged. "Remind you of anyone? Or anything?"

"So he's a little eccentric," Daisy said, struggling to keep her voice calm. "He's an artist."

"Uh-huh."

Daisy turned sideways in her seat. "Just what are you trying to say? Or not say?"

"Well, if he wasn't hanging around with you, I'd say he was a vampire. But I know if that was the case, you would have told me, because keeping a secret like that would put both of our lives in danger. And I know you'd never do that, would you?"

Daisy looked out the window so Alex couldn't see her face. She was a horrible liar and everyone in the family knew it.

"Would you?"

"Of course not."

Alex grunted softly. "You're hiding something, Daisy Mae, and I'll find out what it is, sooner or later."

She hoped it was later. Much later.

"We need to stop for gas. And I'm ready for some breakfast," Alex muttered, glancing at his watch. "Or lunch."

Alex found a drive-through burger place for lunch. For appearance's sake, Daisy ordered a hamburger for Erik, even though she knew he wouldn't eat it. Twenty minutes later, they were back on the road again.

"So," Alex said between bites of his chili burger, "how long have you known him?"

"Erik? Not long."

"How long?"

"I don't know. A couple of weeks."

"Two weeks? That's it? Geez, Daisy, the way you two have been carrying on . . ." Alex shook his head. "Two lousy weeks."

It seemed longer than that, Daisy thought. Sometimes it seemed as if she had known Erik forever . . . forever, she thought, smiling inwardly. He could very possibly live forever, as long as Alex and her father didn't find out what he was.

It was late afternoon when Alex pulled off the highway in search of a place for dinner. They hadn't had anything to eat except an ice cream cone since morning and she was starving. She wondered if Erik needed to feed and how he would manage it here.

Now she felt the tension growing inside her as Alex pulled into the parking lot of a buffet restaurant. The sun hadn't set yet. She really didn't want to see Erik go up in smoke, yet Alex would expect Erik to be hungry by now, since he hadn't eaten breakfast or lunch. Her heart was pounding with dread by the time Alex parked the car.

Before Alex could say anything, she reached over the backseat and shook Erik's shoulder. "Hey," she called softly.

Erik woke immediately. Pulling the blanket away from his face, he looked at her and smiled. "What's going on?"

"We're stopping for an early dinner."

Erik looked out the window. It was an hour until sunset. "Give me a minute," he said, glancing at Daisy's brother. "My leg's asleep."

"We'll meet you inside," Daisy said. "Come on, Alex, I'm hungry."

Alex didn't seem the least bit suspicious as he followed her into the restaurant. He told the cashier a third party would be joining them, paid the bill, and the two of them picked up their trays.

As she filled her plate with salad, Daisy wondered how Erik would get into the restaurant without being burned by the sun, and what excuse he would use for not eating.

She was trying to decide between ham or roast beef when Erik appeared behind her.

"So," he said, "what looks good?"

Alex was standing in front of Daisy. He turned at the sound of Erik's voice, his gaze moving over the corn and potatoes on Erik's tray.

"I'm having the ham," Daisy said brightly. "The roast is too rare for my taste."

Erik grinned at her. "It looks just right for me."

They found a table in a corner, away from the windows. Daisy and Erik sat side by side. Alex sat across from them, a curious light in his eyes as he watched Erik.

"How much longer until we get home?" Daisy asked, hoping her nervousness didn't show.

Erik speared a slice of meat with his fork. "We should be there by late tomorrow night."

Daisy stared at him. Was he really going to eat? Could he?

She glanced at Alex, who had also chosen roast beef, then back at Erik.

"Medium rare," Alex said, taking a bite. "Just the way I like it."

Erik nodded, though he hadn't eaten a thing.

They made small talk for a few minutes, then Alex went back for seconds, leaving Daisy and Erik alone at the table.

"What's going on?" she asked. Erik hadn't eaten a thing, but Alex seemed totally oblivious to that fact.

"Just a little vampire magic," Erik said. "I planted the suggestion in your brother's mind that I'm eating."

"You can do that?"

Erik nodded. Had it not been necessary to allay Alex's growing suspicions, he would have waited for Daisy and her brother in the car. The sound of too many beating hearts, the scent of warm blood combined with the unpleasant odors of so much food, played havoc with his senses and his self-control.

"How did you get in the restaurant without getting burned?"

"I transported myself from the car to here." He would have preferred to do the same thing when he had followed her to the mall. It would have been less painful, but he wouldn't have been able to track her scent that way.

Daisy nodded. While growing up, she and her brothers had heard numerous stories of the remarkable powers that vampires possessed. But it was one thing to hear about them, or read about them, and quite another to know that they weren't stories at all, but fact, and that the man sitting beside her was capable of things she had always regarded as myths.

Alex returned a short time later, the plates on his tray piled high. "Are you two finished already?"

"Not quite," Daisy said. "I want to sample their chocolate cake. And maybe that apple pie. They both look really good."

"You're right," Alex said. "Bring me a slice of that pie, will you?"

With a nod, Daisy left the table.

Alex looked at Erik. "I take it you're not having dessert."

"No."

"No taste for sweets?"

Erik glanced at Daisy, who was standing at the dessert table. "It depends on the sweet," he remarked.

Alex frowned as he followed Erik's gaze. "What are your intentions toward my sister?"

"Intentions?"

"You know what I mean. She said you've only known each other a couple of weeks, but it doesn't look that way to me. I see the way she looks at you," Alex said, leaning forward. "The way you look at her."

"We're attracted to one another," Erik said mildly. "It's quite normal."

"Is it? You're hiding something from her, something . . ." Alex frowned. "I don't know what it is, but you're no good for her."

"Perhaps not," Erik said candidly. "But she's very good for me."

"What's good for you?" Daisy asked, taking her seat beside Erik.

"You are," he said, smiling.

Alex pushed his plate away. "I'll wait for you in the car."

Daisy gestured at the pie on her tray. "What about your dessert?"

"Forget it," Alex said curtly. "I'm not hungry anymore." Rising, he stalked out of the restaurant.

"He's not going to make this easy, is he?" Erik remarked.

"He's never made anything easy," Daisy muttered. "Do you want to go?"

"No, finish your dessert." He turned to look out the window. The sun was still visible above the horizon. "Take as long as you like."

Daisy wasn't sure she could endure another day and night on the road with Erik and her brother.

Last night, after they left the restaurant, the atmosphere in the car had been tense, to say the least. Daisy had managed to distract Alex while Erik transported himself from the restaurant into the backseat. Pleading a headache, he had pulled the blanket over his head. Daisy had taken a turn at the wheel, grateful to have something to occupy her mind. Alex had sulked in the passenger seat.

At dusk, Alex had climbed into the backseat and Daisy had relinquished the wheel to Erik.

And now it was night again, and Erik was driving.

"How much longer?" Daisy asked.

"We should be there a little after midnight," Erik replied. They had made good time since leaving the motel three nights ago. He was reasonably certain they would be safe once they reached Boston. He and Rhys had never exchanged blood; there was no blood link between the two of them, no way for Rhys to find him.

It was different with Alex; Rhys had tasted Alex's blood, which might allow the vampire to track him over a short distance, but even Rhys Costain couldn't follow a scent that was twenty-six hundred miles away. Unless Alex had also tasted Costain's blood.

Of course, that was a question Erik couldn't ask Daisy's brother, since he wasn't supposed to know that a vampire was after the two of them. But it was something they needed to know. He would have to ask Daisy about it. He didn't know why he hadn't thought of it sooner.

Blood was a strong bond. Erik had drunk from Daisy and she had tasted his blood, which had created a bond between them, one that Daisy remained unaware of due to the fact that Erik kept his mind closed to her. He would always be able to find her; if he so desired, he could read her thoughts. If he opened his mind to her, the link between them would work both ways, allowing her access to his thoughts as well. Such a bond grew stronger with each exchange of blood, forging a connection between vampire and mortal that could only be broken by death.

Erik swore softly. If Alex and Rhys had exchanged blood, there was no point in running away. Rhys would be able to home in on Alex's blood whether Alex was across the street or across the country.

Erik slid a glance at Daisy. Her eyes were closed; her lashes lay like dark fans against her rosy cheeks. In all his years, Erik had never created another vampire, never bonded with a mortal, mainly because he had never met anyone, male or female, he wanted to be bound to, until he met Daisy. And now, through some cosmic quirk of fate, he shared a blood link with the notorious Blood Thief.

Needing to clear his head, Erik lowered the car window. A blood-red moon smiled down on him; the cool night air caressed his skin like the hand of a familiar friend. He had learned to love being a vampire just as he had grown to love the night—the sounds, the silence, the sense of belonging. He was a creature of the night now, one with the darkness in ways no mortal could or would ever understand. With his enhanced night vision, nothing was hidden from him. He saw the brown and white dog skulking through the shadows, the barn owl perched in an oak tree alongside the highway, the mouse fool-ishly trying to cross the road.

To be a vampire was to see things, hear things, that were beyond the limited abilities of mortals. Many vampires, drunk on the power of what they were, began to regard mortals as little more than food. Rhys was one of them. He had been a vampire for so long, he had forgotten what it was like to be human.

To Erik's dismay, there were times when he caught himself thinking along the same lines, viewing mortals as little more than sustenance. When that happened, he made himself stop and think about his wife and children, about the love they had shared, their hopes and dreams. Vampire though he might be, he had always tried to hang on to some vestige of his human-ity, to remember what it had been like to be a mortal man, a husband and a father.

His gaze slid over the woman beside him. She was a young female in the prime of her life with her whole future ahead of her. One day, she would give up being a Blood Thief, settle down with a decent young man, and raise a couple of kids. Whether he liked it or not, a 325-year-old vampire had no place in Daisy O'Donnell's life or her future.

Hearing a subtle change in Alex's breathing, Erik glanced in the rearview mirror. Daisy's brother sat up, stretching. He grimaced when he met Erik's gaze.

Erik grinned wryly. Alex made no secret of the fact that he didn't like Erik dating his sister. Good thing he didn't know the truth, Erik mused, his grin widening.

"According to Daisy's directions, we should almost be there," Erik remarked.

"Yeah," Alex said. "Take the next off ramp and turn right at the first stop sign."

Erik glanced in the rearview mirror again. "You want to tell me why you dislike me so much?"

"I don't trust you."

"Any particular reason why you feel that way?"

"Nothing I can put my finger on, but in my gut, I know you're not what you seem."

Erik grunted softly, impressed with O'Donnell's intuition. "Whatever you might think, your sister is safe with me. Believe that if you believe nothing else."

"What do you want from her?"

"What does any man want from a beautiful woman?" Erik grinned inwardly as Alex's face turned an angry shade of purple. "Calm down before you bust a blood vessel," Erik said. "I'm kidding."

"I doubt it," Alex muttered.

Erik met Alex's gaze in the mirror again. "I'm in love with her," he said quietly. "I know you don't approve and you'd rather I wasn't here, but I really don't give a damn what you think. She's in danger, and until she's safe again, I'll be nearby whether you like it or not."

"Turn left here," Alex said gruffly. "We're home."

Daisy woke up when the car came to a stop. She glanced out the window, overcome with a sense of peace when she saw the light shining in the front window. Her mother always left a light burning in the window when one of her children was away from home, whether they were going to be gone for an evening or indefinitely.

She looked up when Erik opened the car door and offered her his hand. "Here we are."

She nodded as she placed her hand in his and let him help her out of the car.

Erik tossed his keys to Alex. "Why don't you get the bags?"

Daisy tugged on Erik's hand. "You're staying here, with us, aren't you?"

"I don't think so."

What was she thinking? Of course he wouldn't want to stay with her, not when her father and brothers were hunters. "Will I see you tomorrow night?"

"I'll be here."

"Where are you going to stay?"

"I'll find a place. Don't worry about me. And don't let that brother of yours do anything stupid. If you're smart, you'll both stay indoors as soon as the sun starts to set. I doubt if Rhys knows where you are, but it's not worth taking the chance. If he finds Alex, he'll kill him. And you, too. Don't doubt it for a minute."

Daisy swallowed hard. If he was trying to scare her, he'd done a first-rate job.

"Do you know if Alex ingested any of Rhys's blood?"

"Drank it, you mean?"

"Yeah."

"I don't think so. Why?"

"Let's just say things will be less complicated if he didn't."

"Less complicated?" Daisy frowned at him. "In what way?"

"Rhys has your brother's scent, but I'm pretty sure he can't track that this far. If your brother and Rhys exchanged blood, Rhys will be able to find him no matter where he goes. If they didn't, then Alex is probably safe here." Erik ran his knuckles down her cheek. "And so are you."

"I never thought to ask him about that."

"Well, if Rhys doesn't show up in the next day or so, there's probably nothing to worry about."

"Should I talk to Alex about it?"

"Probably wouldn't hurt."

"All right."

Needing to touch her, he ran his hands up and down her arms. "Until we know for sure, remember what I said about staying inside."

"I will."

"Hey, Daisy," Alex called from the porch. "You comin'?"

"I'll be right there." She looked up at Erik. "Till tomorrow, then."

"Sweet dreams, Daisy darlin'."

She looked up at him through the veil of her lashes. "Aren't you going to kiss me good night?"

"You bet." Cupping her face in his hands, Erik kissed her long and hard, partly to annoy Alex, who was watching them from the porch, but all thought of aggravating Alex quickly faded from Erik's mind when Daisy's tongue slid across his lips. With a moan that was almost a growl, he crushed her body against his as he deepened the kiss. Maybe he couldn't be a part of her future, but she was here now, and he was determined to make the most of whatever time they had together.

Erik grinned when, a moment later, he heard the sound of the front door slamming shut. "You'd better go," he murmured, dropping a kiss on the tip of her nose. "Before your brother has a heart attack."

"I'll miss you," Daisy said, her gaze searching his. "Come as early as you can."

"Count on it."

"Erik . . ." She stroked his cheek, reluctant to let him go, afraid she might never see him again.

"I won't leave you, Daisy, not as long as he's out there."

"And when the danger's past?" she asked, her voice so low only a vampire could hear it.

"Let's not worry about that now, okay?"

"I don't want to lose you."

"Dammit, Daisy, what do you want from me?"

"I don't know."

"Maybe you'll tell me when you find out." He kissed her again because she was looking up at him, her eyes filled with confusion, because she was so close and smelled so good. Because, oh, hell, when did a man need a reason to kiss a beautiful woman? One last kiss, and then he headed for his car before he took her there, in the damp grass with her brother watching from the window.

Daisy touched her fingertips to her lips as she watched Erik drive away. She could feel Alex's accusing gaze boring into her back, knew that, sooner or later, she would have to go into the house and face him.

Putting it off wouldn't make it any easier. With a sigh of resignation, she went in to face the music.

Chapter 22

Alex was waiting for her when she walked in the door. "I guess you're gonna tell me that was just a good-night kiss between friends?"

Daisy tossed her handbag on the sofa table. "Oh, for crying out loud. He just kissed me like that because he knew you were watching."

"Yeah, right. Dammit, Daisy, Erik Delacourt is after something. Why can't you see that?"

"None of this is any of your business," Daisy retorted. "I'm over twenty-one. You're not my father . . ."

"No, but I am," a deep voice said.

Daisy spun around to see her father coming down the stairs, belting his favorite ratty bathrobe around him.

Noah O'Donnell was tall and lean, with shaggy brown hair and intelligent brown eyes. A narrow scar, souvenir from a fight with a vampire, bisected his left cheek. He glanced from Daisy to Alex and back again. "What's going on?"

Daisy hurried toward her father and threw her arms around him. "Nothing. Alex is just being Alex. I don't know how you stand him."

Noah O'Donnell grinned at his daughter. "Who's Erik Delacourt and what does Alex think he's after?"

"He's after Daisy," Alex said, his tone sour. "If you'd seen the way they were kissing a minute ago . . ."

"Well, you can't blame the man," Noah said. "After all, Daisy is a lovely young woman, and there's nothing wrong with kissing."

"There's something wrong with Delacourt," Alex said sourly. "Something . . ."

"You just don't like him," Daisy said. "I don't know why, and I don't care. I like him."

"Here, now, daughter, how serious are things between you and this man?"

"They're not serious. I hardly know him."

"I see." Noah ran a hand through his hair, his expression suddenly serious. "What brings the two of you home at this hour of the night?"

"Well, uh . . ." Alex cleared his throat. "We had some trouble in LA."

"What kind of trouble?" Noah asked.

"I went looking for Costain," Alex said, "and I . . ." He glanced at Daisy. "We found him."

Noah glanced between Daisy and Alex. "Go on."

"It was a close call," Daisy said. "Alex was badly hurt, at least I thought so at the time." She couldn't tell her brother or her father how close Alex had been to death, couldn't explain how Erik had saved his life. "I took him to Erik's—"

"Why didn't you take him to the nearest hospital?" her father asked.

"I don't know. I guess I panicked. Anyway, Erik gave him first aid and—"

"You didn't tell him Alex had been attacked by a vampire, did you?"

"No, of course not," Daisy said, thinking quickly. "I said he'd been beat up by a man who was stalking me. Anyway, I decided we should get out of town and Erik offered to bring us home."

"I see. And where is he now?"

"He went to find a hotel."

"Why didn't you invite him to stay here?" Noah asked. "After all, we owe him a favor."

Daisy shot a withering glance at her brother. "He didn't want to stay under the same roof as Alex."

"Well, you're both home, safe and sound, and that's what matters most. Why don't you both go get some sleep. We'll talk more about this in the morning."

Daisy nodded, glad for a chance to escape the room and any further interrogation by her brother or her father. "Good night, Dad."

"Good night, daughter."

With a last look at Alex, Daisy went upstairs. The house seemed empty without her mom bustling around, offering cookies and hot chocolate, acting as a buffer between Daisy and Alex. In spite of her affection for her brother, they had butted heads since they were kids.

Going home was like going back in time, Daisy thought as she stepped into her bedroom. It looked exactly the same as it had when she first moved out. Beneath assorted rock-star posters, the walls were pink with white woodwork. Pink polka-dot curtains hung at the windows; a bright pink quilt covered the bed. A dozen stuffed penguins of varying sizes fought for space on the shelf over her desk.

With a sigh, Daisy changed into her pajamas, washed her face, and brushed her teeth. After turning out the light, she climbed into bed and closed her eyes, asleep as soon as her head hit the pillow.

* * *

Erik stood in the shadows outside Daisy's house, watching as the lights inside went out, one by one. He listened as she snuggled into her bed, waited until the soft, even sound of her breathing told him she was asleep before he got into his car and drove away.

With no destination in mind, he drove through the city until he found what he was looking for. The Vampire Vault was a private club similar to La Morte Rouge, a hangout for vampires and those who served them. One had to be a vampire, or be invited by a vampire, to gain entrance. Like La Morte Rouge, the Vault wasn't listed in the phone book or online.

Erik parked his car in the lot, then knocked on the back door. The vampire who opened it looked like he had just stepped off the set of an old Dracula movie. He wore a black suit, white tie, and a long black cloak.

The doorman murmured, "Good evening," in a remarkable impression of a young Bela Lugosi as he gestured for Erik to enter.

A narrow hallway opened onto the club's main floor. A quick glance revealed a long bar at the far end of the room. A trio of waiters served the fifteen or twenty people seated there. High-backed booths lined one wall. Small tables adorned with black cloths were located at intervals around the room. Each table was decorated with a black vase and a blood-red rose. The lighting was dim, the air filled with the scent of beating hearts and the smell of fresh blood.

A young female vampire sat at the grand piano located on a raised platform. Clad in a long white gown, her skin pale, she looked almost ghostlike. It seemed her fingers barely touched the keys as she played. Erik listened a moment, trying to place the song, then shrugged. Perhaps it was a composition of her own making.

He had barely stepped into the room when a leggy blonde clad in a low-cut, skintight emerald green gown and silver high heels slithered up to him. He couldn't help noticing that her figure went in and out in all the right places.

"I've never seen you in here before," she said, her voice a throaty purr.

"I haven't been here in quite some time."

"I hope you'll come back often."

"I might." He couldn't help staring at her. It was obvious that she wasn't wearing anything under the gown. Her skin was smooth and unblemished save for a half-healed bite mark on the inside of her left elbow.

She smiled up at him. "I'm Jade."

Erik nodded. "What are you offering?" Some mortals offered only blood. Some blood and sex.

"Anything you want." She scraped her nails lightly down his cheek. "Are you interested?"

He nodded again. What male in his right mind would be able to refuse such an offer?

Her smile widened as she took his hand and led him up a narrow, winding staircase, then down a long, carpeted hallway. Most of the doors had DO NOT DISTURB signs on them.

Jade bypassed the first empty room, then entered the last room on the right.

Erik followed her inside. It was a large room. The walls were white. Red curtains hung at the window. A round bed covered with a red quilt took up most of the room. A half-open door revealed a bathroom.

Jade sat on the bed. A hidden slit in her skirt parted to expose one long, creamy white thigh. "What's your pleasure?"

"Just a drink."

"Nothing more?"

He shook his head. There was a time when he would have taken everything Jade was offering, he thought with some regret. But that was before a certain sexy Blood Thief entered his life.

Jade pouted prettily. "Are you sure?" She sounded disappointed.

"Yeah." He sat on the bed beside her, his nostrils flaring at the scent of musk and perfume. And warm, fresh blood.

He heard the sudden increase in her heartbeat as she arched her neck, then turned her head to the side, giving him access to her throat. He ran his tongue over his fangs as the hunger rose up within him.

With a low growl, Erik cupped his hands over her shoulders and sank his fangs into the soft skin of her neck. He closed his eyes as her blood flowed over his tongue and down his throat.

It satisfied his hunger, but that was all.

Only Daisy could satisfy his need.

Chapter 23

Frowning, Rhys tossed his cell phone on the dining room table. He'd been calling Erik for the last three nights with no luck. So where the devil was Delacourt, and why wasn't he answering his phone? He considered the possibility that the Blood Thief or a hunter had found him, but dismissed it out of hand. Delacourt was one of the smartest, strongest vampires he had ever met. It was more likely that he'd left town. But where would he have gone? And why?

Rhys muttered an oath as he walked down the hallway to his bedroom. He was the Master of the City. As such, he demanded loyalty from those he allowed to dwell in his territory. To defy him was to court destruction.

Like most vampires, he trusted only a chosen few. Erik was one of them. They had met in Ireland over two hundred years ago. Rhys grinned at the memory. They had both been hunting the same woman, a bonny lass with hair like fire and eyes as green as the Emerald Isle itself. Had Rhys been younger and less in control of his hunger and his anger, he might have challenged Erik. Instead, they had called a truce and shared the wench. A tasty morsel, Rhys recalled. He had been all for draining her dry, but Erik, always gallant where a pretty woman was concerned, had talked him out of it.

Though it had seemed unlikely at the time, the two vampires had become friends.

They had met again by chance in California shortly after Rhys had destroyed the former Master of the City. Erik had been tired of wandering by then and had decided to settle down for a while. Like all the other vampires in the area, Erik had sworn his allegiance to Rhys. Until now, Rhys had never doubted Erik's loyalty.

Rhys grunted softly as he opened his bedroom door. Someone had put a price on his head, and until he knew who it was, everyone was suspect, including his best friend.

The mortal who had tried to destroy him had apparently left the city. And so, it seemed, had Erik. Coincidence? Perhaps, and perhaps not.

Rhys smiled at the woman waiting for him in his bed. He would worry about traitors and bounty hunters tomorrow.

The night was young, the woman was tall, blond, and willing, and he was very, very thirsty.

Chapter 24

Daisy slept until almost noon. Upon awaking, she lingered under the covers, thinking how nice it was to be home again, to sleep in her old bed in her old room. To pretend, for a few minutes, that she was safe, that nothing could hurt her here, in the house where she had spent most of her childhood.

Turning onto her side, she stared at the curtain covering her window. Where was Rhys? Would he come after her and her family? When would it be safe for her and Alex to venture outside during the day? The vampire couldn't enter the house without an invitation, but her family couldn't stay inside indefinitely.

Her thoughts turned to Erik. She wondered if he was awake. Was it too early to call? Warmth curled through her at the thought of hearing his voice. No matter how many times she told herself there was no future for the two of them, she couldn't imagine her life without him. They had spent so much time together lately, being without him now made her feel empty somehow, as if a vital part of herself had gone missing.

When her stomach growled, she threw back the covers and swung her legs over the side of the bed. Padding into the bathroom, she took a quick shower, brushed out her hair, pulled on a pair of lavender sweats, and hurried downstairs.

As was to be expected, Alex was in the kitchen cooking up a storm. She stood in the doorway a moment, watching him. He wore an old Boston Red Sox T-shirt and a faded pair of cut-off jeans. His feet were bare.

Moving into the kitchen, Daisy poured herself a cup of coffee, then sat at the much-scarred oak table, her mug cradled between her hands while she watched Alex flip pancakes. He really was in the wrong business, she mused as she sipped her coffee. The world had lost a great chef when he decided to be a vampire hunter.

Alex glanced at her over his shoulder. "How many pancakes?"

"Six, seven, a dozen. I'm starving!" She was glad he had decided to make a late breakfast instead of an early lunch.

"Bacon or sausage?" he asked with a grin.

"Both."

"Gotcha! Do you want eggs? I've got fried and scrambled."

"No. Yes, scrambled."

Five minutes later, Alex handed her a plate, then sat down across from her. "It's good to be home again, isn't it?"

Daisy nodded. Her roots, the majority of her memories, were here. Birthday parties and Easter egg hunts, camping out in a tent with her dad in the backyard, making brownies with her mom, breaking her arm when she fell out of the big old elm tree in the front yard. Her first kiss on the front porch. No matter what she did, no matter where she went, this would always be home. "The pancakes are wonderful."

"A little orange juice in the batter," Alex said with a shrug, but she could see he was pleased by the compliment. He had always been the best cook in the family.

"I'll have to remember that." Alex tucked into his breakfast and Daisy did the same, thinking again that it was good to be home.

Daisy was on her second cup of coffee when she said, "I've been wondering about something."

"Yeah? What?"

"Your encounter with Costain. Did you drink his blood?"

"Are you nuts? Why would I do that?"

"I know you wouldn't, on purpose. I just thought that, you know, during the struggle . . . we wouldn't have much hope of escaping him if the two of you had exchanged blood. You know that."

"Well, yeah, but it's nothing to worry about."

"You're sure?"

"Of course!" he said emphatically, but Daisy thought he looked a little doubtful.

"Where's Brandon?"

"He got up early this morning to take Paula Christmas shopping."

"Christmas shopping! It's only October."

"Uh, Daisy Mae, I hate to tell you this, but it's the first of November."

She blinked at him. November? It couldn't be, she thought, then shrugged. With all that had been going on in her life the past few weeks, keeping track of the days had been the last thing on her mind.

Her father entered the kitchen a few minutes later, a grin settling over his face as he filled his plate. "It's good to have you back home, boy," he said, taking a seat at the table. "Brandon's not the cook you are. And with your mother gone . . . well, I was getting mighty tired of cold cereal."

The three of them made small talk while they ate, commenting on the weather and speculating on what Irene and Aunt Judy were up to.

"New Zealand will never be the same," Noah said with a grin. Pushing his plate away, he slapped his palms on the table. "So, Alex, you up for a day of hunting?"

Daisy tried to talk the two of them out of leaving the house, but they brushed her concerns aside, confident that the two of them could handle Rhys Costain or any other vampire they encountered while the sun was up.

Daisy prayed they were right as she followed them to the front door. Standing on the porch, she waved as they climbed into her father's pick-up.

Her father tapped the horn a couple of times in farewell as he backed the truck out of the driveway.

Daisy stared after them until they were out of sight; then, too antsy to sit still, she loaded the breakfast dishes into the dishwasher, wiped off the table, and washed up the frying pans. After cleaning the kitchen, she dusted all the furniture, vacuumed the carpets upstairs and down, mopped the kitchen floor, and did a load of laundry, and still Alex and her father hadn't returned.

Taking a deep breath, she told herself not to worry. Her father had been a hunter for over twenty-five years. He knew what he was doing.

Going upstairs to her bedroom, she glanced at the posters on the walls and the stuffed animals on the shelves. Impulsively, she took the posters down, rolled them up, and put them on the top shelf of her closet. The penguins followed the posters, all but the cute little black and white ceramic bird her father had given her for her sixteenth birthday. That remained in the place of honor in the center of the bookshelf.

She ran her fingers over the curtains. Maybe she would replace them, and the quilt, too. Her mother wouldn't mind.

Later, she went into the kitchen for a glass of milk and an apple, then went back upstairs where she spent forty minutes cleaning out her closet, boxing old clothes and shoes she knew she would never wear again, as well as some old games and dolls.

She was almost finished when she came across an old photograph album. Sitting on the floor, she dusted off the cover, then flipped through the pages. Funny, how pictures could instantly transport you back in time. She smiled at the images of herself and her brothers—pictures of the three of them at various ages gathered in front of the Christmas tree on Christmas Eve, all of them wearing new pajamas. Snapshots of them sitting at the kitchen table making cookies, cutting out valentines, decorating Easter eggs, or carving Halloween pumpkins. Funny, how every family took similar photos.

With a sigh, she put the album on a shelf in the closet, then unpacked her suitcase and hung up the clothing she had brought with her.

It was after four when she went downstairs.

"Hey, sis."

"Brandon! Hi. I didn't know you were home." Daisy smiled tentatively at the young woman sitting on the sofa beside her brother. "You must be Paula."

Paula was a pretty girl, with a fair complexion, brown eyes, and shoulder-length bright red hair. A sprinkling of freckles dotted her cheeks.

She stood up as Daisy entered the room. "And you must be Daisy. I've heard so much about you."

"All good, I hope," Daisy said, offering her hand.

"Of course it's all good," Brandon said. "I'm not telling her any of the bad stuff until she says 'I do.'"

"Good idea," Daisy replied.

Paula resumed her seat beside Brandon and Daisy sat in the overstuffed chair across from them.

"Where are Dad and Alex?" Brandon asked.

"Oh, they went out this morning," Daisy said. "They should be back soon. I hear you've been shopping."

"Yeah, Paula bought out most every store in town."

"Really?"

"Not quite," Paula said, poking Brandon in the ribs.

"Really," Brandon said. "This girl has a credit card and she knows how to use it."

"Brandon, stop it," Paula said, blushing.

"She doesn't like people to know her family's rich."

"Oh?" Daisy tried to keep her surprise from showing. Her mother hadn't mentioned that the O'Reilly family had money.

"My dad writes computer software," Paula said with a shrug. "He's very good at it."

"That's great," Daisy exclaimed with a smile.

"Well, we just stopped by to drop off a few things," Brandon said, rising. "And now we're going to dinner. You wanna come along?"

"No, I don't think so. I've been cleaning my room all day and now I just want to relax." It was partly true. She didn't want to leave until she knew her dad and Alex were okay. But mainly she wanted to be here if Erik showed up.

"Okay, sis, catch ya later. Tell Dad I'll be late."

Daisy waited until Brandon and Paula left the house, then grabbed her cell phone and dialed her father's number. There was no answer. Frowning, she disconnected the call and dialed her brother's number. Again, there was no answer.

It would be dark soon, so where were they?

She jumped when someone knocked at the door. She peeked through the peephole, hoping it was her dad and Alex. Her heart skipped a beat when she saw Erik on the front porch.

Unlocking the door, she smiled up at him. "Hi."

"Hi."

She stepped back so he could come in, frowned when he

made no move to enter the house, and then remembered he couldn't enter a home without an invitation. "Come on in, Dracula," she said with a grin.

"Very funny," Erik muttered as he followed her into the living room. He took a quick look around. The walls were off-white, the carpet a deep shade of forest green; the furniture looked worn and comfortable but not shabby. There were books and knickknacks on several shelves, numerous framed family photographs on the fireplace mantel. The morning paper was spread out over the coffee table.

"Sit down," Daisy said, taking a place on the sofa. Her earlier smile had vanished. Worry lines creased her brow.

"What's wrong?" Erik asked, sitting beside her

"My dad and Alex went hunting this morning. They should have been back by now. They're not answering their phones . . ."

"Idiots."

"Can you find them?"

"Maybe, but it's doubtful." Boston had roughly six hundred thousand people. Finding two amongst so many could prove to be difficult. Then again . . . "I might be able to follow their car," he remarked, thinking aloud. Every vehicle carried its own individual scent.

"They took Dad's truck."

With a nod, Erik left the house with Daisy close on his heels.

He paced back and forth across the driveway, then closed his eyes, sorting through the myriad scents of gasoline, trees, and grass until he located the truck's singular smell.

"Well?" Daisy asked.

"Go back inside and lock the door."

"No way! I'm going with you."

"Not this time. You'll only slow me down. Keep your phone on. I'll call you if I find them. You call me if they show up here."

"But . . ."

"Daisy, we don't have time to argue about this."

"Oh, all right." She didn't like the idea of being left behind. She wasn't used to it. After all, in her own way, she was a hunter, too.

He kissed her quickly, and then he was gone.

Moving too swiftly for human eyes to follow, Erik followed the distinctive scent of the O'Donnells' truck, passing ancient red brick sidewalks, Federalist houses, and soaring towers made of glass. The trail ended near Dorchester Bay. Amid the smell of salt water, diesel oil, smoke, and fish, he caught a new scent, that of vampire.

He followed the vampire's scent to a luxury yacht. It took little effort to make the jump from the shore to the deck of the ship. There were humans below, and a vampire. The smell of blood roused his hunger.

Going below, Erik followed the vampire's scent into a stateroom where he found the two O'Donnell men lying on the floor, bound and apparently under some kind of supernatural enchantment. He was moving toward them when he realized he was no longer alone.

Erik whirled around, fangs extended, and came face-to-face with one of his kind. Clad in a pair of black trousers and a loose-fitting white shirt, the vampire was tall and lean and looked to be in his late twenties, though his aura was much older.

"What are you doing here?" the vampire asked. His voice was mild, though his eyes blazed red.

"I know these two," Erik said, gesturing at Daisy's father and brother. "They're not to be harmed."

The other vampire lifted one brow. "Indeed?"

Erik nodded.

"They violated my lair. They tried to destroy me. I am

within my rights to do with them as it pleases me. And it pleases me to kill them."

"I'm afraid I can't allow you to do that."

"No? Who are you?"

"Erik Delacourt."

"Ah."

"You know me?" Erik asked.

"I have heard of you. It is said you are a close friend of Costain's."

Erik nodded, wondering if that was good or bad. "Who the hell are you?"

"Tomás Villagrande."

Erik swore under his breath. Villagrande was the Master of the East Coast vampires, and was even older than Rhys. It was rumored among the ranks of the Undead that Villagrande was one of the first of their kind, that it was Villagrande who had bequeathed the Dark Gift to Dracula himself. Erik didn't know if that was true, but Villagrande's preternatural power was unmistakable.

Villagrande folded his arms over his chest. "Why do you care if these two live or die?"

"They're related to someone I hold dear."

"That does change things, does it not?" Villagrande mused aloud. "And yet the fact remains that they are mine."

Tension thrummed through Erik as he summoned his power. If the other vampire wanted a fight, so be it, although pitting his strength against that of a much older vampire seemed like suicide.

"This someone you hold dear, is it a woman?"

"Yes."

"Ah. And is she young and beautiful beyond compare?"

Erik nodded even as he wondered what game Villagrande was playing.

"You are in love with her?"

"Yes."

"An overrated emotion to be sure," Villagrande remarked, his voice melancholy. "Yet I confess that I, too, have been caught in that snare from time to time. Tell me, are you willing to challenge me in combat to save these two?"

Erik swore inwardly. He had hoped it wouldn't come to that, but he couldn't go back to Daisy and tell her he had failed. Better not to return at all. "If I have to."

Villagrande stroked his chin as he contemplated Erik's decision. "She means that much to you, this woman?"

"And more."

Villagrande laughed softly. "I do not wish to kill you. You have trouble enough. Take them and go."

"Just like that?"

"Just like that." Villagrande smiled, showing a hint of fang. "Never let it be said that Tomás Villagrande stood in the way of true love. As for your inept friends here, I am surprised they have survived as long as they have. They should wake in half an hour or so. You might tell them to be more careful in the future," he said, and with a wave of his hand, he vanished.

Erik stood there a moment, his senses searching for some trace of Villagrande. It was then that he realized he might have made a fatal mistake in giving Villagrande his name. A word from the East Coast Master of the City and Rhys would know where to find Erik, which would lead him to Alex. And Daisy.

Cursing his stupidity, Erik untied Daisy's father and Alex. Hefting a man over each shoulder, he transported himself to the shore. A thought carried him to Daisy's front porch.

She answered before he knocked, making him think she had been looking out the window, waiting for his return.

Her eyes widened when she saw her dad and brother. "Are they . . . ?"

"No, just unconscious."

"Thank the Lord!" She had been terrified that Erik had found them too late. And then she frowned. "What's wrong with them?"

"Nothing. They'll come around in a few minutes."

"How do you know?"

"The vampire they found told me so."

"Oh?" There was a wealth of curiosity in that single word.

Erik lowered Noah O'Donnell onto one end of the sofa and Alex onto the other. "I don't know how we're going to explain this," he muttered.

"Alex has a GPS on his phone. I'll say I called the police and they tracked it, and then I called you. . . . No, that won't work. The police would have taken them to the hospital and doctors would have kept them there until they regained consciousness. What are we going to do? How are we going to explain how they got home?"

"Beats the hell out of me."

Daisy frowned thoughtfully as she glanced at her dad and Alex. "Why didn't the vampire kill them?"

"He was going to." Erik had no doubt that, had he arrived a few minutes later, he would have found Villagrande dining on his captives.

"But he didn't. Why?"

Erik shrugged. "I told him they were important to someone who's important to me." He grinned inwardly. Never in a thousand years would he have figured Tomás Villagrande for a romantic.

"And that made a difference?"

With a nod, Erik took her by the hand and led her out of the living room, through the kitchen door, and out into the backyard.

"What are we doing out here?" Daisy asked.

"Nothing. I just wanted to be alone with you."

"Oh." Anticipation spread through her as he drew her into his embrace. "Thank you for saving Alex and my dad."

"You're welcome." Erik's gaze moved over her face. He traced the outline of her lips with his finger, then lowered his head and kissed her.

Heat unfurled in the pit of Daisy's stomach and spread outward as he deepened the kiss, his tongue stroking hers, his hands moving lightly up and down her spine, drawing her closer, closer, so that their bodies were pressed intimately together, leaving no doubt in her mind that he wanted her.

His lips moved to her brow, the curve of her cheek, her chin, the pulse throbbing in the hollow of her throat. The beat of her heart was faster now, warming her blood. She smelled of musk and desire and woman, of flesh and blood, and he wanted her, needed her.

She stirred in his embrace, inflaming him still more. So easy to take her here, now. So easy . . .

Daisy pressed herself against him, her body trembling with desire as he kissed her again and again. He lowered his head to her breasts, kissing her through the fabric of her shirt while his hands held her body tightly to his. His kisses were like fire, melting her bones, incinerating all thought. There was only Erik, and her desire to please him, to give him whatever he asked. And he was asking. His voice in her ear, begging for a taste . . .

He wanted her, needed her. How could she refuse? With a sigh, she arched her neck, granting him access to her throat. His tongue was like a flame against her skin, the touch of his fangs both pain and pleasure as he drank. And then she was drifting, floating through a red haze of sensation where every touch, every caress, was heightened.

She cried out in protest when he lifted his head, not caring if he took it all if only she could bury herself in the crimson bliss that surrounded her.

Murmuring, "Don't stop," she pulled his head down to her neck once again.

Erik stroked her cheek. "I'm sorry, love, but I dare not take more."

"Please . . ."

He swore softly, then tensed as the back door slammed open and Alex's voice cut through the darkness.

"Daisy? Daisy, are you out here?"

"We're over here," Erik called. Pulling Daisy to him, he quickly licked the tiny wounds in her throat, sealing them, then draped his arm around her shoulders.

"What are you doing out here?" Alex asked, striding toward them.

"Just enjoying the evening air," Erik replied.

"Uh-huh," Alex remarked skeptically. "Daisy, are you all right?"

"I'm fine," she murmured, though it was an effort to focus her thoughts. "Where's Dad?"

"He's talking to Mom on the phone."

"How are you feeling?" Erik asked.

"I feel fine." Alex frowned at him, then looked at Daisy. "What did you tell him?"

"I . . ." Daisy looked up at Erik, wondering what she should say.

"She didn't tell me anything. Why? Is something wrong?"

Alex narrowed his eyes as he gazed from his sister to Erik and back again. "Why should anything be wrong?"

"Alex, we'd like a little privacy, if you don't mind," Daisy said, forcing a smile. "I'll talk to you later."

"Yeah, later." Alex held her gaze for a moment, his

expression puzzled, and then he turned and made his way back toward the house.

"How am I going to explain how they got away from the vampire, and how they got home?" Daisy asked.

"I'm not sure you'll have to."

Daisy frowned. "Maybe you're right. He didn't seem very upset for a guy who'd been captured by a vampire, did he?"

"Exactly. I don't think he remembers any of it."

"Which means my father probably doesn't, either."

"Right. Let's go back inside. I'll hypnotize the two of them and see if they have any memory of what happened. If they do, I'll erase it from their minds, then I'll go get the truck and bring it back here. We'll pretend today never happened. If they don't remember anything . . ." Erik shrugged. "Problem solved either way."

"But . . ." Daisy shook her head, uncertain how she felt about Erik messing with their minds.

"Have you got a better idea?"

"No."

He kissed her lightly on the cheek. "They'll be fine, trust me."

She didn't know why she was surprised by the realization that she did, indeed, trust him. She lifted a hand to her neck, thinking that she had put her life in his hands only moments ago.

"That's my girl." Erik smiled at her as he took her hand and led her into the house.

Chapter 25

Daisy slipped into bed and turned out the light, her mind still filled with images of Erik standing in the living room mesmerizing her father and her brother. She had known such things were possible. She had seen Nonnie put people into trances before. She had known vampires were capable of doing the same thing. The first lesson her father had taught her was never to look directly into a vampire's eyes, something she had totally forgotten upon meeting Erik.

She had watched and listened as Erik had sorted through her father's memories of the day, and then her brother's. Neither her father nor Alex recalled finding Villagrande or anything else about their encounter with the vampire.

"Why would he erase their memories?" Daisy asked.

"I have a feeling he did it just before I took them away, perhaps as a gift to you."

"Me? He doesn't even know me."

"But he knows I love you."

"What? How could he know such a thing?"

"Probably because I told him."

"You discussed me with him?" she exclaimed.

"I explained that you mean a lot to me, and that Alex and your father mean a lot to you."

Thinking back on it now, warm in her bed in the safety of her own room, made her smile. A vampire with a heart of gold. Who'd have thought it?

Erik had left immediately after releasing Alex and her dad from his spell. Brandon had come home shortly thereafter. The four of them had stayed up chatting until well after midnight. Of course, all Brandon could talk about was Paula. She was beautiful. She was sweet and kind and caring, just an old-fashioned girl. She dreamed of going to Niagara Falls when she got married, and she wanted lots of children.

With a sigh, Daisy turned onto her side, thinking she was just a little envious of her brother. Not that she wasn't happy for him. It was just that his future seemed set, while hers seemed to get more complicated every day. Not that she would change her life for Brandon's. Her life might not be perfect, but at the moment, she wouldn't change a thing, not if it meant giving up Erik. Just thinking of him, with his soul-deep eyes, sexy smile, and kissable lips, made her heart skip a beat.

She glanced at the darkness beyond her window. Where was he now? Was he thinking of her, wishing they were together? If only he were there, beside her.

The thought had no sooner crossed her mind than he was lying on top of the covers next to her.

"Oh!" She pressed a hand to her wildly beating heart. "You just scared me half to death."

"Sorry, my little flower," he said, and then grinned. "Any chance I could have the other half?"

"What are you talking about . . . ?" She frowned at him, then recoiled as she realized what he was asking. "No way!"

He ran his knuckles lightly up and down her cheek. "You might like it."

"I doubt it."

"Wouldn't you like to see the world as it is?" He lifted his hand in a gesture that encompassed her bedroom. "Look around you. I can see each stitch in your curtains, hear the ant crawling across the floor, the bird settling in its nest outside your window. When I touch your quilt, I can feel the weave and the texture of the threads. When I touch you . . ." He smiled into her eyes. "Perhaps I'd better not go there."

Daisy stared at him, caught up in the magic of his voice, the wonder of what he was saying. What would it be like, to view the world through vampire eyes? To be able to think yourself across the street or across the country? To hear sounds that others never heard? She recalled watching him carry her father and brother into the house as if they weighed nothing at all. What would it be like to have the strength of twenty men? To drink blood . . .

The thought brought her swiftly back to cold reality. True, Erik had powers far beyond hers, but there was a price to pay for those incredible powers. There was always a price to pay. And the price was far too dear.

"Daisy?"

She closed her eyes, afraid to look at him. He was too beautiful, too tempting. For a moment, she let herself imagine what it would be like to be his equal, a vampire who could share his whole life. Sometimes, when they kissed, she had a taste of what it would be like. With his mouth on hers, she felt strong, invincible, as if she could climb rainbows and touch the stars. But it wasn't real. In a way, he wasn't real.

"Daisy, look at me."

"No."

"What are you afraid of?"

"I'm afraid of you, afraid I'm not strong enough to resist. You make it sound so tempting, but I don't want to be a vampire." She blinked against the burn of tears in the backs of her eyes. "I don't want to give up my family or my life. I like being me."

"It's all right, love." He kissed the tears from her cheeks. "Don't ever let me change your mind."

"But you could, couldn't you?"

He hesitated a moment, pondering the truth versus a lie.

"I know you could," she said. "If that vampire could erase a whole day from Alex's mind, then he could just as easily plant thoughts in his head that weren't his, couldn't he? Couldn't you?"

"I would never do that to you," Erik said quietly.

"But you could?"

"If I wished."

"Promise me. Promise me you'll never do it."

"Very well. I swear it by the love I held for my wife and my children. And by my love for you."

Emotion clogged her throat, making words impossible.

"Sleep now," he said, wrapping her in his arms. "Nothing will hurt you while I'm here."

Yawning, she closed her eyes and snuggled against him. Moments later, she was asleep. Her trust in him was a rare gift, one he wasn't sure he deserved. Like all vampires, he tended to think only of himself, partly out of necessity to ensure his safety in a world that saw him only as evil, partly because it was so easy to forget that he had once been a frail human himself.

Erik brushed a kiss across Daisy's brow. Which of them was the more foolish, he mused.

The woman, for believing he would keep his word?

Or the vampire, for giving it?

* * *

Tomás Villagrande sat atop the city's highest hill. It afforded him a panoramic view of Boston Harbor and Dorchester Bay. He had always loved the ocean. Not surprising, he thought, since he had been a pirate in his youth. In life or undeath, he had lived near the water and owned a ship whenever possible. Boats made unique lairs. He could be ready to move at a moment's notice. No packing involved. Just weigh anchor and be gone.

He had lived in Boston off and on since the early 1850s, back when Fort Warren was being built out on Georges Island. So many years ago, he mused, and yet it seemed like yesterday. But then, time moved differently for his kind.

He had seen much in the course of his long existence. The rise and fall of kings and countries, the decline of nations, devastating plagues and wars without end. Fashions changed. Language changed. Customs changed. But his view of the world remained colored by the era in which he had been born. He had grown up in a time of war and conquest, when men ruled the world and women were little more than pawns, good for providing heirs or cementing alliances with foreign powers. Ah, how times had changed.

He gazed at the moonlight playing over the water and thought about the events of the day. He had been surprised when the hunters showed up. The fact that they had found him made him think it was time to move on, maybe go down to Florida for a while, though the idea held little appeal. There were far too many retired people in the area. Too much old blood. Perhaps New York City, then. The streets were always crowded with tourists, wealthy young men and women eagerly looking for adventure and excitement. Tomás grinned inwardly. He could give them that and more.

He nodded. Yes, tomorrow night he would weigh anchor and head north. It had been a while since he had looked in on those who owed him their allegiance.

And what of Erik Delacourt? What was he doing in Boston? And why hadn't he made his presence known when he arrived, as was proper? It was considered bad form for a vampire to enter a city without obtaining the permission of the Master of the City. But that wasn't the most unusual thing. The big question was, what was a vampire doing associating with vampire hunters? The answer was the woman, of course.

Tomás grinned inwardly. In spite of what he had said about love being an overrated emotion, he had always had a soft spot for young lovers.

His thoughts shifted to the Master of the West Coast vampires. Did Rhys Costain know one of his vampires was protecting hunters? Tomás frowned as a troubling thought occurred to him. What if it was Costain who had sent the hunters? What if Delacourt had shown up to make certain the hunters had done their job?

Vampire, trust no one.

Tomás rubbed a hand over his jaw. Those had been the last words his sire had spoken to him before they parted ways centuries ago, and Tomás had taken them to heart. Was Costain planning some kind of coup? He wouldn't be the first of their breed to want to expand his territory. For eons, vampires had fought for territory. Currently, there were five vampires who claimed sections of the United States as their own. Costain ruled the Western states, Tomás ruled the East. A vampire known as Volger ruled the Midwest; Tristan claimed the North; the South belonged to Morag, one of the oldest female vampires in existence. Other vampires laid claim to the rest of the world. Tomás knew most of them; none were older than he.

His thoughts turned to Costain again. Ruling both the West Coast and the East would be a formidable task. Delacourt was known to be good friends with Costain. Perhaps Costain planned to install his second in command as the new Master of the East Coast.

Tomás frowned into the darkness. Would he be wiser to get in touch with Costain now, or wait until he had more to go on than mere supposition?

Tomás grunted softly. He had sensed Delacourt's power. In another century or two, Delacourt would be a vampire to be reckoned with, even for one as ancient as Tomás himself. He wondered briefly who had sired Costain's friend. Someone extremely powerful, of that there was no doubt.

He lifted his head and drank in the scent of the sea, and with it, the scent of prey. A young man, wandering alone by the shore, unaware of the danger he was in.

Tomás breathed in the lush scent of blood. No need to make a decision tonight. If there was one thing he had learned in his long years as a vampire, it was patience.

His fangs lengthened in response to the lure of hot, fresh, young blood. He had done a good deed today in allowing two hunters to live. Surely he deserved a reward.

"I like being me." Daisy stared at Erik, ashamed of the pleading note in her voice, hating the fear that made her heart pound like a trip hammer. But it was hard not to be afraid when he was looking at her like that, his dark eyes red and glowing, his lips curled back to reveal gleaming white fangs. "Don't," she whimpered. "Please, don't. You promised . . ."

"You won't be any different," he said, and she heard the lie in his voice. "You'll still be Daisy O'Donnell."

She shook her head. "No." She was crying now, tears scalding her eyes and burning her cheeks as he stalked toward her. A long black cape billowed behind him.

She glanced around the room frantically, searching for a

weapon, but the room was completely empty save for the two of them. A distant part of her mind wondered where they were, and then he was a hairsbreadth away, looming above her like the angel of death. Frozen in terror, she could only stare at him as his arm snaked out to curl around her waist, drawing her body against his. His cloak enveloped them, a smothering cocoon.

"Nothing to be afraid of," he said as he bent his head to her neck. "Nothing at all . . ."

She woke with a startled cry. Erik lay beside her. Propped on one elbow, he looked at her, his expression faintly worried.

As though on its own, the bedside lamp came on.

"Are you all right?" Erik asked.

She stared at him, her heart pounding. Was she awake? She lifted a hand to her throat, relieved that there were no telltale bites.

"Daisy?"

As her gaze darted around the room, she was relieved to see she was in her own bedroom, in her own bed. "I . . . I had a bad dream."

"I'm here. There's no need to be afraid."

His words sent a shiver down her spine. *Nothing to be afraid of.*

"Do you want to tell me about it?" he asked.

"No." She shuddered at the memory. "I just want to forget it."

He brushed a lock of damp hair from her cheek. "Go back to sleep. It's hours until dawn."

"I don't know if I can. Tell me more about you, about your life."

"What do you want to know?"

"What's it really like, being what you are?"

"It can be interesting. I've seen much of history in the making. The rise and fall of empires. New inventions. New diseases. Endless wars. I've traveled the world numerous times." He had hunted the famous and the infamous, known great men, courted beautiful women. "As I said, it can be interesting. It can also be incredibly tedious, watching the world change while you stay the same, moving every twenty years or so before people begin to realize that you don't age. It's exciting at first, moving from place to place, learning how to use all your remarkable powers, but after a while . . ."

"Go on."

"After the novelty wears off, you just want what everyone else wants. A place to settle down. Someone to love."

"I've never heard of any vampires staying together. I mean, how does that work, with the whole territorial thing?"

"Bonded vampires can coexist in the same territory."

Thinking of vampires brought Rhys to mind. "How many vampires are there on the West Coast?"

"I'm not sure. Three or four hundred, I imagine."

"That many?"

"It's only a guess."

"And they all answer to Rhys?"

Erik nodded. "To live in the area, one must swear allegiance to him."

She considered that a moment. "You've broken faith with him, haven't you? Because of me."

"Yes, although he doesn't know it, at least not yet." Thoughts of Tomás Villagrande rose in his mind. Had Villagrande contacted Rhys? "There's no law against leaving the city, although vampire etiquette dictates that I should have told him first."

"Do you think Rhys is still looking for us?"

"I don't know. I should probably go back to LA and find out what's going on."

Daisy started to protest, but yawned instead.

He slid his arm under her shoulders and drew her up against his side. "Go to sleep, my little flower."

"You won't leave Boston without telling me?"

"No." His gaze moved over her face. The thought of being away from her for even a day was almost unbearable. "Sleep, my love, there won't be any more bad dreams tonight."

She looked up at him, her beautiful green eyes filled with trust. A moment later, she was asleep.

Erik brushed a kiss across her cheek, marveling at the sweetness of her scent, the warm silk of her skin. He had lived for centuries. He possessed powers beyond compare. Yet this woman, this fragile human woman, had woven a spell around him he couldn't break.

He felt the coming of dawn and with it a sense of heaviness, as if an invisible hand was weighing him down, trying to bury him in the earth where he belonged. Though he hated to leave Daisy, he needed to be away from her house and safely out of the sun's reach.

He brushed a kiss across her brow. She smiled faintly, making him wonder if she was dreaming of him, dreaming of the two of them locked in each other's arms. The thought of holding her body against his, of running his tongue over her skin, tasting her lips, her blood, aroused him instantly.

Muttering an oath, he dissolved into mist and fled the house before he put thought to deed. Moments later, he materialized inside his hotel room. He had left strict instructions at the desk that he wasn't to be disturbed during the day. Still, he had not survived this long by trusting his fate to others. He quickly set wards around the door and the windows. His preternatural power, combined with his witchcraft, afforded all the protection he needed.

He took a quick shower and then, with his strength being leeched away by the rising sun, he fell facedown on the bed and surrendered to the darkness. And though he hadn't dreamed since the night he became a vampire, on this day, he dreamed of making love to Daisy.

And in his dream, he wasn't a vampire and she wasn't the Blood Thief.

Chapter 26

Daisy awoke slowly, reluctant to leave the beautiful dream she had been having. Sighing, she turned onto her side and closed her eyes, hoping to recapture the wonder of it. The magic of it. It had seemed so real . . . just her and Erik, sharing a candlelight dinner beneath a canopy of summer stars, dancing to music only they could hear, walking along a moonlit path, pausing now and then to kiss in the shadows. And then, in the way of dreams, the scene had changed and they were lying on a pile of furs in a room with a ceiling made of glass. The moon smiled down on them as Erik drew her into his arms. And in the way of dreams, she never thought to wonder where their clothing had gone. It was too wonderful to feel his bare skin against hers, to run her hands over his broad chest and shoulders, to bask in the touch and the taste of him. There was no time in this place of dreams, and they had explored each other at their leisure. She was ticklish. He was not. Her skin was soft and warm. His was firm and cool. Two halves, fashioned differently, yet they fit together to make a perfect whole . . .

"Erik . . ." Breathing his name, she opened her eyes. The

dream had seemed so real, she half expected to find him lying in bed beside her.

"Hey, sis, you ever gonna get up? Breakfast is ready."

The last vestiges of her dream vanished at the sound of Brandon's voice.

When she entered the kitchen some ten minutes later, Brandon, her father, and Alex were waiting for her.

"'Bout time you got up," Alex remarked.

Daisy stuck her tongue out at him as she took her place at the table. As usual, Alex had prepared enough food for a small army. This morning he served ham and cheese omelets, toast, fried potatoes, and a bowl of fruit.

They were halfway through their breakfast when Brandon cleared his throat.

Daisy and Alex exchanged knowing grins. Brandon always cleared his throat when he had something important to say.

"Well, go on, son, spit it out," Noah said.

Brandon cleared his throat again. "Last night, after dinner, I asked Paula to marry me."

Alex slammed his hand on the table. "Judging by that grin on your face, I'm guessing she said yes."

"You guessed right, big brother. We're getting married the week after Christmas."

"So soon? Damn, bro," Alex exclaimed. "You've only known her a few weeks."

Brandon shrugged. "Long enough to know she's the one for me."

"I think it's wonderfully romantic," Daisy said. "Congratulations."

"Thanks, sis."

"I know your mom will be pleased," Noah said. "You'll have to call her later and let her know."

Brandon nodded, his grin stretching ear to ear.

"How do Paula's folks feel about it?" Alex asked. "I assume you've already told them."

"They gave us their blessing, although I think they'd rather we waited a while."

"Have you told Paula what you do for a living?" Daisy asked.

"No." Brandon cleared his throat yet again. "I've decided to give it up."

Daisy glanced at Alex and her father. Alex looked chagrined. Noah looked relieved.

Brandon looked at his father, waiting for his response.

"I think that's a wise choice," Noah said. "Being a hunter is a dangerous business, and it's a hard secret to keep. If your mother hadn't been a hunter when I met her, I would have taken up another line of work. Any idea what you'll do?"

"Mr. O'Reilly said I could work for him."

Noah nodded. Paula's father ran an enormously successful software company.

"You're gonna become a computer nerd?" Alex asked disdainfully.

"It's a perfectly respectable line of work," Brandon retorted, obviously stung by his brother's disapproval. "It's going to be a small wedding, just family and a few close friends." Brandon looked at Daisy. "Paula's going to ask you to be a bridesmaid."

"Me? She doesn't even know me."

"Well, we're keeping it in the family. Alex, I was hoping you'd be my best man . . ."

Alex grinned. "I hate to break it to you, little brother, but I've always been the best man."

"Her brother, Kevin, will be an usher," Brandon said, ignoring Alex's jibe.

Kevin, the ubiquitous Mr. Right, Daisy thought glumly. Not wanting to think about having to spend an evening with

Kevin O'Reilly or sidestepping her mother's matchmaking efforts, Daisy began to clear the table. Maybe, if she was lucky, she could get Erik invited to the wedding.

Since Brandon was giving up the family business, they decided to take Daisy's compass and go for one last hunt together. After gathering their gear, Daisy and Brandon climbed in the front seat of Brandon's old Firebird, Alex and Noah squeezed into the back, where they played Rock, Paper, Scissors to decide which way to go. Noah won and chose east, and Brandon headed toward the ocean.

"Hey, Daisy Mae," Brandon said. "Any sign?"

Daisy glanced at her compass. "Go straight." She watched the needle grow brighter, darker. "Turn left here." They were nearing Boston Harbor now. "Left at the corner—stop!"

Brandon pulled up in front of a small bungalow located on a quiet side street.

Daisy stared out the window. The door to the bungalow was closed, the windows shuttered. There was no sign of life.

"Is this the place?" Noah asked.

Daisy nodded. The needle was bright red.

"Let's go!" Alex said.

As they piled out of the car, they each grabbed their gear, then walked single-file up the narrow, rock-lined path.

Alex made short work of the lock on the security screen door and the three deadbolts on the front door, and they were inside the house.

As in most lairs, heavy blackout curtains covered the windows.

"Daisy, which way?" Alex asked.

Heart pounding, she murmured, "Straight ahead."

Moving quietly, they passed through the living room, down a narrow hallway, and into a large bedroom.

"There's nothing here," Alex said. "Are you sure that compass is working?"

"In there," Daisy said, pointing at the closet door.

Brandon opened the door and stepped inside, his flashlight making a sweep of the interior.

"There," Noah said. "Another door."

It was locked but Alex's trusty lock pick made short work of it. Daisy followed her father and brothers into another room. In the eerie light cast by Brandon's flashlight, she saw four caskets lined up side by side.

"Let's go to work," Noah said.

Alex lifted the lid on the first coffin. Brandon filled several vials with blood for himself and Daisy, then backed away. Daisy closed her eyes as Alex staked the vampire, then cut off its little finger as proof that he had destroyed the vampire. Those who paid the bounty on the Undead required some kind of proof—blood or a finger in the case of young vampires, the vampire's ashes in the case of the ancient ones, since they disintegrated when they were staked or beheaded.

They moved to the second casket and quickly took care of business.

Brandon was about to open the third coffin when the lid flew open and a female vampire sat up, her eyes blazing red, her fangs bared.

"Stake her!" Noah cried, but before Alex could move, a male vampire burst out of the fourth coffin. Alex and Noah charged toward the male. Their combined strength drove the bloodsucker to the floor. He lashed out, his nails drawing blood as he tried to defend himself.

The female had her arms wrapped around Brandon. Her fangs were only inches from his throat.

Daisy jumped on the vampire's back, hoping to distract her.

With all the stubbornness of a pit bull, the female vampire tightened her hold on Brandon and sank her fangs into his throat.

Daisy screamed as Brandon sank to the floor, his hands trying to dislodge the vampire. Daisy raked her nails across the vampire's cheek, then pummeled the creature's back and shoulders, but the vampire seemed oblivious as she continued to feed on Brandon.

With a wild cry, Daisy slid off the female's back. Fishing in her pocket, she pulled out a stake and drove it into the vampire's back.

Shrieking in pain, the vampire lifted her head, blood dripping from her fangs, but didn't loosen her grip on Brandon.

Summoning all her strength, Daisy jerked the stake from the vampire's back and drove it in again. She hit the heart this time, she was sure of it. A horrible cry erupted from the vampire's throat as she rolled off Brandon. She twitched once and then lay still, her sightless red eyes wide and staring. A single red tear slid down her pale cheek.

"Brandon!" Daisy dropped down beside her brother. "Dad! Help!" Sobbing, she cradled Brandon's head in her lap. "No, no, Brandon, stay with me," she pleaded as his blood, still warm, soaked into her jeans. "Please, stay with me. You'll be all right. Just hold on . . ."

She looked up through eyes blurred with tears as Alex and her father, both splattered with blood and gore, raced toward her.

Noah fell to his knees beside his son. Tears rolled down his cheeks as he drew Brandon into his arms and rocked him back and forth.

Daisy stared at her father and brother in disbelief. No one in their family had ever been killed by a vampire. They'd had some close calls, sure, but nothing like this. Even now, with the proof in front of her, she couldn't believe Brandon was gone.

It was a somber group that gathered around the kitchen table later that evening. Alex had fixed a dinner that no one ate, and now they sat there, too numb with loss and grief to speak. They had done what needed to be done before leaving the lair near the harbor.

Noah had wrapped his son's body in a quilt pulled from a closet and carried him out to the car.

Alex had decapitated the vampires to make sure they wouldn't rise again, then collected the necessary proof that the kills had been made.

Daisy had stowed the vials of blood in the cooler. She had been tempted to leave them behind, but she couldn't. The liquid in those vials had cost her brother his life.

Daisy and Alex had been about to leave the house when Alex paused. "Do you smell that?"

Daisy had sniffed the air. "It smells like death."

Alex grunted softly.

Daisy followed Alex down a narrow flight of stairs to the basement where they made a grisly discovery—the bodies of a middle-aged man and woman shoved inside an old coal chute.

"They've been dead a while," Alex said. "We need to notify the police."

Daisy had turned away, sickened by the sight and the smell of the house's former owners.

Alex called the police. The rest of the afternoon had passed in a blur of police reports and endless questions. There was no law against destroying vampires. Once the police had ascertained that the deceased were indeed vampires, Daisy and her family had been free to go. They had taken Brandon's body to the local mortuary and made the necessary arrangements for the funeral, and then driven home.

"Your mother and Aunt Judy will be home day after tomorrow," Noah said, breaking the stillness.

"How's Mom taking it?" Alex asked.

"Hard."

"Someone needs to call Paula," Daisy remarked.

"I'll do it." Alex blew out a sigh. "I guess now's as good a time as any." Rising, he left the kitchen.

Daisy stared blankly out the window. Instead of a wedding, there would be a funeral. She still couldn't believe her brother was dead. Brandon had been such a gentle, fun-loving young man. Once, he had confided in her that he didn't like being a Blood Thief. When she had asked why he didn't quit, he had admitted, somewhat sheepishly, that he knew Alex would tease him unmercifully. Daisy blinked back her tears. If only he had quit before it was too late. Funny, she had never really believed anyone in her family would be hurt. They were the good guys, after all.

She looked up, startled, when the doorbell rang. "I'll get it, Dad," she said, thinking it was probably the police with more questions. Her father had been through enough for one day.

It wasn't the police. Opening the door, she found herself staring up at Erik. The word *vampire* screamed in the back of her mind. In that moment, if she'd had a stake at hand, she would have destroyed him without a qualm.

"What's wrong?" There was no mistaking the hatred in her eyes, though he could think of nothing he had done to put it there.

"My brother . . . Brandon . . . he's . . . he's dead."

"I'm sorry. How did it happen?"

She clasped her hands together to still their trembling. "He was. . . ." She took a deep breath and said it all at once. "He was killed this afternoon. By a vampire."

"Ah." That explained everything. "Do you know who did it?"

"Yes. She'll never hurt anyone again."

"I can see I'm not welcome here," Erik said quietly. "I'm sorry for your loss."

Rage and impotent anger boiled within her. She wanted to strike out, to hurt as she had been hurt. Conversely, she had an almost overwhelming urge to invite him in, to rest her head on his shoulder and let him comfort her, but she couldn't. He was Nosferatu. For all she knew, he might have been friends with the vampire who had killed Brandon.

Distraught, she could only stand there, drowning in grief that was too painful, too fresh, for words.

"Good-bye, Daisy."

He was gone before she had time to respond.

Chapter 27

After leaving Daisy's house, Erik told himself that their parting was for the best and would have come sooner or later. Still, even knowing there could be no future for the two of them, he had hoped they could find a way to make it work. Of course, that was impossible now. A vampire had killed her brother, something Daisy would never forget or forgive. Still, he had promised not to leave her until she was safe.

He stood in the shadows for a moment, and then, feeling a need to be with his own kind, at least for an hour or so, he closed his eyes and willed himself to his lair in Los Angeles. He took a quick shower, then slipped into a pair of black slacks and a T-shirt. Since he had left his car parked in front of Daisy's house, he spent a moment deciding how to get to La Morte Rouge.

Not sure what his welcome would be, he opted to walk.

It was a beautiful clear night.

He found Rhys sitting at the bar in the nightclub, a willowy blond on one arm and a buxom redhead on the other.

"Well, well, well," Costain drawled, shooing the two females away, "look who finally showed up. Where in hell have you been?"

Erik took the seat at Costain's right. "I decided to get out of town for a while. You got a problem with that?" He knew he had made a mistake as soon as the words were spoken. He was supposed to be keeping an eye on the West Coast. Hadn't he insisted on staying here? Of course, his only motive at the time had been to be near Daisy. He hadn't given a thought to Costain, or to trying to find out who had offered a reward for his head.

"I've got a problem, all right," Rhys said. "A mighty damn big one. It might have slipped your mind, but someone's out to get me, and they're not fooling around."

"Have you been attacked again?"

"No, but the word's spreading. LA is crawling with hunters." Rhys glanced around the club. "Next thing you know, they'll be coming in here."

"I doubt that," Erik said dryly. La Morte Rouge had more security than Fort Knox and the White House put together.

"So, where were you?" Costain asked. His voice was deceptively mild, at odds with the predatory gleam in his eyes.

Erik made a vague gesture with his hand. "I went East for a few days."

"East?"

Erik hesitated. How much did Costain know? Had Villagrande called him? "Boston."

"Four vampires were killed there this afternoon," Rhys remarked, his voice still mild. "Did you have anything to do with that?"

"Why would I?"

"You tell me."

"I don't know anything about it."

"What do you know about the two hunters who tried to destroy Villagrande?"

Erik swore softly. Damn. He had been counting on Villagrande to keep his mouth shut. How much had he told Costain?

"I'm waiting," Rhys said, and now his voice was like ice.

"I know one of the hunters. He's the friend of a friend." No way would he mention Daisy, her brother or her father by name. "I knew he was in trouble and I asked Villagrande to spare his life, and he did. There's no more to it than that."

"Is that so?"

Erik nodded, every muscle tense. Those who underestimated Rhys Costain rarely lived long enough to regret it.

"And where is he now, this hunter?"

Erik shrugged. He couldn't reveal Alex's whereabouts without disclosing Daisy's, too.

"Mariah thinks you're the one who betrayed me," Rhys said thoughtfully. "Villagrande thinks I sent you East with an eye to challenging him for his territory. Perhaps you went East to challenge Villagrande yourself, or perhaps the two of you are conspiring against me. Is it mere coincidence that your name keeps coming up?"

"I've got no reason to want you dead," Erik replied. "I don't have two hundred grand to pay for your head. I don't want to take over your territory, or Villagrande's, for that matter. Perhaps you should look closer to home."

Costain's eyes narrowed. "Do you know something I should know?"

Erik shook his head. Why hadn't he stayed in Boston?

"You're keeping something from me," Rhys said, his voice sharp. "What is it?"

"Nothing you need to know."

"We've been friends a long time. I'd hate to see anything change that."

Erik took a deep breath. "Do you want me to leave the city and find a new lair?"

Rhys leaned forward, his eyes glowing red. "I want the truth."

"I've given it to you."

Rhys shook his head. "I don't think so."

Before Erik realized what Rhys had in mind, two mortals, obviously under some kind of thrall, came up behind Erik. One dropped a thick silver chain around his neck and jerked it tight while the second dropped a chain around Erik's chest, pinning his arms to his sides.

Erik hissed as the silver burned through his clothing and singed the skin beneath. Rendered powerless, he glared at Costain. "You're making a big mistake."

"We'll see. Take him downstairs."

"Dammit, Rhys . . ."

"Enough! Get him out of here!"

Erik cursed as the two mortals dragged him down a flight of stairs to Costain's personal dungeon. In years past, Rhys had kept mortals here that he intended to prey on at a later date.

The building that housed La Morte Rouge had once been a warehouse with a large basement. Before turning the upper floor into a nightclub for the Undead, Rhys had used the warehouse as a lair. He had turned the basement into a dungeon for his own amusement, complete with cells and chains and other ancient implements of torture.

Erik swore softly as he was dragged into the dark interior. The dungeon was cold and musty and smelled of death and old blood.

One of Costain's thralls opened the door to the nearest cell. The second thrall shoved Erik inside. They fastened silver shackles around his wrists and ankles, then attached the shackles to iron rings set in the wall. When that was done, they removed the chains from his neck and chest, and then the two mindless creatures shuffled out of the cell. After closing and locking the door, they left the dungeon.

Erik tugged on the heavy shackles, but the silver drained his vampiric strength. Weak and helpless, he sank down on the cold stone floor and wondered, morbidly, if Rhys intended to destroy him.

Chapter 28

The next four days were the worst of Daisy's life. She felt as if she were living a nightmare from which there was no escape. No matter how she tried to shake it off, she couldn't. Her brother was dead, and Erik was gone. She knew, in her heart, that his last good-bye had been final. She would never see him again. She didn't know which loss had left a bigger hole in her heart.

Life seemed suddenly unreal, as if she were standing in the background watching a movie that had nothing to do with her.

Her mother and Aunt Judy came home from New Zealand.

Friends and extended family were notified of Brandon's death.

They went to the mortuary to arrange for the funeral. They selected a casket. Arranged for flowers.

Worst of all was the evening when the O'Reilly family came by to express their condolences.

Daisy's mother and Mrs. O'Reilly clung to each other, both weeping softly.

Noah and Mr. O'Reilly eased their sorrow in a bottle of Irish whiskey.

Paula said very little, but Daisy could hardly blame her.

Surprisingly, Alex planted himself by Paula's side and stayed there the whole night.

Later that evening, Daisy found herself alone with Paula's brother. Kevin O'Reilly was a tall, handsome young man, with dark red hair and deep brown eyes. Daisy liked him immediately. He had a winning smile and a quiet sense of humor that she found charming. If she hadn't already given her heart to Erik, she would have been happy to get to know Kevin better.

As the O'Reilly family took their leave, Kevin took Daisy aside.

"I know I shouldn't be asking this now, but I'm afraid if I wait, you might go back to LA before I, well, I'd really like to see you again, you know, in a couple of weeks, or whenever you're ready. I'm sorry, I . . ."

"It's all right, Kevin."

"I can call you, then?"

"Yes."

"If there's anything we can do, don't hesitate to ask."

"Same here."

Kevin nodded, shook hands with Alex and Noah, and left the house.

They held the funeral the following afternoon. At the graveside, Daisy stood between Aunt Judy and Alex as the minister said a few final words of assurance and the promise that they would see Brandon again. Her mother and father clung to each other, their cheeks damp with tears. Aunt Judy sobbed into a handkerchief. Dry-eyed, Alex looked like he had been carved from stone.

Daisy held up pretty well until they lowered the casket into the ground and the mourners dropped handfuls of dirt onto it. It hit her then, really hit her. Brandon was dead and she would never see him again. Almost, she wished that he was a vampire, that he would rise again when the sun went down. Her tears came then, tears of sorrow for the loss of her brother, tears of regret because Erik wasn't there to comfort her. Where had he gone? And why did she care? He was a vampire, the same kind of godless, soulless creature that had killed Brandon.

She should hate him.

She wanted to hate him.

If only she could.

Kevin waited two weeks before calling on Daisy. She went out with him in hopes that it would ease her sorrow, that it would help her to forget Erik. It did neither. She tried to tell herself the reason she couldn't warm up to Kevin was because it was too soon, but that wasn't the reason. There just wasn't any spark between them, and there never would be.

"It's not working, is it?" Kevin remarked at the end of their third date.

"I'm sorry," Daisy said. "It's not you, it's me."

"Is there someone else?"

"There was. I guess I'm not over him yet." It wasn't Kevin's fault that she was forever comparing him to Erik, nor was it Kevin's fault that he fell short in every way.

"I understand. If you'd like to try again, give me a call."

Daisy nodded, uncertain whether she felt relief or regret as she watched him walk away.

Thanksgiving came and went with little fanfare. The family shared a quiet dinner and went to bed early.

Alex and Daisy had rarely left the house since returning home. Alex started complaining that he was going stir-crazy. Daisy could relate. Not only that, she missed her own place in LA. They were both heartily sick of being housebound.

Hardest to bear was the emptiness Daisy felt inside. She missed Brandon. She hated seeing the sorrow on the faces of her parents. The world around them was dressing up for the holidays, but there was little joy in the O'Donnell house. Daisy wondered if her mother would ever smile again.

Most of all, Daisy missed Erik. She thought of him constantly during the day and dreamed of him at night—strange imaginings that were always the same. Sometimes they seemed more like visions than dreams. You weren't supposed to feel pain in a dream, yet her body felt like it was burning, and her stomach felt like it was on fire. When she woke in the morning, she was always thirsty, as if it had been weeks since she'd had anything to drink. She told herself time and again that she hated him even though she knew it was a lie. She might hate what he was, but she couldn't hate him.

By the end of November, she couldn't stand it anymore. Her dreams were nightmares now, becoming more vivid, more realistic, each night. She had never been psychic, never had visions of any kind, but she was continually plagued by the very real fear that Erik's life was in danger. Her worries increased when she called his cell phone and no one answered.

Where was he?

Finally needing to talk to someone, she shared her worries with Alex one night after their parents had gone to bed.

Alex listened patiently, then said, "Forget him, Daisy Mae. I never liked him anyway. Now, Kevin . . ."

"I am *not* interested in Kevin O'Reilly! I'm interested in Erik, and I don't give a flying fig whether you like him or not."

"You hardly know the guy. I don't understand what you see in him."

"I love him," Daisy said, and felt the truth of it sink deep into her heart and soul. "It doesn't matter if you don't like him. It doesn't matter that he's a vampire—" She clapped her hand over her mouth, horrified by what she had let slip.

Alex stared at her, his eyes wide with disbelief. "I knew it. Dammit, in my gut I knew it all the time." He shook his head. "A dirty, bloodsucking vampire."

"And a good thing, too," Daisy retorted, "or you'd be dead now."

"What are you talking about?"

"When I took you to his house that night after Rhys almost killed you, Erik saved your life."

Alex gained his feet and stared down at her, his brow furrowed. "Oh, come on, Daisy, I wasn't hurt all that bad. Hell, I was up and around the next day. I didn't have a scratch on me."

"That's right, because Erik gave you his blood!" She hadn't intended to tell him that, wished she could recall the words the minute they were spoken.

"A vampire." Alex speared a hand through his hair.

"Yes, and you should be damn glad he is, or Brandon wouldn't be the only one of my brothers who's dead now."

Muttering under his breath, Alex dropped down on the sofa again.

"I have to find him," Daisy said. "I just know he's in some kind of trouble. I can feel it."

"You can . . . ?" Alex looked at her sharply, his eyes narrowed. "You didn't . . . tell me you didn't drink his blood."

"Just a taste, once."

"And he drank yours?"

Her gaze slid away from his. "Yes."

"So, the two of you share a blood bond," Alex said, unable to keep the disgust out of his voice. "That's why you can feel what he's feeling."

"I hope not," Daisy murmured. "Oh, Lord, I hope not." The thought that Erik might actually be experiencing what she had been dreaming about was horrifying beyond words. And yet she knew it was true.

Erik stared into the blackness. He had lost track of the hours, the days, he had spent shackled in the dark. It could have been a month, it could have been a year. All he was really aware of was the pain that burned through his body. The searing agony of the silver that bound his wrists and ankles. The knifelike hunger pains that speared through his insides, growing sharper, longer, with every passing night.

He had expected Rhys to visit him, but no one came to torment him or check on him. Nothing except a large gray rat that scurried across the floor from time to time. Driven to near madness by the pain, Erik had called the rat to him. He had never dined on the blood of rats, but after three weeks, he would have dined on a corpse.

In an effort to forget the excruciating pain, he closed his eyes and summoned Daisy's image. She was the only one who could help him now. If he dropped the mental barrier he had erected between them, he could call her to him. She would be able to see into his mind and determine where he was and what he was going through. It was tempting, so tempting. But he couldn't bring her here, couldn't put her life in danger, not even to preserve his own wretched existence.

If he was to meet his end here, so be it. His only regret would be that they had never made love.

"Daisy." Lost in a world of external pain and internal thirst, he whispered her name into the darkness like a prayer.

During the next week, Daisy's nightmares grew worse. Night after night, she woke in tears. She couldn't eat, was afraid to sleep. Tonight was no different. She woke with a start, the sound of her own cries echoing in her ears.

She sat up as the light came on and her mother entered the room and perched on the edge of the bed, a frown wrinkling her brow. "Daisy, are you all right?"

"Oh, Mom . . ." With a sob, Daisy fell into her mother's arms and, between sobs and hiccups, poured out the whole story of meeting Erik and everything that had happened up to the time she came home. "Mom, I don't know what to do."

"There's nothing you can do, honey," Irene said, stroking Daisy's hair. "You can't fix this."

"I have to try. I . . . I've got to go to him."

"Daisy, what are you saying? Thinking? You can't go back there. I won't let you put your life in danger."

"Mom, I'm in love with him."

"Daisy, what are you saying? He's not human."

"I don't care! I love Erik. He saved Alex's life. He saved my life. I can't just leave him where he is." Daisy rubbed her hands up and down her arms. "He's suffering horribly. I know he is. I can feel it."

"But you don't even know where he is."

"I'll find him."

"Find who?" Noah asked, coming into the room. "What's going on?"

Irene looked up at her husband. "Tell her she can't go."

"Go where?" Noah asked. "Do you two know what time it is? What the heck is going on?"

As quickly as possible, Daisy repeated what she had told her mother only minutes ago.

By the time she finished, her father was sitting on the foot of the bed, his head cradled in his hands.

"Noah, tell her she can't go."

"Dad?"

Slowly, Daisy's father looked up and met her gaze. "You're a big girl, daughter. I don't approve of your involvement with Delacourt. I don't understand how you can even associate with him after what happened to Brandon but, like I said, you're a big girl. This is a decision you have to make on your own, but I'll back you up, whatever you decide."

"Noah! What are you saying?"

"We owe it to him, Irene. He saved Alex's life."

"But—"

Noah patted his wife's hand. "Don't worry, honey, I'll be with her."

"No, Dad," Daisy said. "Mom needs you here."

"Hell, I'll go with her."

Daisy glanced at the doorway as Alex sauntered into the room.

"It's the least I can do, seeing as how the bastard saved my life."

"I won't hear of it!" Irene said, her voice rising. "I've already lost one son. I won't risk losing the two of you. I can't! I won't!"

"All right, Mom," Daisy said quietly. "Maybe you're right."

"Of course I am. I appreciate what your . . . what the vampire . . . did, but . . ."

Daisy squeezed her mother's shoulder. "It's all right, Mom, I understand where you're coming from. I don't know what I was thinking," Daisy said, yawning.

"Come on, Irene, let's go to bed." Noah bent down and kissed Daisy on the cheek. "I love you, daughter."

"I love you, too, Dad. Good night, Mom. Dad."

Alex followed his parents out of the room. Pausing in the doorway, he looked back at Daisy and mouthed the words, "An hour."

* * *

Erik breathed a sigh of relief as he felt the change in the atmosphere that signaled the rising of the sun. Closing his eyes, he waited for the Dark Sleep to carry him away into oblivion. It was his only relief from the pain, the hunger, that engulfed him every waking minute. He had not prayed in years, but he prayed now, prayed that Costain would come to end his existence, and with it, the agony that knifed through him with every breath. Never, in all his years as a vampire, had he known such pain, such hunger. Never had he been so desperate to end his existence. No matter what awaited him on the other side, it had to be better than this.

"Mom and Dad are never going to forgive us for this," Daisy said as she tiptoed down the stairs behind Alex. She hadn't taken time to pack anything except her compass, her kit, and her handbag.

"Yeah, well," Alex whispered back. "If this turns out the way I think it will, we won't have to worry about it."

Daisy didn't say anything, but she was afraid her brother was right. Going back to LA when the Master of the City was looking for the two of them certainly wasn't the brightest thing they had contemplated, but she knew she would never be able to live with herself if Erik really was in trouble and she didn't try to help. She owed him that much, and so much more.

And she loved him. She just hoped she had a chance to tell him so before it was too late.

Outside, Alex called the airport and booked a midnight flight, then called for a taxi to pick them up on the corner. "No sense leaving one of our cars in the lot," Alex remarked, "since I'm gonna pick up my car while we're in LA."

If she hadn't been so anxious to get to LA, she would have

suggested they take Erik's car, which was still parked in front of their house.

Since it was late, they didn't have to wait long for a taxi. Daisy stared out the window at the sleeping city. She hoped her dreams were just dreams, that when they reached LA, Erik would be safe at home. And if he wasn't . . . she bit down on her lower lip. If he wasn't, then she intended to find him even if she had to turn the city upside down.

It was cool and cloudy when they arrived at LAX. Due to some engine trouble and a layover in Las Vegas, Daisy was a nervous wreck by the time they pulled out of the airport parking lot in the rental car Alex had arranged for. It had been one thing to talk about saving Erik when she was safe in her parents' home in Boston, quite another now that she and Alex were here, in the heart of Rhys Costain's domain.

The signs of the upcoming holiday could be seen everywhere, she thought as they drove through the dark streets, but it hadn't felt like Christmas in her parents' home even though her father had insisted on putting up a tree. No one in the family felt like shopping and they had decided that, in lieu of presents, they would make a donation to Brandon's favorite charity.

Daisy was exhausted when they reached her house an hour and a half later. Every yard but hers sported Christmas lights and Nativity scenes. After unlocking the door, she switched on the lights, then dropped her handbag on the sofa. She glanced around the room. Everything looked the same, but she was different. So much had changed since she had been here last. In some ways, her life and that of her family would never be the same again.

"I'm not going to be worth anything if I don't get some sleep," she said, smothering a yawn.

Alex stretched his arms over his head. "I know what you mean. We can't do much today, anyway, so what do you say we get a few hours of sack time and then figure out what we're going to do."

"Sounds good to me."

Still, as tired as she was, it was a long time before sleep found her.

Chapter 29

Awareness returned slowly. Erik knew it was a sign of his waning strength that it took him a moment to remember where he was. Ah, yes, Costain's dungeon, he thought bleakly. His body ached; his veins felt tight, shriveled.

If he didn't feed soon, he thought he might go mad, but even that seemed preferable to the hunger that clawed at him relentlessly, demanding to be satisfied.

The faint click of metal against metal told him someone had opened the door. Her scent preceded her.

It took an effort for him to gain his feet, but his pride wouldn't let her find him on the floor. "Mariah, what in hell brings you here?"

Her smile was decidedly nasty as she gestured at the chains that bound him. "How could I miss seeing you like this?" Her gaze moved over him. "Hungry, Erik? I'll bet you'd like a drink." Mariah snapped her fingers and a young man appeared at her side. Using her thumbnail, Mariah made a gash in the man's wrist.

The rich, sweet, coppery scent of hot fresh blood filled the air, so thick, so rich, Erik could almost taste it on his tongue. He moved toward the bars, his fangs aching, everything else forgotten but the man. The mortal, an end to his torment, was close, so close. Erik tugged on the chains that bound him. If he could just reach the man, he could quench the relentless thirst that burned through him . . .

Mariah's laughter rang off the stone walls as Erik tugged against the chains. "He's sweet," she said, her voice a throaty growl, "so sweet." Her eyes went red as she sank her fangs into the man's neck. The hapless mortal winced but made no sound, no effort to push her away.

Mariah drank, her gaze never leaving Erik's face. When she finished, she let the mortal fall to the floor.

"I'll be back," she said, a smug smile twisting her lips. "I'll be the last thing you see before I send you to hell."

And so saying, she vanished from sight.

Erik stared at the place where Mariah had stood only moments before, her threat replaying itself in his mind. He was trying to determine what it meant when the man moaned softly. Lifting himself on his elbows, he tried to crawl away, but he was too weak to drag himself for more than a foot or two.

A string of curses rose in Erik's throat. The man wasn't quite dead. Blood oozed from the wounds in his neck. The smell of it wrapped around Erik until he could think of nothing else. In spite of the pain, he tugged against the chains, his only thought to reach the mortal who lay slowly dying just out of reach.

If he could bring the mortal nearer the bars before it was too late. . . . Closing his eyes, Erik tried to focus his thoughts, to meld his mind with that of the mortal, but he couldn't think, couldn't concentrate.

And then it was too late. The tantalizing scent of blood was replaced by the sharp stink of urine and the musty smell of death.

Shrouded in despair, Erik huddled in a corner of his cell and prayed that Rhys would soon grow weary of whatever game he was playing and end it.

Chapter 30

When Daisy awoke the next morning, she wasn't surprised to find Alex in the kitchen fixing breakfast. As usual, he didn't know the meaning of the word *small*, and she didn't think he'd eaten cereal since they were kids. They weren't having cereal this morning, either. Bacon sizzled in one frying pan, there were scrambled eggs in another.

With a shake of her head, Daisy sat at the kitchen table.

"Hey, sis, you hungry?"

"I'd better be," she muttered, "or a lot of this is going to waste."

Alex shrugged as he expertly flipped one pancake after another. "Breakfast is the most important meal of the day, you know that, and if we're going after Costain, well . . ."

He didn't finish the sentence, but then, he didn't have to. If they were hunting Costain, they'd need their strength.

The *Star Wars* theme cut across the silence. With a shake of her head, Daisy reached for Alex's cell phone, which was sitting on the table.

"Don't answer it!" Alex warned. "It's either Mom or Dad. They've been calling since daybreak."

Daisy stared at the phone until it stopped ringing. "We probably should have left a note. I wonder why they haven't called me."

"Have you checked your phone? Maybe it's dead."

"Maybe. I'll check it later."

Alex handed Daisy a plate, then sat down across from her. "I'm sure they've figured out what we're up to."

"I guess so. Still . . ." Daisy picked up her fork. "You don't think Dad will come here, do you?"

Alex shrugged. "I doubt it. You know how he is. He's always let us make our own choices."

Daisy nodded. Her parents had never tried to control the lives of their children. Noah and Irene had taught them right from wrong, then let them discover for themselves that there were rewards or consequences for every act and every decision.

They ate in silence for several minutes before Alex said, "So, how do you want to play this?"

"I'm not sure. I just know we need to find Erik before it's too late. He's hurting, Alex. He might be dying."

"Come on, Daisy, he can't be dying. He's already dead. The only way to take a vampire out now is by lopping off their head. Or impaling them with a well-placed stake."

"All right, maybe what's happening to him won't kill him, but he's in pain unlike anything you can imagine. I dreamed about him again last night, and it was awful. I could see him. He's in a dungeon, chained to a wall. He hasn't fed in days . . ."

Alex blew out a sigh. "You know they don't have to feed every day."

"Stop it! I know what I'm feeling, what I've seen. We came here to help him, remember?"

Alex rolled his eyes. "All right, all right." Taking up his cell phone, he turned it off and shoved it into his pocket. "Let's get this show on the road."

* * *

Finding Erik's whereabouts proved to be much easier than Daisy had expected. She didn't need her compass, although it was open in her lap as she drove. All she had to do was concentrate on Erik. As if guided by an internal GPS, she knew which streets to take, where to turn, and where to stop.

"You're sure he's in there?" Alex asked as she parked the Lexus.

"Yes," she said, but she couldn't help frowning as she read the small hand-lettered sign above the door. LA MORTE ROUGE.

"Looks like a nightclub or a fancy whorehouse," Alex remarked. "Are you sure he's in trouble and not just . . . ah, scratching an itch?"

"I'm sure," Daisy replied succinctly.

"Uh-huh. So, where do we go from here? This is your party. You call the shots."

Daisy closed her eyes. She could sense Erik's presence, but only faintly. At this time of the day, she figured he was resting. So, what now? Did they try to go in the front door, or find a back entrance? She glanced at the compass in her hand. The needle glowed red. If only it could tell her how many vampires were inside.

"Daisy?"

She glanced up and down the street. There was no one in sight. "Let's see if we can find another entrance."

"You're the boss."

Daisy grimaced. That was a scary thought. Taking a deep breath, she got out of the car and walked around the corner of the building. The property in the rear of La Morte Rouge sloped downward. A narrow stone staircase led to a lower level.

She breathed a sigh of relief when she reached the bottom of the stairs. The hill leveled out; the ground was mostly flat, dotted with weeds. There were no windows on the back side of the building. There was, however, a corroded iron door. It had a lock, but no handle.

"Alex?"

"I'm on it." Pulling out his trusty lock pick, he set to work.

"What's taking so long?"

"Don't get your panties in a twist. It's an old lock."

Daisy tapped her foot impatiently. If they couldn't get in this way, they'd have to go through the front door. She frowned inwardly. Maybe the front door would have been the way to go. Maybe the lower floor was some kind of lair. For all they knew, Rhys could be inside.

She was about to ask Alex if they were doing the right thing when he murmured, "Bingo!" He gave a little push on the door and it swung open with a rusty creak.

Daisy took a few steps forward. She peered into the darkness beyond the doorway, wrinkled her nose against the musty smell emanating from the inside.

"Smells like something died in there," Alex muttered as he pulled a flashlight from his pocket. "Come on."

If she hadn't been one hundred percent sure that Erik was in there somewhere and that he needed her, she never would have followed Alex into that foul-smelling cavern.

The corridor seemed to go on and on, with the smell of decomposing flesh growing increasingly odious until, abruptly, the corridor opened into a cavernous room that looked like something out of an old horror flick.

Alex swept his flashlight back and forth, revealing a dozen small animal cages along one wall, and six larger cells on the other.

They found the source of the horrible smell lying on its stomach a foot or so from the last cage.

Erik was in the last cell. He was sprawled on his back, his eyes closed, his arms shackled to the wall behind him.

Daisy gasped when the flashlight's beam settled on his face. His cheeks were sunken, his skin looked like old parchment.

"I think we're too late," Alex whispered. "Let's get the hell out of here."

"Erik? Erik, wake up!" She moved closer to the cell, her hands curling around the bars. Was he breathing? He couldn't be dead! There was no stake in his heart; his head—she shuddered—was still attached to the rest of him. "Erik, it's Daisy. Please wake up." She glanced over her shoulder, her unease at being in this horrible place growing by the minute. The sooner they got out of there, the better. "Erik!"

He jackknifed into a sitting position, his movement so fast, so unexpected, she jumped backward, colliding with Alex, who had been standing behind her.

Pressing a hand to her heart, Daisy murmured, "Thank the Lord!"

"Daisy?"

"I'm here." She reached through the bars, wanting, needing, to touch him.

Erik shook his head. "Get out of here," he said hoarsely. "Now." He looked at Alex. "Get her out of here."

"We're not leaving without you," Daisy said.

"Dammit! Rhys owns this club. He's probably upstairs right now. Get out of here!"

"Alex, the door, hurry." Daisy glanced over her shoulder, her memory of the last time they had encountered Rhys all too vivid in her mind.

Unlike the lock on the door to the dungeon, the lock on the cell door clicked open on the first try.

Erik hissed as Alex stepped inside. "Get out of here! Dammit, do you want to die? I haven't fed in weeks."

Alex took a quick step backward, putting himself out of reach. "All right, Daisy Mae, now what?"

"Give me the pick," Daisy said.

"No way! Going in there is suicide. Look at his eyes."

Daisy took a deep breath as she plucked the lock pick from her brother's hand. "He won't hurt me."

"Are you willing to bet your life on that?"

"Yes, because we don't have time to stand here arguing about it."

"Daisy, no!" Erik scrambled to his feet. "Get out!" He closed his eyes as the hunger rose up within him, hot and heavy. "Go. Please, Daisy."

"No."

He didn't have to open his eyes to know she was standing beside him. Her scent teased his nostrils, the rapid beat of her heart was like thunder in his ears as she picked the lock on the silver shackles that bound him.

As soon as the chains fell away, his arms closed around her.

Daisy stared up into his eyes, eyes burning with the need for blood. She took a deep breath. It wasn't wise to show fear in the face of a predator. "Erik, just wait a few more minutes, until we're out of here, and then I'll give you what you need, I promise."

It was hard to concentrate on her words when her blood was singing so sweetly, promising an end to the pain knifing through him. She was here, warm in his arms. Her blood . . . he needed it as she needed air to breathe. The urge to bury his fangs in her throat grew stronger. He could take her, and her brother, too. It would be so easy.

"Erik." She stroked his cheek with her fingertips. "We need to go."

He stared at the love shining brightly in the depths of her eyes and then, with a murmured curse, he released her and staggered out of the cell. "We need to hurry," he said, his voice tight with pain. "Rhys is coming."

Muttering, "I've got a bad feeling about this," Alex grabbed Erik, slung him over his shoulder, and headed for the door with Daisy hot on his heels.

She blinked against the sunlight when they emerged. "Wait! The sun!" Tugging off her sweater, she threw it over Erik's head. "The door! Shouldn't we lock the door?"

"It won't slow him down," Erik said, his voice muffled by her sweater.

Daisy followed Alex up the stairs to the street, her heart pounding. She dared not look behind her for fear she would see Rhys. If she lived to be a hundred, she would never forget how it had felt to drive a stake into his back. Never forget the way he had looked at her, his eyes red and wild, his fangs dripping with Alex's blood.

When they reached the car, Alex shoved Erik none too gently into the backseat and slammed the door. Daisy scrambled into the passenger seat while Alex slid behind the wheel, jammed the key in the ignition, and peeled away from the curb, leaving a wide swath of rubber behind.

"Go to my place," Erik said.

Alex shook his head. "No. I don't like that idea at all."

"It's closer," Daisy said. "We don't have time to argue."

"Daisy, maybe he's right for once," Erik said. "Rhys has never been to your house. The threshold should keep him out."

"Should?" Alex careened around a corner on two wheels. "Will it or won't it?"

"I don't know." Erik closed his eyes in an effort to shut out the beating of mortal hearts, but it was no use. The sound of their rapidly beating hearts, the scent of their blood, was overpowering. The heat of the sun coming through the back window made his skin tingle, rivaling the burning pain in his hands and legs where the chains had burned his skin. Damn, he couldn't remember when he'd felt this bad.

Twenty minutes later, Alex pulled into Daisy's garage. Erik breathed a sigh of relief as the garage door came down, shutting out the sun.

For a moment, the three of them sat there, then Alex got out of the car, a stake in one hand.

"What are you doing?" Daisy asked, getting out of the car.

"Look at him and then ask me that. You've brought a monster home with you, and a damn hungry one from the looks of him."

"He's right, Daisy." Erik clenched his hands at his side. "You're in more danger from me than from Rhys."

"I'm not afraid."

"Dammit, you should be!"

"Let's go inside."

"Are you out of your mind?" Alex asked.

"Erik needs to feed," Daisy said with a calmness she was far from feeling. "So, this is what we'll do. I'll let him drink from me, and you . . "

"No way!" Alex said.

"And you," Daisy continued, "will stand behind me to make sure he doesn't take too much. And then he's going to drink from you."

"Like hell!"

Daisy glanced at Erik. She had never truly been afraid of him before, never believed she was in any danger from him, until now. "Alex, we don't have time to argue."

"Dammit, Daisy, this is the dumbest idea you've ever had!"

Daisy didn't reply. Sweeping past her brother, she unlocked the door that connected the garage to the kitchen and went inside.

After a moment, Erik exited the car and followed her.

Alex glared at the vampire's back. Muttering an oath, he

slammed the car door, then stomped into the house. He found Daisy and Erik facing each other in the living room. Erik looked like death warmed over. Alex looked at his sister, wondering if she was as relaxed as she appeared.

"All right, let's get this over with." Daisy turned toward Erik. After taking a deep breath, she held her hair away from her neck. "Go on. If Rhys shows up, you'll need to be strong."

Erik stared at her. He wanted to refuse, but her blood called to him, screamed to him. "Don't let me feed for more than a few minutes," he told Alex, and then, uttering a vile oath, he wrapped his arms around her.

Alex stood close behind Erik, his gaze fixed on the vampire. He had hunted vampires since he turned seventeen. He had staked them. He had beheaded them. But he had never actually seen one feed. It was totally revolting and yet he had to admit that watching Erik drink from Daisy held a certain morbid fascination.

A glance at Daisy showed that she didn't find it the least bit revolting. Her eyes were closed, her expression was one of a woman in the throes of ecstasy.

With a shake of his head, Alex glanced at this watch. Erik had said not to let him feed for more than a few minutes. How many minutes in a few? Two? Three? Five? How the hell was he supposed to know how long was too long?

He looked at Erik. The vampire's eyes were also closed. Grimacing, Alex shook his head. If he didn't know better, he would have sworn Erik and Daisy were making love. Hell, maybe they were. What did he know about vampire lovemaking?

Another minute ticked past, and then another.

Taking a deep breath, Alex poked Erik in the back with the point of the stake. "That's enough!"

With a low hiss, Erik lifted his head from Daisy's neck.

Alex recoiled a step, then held his ground, the stake held high. "You said not to let you feed too long."

Erik nodded. "You were right to stop me." A swipe of his tongue closed the two tiny puncture wounds in her throat.

Daisy's eyelids fluttered open. For a moment, she stared up at Erik, a half smile on her lips. And then she looked at her brother. "Your turn."

Alex stared at Erik.

Unblinking, Erik looked back at Alex, an unspoken challenge in his eyes.

Alex thrust out his arm, his expression defiant. "Go ahead, bloodsucker, take what you need."

"How very gracious of you to offer," Erik said dryly.

"Yeah, well, don't get carried away." Alex held up the wooden stake clutched tightly in his hand. "I've still got this."

Murmuring, "I'm terrified," Erik took hold of Alex's arm.

Alex swore softly as Erik sank his fangs, none too gently, into the vein in his wrist.

Daisy sighed as she glanced from one man to the other. She loved them both, but she didn't have much hope that they would ever be friends. Time seemed to slow to a stop as she watched Erik feed. She glanced at her watch, then back at Erik. She could see him growing stronger right before her eyes.

Her gaze moved over Alex. His whole body was rigid, his knuckles white around the stake clutched in his hand.

Daisy was beginning to worry that she would have to do something to stop Erik when he ran his tongue over the bites in Alex's wrist, then lifted his head.

Alex took a step backward, his expression uncertain.

Erik's gaze met hers. His eyes were still red and glowing; a drop of bright red blood stained his lower lip. With his gaze still on hers, he licked it off.

"Waste not, want not," he muttered.

Chapter 31

Rhys Costain stared into the empty cell. How the devil had Erik slipped his bonds and escaped? Silver rendered a vampire powerless. Erik couldn't have dissolved into mist and floated away.

Stepping into the cell, Rhys nudged the shackles with his foot. Someone had picked the lock.

Closing his eyes, he took a deep breath, then spat out a string of curses as two familiar scents mingled with Delacourt's.

"Dammit!" He drove his fist into the wall, shattering brick and mortar as if it were cardboard. "Traitor!" The word echoed off the cold stone walls. "Traitor!"

Damn her! Mariah had been right all along. Delacourt had been in league with the hunters who had tried to destroy him. But why now, after all this time? And what the hell difference did it make?

Rhys slammed the cell door shut. The clang of metal against metal echoed off the walls.

"Vampire, trust no one," he muttered.

Turning on his heel, he stalked toward the stairway, his anger growing with every step.

"Damn your black soul, Delacourt. You can run, but you can't hide from me. I'll find you. All of you. And death will be a long time coming!"

Chapter 32

"So, what now?" Daisy asked.

At Erik's request, she and Alex had both had something to eat and drink and now the three of them were sitting in the living room. Erik sat in the chair facing the sofa, his expression pensive. Alex sat on the sofa beside Daisy. He looked wary and apprehensive. Daisy couldn't blame him. She wasn't anxious to face Rhys Costain again, even with Erik on their side. She knew Erik was a powerful vampire, but Rhys was far older, and vampires grew stronger with every passing year.

Alex straightened in his chair. "What are you staring at, vampire?"

"I was thinking about the reward on Costain's head. Who told you about it?"

"I found it on a Web site. You know, sort of a vampire hunter's craigslist."

"Who offered it?"

"I don't know. There was no name, just an e-mail address."

Erik ran a hand over his jaw, his expression thoughtful. "How were you supposed to claim the reward?"

"I was instructed to send an e-mail saying it was done, and then we were supposed to arrange a meet."

"What were you going to take as proof? Once you kill him, he's dust."

Alex shrugged. "I was told to collect whatever was left and take it with me."

"Only another vampire would be able to tell if the remains belonged to Rhys or not."

Alex frowned. "So, you're saying a vampire put out a hit on another vampire?"

Erik nodded.

"Why would they do that?" Daisy asked.

"Could be a lot of reasons. Anger. Jealousy. Someone wanting to take over Costain's territory." Erik grunted softly. "I wonder . . ."

"What are you thinking?" Daisy asked.

"Costain has made a lot of enemies in his time. Some of them are right here, in LA. I'm thinking we might be able to set a trap."

"Yeah? Before or after Costain kills us?" Alex asked.

Daisy glared at him. "That's not funny."

"Damn right!" Alex retorted.

"Calm down, you two," Erik said impatiently. "If we can hand the traitor to Rhys, maybe it'll let us off the hook."

"And if it doesn't?" Alex asked.

"We'll be no worse off than we are now. Besides, I've got a pretty good idea who it is."

"Why did Costain turn against you?" Daisy asked.

"He thinks I'm the one who put the hit out on him."

"Did you?" Alex asked.

"Alex, don't be a bigger idiot than you are," Daisy said with a huff of annoyance.

Rising, Alex began to pace the floor. "Okay, suppose you

convince Costain that you're innocent. How's that gonna help us? We tried to take him out."

"I'm pretty sure I can persuade him to leave you alone."

"Pretty sure?" Alex said. "That's a real comfort."

"We've got to start somewhere," Erik said. "Rhys is the most powerful vampire I know. I don't want to fight him if I can help it. I'd rather try to reason with him. If that doesn't work . . ." He shrugged. "Then it's the three of us against him."

Muttering under his breath, Alex paced the length of the room.

Daisy leaned toward Erik. "Do you think the three of us can beat him?"

"I'm betting my life on it."

"Yeah," Alex said glumly. "And ours, too."

"I want to see that ad," Erik said, rising.

Daisy led the way into her office and switched on the light. Alex sat at the computer, with Daisy and Erik standing behind him.

It took him only a few moments for Alex to find the right listing.

Daisy grimaced as she read the ad, which was short and to the point.

> Two-hundred-thousand-dollar reward
> for the head of Rhys Costain.
> Contact MC at hunterz666.net
> when the job is done.

"Now what?" Alex asked.

"I need to go out for a while," Erik said. "Then I'm going to get in touch with Rhys and see if he'll listen to reason. I'm going to tell him what I think is going on. If he's willing to be reasonable, we'll see about setting that trap."

"And if he isn't willing to be reasonable?" Daisy asked. "What then?"

Erik shook his head. "Then it's a whole new ball of wax."

"Why are you going out?" Alex asked, suspicious as always. "How do we know you're not going behind our backs to make a deal with Costain? You know, our lives for yours?"

"Alex, enough! Erik saved my life. He saved *your* life. I won't have you talking to him like he's our enemy."

"It's all right, Daisy," Erik said. "He has no reason to trust me, any more than I trust him. Like I said, I need to go out."

Daisy watched him leave the room, and then hurried after him.

"Erik, wait!"

He turned at the sound of her voice.

"When will you be back? What if Rhys comes here?"

"Don't worry, darlin'." Erik put one finger under her chin. "I'll be back as soon as I can. If Rhys comes here, don't talk to him. Don't open the door. Don't ask him inside."

She looked up at him, her eyes wide. "What if you don't come back?"

Erik's gaze moved over her face. "If I don't come back, get the hell out of LA just as fast as you can." Forcing a smile, he kissed the tip of her nose. "Don't worry, little flower, I'll be back."

Daisy stared after him. How could she let him go? What if she never saw him again? "Erik!"

He paused on the sidewalk. "I'll never get back if you don't let me go."

"I'm afraid."

"Don't be. I won't let anything happen to you. Or that brother of yours."

"That's not what I'm afraid of."

He closed the distance between them. "Daisy . . ."

She pressed her fingertips to his lips, silencing him, everything she was thinking, feeling, shining in the depths of her eyes.

"Ah." His gaze moved over her face, as if to memorize every line.

"Please, Erik. I want this night to remember."

"You're sure?"

"Yes," she said tremulously. "I'm sure."

He knew he should refuse, tell her this wasn't the time, and definitely not the place, but if he were honest with himself, he was just as afraid as she was.

"You need to tell Alex you're leaving."

"He won't like it."

"Do you want him to spend the rest of the night worrying?"

"No, but . . ."

"Do you want me to tell him?"

"No, I'll do it."

"That's my brave girl."

Nodding, Daisy went back into the house. She didn't feel brave, but Erik was right. She couldn't just leave without letting Alex know.

She found him in the living room, watching the news on TV. "I'm going out with Erik for a while."

"What?"

"You heard me."

"Do you think that's a good idea?"

"Probably not, but I'm going, so don't try to stop me."

"I don't suppose it would do me any good."

"I love him, Alex. Please try to understand."

"I don't understand, and I never will. When will you be back?"

"I'm not sure. Before sunrise, I guess," she said with a bittersweet smile.

"Keep your phone on."

"I will." Impulsively, she threw her arms around him and hugged him tight. "I love you, Alex. Thanks for always being there for me."

"Yeah, go on, get out of here."

Daisy held his gaze for a long moment, and then she ran out of the house. "Let's go."

"I didn't think he'd let you out of the house."

"Is that why you sent me in there? Because you thought he'd make me stay?"

"Foolish girl," he said, and wrapping her in his embrace, he transported the two of them into the hills, far from the city, to a four-star hotel that catered to the very wealthy who wanted to get away from it all.

A quick stop in the office and a bit of vampire magic procured the best suite in the hotel.

Daisy glanced around the room, her eyes wide as she took it all in. The walls and carpet were a pale, pale blue. Tall windows overlooked the twinkling lights of the city below. A cheery blaze sprang to life in the white marble fireplace when Erik closed the door. Soft music and lighting added to the seductive ambience as Erik took her in his arms.

"Daisy . . ."

"You're not going to try and talk me out of this, are you?"

"No." He had wanted her too long, waited too long for this moment. He folded his hands over her shoulders and drew her into his embrace. She leaned into him, the soft curves of her body pressing against his as she lifted her face for his kiss.

Her eyelids fluttered down as his mouth covered hers. His lips were firm and cool, his tongue a flame as it dueled with hers in a mating dance that was as old as time and yet forever new. She clasped her hands behind his neck, wanting to be closer still.

He kissed her again and yet again, his mouth as hot and

hungry as the hands that glided over her body, sending shivers of delight coursing through her. Lifting her into his arms, he carried her swiftly into the bedroom, his mouth never leaving hers.

He laid her on the bed, then followed her down, his hands again moving over her body, until she lay naked beside him. He shed his own clothing and then drew her up against him. She basked in the touch of his bare skin against her own, the heat of his mouth on hers. The stroke of his tongue was like lightning, igniting a fire deep within her very core.

His hands drifted over her shoulders, her breasts, her thighs, each touch slow and sensual, teasing her senses. Clever hands that knew when and where to stroke, to softly caress, until she writhed beneath him, helpless, mindless, aware of nothing but the heat of his kisses, the warmth of his touch.

She clung to him, afraid that if she let go, she might float away. What magic had he wrought upon her senses? He was life itself, more vital to her existence than the air she breathed. How would she survive if he took his mouth from hers?

When he rose over her, she lifted her hips to receive him, a muffled cry of pain rising in her throat as his body melded with hers, but the discomfort was quickly forgotten as he moved inside her, each stroke of his flesh building the tension within her. She buried her face in his shoulder as, with a last thrust, he brought her to fulfillment. His own release came quickly, filling her with warmth and a sense of pleasure unlike anything she had ever known.

Erik kissed her as he rolled onto his side, carrying her with him, so that they lay facing each other, their bodies still entwined. With a sigh, she wrapped her arms around him and closed her eyes.

His gaze moved over her face, noting the sweep of her lashes against her cheeks, the faint perspiration on her brow. Her breasts were warm against his chest.

It had been wrong of him to take her innocence. Had he known she was untouched, his honor would have forbidden him to take her. But he had wanted her for so long, needed her so badly, he hadn't taken the time to ask if she was still a virgin. And yet he should have known. Perhaps, deep down, he had known. But he couldn't be sorry for what he'd done. A woman never forgot her first lover. Whatever happened in the future, she would always remember him, always remember this night, just as he would.

He brushed a kiss across her cheek and then, still holding her in his embrace, he brushed the hair from her neck. A taste, he told himself. He would only take a taste. If things went wrong when he met with Rhys, he wanted to carry the memory of this night and the sweet taste of Daisy's blood with him when Rhys sent him to hell.

It was after midnight when Erik tucked Daisy into her own bed and kissed her good night. Outside, he paused in the shadows. Gathering his power around him, he placed protective wards around her house just in case Rhys showed up. Erik was certain that the threshold of the O'Donnells' house was strong enough to repel an angry vampire, but in Daisy's case, he wasn't willing to risk being wrong.

When he was satisfied with the wards he had erected, he willed himself to his own home. Although going up against Rhys wasn't something he was looking forward to, it had to be done, but not before he had afforded himself a little extra added protection.

He hadn't practiced witchcraft in centuries. Until now, his supernatural powers had been enough, but tonight he felt the need for all the help he could get.

Going out into the backyard, he erected an altar on which

he placed a black candle, an aged athame, a cup of his own blood, and a quick sketch of Costain's face.

Lifting his arms toward the moonlight sky, Erik reached back in time, sifting through his memories until he found the spells his mother had taught him. Using the toe of his shoe, he drew a circle that encompassed himself and the altar and then, chanting softly, he cast his spell. He just hoped he hadn't lost his magic after letting it lie dormant within him for so many years.

When he finished the incantation, he broke the circle, doused the candle, and spilled the blood onto the ground.

Now there was only one more thing to do before he faced Rhys. Leaving the backyard, he moved into the shadows alongside the house, his nostrils scenting the wind for prey.

He didn't have to wait long. From his place beneath a pepper tree, he watched a young man stride down the street toward him. He waited until the man passed by, then moved up behind him. A word spoken to the man's mind brought him to a stop. Erik moved off the sidewalk and the young man followed. Knowing he would need all his preternatural strength, Erik fed quickly, taking as much as he dared without doing the man any permanent harm. After freeing the man from his hypnotic state, Erik sent him on his way.

"Now for the hard part," Erik muttered, and headed for his old friend's lair.

Chapter 33

Rhys Costain's primary lair was located in a high-rise building that he owned in West Hollywood. The first floor housed a bank, the next five floors housed a variety of small businesses. Rhys used floors six to ten to store the furniture and memorabilia he had collected in the last 512 years. His residence occupied the eleventh-floor penthouse. A private elevator that required a key and a password known only to Rhys ran from the tenth floor to the eleventh, where a solid steel door assured his privacy and his security.

Erik thought it odd that Rhys was such a fanatic about protecting this lair and so lax when it came to protecting the house he used for his meetings with the other vampires in the city. It had been a mere fluke that Alex and Daisy had found Costain resting in the meeting house.

It took only moments to transport himself to Costain's penthouse lair. Erik stood on the sidewalk, looking up, his senses probing the interior of the building. There was no one inside save for one security guard. And one vampire.

A thought took Erik to the penthouse balcony. His feet had barely touched the floor when the French doors flew open.

"Well, well," Rhys drawled, "look who's here."

"We need to talk." Erik stepped across the threshold and as he did so, he felt the full weight of Costain's anger slam into him with the force of a blow. Erik immediately summoned his protection spell, praying that it would block the other vampire's preternatural power.

"Yeah, let's talk." Rhys lifted his head, his nostrils flaring. "You've been with her, haven't you? That tasty little mortal who tried to destroy me." He sniffed the air again. "And her brother, too."

"Listen to me . . ."

"No! You listen." Costain slammed the French doors with a wave of his hand. He glared at Erik, his eyes burning red. "You're going down this time."

Fury sheathed in ancient power rolled toward Erik in an angry wave, met his protective spell, and dissipated.

Rhys bared his fangs as he summoned his power and unleashed it a second time with the same impotent result.

"We need to talk," Erik said again.

Uttering a low growl, Rhys took a step forward, fangs and claws extended, only to come to an abrupt halt. "What the hell . . . ?"

"I don't want to fight you."

Rhys spat out a string of oaths as he tried, without success, to penetrate the invisible barrier that held him immobile. "What kind of stunt is this?"

"Just a little old-fashioned witchcraft."

Rhys swore again. "Witchcraft?"

Erik nodded, immensely relieved that the ancient spell had worked. "Just listen to me for a minute. I'm not the one who put the price on your head, but I know how to find out who's behind it."

The red faded from Costain's eyes. "Go on, I'm listening."

As briefly as possible, Erik told Rhys about Alex and how he had found the offer of a reward for Rhys's head online.

"So, you want me to play dead so this Alex can meet with the hunter and collect the reward?"

Erik nodded. "You got it."

"What are you gonna use for my remains?"

"Fireplace ashes. By the time the hunter discovers it's not you, it'll be too late for him to get away."

"Whoever the hell it is, he's mine," Rhys said. "And after I dispatch him, I'm going after, what was his name? Alex? And his sister, too."

"No! You can't touch them."

"Like hell!"

"Come on, Rhys. They're hunters. They were only doing what hunters do, the same as you."

"Except *these two* were hunting *me*."

Erik sighed impatiently. "It's my way or no way."

Costain regarded him a moment, his eyes narrowed. And then he grunted softly. "She means that much to you?"

"And more. I won't let you hurt her."

"Fine, I'll spare the girl, but the boy dies."

Erik shook his head. "No."

"Dammit! They tried to destroy me!"

"I know, but if you lay a hand on either one of them, I'll come after you with everything I've got."

Rhys hadn't survived as long as he had by being stupid. "So, when do we start?"

"Your word, Rhys. I want your word of honor that you won't touch Alex or his sister."

"Fine, you've got it. Now turn me loose!"

"You believe me, then?"

"Yeah, I guess so."

"How do I know you won't take my head off when I release you?"

"'Cause I'm telling you I won't. Now turn me loose, dammit!"

Hoping he wasn't making the biggest mistake of his existence, Erik released Costain.

The vampire took a tentative step forward. And then, before Erik realized what he was about, Rhys was on him, his hands locked around Erik's throat, his eyes blazing, his fangs bared.

Erik stared up at Rhys and knew he was looking death in the face. And even then, his only regret was that he wouldn't be able to see Daisy one last time.

"Don't. Ever. Do. That. To. Me. Again." Rhys bit off each word; then he dropped his hands and took a step backward. "Why didn't you tell me you were a witch?"

Erik rubbed his throat. "The subject never came up."

"So, what now?"

"Meet me at my place tomorrow night."

"I won't find any hunters waiting for me when I get there, will I?"

"Give it a rest, will ya? My place, tomorrow night. And leave the attitude at home."

For the tenth time in as many minutes, Daisy glanced at her watch. She hadn't heard from Erik since last night. Why hadn't he called? She knew he couldn't go out until after sundown, but she had expected to hear from him before now. Surely he knew she would be worried about him, curious to know how his meet with Costain had gone. She chewed on her thumbnail. Maybe it had gone horribly wrong.

"Stop fidgeting," Alex said. "I'm trying to watch the news."

Daisy shook her head. The news was always the same—

a horrible accident on the freeway, fires in the mountains, floods in the South, and a stock market that went up and down like a yo-yo. "Do you think something went wrong last night?"

"How the heck should I know? Damn, look at that pileup on the 101."

"Alex, I know you don't like Erik, but he's trying to help."

"Yeah, right. He probably made a deal with the devil last night."

"Alex."

"All right, all right, I'm sorry. I just don't trust him." He held up his hand when she started to speak. "I know, he saved our lives, but . . ." Alex shook his head. "He's a vampire. Killing mortals is what they do. We're mortal, natural enemies, you know? No matter how much you might want to keep a tiger for a pet, it's never a good idea because you never know when they'll turn on you."

"He's not a tiger."

"No, he's worse." Daisy glared at him and Alex shook his head.

"It's like talking to the wall," he muttered sourly. "Have you forgotten a vampire killed Brandon?"

"Of course I haven't forgotten!"

Daisy glanced at her watch again. She had awakened in her own bed this morning with no recollection of how she had gotten there. But, oh, she remembered everything that had happened before she fell asleep. Just thinking about it now, recalling how she and Erik had made love, brought a rush of heat to her cheeks. She had read books and seen movies depicting love, she had daydreamed about making love, but the reality had been far more than she had ever imagined.

Her cheeks grew hotter under Alex's suspicious gaze.

"Why are you blushing?" he asked.

"Am I?"

Alex stared at her, his eyes narrowing. "Anything you want to tell me, little sister?"

Daisy shrugged, her gaze sliding away from his. "I can't think of a thing."

"I never heard you come in last night. Where'd you go with him?"

"We just . . . we went for a drive up in the mountains."

"Is that right?"

"You're not my father," Daisy retorted, lifting her chin defiantly. "I don't have to answer to you."

Alex grunted softly. "You don't have to say anything. I've got a pretty good idea what you were up to last night." He shook his head. "How could you? Dammit, Daisy . . ."

She turned her back to him when her cell phone rang. After a quick glance at the caller ID, she flipped open the phone. "Erik! Are you all right?"

"Yeah. Is Alex home?"

"Yes, why?"

"Rhys is here with me. We're coming over."

Daisy glanced over her shoulder at Alex, who was still engrossed in the news. Lowering her voice, she said, "Rhys is coming here?"

"Is that going to be a problem?"

"Not for me, but . . ."

"We'll be there in about twenty minutes," Erik said, and hung up. They could have been there in moments, but Erik wanted to give Daisy time to prepare Alex for their visit.

"Who was that?" Alex asked as she disconnected the call.

"Erik." She debated whether to tell him Rhys was also coming and decided against it. "He'll be here in a little while."

Daisy fought down a rising sense of panic as the minutes ticked past. She told herself there was nothing to be afraid of. Erik wouldn't bring Rhys to her house if there was any danger.

* * *

"Are they coming here?" Rhys asked.

Erik slipped his phone into his pocket. "No, we're going there."

Rhys lifted one brow in obvious consternation.

"What's the matter? Don't tell me you're afraid of meeting with Alex and his sister?"

"Don't be an idiot. But if either of them tries anything, the deal's off and they're dead." Rhys drummed his fingers on the arm of the sofa. "So, who do you think it is? Some stupid mortal, or one of us?"

Sitting back in his chair, Erik stretched his legs out in front of him. "I don't know, but my money's on one of us."

"Why?"

"Why would a mortal offer a reward to have you destroyed? Most mortals don't even know you exist. A hunter would do it on his own."

"Yeah, but the government isn't offering hunters two hundred grand."

Erik grunted softly. Fifty years ago, the government had offered a thousand-dollar reward for every vampire destroyed. Those had been dangerous times. More than one Goth had been killed by mistake. As more and more innocents were killed, the government's reward had dropped to five hundred dollars, and then two hundred and fifty. When people decided two-fifty wasn't worth dying for, the frenzy to hunt vampires had dwindled until only dedicated hunters remained. Now there was more money to be made by selling vampire blood than by destroying them.

"Come on," he said, rising. "It's time to go."

* * *

Rhys stood beside Erik on the O'Donnells' front porch. Thrusting his hands into his pants pockets, he took a deep breath as two familiar scents reached his nostrils. Scents he remembered all too well.

"Behave yourself," Erik admonished, and knocked on the door. From inside, he heard Daisy telling Alex that Rhys was also coming, and Alex's stunned silence in reply.

Moments later, Daisy opened the door, a tentative smile on her face. Clad in a pale yellow sweater and a pair of faded jeans, she looked as lovely and fresh as the flower she had been named after.

For a moment, he forgot everything else as the memory of the hours they had spent together at the hotel flashed through his mind. Erik had never been one for wishful thinking, but at the moment, he wished he could sweep Daisy into his arms and carry her back to that suite in the hotel. The flush that rose in Daisy's cheeks told him she was remembering it, too.

"Come in," Daisy said, and then she saw Rhys, who was standing slightly behind Erik, his long legs slightly spread, his arms crossed over his chest. Attired all in black, he looked both forbidding and formidable. "Come in," she said again, and hoped she wasn't making a horrible mistake.

Erik and Rhys followed her into the living room.

Alex had gained his feet and now stood in front of the sofa, a wooden stake tightly clasped in one hand. He glared at Erik. "What's *he* doing here?"

"Relax, both of you," Erik said, glancing from Erik to Daisy. "He's just here to talk."

"Yeah, right." Alex moved up beside Daisy, then took another step forward, putting himself between Daisy and Rhys.

Erik's gaze met Daisy's. "Do you trust me?"

"Of course." Stepping around Alex, she put her hand in Erik's.

Erik glanced at Daisy's brother, who stood there glowering at him. "What about you?"

"Not as far as I can throw you," Alex retorted.

Costain's amused laughter washed over them.

Alex glared at him. "What's so funny, bloodsucker?"

"Take it easy, hunter," Rhys said. "The fact that you're still breathing should prove you're in no danger."

"He's right, you know," Daisy said. "Come on, Alex, let's all sit down and see what he has to say."

The tension in the room was palpable as Alex resumed his seat on the sofa. His gaze never strayed from Costain.

Daisy sat beside her brother, her hands folded tightly in her lap. Despite her outward calm, she was trembling inside. The combined power of Erik and Rhys danced over her skin like static electricity.

Erik sat on the arm of the sofa.

In an effort to put Daisy and Alex at ease, Rhys moved to the far side of the room, where he stood with his arms crossed over his chest.

Alex and Rhys eyed each other warily as Erik outlined his plan. "It's pretty simple, really. Alex, you'll e-mail your contact and tell them you've destroyed Rhys and you want to set up a time to collect the reward . . ."

"He's not gonna take my word for it," Alex said, crossing his arms over his chest. "What are you planning to use for bait?"

"Fireplace ashes," Erik replied.

"It might work," Alex said. "But not for long."

Erik shrugged. "By the time he realizes it's a trap, we'll have him."

Rhys glanced from Erik to Alex. "Just remember, he's mine."

Daisy would have objected, but the hard edge in Costain's voice and the predatory gleam in his hooded gaze brooked no argument, and neither Erik nor Alex offered any.

"So, what do you say, Alex?" Erik asked.

Alex blew out a sigh. "I'm in, but I'm sure gonna miss that two hundred grand," he said glumly.

Rhys grinned at him. "If this works, I'll make good on the reward."

"Well, hell!" Alex exclaimed. "Let's do it!"

It took only minutes for Alex to sign on to Daisy's computer. Rhys, Daisy, and Erik stood in a semicircle behind his chair as he opened his e-mail program.

His message was short and to the point.

> Have destroyed Costain.
> Proof is in my hands.
> Where and when can we meet?
> A.

Alex hit Send, then sat back in the chair, his elbows resting on the arms, his gaze focused on the screen. "All we have to do now is wait for a reply."

Erik looked at Rhys. "You'll have to lay low until we hear something."

"Yeah, I hadn't thought about that."

"You can stay here." Daisy glared at Alex, silencing the argument she saw in his eyes. "No one will think to look for you here."

"Thanks." Rhys grinned at Erik. "I guess I owe you an apology. Remind me to say I'm sorry in a hundred years or so."

"Right. And now. if you two don't mind, I'd like to spend a little time alone with Daisy."

"I don't mind," Rhys said with a leer.

Alex pushed away from the desk and stood up, his hands clenched at his sides. "Well, I do."

"It's not up to you," Erik retorted. Taking Daisy's hand in his, he gave it a squeeze. "What do you say, darlin'?"

"I say, let's go."

"Dammit, Daisy," Alex muttered, "I don't like you going off with him."

"I know."

Alex glared at Erik, then stomped out of the room.

Daisy smiled tentatively at Rhys. "Make yourself at home."

"Thanks."

"Remember," Erik warned, "you can't let anyone know where you are. And you can't leave here until this is over."

"Yeah, yeah," Costain muttered irritably. "But if we don't hear something soon . . ." He looked at Daisy, his gaze lingering on the pulse throbbing in the hollow of her throat. "I'll need something to nibble on."

Daisy blew out a sigh. "How long do you think it will be before Alex gets an answer to his e-mail?"

Erik shook his head. "I don't know, and right now, I don't care." Lowering his head, he brushed a kiss across Daisy's lips. "Where would you like to go?"

"I don't care. Anyplace where we can be alone."

Grinning, Erik wrapped Daisy in his embrace and then, with an effort of will, he transported the two of them to the balcony of Costain's primary lair. A wave of his hand unlocked the French doors and he ushered her inside.

"Where are we?" Daisy wandered around the room, thinking she had never seen anything so luxurious. The carpet beneath her feet must have been two inches deep. The furniture was butter-soft black leather. The fireplace was white marble veined with gold.

"This is Costain's place."

"You're not serious?" She glanced at the statue of a golden-haired Madonna standing in one corner, thinking such a thing was an odd decorating choice for a vampire's lair.

Erik shrugged. "He won't be using it tonight."

"But . . ." Her protest died in her throat when she spied the painting hanging over the fireplace. "Is that a genuine Matisse?"

Erik nodded. Rhys was quite the collector. The floors below were filled with antiques and original masters from the last four centuries, along with Persian carpets and dozens of artifacts that were presumed lost or destroyed.

"I take it your friend is pretty well off financially."

"You could say that."

"I guess it's not surprising. He's had a long time to save his money."

Erik chuckled as he drew her into his arms. "Do you want to talk about Rhys all night?"

"What did you have in mind?"

"Giving you a tour of the place," he said with a wicked grin. "Starting here, and ending in the bedroom."

"That's a short tour," Daisy teased.

"That's all there is to see, except for his office and the view from the balcony."

Daisy slid her hands up and down Erik's chest, then rose on her tiptoes and kissed him. "Let's save those for later."

"Much later," Erik agreed as he drew her sweater over her head, revealing a lacy white bra.

Daisy kicked off her sandals and shimmied out of her jeans.

"Beautiful," Erik murmured as he removed her bra and caressed her out of her bikini briefs. "More than beautiful."

He undressed quickly, grinning under Daisy's avid gaze.

Swinging her into his arms, he carried her down a short hallway. A flicker of energy brought a dozen candles to life, revealing the largest, most garish bedroom Daisy had ever seen. She glanced around, somewhat awed by what she saw. The walls were papered in a dark red print. The carpets were the same shade, as were the heavy velvet drapes drawn over the single window. An enormous bed covered with a black spread took up a good portion of the room. A black stone fire-place took up one entire wall; a TV screen took up another wall from floor to ceiling. There were more paintings in this room, all originals, Daisy assumed, and all beautiful. Figurines of varying sizes—all depicting demons, dragons, or vampires stalking their prey—occupied an antique curio cabinet.

"It's like being in hell's waiting room," Daisy murmured.

Erik laughed as he placed her in the center of the bed. "You make it heaven."

"Flatterer."

"Have I told you that I love you?"

"Not lately."

"I love you, Daisy O'Donnell, Blood Thief extraordinaire, with everything that I am, my whole being."

His words warmed her heart, her soul. "I love you, too, but you know that, don't you?"

He nodded.

"Is it enough, Erik? Can love be enough for two people who are as different as we are?"

He ran his knuckles up and down her cheek, then cupped her face in his hands. "I don't know, Daisy darlin'. I hope so."

She didn't want to have to think about it now, didn't want to worry about the past or the future. She wanted only to live for this moment, with his body covering hers, his hands lightly caressing her while he rained kisses over her face, her neck, her breasts.

A soft moan rose in her throat when she felt his fangs lightly scrape the skin along the side of her neck. Threading her fingers through his hair, she drew him closer, her body arching up to meet his as his tongue laved the tender skin beneath her ear. His body melded with hers, stroking lightly, as his fangs pierced her skin.

She folded her hands over his shoulders, her nails digging into his flesh as sensation after sensation washed over her. She had heard of two becoming one, but she had never experienced anything like this. It was beyond pleasure, beyond ecstasy. Belatedly, she realized she was also feeling what Erik was feeling, what he was thinking.

She sobbed his name as wave after sensual wave exploded deep within her. A moment later, he shuddered and then, with a sigh, buried his face in her shoulder.

He held her for several minutes while their breathing returned to normal and the perspiration cooled on their flesh. When he would have rolled away, she wrapped her arms around him and held him close.

"I'm too heavy for you," he murmured.

"No." It was a welcome weight. She smiled inwardly, thinking about what she had learned while they made love. He adored her. He thought she was beautiful, that her skin was baby soft, that her hair was like russet-colored silk, that her blood was sweeter than the finest wine.

"You heard all that, huh?"

"Oh, yes," she replied. "And more."

Erik grunted softly. "I'll have to be careful about what I'm thinking in the future."

"Did you feel what I was feeling, too?"

"Sure. It goes both ways, you know."

He eased up onto his elbows and gazed down at her. "I never thought of myself as a hottie."

"I wasn't thinking that!"

"No?"

"Well, maybe for a minute."

He lifted one brow.

"Okay, two minutes, three at the most."

His laughter washed over her. "Ah, Daisy, my little flower, do you know how much I love you?"

She ran her hands over his shoulders, down his chest to where their bodies were still joined. "How much?"

Leaning down, he kissed the tip of her nose. "More than words can say."

"Really?" She raked her nails over his chest. "Then I guess you'll just have to show me."

"Like this?" Rolling onto his side, he dropped butterfly kisses on her brow, her cheeks, the curve of her throat.

She shivered with delight as he continued his slow assault on her senses, his tongue like a flame as he licked her breasts and belly, then kissed his way down the sensitive skin along the inside of her thigh.

Only when she was writhing in delicious torment did he cover her body with his.

Daisy was hovering on the brink of sleep when her cell phone rang. Rolling onto her side, she reached over the edge of the bed, searching for her handbag. "Hello?"

"Where are you?"

"Alex!" She sat up, suddenly wide awake. "What time is it? Is something wrong?"

"I don't know what time it is. Four thirty, five. Just get home. And bring the vampire with you."

"The vampire?" Erik's deep voice rumbled from the other side of the bed.

Daisy's heart skipped a beat at the sound of his voice. "Alex wants us to come home," she told him, and then wondered why she bothered. No doubt Erik had heard every word Alex had said.

"Daisy, you still there?"

"Yes, Alex. What's going on?"

"I got an answer to that e-mail."

"Oh! We'll be there as soon as we can." Daisy looked at Erik and whispered, "It'll be light out soon. Will that be a problem for you?"

"Not if you don't mind my spending the day at your house."

"I don't mind," she said with a mischievous grin. "You can sleep in my bed, like Sleeping Beauty. And I'll wake you later with a kiss."

"Very funny."

"Daisy?"

"Alex, I said we'll be there as soon as we can." After disconnecting the call, she looked at the time. "Five fifteen." The sun would be rising in another hour or so. "What's he doing up at this time of the morning, anyway?"

"Probably waiting for you to come home," Erik replied with a wry grin.

Tossing the phone onto the floor, Daisy slid under the covers again. "I hate to leave."

"Me, too." Erik stroked her back, loving the warmth of her skin beneath his hand, the little purr of pleasure that rose in her throat at his touch.

Daisy sighed. "I guess we should go."

"How about a quickie first?"

"But Alex said to hurry."

"So, we'll hurry."

"But not *too* fast," Daisy said with a smile.

"No," Erik agreed, drawing her body against his. "Not too fast."

Chapter 34

Alex was waiting for them at the front door. "What the hell took you so long to get here?" he asked irritably, and then grimaced as he took in his sister's tousled hair and swollen lips. "Never mind. I don't wanna know."

Shaking his head in disgust, he turned on his heel and stalked into the living room.

"Where's Rhys?" Erik asked, his gaze sweeping the room.

"I don't know."

"What do you mean, you don't know? Dammit, he didn't go out, did he?"

"No, I think he's sacked out in Daisy's closet."

"My closet!" Daisy exclaimed. "What's he doing in there?"

Alex shrugged. "He wanted a room without a window."

"So, he doesn't know about the e-mail you received?" Erik asked.

"Hell, no! I wasn't about to wake him up!"

"Probably a wise decision," Erik said, chuckling. "Let's go have a look at that e-mail."

Muttering under his breath, Alex headed for Daisy's office

and sat down at the desk. It took only moments for him to boot up and find the anticipated message.

Daisy stood behind him, reading over his shoulder.

> Meet me tonight at the back door
> of La Morte Rouge at midnight.
> Bring the proof with you.
> Come alone.
> RD

"Alone?" Daisy said. "No way!"

"He won't be alone," Erik said. "I'll be there with Rhys."

"And I'll be there," Daisy said.

Erik and Alex both said, "No," at the same time.

"Why not?" Daisy asked. "I've got just as big a stake in this—you should pardon the pun—as you do."

Alex scowled at her.

Erik laughed. "You're staying home because I said so, and because I have a pretty good idea who's behind this, and I don't want you anywhere around when we meet. Got it?"

Daisy glared at him, her hands fisted on her hips. "And if I refuse, what are you going to do, tie me to a chair?"

"Or to the bed," Erik retorted with a wicked grin.

"Do you think you could keep it down in here? Some of us were trying to sleep."

Erik glanced over his shoulder as Costain entered the room. "I've never known you to turn in before sunrise."

Rhys snorted softly. "There's nothing else to do here." He jerked his chin toward the computer. "So, what's going on?"

"We got an answer to Alex's e-mail."

Rhys moved up behind Alex, his gaze moving quickly over the words on the screen. He grunted softly. "They want a meet, at midnight, at my place?"

Erik nodded. "So it seems. Does that strike you as odd?"

"For a mortal, yes," Costain replied, his voice deceptively mild.

"But not for one of us," Erik mused.

"Exactly."

A slow smile spread over Costain's face. Looking at it sent chills down Daisy's spine. She didn't know who had put out a hit on the Master of the City, but she was glad it wasn't her.

Erik's head snapped up as a sliver of light penetrated the window over the computer. As one, he and Rhys stepped away from the desk.

Daisy reached over Alex's head to draw the curtains. "Sorry about that."

Rhys shrugged. "Force of habit. It doesn't really bother me much anymore."

"Speak for yourself," Erik muttered.

"Well, I don't know about the rest of you, but I'm going to bed," Daisy said, and then bit down on her lower lip as she recalled that Rhys had been sleeping in her closet.

Erik slipped his arm around Daisy's shoulders. "Rhys will find another closet, won't you?"

"Never let it be said I stood in the way of true love," Rhys muttered.

Alex frowned at Daisy, clearly not liking the fact that Rhys would be sleeping in his closet, since Daisy's house only had two bedrooms.

"Sorry," Daisy said, smiling sweetly at Alex. "Only one vampire to a bedroom, and Erik is sharing mine."

And so saying, she took Erik by the hand and led him up the stairs to her room.

Erik closed the door behind them. "Second thoughts?" he asked.

"No, why?"

He shrugged. They had made love, they had slept together, but he had never succumbed to the Dark Sleep in her presence. Or in anyone else's, for that matter.

Daisy looked at him, her brow furrowed, and then murmured, "Oh," as comprehension dawned.

"I can rest outside."

"Outside? Where?"

"In the ground."

"Why would you want to do that?"

"I didn't say I wanted to. I was just thinking about you, about how you'd feel sharing your bed with . . ."

"A sleeping vampire?"

"Exactly."

"You don't snore or talk in your sleep, do you?"

"No, I'm pretty sure I don't."

Daisy yawned behind her hand. "Well, I don't know about you, but I can't stay awake any longer."

Feeling a little shy, she turned her back to Erik. After toeing off her sandals, she pulled her sweater over her head and tossed it on a chair.

"A little late for modesty, isn't it?" Erik asked, a smile in his voice.

Crossing her arms over her breasts, Daisy glanced at him over her shoulder, surprised to see that he was already undressed save for his briefs.

"Here," Erik said, "let me help you."

"This is getting to be a habit," she murmured as he unfastened her bra and tossed it aside.

"But a nice one," he said, waggling his eyebrows.

Her cheeks grew hot as Erik unzipped her jeans and slid them down over her hips. When she stepped out of them, he tossed them on top of her sweater. Her panties and his briefs followed.

"I think you've bewitched me, woman," he said as he slid into bed beside her.

"I think you've got that backwards," Daisy remarked, cuddling up against him. "You're the witch."

"That's one kind of magic," Erik replied, "but it's nothing like the magic you've worked on me."

"Really?" She smiled, pleased that he thought himself under her spell. And then she yawned.

"Sleep, love."

"When I wake up, will you still be sleeping?"

"Most likely."

She worried the corner of her lower lip. "Is it really like death?"

"In a way, I suppose it is." He stroked her cheek. "Vampires aren't supposed to dream, you know, and I never did, until I met you. Thank you for that."

"You're welcome." She wanted to know more about the Dark Sleep, but her eyelids were heavy, so heavy. Resting her head on Erik's shoulder, she closed her eyes. She would ask him more in a minute . . .

Erik watched Daisy's eyelids flutter down, heard the change in her breathing as sleep claimed her. She was beautiful, he thought, an angel come to earth.

He kissed her cheek, the lethargy that came with the rising of the sun weighed him down. Wrapping his arm around Daisy's shoulders, he closed his eyes and tumbled into the Dark Sleep of his kind.

Alex prowled from one room to another, his hands clenched, his thoughts chaotic. He had tried going back to bed, but knowing one of the world's oldest vampires was resting in his closet made sleep virtually impossible. He had stretched out on the sofa, but again, sleep eluded him. How was a hunter supposed to get any rest with two vampires in the house? He didn't trust Erik Delacourt any more than he trusted Rhys Costain.

At the sound of thunder, he moved to the living room window and drew back the curtains. He had been so preoccupied, he hadn't even realized it was raining. Lightning sizzled across the skies. He stared at the rain. Why was he standing here, watching the storm, when he should be taking Costain's head, and Delacourt's, too?

Alex slammed his fist down on the sill. Dammit, he was a vampire hunter, not a nursemaid. He had been trained from childhood to hunt the Undead, not babysit the Master of the City and his sidekick. And what about Daisy? How could she be in love with the same kind of scum that had killed Brandon?

Alex muttered a vile oath. What kind of brother was he, to stand here and do nothing while a vampire bedded his sister? What would his parents think if they knew? And what about Brandon? His brother must be turning in his grave. Alex groaned as a wave of guilt swept over him. Brandon had always been the smarter of the two of them, the one who had known what he wanted out of life, the one who hadn't been afraid to tell their dad that killing just wasn't in his blood. Brandon should have lived. He would have made a good husband, a good father, done something important with his life.

"It should have been me, bro," Alex murmured. "It should have been me."

He glanced at his watch. It was a quarter after one. Most vampires were rendered helpless until sundown, but Delacourt and Costain seemed to be exceptions to that rule. Alex snorted softly. So, they could be awake during the day, but how deeply did they sleep when they were at rest? If he grabbed his blade and opened the closet door, would Costain awaken?

Turning away from the window, he began to pace the floor.

Instead of fireplace ashes, why not go to the meet with the genuine article and collect the reward? Of course, he'd have to take Delacourt out first. Alex raked his hands through his hair. Daisy would never forgive him. Oh, hell, she'd just have to get over it.

Digging into his vampire hunting kit, Alex withdrew mallet and stake, then dropped a bottle of holy water into his pocket. Delving into the bag again, he withdrew a long-bladed knife and a whetstone. He held the blade up to the light, turning it one way and then another. Maybe with Delacourt out of the way, his sister would give Kevin O'Reilly a chance.

"What do you think you're going to do with those?"

Alex pivoted on his heel at the sound of his sister's voice. "Avenge my brother's death and my sister's honor."

"Alex . . ."

"Don't try to stop me. We're hunters, Daisy, or have you forgotten that? I don't know what kind of supernatural spell Delacourt's worked on you, but you seem to have forgotten who you are."

"And you seem to have forgotten that Erik saved your life."

"What about Brandon?" Alex glanced toward the stairs. "It was creatures like those two that killed him."

"Erik didn't do it, and neither did Costain."

Alex made a dismissive gesture with his hand. "Same smell."

"You're not thinking clearly," Daisy said, moving farther into the room. "All vampires aren't the same, just as all humans aren't the same."

"Oh, please," Alex said, grimacing. "Get hold of yourself and think with your brain instead of your hormones!"

"You're not thinking at all! I won't let you do this. This is my house and I want you out of it, now!"

"You're kicking me out?" he asked in astonishment. "Your

own brother? You're choosing that bloodsucker over your own flesh and blood?"

"I told Erik and Costain they would be safe here," Daisy said, and then frowned. "This is about the money, isn't it? You're still hoping to collect that reward!"

"What if I do?" Alex asked sullenly. "It's two hundred thousand dollars! One last kill and I could retire."

"Rhys said he'd make it good," Daisy reminded him.

"Yeah, right! Like I'd trust the word of a vampire."

Daisy stared at her brother as if she had never seen him before, unable to understand his sudden about-face. Was it just nerves? Had he been drinking? Or had the lust for the reward overridden every other consideration?

"Alex, please tell me what's going on. You're scaring me."

"I just feel like we're on the wrong side, helping vampires, when a vampire killed Brandon. Why," he asked, his voice dropping to little more than a whisper, "why couldn't it have been me?"

"Is that what this is all about? You're feeling guilty because you're alive and Brandon is . . . is gone?"

"He had everything to live for. Everything."

"Oh, Alex." Closing the distance between them, Daisy took the knife from her brother's hand and laid it on the table, then drew him into her arms. He resisted for a moment, then seemed to go limp in her embrace.

All this time, she thought, and she had never known her brother felt this way. Alex had always been the joker in the family, never taking anything too seriously, never letting himself get involved with anyone other than his own family. Had he secretly been jealous of Brandon the whole time? In some warped line of thought, did he think that destroying Erik and Rhys would somehow make up for the fact that he was alive and Brandon was dead?

Murmuring words of comfort, she patted Alex's back, her heart breaking when she realized he was crying. They were the first tears he had shed since their brother's death.

"I loved him," Alex said between sobs. "I don't think I ever told him."

"You didn't have to say it. Brandon knew."

"I need to talk to him, tell him I'm sorry that I let him down."

"We'll go to the cemetery together, after this is over, all right?"

"Yeah." Somewhat embarrassed, Alex turned his back to her. Pulling a handkerchief out of his back pocket, he blew his nose. "I'm sorry, Daisy Mae, I didn't mean to . . . to . . . you know."

"I know. Why don't you get a few hours' sleep? I'll make up the sofa for you."

Daisy sat in the chair across from the sofa, watching her brother sleep. Every now and then, he mumbled something incoherent. Once, she caught Brandon's name. Alex had been so strong since the funeral, comforting everyone in the family, helping her parents get through the first few weeks of grief when it seemed none of them would ever smile again, finding humor where none existed. She should have known he was hurting inside, tearing himself apart because of what had happened to Brandon. As the oldest, Alex had always seen himself as the defender of his younger siblings. He had believed that he was invincible, able to leap tall buildings in a single bound, to protect them against anything and everything. No wonder he felt he had failed.

With a sigh, Daisy glanced at her watch. It was almost five. She should wake Alex. Erik would be rising soon, and Rhys, too.

The thought had no sooner crossed her mind than Erik appeared in the doorway.

Daisy eyed him appreciatively. Clad in a black T-shirt, khaki slacks, and black cowboy boots, he was the epitome of tall, dark, and sexy.

He lifted one brow, a wry smile curving his lips as he walked toward her. She had no doubt that he knew exactly what she was thinking.

Bending down, he kissed her lightly. "Good evening, love."

Daisy grinned, thinking he sounded just like Dracula.

Erik glanced at Alex, snoring softly on the sofa.

"Did you hear what he said?" Daisy asked.

Erik nodded, then sat down on the floor beside her chair. "Do you think we can count on him?"

"I don't know. I hope so."

"It might be best if Rhys and I do this alone."

"Or I could take Alex's place."

"No!"

"You need someone to make the initial contact," Daisy said. "Someone he won't suspect."

"We've already had this discussion. I won't put your life in danger."

"My life's been in danger since I was eighteen years old," Daisy retorted.

"Be that as it may, I want you to stay here. I don't want to be worrying about you when this goes down."

"You know who it is, don't you?"

"I have a pretty good idea."

Daisy leaned forward. "Does Rhys know?"

"I'll tell you what Rhys knows," Costain said, coming into the room. "He knows he's sick and tired of being cooped up."

Erik shook his head. "Is that right? Try spending a few days in that dungeon of yours."

"Yeah, yeah, I said I was sorry," Rhys muttered, pacing the floor in front of the fireplace. "I need a drink."

Daisy froze as Costain stopped pacing to stare at her.

Rising smoothly to his feet, Erik moved to stand in front of Daisy. "Forget it."

"I have some wine, if that will help," Daisy said, disliking the tremor in her voice.

Rhys snorted with derision.

Daisy shrugged. "Take it or leave it, but that's all I'm offering."

"Fine, I'll take it. Some hostess," Rhys muttered after Daisy went into the kitchen. "Doesn't keep anything on hand for her guests."

"I don't think she was expecting you," Erik remarked.

"Yeah, well, I'm just edgy from being cooped up." Rhys spun around when, with a low groan, Alex sat up, stretching.

"What are you looking at?" Alex asked.

"Dinner?" Rhys asked hopefully.

Alex sprang to his feet. "No way!"

"Whatever happened to hospitality?" Rhys complained.

"It went the way of the cassette tape and the phonograph," Erik said with a grin. "Hell's bells, suck it up, Costain. You're whining like a week-old fledgling who hasn't fed yet."

"Maybe you're right." Rhys smiled at Daisy as she offered him a crystal glass of red liquid. "My thanks, dear lady."

"You're welcome."

"Well," Alex said, "it's dinnertime and I'm hungry. Daisy?"

"I could eat."

"Yeah." Rhys looked at Daisy, his gaze lingering on the pulse throbbing in the hollow of her throat. "Me, too."

"Rhys." The warning was clear in Erik's tone.

"Come on, Alex, I'll help you fix dinner," Daisy said, and made a hasty retreat into the kitchen.

Rhys laughed softly as he watched Daisy hurry out of the room. "Is she as tasty as she looks?"

"You'll never know," Erik replied. "Not as long as I draw breath."

Dinner was over, the dishes were done, and Daisy was a nervous wreck. She sat on the sofa in the living room, pretending to watch TV, while Erik, Alex, and Rhys sat in the kitchen formulating a plan for the midnight meet. From what little she could overhear, their plan was ridiculously simple. Alex would show up for the meet. Erik and Rhys would stay out of sight until the deal was made, and then Rhys would take control of the situation. Apparently Erik's only function was to act as backup for Rhys.

In theory, it sounded simple enough, but doubts plagued Daisy. What if the one offering the reward didn't come alone? What if something happened to Alex? How would she explain it to her parents? They would never forgive her if he was injured or, worse, killed. She would never forgive herself.

She glanced at the clock, certain it must be near midnight. It was only a quarter after nine. She had never known time to pass so slowly!

At nine thirty, the meeting in the kitchen broke up. Rising, Daisy grabbed Erik by the hand and gave it a tug.

"Something wrong?" he asked.

"Yes. No. I just need some time alone with you."

"Sounds good to me," he said, smiling. "What did you have in mind?"

She looked at him as if he wasn't too bright. "What do you think?" she asked, her voice pitched low so that only he could hear.

"Ah." Erik glanced over his shoulder.

Rhys stood in the kitchen doorway, his arms folded over his chest, a knowing look in his eyes. Alex glowered at him from in front of the fireplace.

Chuckling softly, Erik looked back at Daisy. "I'm yours to command."

Alex swore long and loud as he watched Daisy lead Erik up the stairs to her bedroom. If he was going to be totally honest with himself, Delacourt wasn't such a bad guy, all things considered. He treated Daisy with respect. If Daisy was to be believed, Delacourt had saved his life. But still . . . it just wasn't right!

"It bothers you," Costain said, "the two of them?"

"Damn right!" Unable to stand still, he began to pace the floor. He glanced upward. It didn't take a genius to figure out why it was so quiet up there. It made him sick to his stomach to think about what Daisy was doing, and who she was doing it with.

Rhys grinned as he took a place on the sofa, one arm resting along the back. "He's a good man."

"He's not a man at all. And neither are you."

"No?" Rhys shrugged. "I would wager I'm as much a man as you are. More, perhaps."

"All right, then. He's not human," Alex amended, his voice gruff. "And neither are you."

Rhys laughed out loud. "Mortals!"

"Jealous?"

"Hardly," Rhys said with a huff. "We are superior to you in every way. In another hundred years, I'll be more powerful than I am now, and still making love to beautiful women. Where will you be?"

Faced with his own mortality, Alex dropped into a chair. He had hunted vampires. He had killed vampires. But he had never really talked to one. Never tried to understand them. He leaned forward, his elbows resting on the arms of the chair. "You really like being a vampire?"

Rhys grunted softly. Mortals were so predictable. They always asked the same questions, as if there were no more to being a vampire than blood and death. "Yes," he said. "I like being a vampire."

"So, drinking blood? Killing innocents? None of that bothers you?"

"Blood is a necessity. Killing is a choice. A choice you've also made."

"It's not the same. You can't kill something that's already dead."

"You're judging a way of life for which you have no experience. You have no idea what it's like, to have the strength of twenty men, to be able to transform into mist, to move faster than the human eye can follow, to scale a building or leap a barrier with no effort at all, to cross the country with a thought, to see and hear and touch the world in ways that mortals can never know. You don't know how addicting that power can be."

Alex stared at Costain, mesmerized by his voice, by the picture he had painted. Maybe being a vampire wasn't such a bad thing after all. To always be young, powerful, in control.

Rhys smiled faintly. "The thought of being a vampire no longer seems so repellant, does it?"

"Of course it does!" Alex exclaimed, but they were just empty words, and Rhys knew it.

"You're a hunter. You've killed my kind. Have you never tasted our blood?"

"Of course not!" Alex said adamantly, and even as he denied it, he heard Daisy's voice in the back of his mind. *Erik saved your life.* He had never asked how, never let himself dwell on it, until now. Had Erik given him his blood? Even as the thought rose in his mind, he was afraid the answer was yes.

"Never been curious?" Rhys asked.

"Sure, I've wondered. They say it gives you a high like no other, that it lets you experience, for a short time, what it's like to be a vampire."

Rhys nodded. "So they say."

"They also say that too much will kill you, and that some people come down hard, and some never come down." Just his luck, Alex thought. The one and only time he'd had a chance to find out what it was like, and he'd been unconscious.

"So they say." Rhys bared his fangs. "It's better straight from the source."

Alex stared at the vampire, at the gleaming white fangs. What would it be like to taste vampire blood? He had tasted his own blood. What human hadn't pricked a finger or received a small cut and licked the blood away? It was a natural reaction. But to drink vampire blood—Undead blood—to feel what it was like to be a vampire—the power . . . the invincibility . . . he wasn't unconscious now. What would it be like?

With a shake of his head, Alex sat back in his chair. What the hell was he thinking?

Rhys laughed. "Where's your courage, hunter?"

Erik stared at the woman lying so trustingly in his arms. Never in all his existence had he expected to feel this way about a mortal woman. With Daisy, he felt anything was possible. Almost, he could believe he was just an ordinary man in love with a woman, that they could have a future together. A nice dream, but that's all it was. There was no place for them in the world he lived in, and certainly no place for him in hers.

She smiled up at him, a sleepy, satisfied smile, one that stroked his ego because he had put that smile on her face.

"What are you thinking about?" she asked.

"How incredible you are."

"You are."

"There is something I've been wondering about," Erik said. "How did you find me at La Morte Rouge?"

"I felt your pain, and I followed it." She frowned at the memory, then reached up to cup his cheek. "How did you stand it? I've never experienced anything so awful, so . . . I don't know. I can't describe it."

Erik shook his head. "How could you feel it? I blocked the link between us so that you wouldn't."

"Well, I guess it didn't work."

"You really are incredible." He kissed her lightly. He hadn't wanted her to know what he was going through, had been afraid she would do exactly what she had done and ride to his rescue. "My brave, foolish flower." He glanced out the window. It was time to go. "It's a quarter after eleven, Daisy darlin'."

"I wish you didn't have to go."

"I know." Erik trailed his fingertips down her cheek. "Don't you think I'd rather stay here with you?"

With a sigh, Daisy snuggled closer to his side. Some people were addicted to vampire blood, she thought, but not her. She was addicted to a vampire. Just looking at him made her high. His kisses were as intoxicating as the touch of his hand—that big, powerful hand that was gently stroking her thigh, making her quiver for more.

She sat up, reluctant to let him go, but knowing she couldn't ask him to stay. She didn't trust Rhys Costain to watch out for Alex, but she knew Erik would take care of him, not because Erik cared whether her brother lived or died, but because he loved her.

It was eleven forty-five when Erik followed Daisy into the living room. Rhys was stretched out on the floor in front of the TV. Alex sat on the sofa, going through his vampire hunting kit.

Erik felt the tension in the room rising with each tick of the mantel clock.

He glanced from Rhys to Alex and back again. "So, what have you two been doing?"

"Not much," Rhys said with a shrug. "We spent some time comparing the merits of being a vampire as opposed to being a mortal."

"Is that so?" Erik looked at Alex, one brow raised. "Don't tell me you're thinking about joining the ranks of the Undead?"

"Hardly." Alex glanced at his watch. "Isn't it about time we were going?"

"Finally." Rhys stood and moved toward the door in a single fluid movement.

Daisy took Erik's hand in hers. "You'll be careful, won't you? You won't let anything happen to Alex?"

"Stop worrying." Erik slipped his arm around Daisy's shoulders and gave her a squeeze. "We'll be back before you know it."

"That's right, kid," Rhys added as he went out the door. "And your brother will be two hundred grand richer."

Chapter 35

Daisy blew out a sigh as the door closed behind Rhys Costain. She tried to tell herself there was nothing to worry about. Rhys was a powerful vampire. Erik was a powerful vampire. Between them, they would make sure that nothing happened to Alex.

But what if Rhys was just stringing them along?

What if Rhys couldn't be trusted?

What if he intended to kill whoever it was who had put the hit out on him, then kill Alex, and maybe Erik, too?

What if the man who had hired the hit brought backup with him?

She told herself she was worrying for nothing, that she was just letting her imagination run wild.

What if she wasn't?

Was she just going to sit home and wait and worry?

"No."

She filled her pockets with vials of holy water, grabbed a handful of sharp stakes, a silver-bladed knife, and her keys, and left the house.

Whatever happened tonight, she was going to be there, hopefully only as an observer.

A light rain began to fall as Alex pulled up in front of La Morte Rouge. He had dropped Costain and Delacourt off a few blocks back, just in case the man he was supposed to meet was holed up somewhere nearby, watching.

After killing the engine, Alex spent a few minutes checking the place out. It looked deserted. No lights shone from inside. There were no other cars along the curb; from where he sat, he couldn't see any cars parked in the lot.

He glanced behind him, wondering where Costain and Delacourt were hiding. Damn! How had he gotten mixed up in all this? Maybe it was time to rethink his career choice. He had always loved the excitement of the hunt, but lately . . . hell, he had put Daisy's life in danger, not to mention his own. He'd wager he'd had more close calls in the last month than he'd had since he staked his first vampire. His hands tightened on the steering wheel. Putting his own life in danger had been one thing, but now Brandon was dead and Alex couldn't help feeling it was his fault. And if that wasn't bad enough, he owed his life to a stinkin' bloodsucker. He pounded his fist on the steering wheel. A bloodsucker who was in love with his sister. And, worst of all, Daisy was in love with him.

Alex glanced out the window. He'd farted around long enough. It was time to go. Muttering, "Ready or not, here I come," he stepped out of the car. Turning his collar up against the rain, he reached into the backseat for his backpack. After slinging it over his shoulder, he slammed the door shut, then sprinted across the parking lot. He paused a moment at the top of the stone stairway, wishing, however briefly, that he possessed a vampire's enhanced sense of sight and smell.

Screwing up his courage, he walked cautiously down the rain-slick stone steps that led to the club's back door. He knew it was only his imagination, but the night seemed to grow darker and more ominous with every step he took.

He saw the figure near the back door as soon as he rounded the corner of the building. Even in the dark, he could see that it was a woman. A beautiful woman, he thought as he closed the distance between them. Her skin was pale, almost translucent. Wisps of light blond hair peeked out from the hood of her long red cloak.

"Alex?"

His surprise turned to uneasiness when he looked into her eyes. Dark brown eyes with a hint of madness. "You're MC?"

"Mariah, actually."

"But . . . you're one of them. A vampire." Alex didn't know what shocked him more, the fact that MC was a female, or the fact that he knew she was a vampire. He frowned inwardly, wondering how he knew, and then realized it had to have something to do with the fact that Erik's blood was running in his veins. But there was no time to think about that now. "Why do you want to kill Costain?"

"What difference does that make to you?"

"None," Alex said, shrugging. As inconspicuously as possible, he checked the surrounding area. Where the hell were Costain and Delacourt?

"Where's the proof?"

"What? Oh, right." Alex delved into his backpack for the jar filled with ashes from Daisy's fireplace. "Where's the money?"

She held out her hand. "Give it to me."

Alex hesitated, then offered her the jar. Dammit, where was his backup?

Mariah unscrewed the cap. She looked at Alex, then sniffed the jar's contents. "What kind of joke are you playing?"

"What do you mean?"

Mariah hurled the jar against the side of the building, where it shattered. "You fool! Did you think I wouldn't know the difference?"

Alex took a step backward as her eyes blazed red.

Mariah glided toward him, her hands curled into claws, her fangs running out.

Muttering an oath, Alex turned on his heels and sprinted toward the staircase. And barreled into one very angry vampire.

She hissed at him as she dug her claws into his shoulders. "You stupid, puny mortal. Did you really think you could get away from me?"

Alex glared at her. Swallowing his fear, he lifted his chin defiantly. "Kill me if you want. It won't save you. Rhys knows all about you."

A flicker of fear sparked in her eyes. "I don't believe you."

"He's here," Alex said, praying he was right.

Mariah's gaze darted from right to left. "Lies won't save you."

"Nothing will save you," Alex said with more bravado than he felt.

"Let him go!"

Alex's head jerked around. "Daisy! What the hell are you doing here?"

Daisy waved the wooden stake in her hand. "Backing you up, of course."

An unladylike snort rose in Mariah's throat. "You think you can save him with that sliver of wood?"

"Just let him go!" Daisy said, her voice rising. "Let him go now!"

Mariah snorted with disdain. "Stop waving that silly thing around. I can rip his throat out before you reach me, and kill you before you realize what's happened."

"You can try."

Mariah's laughter sliced through the air. "You're a cheeky little broad," she said, and then frowned. "You're the Blood Thief, aren't you?" She laughed again, genuinely amused. "To think, Rhys was concerned about a puny little female like you."

"We almost killed him," Daisy said. "I don't think you'll be a problem."

Alex glared at his sister. What did she hope to gain by antagonizing the vampire? He slid a glance at Mariah's face. Was it just wishful thinking, or did the vampire look worried?

Alex held his breath. Apparently distracted by what Daisy had said, the vampire had loosened her grip on his shoulders.

"If you don't let him go, I'll come after you," Daisy said. "And I'll find you. The same way I found Rhys. The same way I found Saul."

Mariah's eyes narrowed when Daisy mentioned the vampire she had destroyed.

It's now or never, Alex thought. He jerked his arms straight up, breaking the vampire's hold, and then he drove his fist into her face just as hard as he could.

With a startled cry, Mariah reeled backward as blood spurted from her broken nose.

Alex raced toward Daisy, delving into his backpack for a stake as he went. "Let's get the hell out of here."

Daisy didn't argue. Side by side, they raced up the narrow stairway to the top of the hill.

"Where's Erik?" she asked, gasping for breath.

"Damned if I know. Let's get the hell out of here while the getting's good."

Daisy risked a glance down the hill. She had expected to see the vampire coming after them, but nothing moved on the stone stairway behind them. That was odd, she thought. Surely a broken nose wouldn't put Mariah out of commission for long.

Daisy breathed a sigh of relief when Erik materialized in front of her.

"Where the devil were you?" Alex demanded. "Some backup you turned out to be! You almost got us killed."

"Mariah wasn't alone," Erik replied. "She had a dozen zombies hidden around the building. It took us a few minutes to dispatch them all."

Daisy shuddered as she imagined Erik and Rhys battling an army of zombies. She wasn't sure how you made a zombie, or how you went about killing one, but then, she didn't really want to know.

She glanced around, then asked, "Where's Rhys?"

A muscle twitched in Erik's jaw. "He's taking care of business."

"Taking care of—oh. What will he do to . . . ?" The question died in Daisy's throat as a horrible keening sound rose in the air. She shivered as the anguished cry went on and on, scraping along her nerves like fingernails on a blackboard. Pressing her hands over her ears, she buried her face in Erik's shoulder.

"Damn!" Alex exclaimed. "What's he doing to her?"

Erik shook his head. "You don't want to know. Come on, let's get out of here." Wrapping his arm around Daisy's shoulders, he led her across the damp parking lot toward the car.

He opened the passenger door for Daisy, then opened the rear door and motioned for Alex to get in the backseat. "I'll drive."

"I can drive my own damn car," Alex said belligerently.

"I said I'll drive. The way your hands are shaking, you'd probably run us into a ditch."

Alex glared at him but didn't push it. Truth was, he was more rattled by what had happened than he wanted to admit.

Erik shut the rear door, then slid behind the wheel. A thought started the engine.

As he pulled away from the curb, another high-pitched wail pierced the quiet of the night.

Daisy's pulse had returned to normal by the time Erik pulled up in front of her house.

As soon as they were inside, Alex poured himself a good stiff drink. He downed it in one long swallow, and quickly poured another.

Erik stood near the fireplace, his expression thoughtful. Curious to know what he was thinking, Daisy tried to read his thoughts, but his mind was closed to her.

After excusing herself, Daisy went into the kitchen and called home to let her parents know that she and Alex were okay.

After she bade her mother good night, her dad insisted on getting on the phone and hearing all the gory details. "What about Rhys?" he asked. "Did you take him out?"

"No, Dad, he was helping us."

"A vampire helping hunters? I don't believe it."

"Believe it. And you can cross Mariah off the list."

"You destroyed her?"

"Rhys did."

Daisy could almost hear her father frowning as he tried to wrap his mind around the idea of one vampire destroying another.

"And Erik?"

"He's here with us."

"I see."

"I love him, Dad."

"Are you sure?"

"Of course I am."

"Are you sure your feelings are your own, and that the natural allure of the vampire hasn't colored your emotions?"

"I'm sure," she replied. "Listen, Dad, I've got to go. I can hardly keep my eyes open."

"Good night, daughter."

"Night, Dad. I love you."

Daisy ended the call, then stared at the phone. What if her dad was right? What if what she felt for Erik wasn't real at all? There was no denying that vampire glamour was real. They used it to attract their prey. But she wasn't prey.

And yet, even as she assured herself that what she felt for Erik was the real thing, a tiny voice in the back of her mind echoed her father's question: *Are you sure your feelings are your own?*

Daisy took a deep breath before returning to the living room. Judging from the way Alex was slumped in his chair staring into space, she guessed he'd consumed another couple of drinks.

Erik remained by the fireplace, one arm resting on the mantel. His gaze caught hers the moment she entered the room.

"Is everything all right?" he asked quietly.

Her defense mechanism immediately went on alert. "Yes, of course. Why wouldn't it be?"

"I don't know. You tell me."

"Uh-oh, sounds like a serious talk comin' on," Alex mumbled, lurching to his feet. "Me and my good buddy, Jack Daniel's, are gonna go on up to bed and think about how to spend that two hundred grand."

Daisy nodded at her brother as he staggered out of the room; then, taking a calming breath, she looked at Erik.

"It's late," she said. "I think I'll turn in, too. You're welcome to spend the night here."

"Am I?"

Daisy's heart skipped a beat, and then seemed to sink into the pit of her stomach. Had he overheard what her father said? Of course he had. He had ears like a lynx.

Erik pushed away from the mantel. "It's all right, Daisy. I think we both knew this night was coming."

"I don't know what you mean."

"This isn't the time to start lying to each other."

She looked up at him, her mind running in a dozen directions all at once.

"I don't want you to mistake lust for love, or gratitude for affection."

"But . . ." She crossed her arms over her breasts, certain she didn't want to hear whatever was coming next.

"Hear me out. We've been through a lot together in the last few weeks. I think you need to spend a little time by yourself to sort out your feelings."

"You were listening, weren't you?"

"I didn't mean to eavesdrop," he said with a shrug. "In any case, I would have suggested we spend some time apart anyway. I'm a vampire . . ."

"Really?" she exclaimed with mock surprise. "I had no idea."

"Daisy." He closed the distance between them, his hands folding lightly over her shoulders. "You need to think this through. Are you ready to spend your life with me, with a vampire? In a good relationship, each party gives fifty percent. If you stay with me, you'll be giving up much more than I will. I can't conform my life to yours. You'll have to conform your life to mine. Can you do that? Do you want to do that?"

She blinked up at him, doubt and confusion evident in her expression.

"The fact is, affairs between vampires and mortals rarely last. I care for you more than I've ever cared for anyone, mortal or otherwise. And because of that, I don't want to hurt you. I don't want to steal your youth or your dreams. I don't want to look in your eyes years from now and see regret for the sacrifices you had to make to stay with me." He took a deep breath. "Most of all, I'm afraid I won't be able to keep my promise, that the day will come when I'll turn you against your will."

She continued to stare up at him, mute, a single tear glistening on one cheek.

"Good-bye, Daisy." Leaning down, he kissed the tear away, then brushed her lips with his. "God bless you."

Odd words coming from a vampire, Daisy thought. But before she could remark on it, before she could ask him to stay, he was gone.

Chapter 36

Rhys stood over what was left of Mariah. He felt neither regret nor remorse for what he had done. She had brought it on herself, the ungrateful traitor.

Thunder rolled across the skies and he lifted his face to the storm, wondering, as he did from time to time, what his ultimate fate would be. He had never professed to believe in either heaven or hell, but if there was an afterlife, he supposed he was bound for hell. At least he wouldn't be alone.

Rhys grunted softly. He'd have a few friends there in the pit with him, and a lot of enemies, he thought, looking at Mariah's remains. He wondered if his old buddy ever thought about where they would spend eternity. Of course, Erik had other things on his mind just now.

Rhys smiled faintly. She was a pretty little thing, Erik's Daisy. And head over heels in love with a vampire. He wondered if she realized what living with a vampire would mean. Delacourt was a decent guy, but he was still a vampire, with a vampire's needs. Had Daisy considered what would happen in thirty or forty years, given any thought to how she would feel when Erik was still young and virile and she was an old woman? She didn't have to age, of course. She could surrender to the Dark Gift, give up her humanity, her family, any hope she had of bearing children.

There was a reason why few vampires became vampires by choice. As exciting as it was to be Nosferatu, there was a heavy price to pay. You could live forever, but those you loved would wither and die. Food became a distant memory. The moon became your sun. Humanity became your enemy.

He glanced at Mariah's remains again, bemused by his maudlin thoughts. She had betrayed him and she had paid the requisite price for her treachery. Tomorrow, the sun would take care of what little was left.

A thought took him to the flat roof of La Morte Rouge. Standing there, he looked out over the city, the undisputed master of all he surveyed.

He turned as he sensed a presence behind him. "Erik. What brings you here? I thought you'd be curled up with that pretty little flower."

"I thought so, too," Erik replied. "But who would know better than you that life rarely turns out the way we plan."

"Indeed. So what happened?"

"Nothing. I just decided to let her go."

"How very noble of you," Rhys muttered. "What brought that on?"

"A lot of things." It was more than just the doubts her father had planted in her mind. He couldn't help thinking that circumstances more than anything else had brought them together. There was nothing like danger to intensify emotions. Maybe Daisy truly loved him. Maybe what she felt was nothing but affection multiplied by gratitude because he had saved her life. Of course, he had put her in danger, too. But mainly, he had decided to let her go because he loved her. She deserved far more from life than he would ever be able to give her.

"Erik?"

"I don't want to talk about it."

Rhys nodded. "Fair enough. I've found fresh blood and a new woman to be a remarkable cure for most of life's problems." Lifting his head, he sniffed the wind. "I smell prey nearby." He slapped Erik on the shoulder. "What say you, Lord Erik? Shall we hunt?"

Erik glared at Rhys. Lord Erik, indeed. How many years had it been since that title had been his? He wondered what had become of the land that had once belonged to his family. Was it still in Delacourt hands, or had others laid claim to his family's birthright? And what the hell did he care?

Feeling the weight of Costain's gaze, Erik faced his old friend. "Fresh blood," he murmured. "Let's hunt."

She wouldn't cry. Daisy sat by the living room window, staring out into the darkness. Erik was out there somewhere. If she homed in on the link they shared, would she be able to read his thoughts, or had he erected a barrier between them? The last time he had tried that, he had failed, but he had been hurting then, weak from pain and hunger.

He had left her with nothing more than a quick kiss and a hasty good-bye. Left her flat because he had listened in on her conversation with her father. She tried to summon some measure of anger, but she couldn't. All she felt was a sense of overwhelming weariness and loss. She thought she might feel better if she cried, but she didn't seem to have any tears. Just emptiness.

She stared up at the painting over the fireplace, remembering how thrilled she had been when Erik gave it to her. At least she had something to remember him by.

After turning out the lights downstairs, she went up to her

bedroom. She undressed, brushed her teeth, combed out her hair, then crawled into bed, only to lie staring up at the ceiling, while a little voice inside her head kept repeating, "He's gone. He's gone. He's gone . . ."

She told herself it didn't matter. He was a vampire, after all. Human, but not human. Real, but not real. Alive, but not alive.

"Why would you want him anyway?" queried her conscience. "What kind of life could the two of you have? Even though he saved Alex's life, your parents will never really accept him. He can't give you children. You can't grow old together. You're so different. You'll never be equal, you'll never truly understand him. It's like you're Lois Lane and he's Clark Kent. His supernatural powers will always overshadow your humanity."

All true, Daisy admitted. *And you haven't even mentioned the worst part. I'll grow old and wrinkled and one day, I'll die. And he won't.*

"I didn't want to bring up the obvious," her conscience said.

A single tear leaked out of Daisy's eye and slid down her cheek. When she reached up to wipe it away, she remembered how Erik had kissed her tear from her cheek before he left her.

That memory, that last tender act of affection, unlocked the floodgates and unleashed the tears she had been holding back.

Sobbing now, she turned onto her side and wept.

Erik paused in the act of calling his prey to him as his mind filled with images of Daisy. She was lying in bed, crying, because of him.

"What's wrong?" Rhys also paused, his eyes narrowed as he lifted his head to sniff the wind.

Erik shook his head. "Nothing."

"Uh-huh." Rhys turned his attention back to the women he and Erik had chosen as prey. Wrapping his arm around the waist of the taller woman, he lifted her hair away from her neck and sniffed her skin.

Erik blew out a sigh as he glanced at the second woman. She stood unmoving, her brow furrowed. Muttering an oath, Erik exerted his will and she walked toward him, her face wiped clean of expression.

Rhys smiled knowingly. "You'll feel better after you've eaten," he promised, and drawing the woman into his embrace, he bent his head to her throat.

Erik stared at the woman standing in front of him. She was plump and pretty, with curly blond hair and vivid green eyes. Probably a nice girl. But she wasn't Daisy. And although the woman's blood called to him, he found no pleasure in taking it. It was sustenance, nothing more. It was like craving champagne and settling for beer. It quenched his thirst, but that was all.

Pulling her roughly into his embrace, he drank quickly and released her from his thrall, then watched as she walked away, weaving slightly.

Rhys shook his head; then, with an aggrieved sigh, he sent his prey away.

Erik shoved his hands in his pants pockets. "What are you looking at me like that for?"

"I should have known you wouldn't take it all."

"Yeah? Well, I'm surprised you didn't."

"Yeah? Well . . . oh, forget it. Let's get out of here."

Erik fell into step beside Rhys. "Any idea why Mariah wanted your head?"

"Sure. She wanted to be Master of the City."

"You're kidding! She never could have pulled it off. She wasn't strong enough."

"Or smart enough." Rhys turned his gaze on Erik. "In case she gave you any ideas, just remember that I'm older and—"

"Wiser and stronger," Erik finished, grinning.

"And don't you forget it."

Erik grunted softly. "As if you'd let me."

Side by side, they wandered the city's dark streets. Erik didn't know where Costain's thoughts lay, but his own thoughts were lodged in a small white house with yellow trim where a precious flower shed tears over a soulless monster.

Chapter 37

It was midmorning before Daisy found the energy to get out of bed. As she stepped into the shower, memories of the past week splashed over her like drops of water.

The night after Mariah had been destroyed, Rhys had shown up with a diamond necklace and a bouquet of flowers for Daisy, and a bank draft for two hundred thousand dollars made out to Alex. The Master of the City had made no mention of Erik, and as much as she had wanted to, Daisy hadn't been able to bring herself to ask about him.

After Rhys left, Alex had insisted on taking Daisy out to dinner at the most expensive restaurant in town, even though Daisy hadn't felt much like celebrating. How could she, when her heart was breaking?

The next day, Alex had surprised her by taking her to the bank, where he deposited a hundred thousand dollars into her savings account.

"You can take a long vacation now," he had said with a wink. "I know that's what I'm going to do. Why don't you come with me?"

But Daisy wasn't in the mood for a vacation. She just wanted to be alone. As though sensing that, Alex decided to go back to Boston and spend some time with their parents.

Daisy had agreed that was probably a good idea. No doubt the folks were feeling pretty lonely, with just the two of them rattling around that big old house. Alex had left for home the next day.

Daisy sighed as she stepped out of the shower. Her house had been feeling pretty empty ever since Alex left.

After slipping into her favorite sweats, she tied her hair back into a ponytail, brushed her teeth, and then went downstairs.

She hadn't been functioning very well since their encounter with Mariah. Every time she thought she had shed her last tear over Erik, a new flood arrived. At night, her dreams were plagued by nightmares, fragmented dreams that quickly shifted from one hazy scene to another, dreams that made no sense, even while she was asleep.

Last night had been the worst of all. Her nightmares had been peopled with monsters—a ravening ghoul preying on baby dolls with painted faces had transformed into a huge black bat devouring a lamb. The bat had metamorphosed into a big black wolf stalking a rabbit. Lastly, the creature had turned into a red-eyed vampire draining a young girl with russet-colored hair and green eyes. . . .

Daisy paused in the act of opening the refrigerator. How could she have been so blind? Of course the monsters in her nightmares represented Erik, her unconscious fear of what he was. She, of course, had been the prey in each scenario, help-less to save herself from the ravening beast.

She pulled a bottle of orange juice from the fridge and poured herself a glass, then dropped two slices of bread into the toaster.

"You're better off without him," she muttered. If only she could make herself believe it.

After buttering the toast, she put it on a plate, then sat down at the kitchen table, the toast forgotten. Maybe it was time to move back to Boston. As much as she loved living on her own in LA, she felt a sudden need to be with her family.

She gave herself permission to spend the rest of the day grieving for what might have been. She relived every memory, recalled every word Erik had spoken, wept for the love they had shared, and then wrapped up all the memories and locked them away in the back of her mind. Later, she took down the painting he had given her, wrapped it in plastic, and stowed it in the back of her closet. From now on, she would concentrate on the future and forget about the past.

Tomorrow, she would call a real estate agent and put the house up for sale.

The decision brought with it a sense of peace. She would go home and lick her wounds. Thanks to Alex's generosity, she could take a long vacation. Maybe she would look for a new line of work. One thing was for certain. She, Daisy Louise O'Donnell, had had her fill of vampires.

Damon stood outside the woman's house for the second time in as many nights, his anger growing with every moment. From time to time, she passed in front of one of the windows. He stared at her, imprinting her features on his mind. She was a pretty woman, but he was blind to her physical beauty. He saw only a puny mortal who was partly responsible for killing the woman he loved.

He cursed softly. Had Mariah been honest with him, had she taken him into her confidence about what she had planned, she would still be alive. But she had always treated him like he was still a punk kid, forcing him to sneak around, trailing after her like some pathetic creature who couldn't be trusted, leaving him to watch from the shadows while she put her plan into action, just as he had stood in the shadows and watched this mortal female and her brother betray Mariah into the hands of the Master of the City.

Damon expelled a deep breath. He knew what he was doing was dangerous, knew that should he be caught, he would be destroyed, but it didn't matter. Nothing mattered now but avenging Mariah's death. How she would laugh at that, Damon thought bitterly. A muscle clenched in his jaw. Perhaps if he had been more assertive, she would have treated him with respect. But it was too late to think about that now.

Damon closed his eyes, remembering how he had followed her that last night. Hands clenched into tight fists, he had watched her walk into a trap. As much as he had loved Mariah, his sense of self-preservation had kept him from going to her aid. Not that he could have stood against the Master of the City. Rhys Costain's fury was something Damon hoped never to see again. Mariah had been powerless against the older vampire.

Damon grinned into the darkness. He might not be able to best Costain in a fight, but he was strong enough to execute Costain's two mortal accomplices. It wouldn't bring Mariah back, Damon mused as he crossed the street toward the woman's house, but it would do wonders for his self-esteem.

Daisy was getting ready for bed when the doorbell rang. She knew it wasn't Erik, told herself she didn't want it to be Erik, but she couldn't suppress the rush of anticipation that swelled in her breast as she slipped into her bathrobe, then hurried down the stairs to answer the door.

Even though she hadn't really been expecting Erik, she couldn't stifle her disappointment when she saw the young man standing on the other side of the door. "Can I help you?"

"I hope so." He gestured at his oil-stained jeans. "My car broke down and my cell phone's dead, and . . ." His eyelids fluttered down and he swayed unsteadily on his feet.

"Are you all right?"

"Yes, ma'am, it's just that . . ." He braced one hand on the door frame. "I lost someone I loved recently, and I haven't felt much like eating the last few days."

"I know how you feel," Daisy said. "My brother passed away not long ago."

"I'm sorry to hear that, ma'am. I hate to ask this, but could I use your phone?"

"Sure, just let me get it." Drawing her robe around her, Daisy went into the living room to retrieve her phone. When she returned, the young man was sprawled facedown on the porch.

Kneeling beside him, Daisy rolled him onto his back, then shook his shoulder lightly. "Don't move," she said. "I'm gonna call 911."

"No, that won't be necessary. I'll be fine if I could just have a glass of water."

Daisy bit down on her lower lip. She was alone in the house. He was a stranger. But he was just a skinny kid, not more than sixteen or seventeen. She couldn't just leave him lying out here on the porch. Besides, she had a Crocodile Dundee–sized knife in her kit. And with that in mind, she helped him to his feet.

"Why don't you come in for a minute, until you feel better," she suggested.

"Are you sure it won't be too much trouble?"

"Of course not." Slipping her arm around his waist, Daisy helped him inside.

She knew she had made a terrible mistake the minute they crossed the threshold, when the seemingly innocuous young man flung her across the floor. She cried out as the back of her head slammed against the wall.

She stared up at him, mute, her eyes widening with horror when his lips drew back, revealing his fangs. *Never show fear.* How often had her father drummed that warning into her head? Unfortunately, her courage seemed to have deserted her and all she could think was that she was going to die, and she would never see Erik again.

She cried out when the vampire grabbed her by the throat and jerked her to her feet. "Why?" she asked, gasping for breath. "At least . . . tell me why."

"You were there when Costain took her life. Now I'm going to take yours."

Daisy looked into his eyes and knew it was pointless to ask for mercy. She tried to speak, tried to rescind her invitation, but fear trapped the words in her throat. Knowing it was useless, she struggled to free herself, but her hands and feet were puny weapons against the strength of a vampire.

She was going to die. She gasped for breath as his hand tightened around her throat, and then he was bending over her, brushing her hair away from her neck.

A choked cry of pain rose in her throat as he buried his fangs in her neck. Erik's bite had been sensual, pleasurable. This bite brought only pain and fear. Darkness ate away at the edges of her vision. The frantic beat of her heart echoed loudly in her ears and then, gradually, slowed. The strength went out of her limbs.

Whispering Erik's name, she fell into blackness.

Rhys leaned one elbow on the bar as he regarded the man beside him. And then he shook his head. "You look like one of the walking dead," he muttered.

"Very funny," Erik replied sourly.

"Come on, snap out of it. The world is filled with young, beautiful women, and they're all ours for the taking."

"They aren't her."

Rhys muttered a pithy oath. "They're all the same in the dark."

"You've turned cynical in your old age, haven't you?"

Rhys grunted softly. "It never works out, you know that. You love them for twenty or thirty years and then they die on you, and what have you got left? Memories and a broken heart." He shook his head. "I learned my lesson the first time around."

"Are you ever sorry you killed her?"

Rhys blew out a sigh that seemed to come from the very depths of his being. "Every damn day."

Erik had never felt sorry for Rhys Costain. The man was diamond hard and bulldog tough. If Rhys had ever had any qualms about being a vampire, ever entertained any doubts, he had never given a hint of it, at least in Erik's presence. Erik had long suspected that killing Josette was a wound that had never healed. Now, seeing the pain in Costain's eyes, he knew he had been right.

"You should go back to your little mortal," Rhys said quietly.

"I thought you said such relationships never work."

Rhys lifted one shoulder and let it fall in a negligent shrug. "There's a first time for everything. Who knows? Maybe you'll break the mold."

Erik shook his head. "I can't."

"Why the hell not? You've been pining away for her for days."

"I'm afraid . . ." Erik blew out a breath. "The more I'm with her, the more I want her."

"You're afraid you'll bring her across."

"Exactly. And she'll hate me for it."

"Did you ever talk about it?"

"She doesn't want me. She made me promise I wouldn't turn her against her will."

"So make her think it's what she wants."

"I won't do that. I can't do that."

"My love is dead. You've abandoned yours. What do you say we go find ourselves a couple of good-looking babes and drink until we can't drink any more?"

Erik snorted softly. "That's your answer for everything, isn't it?"

"What else is there?"

He had a point, Erik thought. If he'd been a mortal man, he would have drowned his sorrows in a bottle of booze, but, since he was a vampire, that wasn't an option.

He was about to accede to Costain's wishes when a terrified shriek broke through the barrier Erik had erected between himself and Daisy.

Spurred by a soul-deep fear such as he had never known, he left the club, streaking with preternatural speed across town toward a little white house with yellow trim, and praying he wasn't too late.

Erik burst into Daisy's house, the scent of human blood almost overpowering the scent of vampire. Erik's fangs lengthened in response to the threat as he crossed the threshold.

The sight that met his eyes brought him up short. For a moment, he could only stare at the scene before him. Daisy lay on the floor, her face ashen. Damon hovered over her like a bird of prey. He sprang to his feet when Erik entered the room, his hands curled into claws, his fangs dripping blood.

"What have you done?" Erik demanded, the words little more than a snarl. He didn't wait for an answer. In the space of a heartbeat, he was on the other vampire.

Under ordinary circumstances, he would have taken Damon down without much effort. But Damon was high on the blood he had just consumed. Daisy's blood. With a hiss, Damon twisted out of Erik's grasp.

Fangs bared, they came together in a rush. Damon let out a howl as Erik sank his fangs into his shoulder and ripped off a hunk of flesh. Blood sprayed from the wound. Fighting for his life, Damon found the strength to break Erik's hold. He retreated a moment and then, with a wild cry, he lunged at Erik.

Erik stood his ground. At the last moment, he sidestepped and as Damon's momentum carried him forward, Erik grabbed him around the throat. A sharp twist broke Damon's neck; a stick of wood plucked from the fireplace assured that the other vampire wouldn't rise again.

"Daisy!" Crying her name, Erik dropped to the floor beside her. Lifting her into his arms, he cradled her against his chest. She was dying, her heartbeat slow and irregular, so faint he could scarcely hear it. Her skin was cool beneath his fingertips. "Daisy. Dammit, don't do this!"

"Erik?" Her eyelids fluttered open. "Erik, are you there?"

"I'm here."

"Are you holding me?"

"As close as I can."

"I love you," she murmured. "I never stopped."

"Let me bring you across before it's too late."

"No . . ."

She didn't want to be a vampire.

She didn't want to die.

She didn't want to leave Erik, but she couldn't endure the pain that burned through her any longer. With each labored breath she took, the world around her grew darker. In the distance, a faint light grew bright, brighter, beckoning her. Indistinct shadows moved beyond the light.

Gradually, one of them took on shape and substance until it resembled her grandfather. Smiling, he held out his hand. "Come along, Daisy, it's time."

"Grandpa O'Donnell," she murmured, "is that you?"

"Yes, poppet."

She reached for his hand and as she did so, the pain disappeared.

"Daisy!" Erik's arm tightened around her. "Don't leave me! Dammit, don't leave me here in the dark without you."

His words, so filled with love and sorrow, pulled her back. How could she leave him when he needed her so? Was this what Grandmother O'Donnell had meant when she said Daisy's compass might guide her in paths she had never thought to follow? Erik's arms tightened around Daisy. He could feel her slipping away. "Daisy, hang on." Perhaps a doctor could help her, yet even as the thought crossed his mind, he knew she was beyond medical help. "Daisy." He hadn't wept in centuries, but now, at the thought of losing her, tears scalded his eyes.

Daisy blinked as his tears dripped like red rain onto her cheeks. "Erik . . ." With a sigh of resignation, she closed her eyes. Hadn't she always known, deep down, that it would come to this?

"Do it," she murmured, and went limp in his arms.

Erik choked back a sob. Had he waited too long?

Praying it wasn't too late, he bent his head to her neck and drank.

Chapter 38

She was drifting, floating. The beautiful bright light had enveloped her grandfather, then faded and disappeared, leaving her frightened and alone in a world of darkness and pain. Had she lost her chance at heaven? Was she in hell? Was that why her blood seemed to be on fire, why everything seemed bathed in crimson? She tried to fight her way out of the darkness but her body felt heavy, lethargic. She willed her toes and fingers to move, felt a sharp stab of fear when nothing happened.

Was this death, this horrible sense of loss?

Of nothingness . . .

Erik sat at Daisy's side all through that long, seemingly endless night. Earlier, he had removed her bloody clothing, washed the blood from her neck, then slipped a nightgown over her head. When that was done, he had brought her to his place and put her in his bed. Since then, his mind had been filled with doubts. Had she known what she was asking for? Would she regret her decision when she regained consciousness and realized the full extent of what he had done?

He groaned low in his throat. Had he done the right thing? She would be alienated from her family and friends now. Damn. He could only imagine what Alex would say. Nothing good, that was for sure.

With a sigh, he caressed Daisy's cheek. Her skin was cool, her face pale, her breathing so shallow, he could scarcely hear it even with his vampiric senses.

Bending down, he kissed her brow. "Fight, Daisy," he murmured. "I've done all I can. Now, it's up to you."

With the coming of dawn, he carried her down to his lair. Tucking her close to his side, he stared into the darkness. Tomorrow night would tell the tale. If she awoke at the setting of the sun, she would be his forever.

A voice penetrated the thick darkness, a voice speaking her name. "Erik?"

Daisy fought her way through the smothering darkness and when she opened her eyes, the first thing she saw was Erik sitting beside her on the bed, his brow creased with worry.

She stared at him. He looked the same, yet different somehow. "Is something wrong?"

He shook his head. "No. How do you feel?" Because he hadn't wanted her to be frightened by waking in his lair, he had brought her upstairs to the bedroom before she regained consciousness.

"I don't know. I feel . . . I don't know. Why does everything look so bright?" she asked, squinting, and then she covered her ears with her hands. "What's that noise?"

"Just a truck going by."

"It sounds like a tank."

Erik nodded. "Just take it easy. What do you remember from last night?"

"Last night? There was a young man . . ."

"Damon."

"He was a vampire!" She lifted a hand to her neck. "He bit me! It hurt more than anything . . . not like when you bite me . . ." She frowned. "And then you were there, and . . ." Her eyes widened as her memory returned. "What have you done? Oh, Lord, what have you done!"

"Daisy . . . it's all right."

"No! How could you?"

"You asked me to, don't you remember?"

She shook her head. "No . . . no, I wouldn't. I never wanted . . ." She paused, her gaze sliding away from his as another memory surfaced. Erik's voice, pleading with her. *Don't leave me! Dammit, don't leave me here in the dark without you.* The anguish in his voice had pierced her heart and she had asked him to bring her across, to make her what he was.

She could feel Erik watching her, his gaze wary as he waited for her reaction.

Sitting up, she ran her hands over her arms, her face. She was a vampire now, and there was no going back. She should be furious with him, with herself, yet she couldn't seem to work up any anger, couldn't even decide how she felt about what had happened. She wasn't happy to be a vampire, but she was glad to be alive. Or Undead. She wasn't crazy about the idea of existing on blood, either, she thought, and then she looked at Erik and grinned in spite of herself. At least she wouldn't have to drink alone.

Erik frowned at her. "Is something funny?"

"Not really."

"What are you grinning at?"

"I was thinking how happy I am that I don't have to drink alone."

He stared at her, bemused, and then he laughed.

Daisy laughed with him. She laughed until her sides ached. And then she wept for all she had lost.

At a loss as to what to do, Erik could only sit there. He had never turned anyone before; he had no idea what to expect or how she would react. The main thing he remembered from his first night as a vampire was a horrible thirst, but Daisy didn't seem to be plagued by that, perhaps because, in desperation, he had given her as much of his blood as she could hold.

He swore softly. He yearned to take her in his arms, but wondered if his touch would be welcome. Listening to her cry was the worst pain he had ever known—worse than the touch of the sun, worse than the agony he had suffered in Costain's dungeon. Worse, because he had caused it. Had he done what he'd known to be right, he never would have let things go this far. Instead, he had selfishly sought her out, thinking more of easing his own loneliness than worrying about where their relationship would lead.

With a last sniff, Daisy wiped her eyes and face with a corner of the sheet. "I'm sorry, I . . ."

"Don't apologize. What the hell do you have to be sorry for?"

She blinked at him. "Are you mad at me?"

"What?" He stared at her, completely baffled. "Why would I be mad at you?"

"I don't know."

"Daisy, I . . ." He raked his hand through his hair. "I'm the one who should be asking your forgiveness."

"For what? You didn't do anything wrong. I . . . I asked you to bring me across."

"Yeah." He blew out a breath, remembering how he had begged her not to leave him.

"I knew what I was doing."

"Did you?"

"Of course." She tilted her head to the side. "Are you sorry you brought me over?"

"No." His gaze moved over her face. She had always been beautiful; she was even more so now. Though subtle, changes in her appearance assured that when she called, no man would be able to resist her. "Are *you* sorry?"

"No," she said quickly. How could she be sorry when it meant spending an eternity with the man she loved? "Unless you don't want me anymore."

"Not want you? Are you out of your mind?" He had never been less than confident around women before, but this new Daisy put him off his stride. He had expected her to be angry, to berate him for what he had done; instead, she seemed to be waiting for something, though he had no idea what it might be.

"Erik?"

"Yes, love?"

"Aren't you going to kiss me?"

Was that what she had been waiting for? He blinked at her, and then he smiled. "As you wish," he said. "But I don't think I'll be able to stop at just a kiss."

Eyes twinkling with merriment, she smiled a seductive smile. "Who asked you to?"

Murmuring her name, he wrapped her in his arms. She was his now, he thought as he claimed her lips with his, always and forever his.

Chapter 39

Daisy shook her head as they neared her parents' home. "I don't think I can do this."

"Of course you can," Erik said patiently. "There's nothing to be afraid of."

"Hah! That's easy for you to say." Daisy glared at him. Becoming a vampire hadn't been nearly as awful as she had expected. With Erik to guide her, she had learned to use her preternatural powers until they were almost second nature. Sometimes, she wondered how she had ever existed without them.

Erik had taught her to dissolve into mist, to scurry up the side of a building as easily as a spider, to leap tall buildings, move faster than the human eye could follow. Most importantly, he had taught her the intricacies of hunting, how to attract her prey and call it to her, how to take what she needed without taking too much or doing any lasting harm to her victim. She had resisted the urge to feed as long as she could, certain that she would never be able to do it. Convinced that existing on human blood would be revolting, she had been shocked to find it immensely pleasant and not the least bit repulsive.

But nothing in the last five months had scared her as much as going to Boston to visit her family.

Daisy stared at the front door of her parents' home. Even with the door closed, she could smell their blood, hear the beating of their hearts. "Will they be able to tell that I've changed?"

Erik shook his head. "Not unless you tell them."

She had kept in touch with Alex and her parents. Her mom and dad were still mourning Brandon, of course. To Daisy's surprise, her mother had informed her that Alex was spending a lot of time with Paula O'Reilly.

"I think he's in love with her," Irene had remarked during one conversation. "Perhaps it was inevitable. They started out comforting each other and, well, it looks like Paula might eventually be a part of the family after all."

Daisy was summoning the nerve to knock on the door when she heard footsteps behind her. She didn't have to turn around to know that Alex was coming up the walk, and that he wasn't alone. Paula was with him.

"Hey, sis!"

Slowly, she turned to face him. "Hi, Alex. Paula."

Alex nodded at Erik, then threw his arms around Daisy and gave her a quick hug. "I didn't know you were coming."

"It was kind of spur of the moment," Daisy said. "Paula, I don't think you've met Erik."

Erik extended his hand. "Pleased to meet you, Paula."

"Likewise."

Annoyed with the amenities, Alex opened the door and ushered everyone inside.

The next few minutes were spent on introductions as Erik met Daisy's parents. Even though Daisy knew her mother and father were uncomfortable with having a vampire in the house, they handled his presence better than she had expected. Her mother invited Erik to sit down and soon they were all seated in the living room, with Erik and Daisy on the love seat, Alex, Paula, and Irene on the sofa, and Noah in his favorite chair.

"So, daughter, how was your trip?" Noah asked. "Did you fly or drive?"

Daisy slid a glance at Erik. "We flew." *In a manner of speaking,* she thought, smiling inwardly.

"How'd you get here from the airport?" Alex asked. "I didn't see a rental out front."

"We took a taxi," Daisy said. She didn't like lying to her family, but the truth was out of the question.

"Of course, no need for a car," Noah said, "since you'll be staying here."

"Thanks, Dad, but we're staying at a hotel."

"Now, you know I won't hear of that," Irene said, her hands fluttering. "You can stay in your old room and Erik can . . . can . . ."

"Erik can stay in Brandon's room," Noah finished.

"Thanks, Dad, but we've already made reservations."

"Oh, well, if that's what you want," Irene murmured.

Daisy didn't miss the look of relief in her mother's eyes when she realized Erik wouldn't be staying the night.

"Well," Irene said briskly, "where are my manners? Can I get you all anything? I made a devil's food cake this afternoon."

"Sounds good, Mom," Alex said with a wink.

"None for me, thank you," Erik said.

"Me, either," Daisy said. "We ate just before we got here."

"But, Daisy," Irene said, "it's your favorite."

"I know," Daisy said, smiling. "Maybe later."

"I'll have some of that cake," Noah said, "with a little ice cream on the side. And a cup of coffee."

"Let me help you, Mrs. O'Donnell," Paula said. Rising, she followed Irene into the kitchen.

"You seem a little uptight, daughter," Noah remarked after Irene and Paula left the room. "Is anything wrong?"

"Why should anything be wrong?"

"I don't know." He leaned forward in his chair, his eyes narrowed. "You tell me."

"I'm fine, Dad, just a little, ah, jet-lagged."

"Uh-huh."

Daisy looked at Erik for reassurance. *Should I just tell them the truth?*

It's up to you, love.

"All right, Daisy, spit it out," Alex said. "You're hiding something." He sent a suspicious glance at Erik, and then swore softly. "You didn't. Dammit, you bloodsucker, tell me you didn't!"

Noah looked at Alex, then at Daisy, and then at Erik. "Didn't what?" he asked, and then comprehension dawned in his eyes. "Daisy, no."

She couldn't face the disappointment in her father's eyes, the disgust in Alex's. Sobbing, "I knew this was a bad idea," she fled the house.

When Erik started to follow, Alex stood and blocked his path. "You filthy bloodsucker! How could you?"

"It was her decision."

"I don't believe that for a minute," Alex said, his voice tinged with bitterness.

"Remember Mariah? Well, she had a boyfriend. Damon wasn't very happy about what happened to his lady love. He attacked Daisy. My guess is that you would have been next. Of course, that's neither here nor there. Daisy was dying when I found her. I gave her a choice."

"No." Noah O'Donnell gained his feet and took a menacing step toward Erik. "She would never agree to that."

Erik swore under his breath. Daisy had been right. Coming

here had been a bad idea. Judging by the looks on the faces of Daisy's father and brother, things were about to get really ugly really fast. Unable to think of a safe way to defuse the situation, he was about to dissolve into mist when Daisy materialized beside him.

"Erik's telling the truth," she said, taking his hand in hers. "It was my idea."

The sound of breaking dishes rang out from the kitchen. Before anyone could go see what had happened, Irene appeared in the doorway. Tears cascaded down her cheeks as she murmured, "Oh, Daisy, no."

"I'm sorry, Mom." Daisy tugged on Erik's hand. "Let's go."

"No!" Hurrying across the room, Irene O'Donnell threw her arms around her daughter. "I don't care what you are. All that matters is that you're still here, with us."

"Irene—"

She turned on her husband like a mother grizzly defending her young. "Hush up, Noah Patrick O'Donnell. Would you rather she was gone forever, like Brandon?"

Shoulders sagging, Noah shook his head. "No." Head bowed, he took several deep breaths and then, heaving a sigh, he straightened his shoulders and offered Erik his hand. "Welcome to the family. Son."

With tears in her eyes, Daisy threw her arms around her father. "Thank you, Daddy," she whispered.

Alex snorted softly, and then he, too, offered Erik his hand. "Welcome to the family. Vampire."

Sitting on the edge of the bed in their hotel room, Erik pulled Daisy onto his lap. "I told you everything would be all right."

"All right? Is that what you call all right?"

"Well, at least your old man didn't drive a stake through my heart," he said with a wry grin. "Or yours."

"Very funny."

"They'll get used to the idea. Just give them a little time."

"Strange advice coming from you," Daisy retorted. "You said you left your home and your family after you were turned, and never went back."

"It's not the same thing. I didn't have anybody to show me the ropes when I was turned. No one to tell me I didn't have to kill to survive. I didn't know anything about vampires, and there was no one with me when I woke up that first night, no one to tell me what to expect. All I had was a raging thirst."

Daisy nodded. He was right, of course. She didn't know what she would have done if Erik hadn't been there. He had made her transformation from mortal to vampire almost painless. He had even made a joke the first night he had taken her hunting, asking her what she was in the mood for, Italian, French, or Chinese. She hadn't been amused at the time, but she saw the humor in it now. What couldn't be changed must be accepted. And if you could do it with a smile, so much the better. And looking at Erik always made her smile.

He was watching her, his dark eyes filled with concern, and she loved him the more for it.

"Stop worrying about me. I'm okay."

"You're better than okay, darlin'. You're perfect. And you know what else? I don't think we should let Alex and Paula beat us to the altar."

"What?"

"Marriage, Daisy Mae. I'm asking you to marry me."

She blinked at him. "You want to marry me?"

"Well, I thought I did. But if you don't want to . . ."

"Of course I want to. Now, hush up and kiss me."

Stifling a laugh, he said, "You sound just like your mother.

Maybe we can have a double wedding. Rhys can be the best man."

The very thought made Daisy burst out laughing.

"I love you, Daisy darlin', more than you'll ever know."

Warmth and affection flooded Daisy's heart and soul as she wrapped her arms around him. "And I love you. Only you. All of you."

He knew what she wanted even before she did. Falling back on the bed, he finessed her clothes away, then drew her down on top of him, his hands sliding up and down her bare back.

There were a lot of perks to being a vampire, Daisy mused when he kissed her. All of her physical senses were enhanced, which served to heighten her pleasure when they made love, so that every kiss, every touch, was experienced on a deeper, more sensual level. She slid her hands under Erik's shirt, loving the way his muscles bunched and quivered beneath her fingertips, the latent sense of power that radiated from him. But best of all, he never got tired, and neither did she.

With a heartfelt sigh, she surrendered to the sensual magic of Erik's touch, reveling in each tender kiss, each languid caress.

There was no need to hurry.

Dawn's first light was hours away.

Dear Reader:

I hope you enjoyed the tale of the Blood Thief. I found myself reluctant to see the last of Rhys, and so I decided he should have his own story, which is currently in the works. If he cooperates, and my Muse doesn't let me down, his story should be coming soon.

May God bless you and yours.

Amanda
www.amandaashley.net

If you liked this Amanda Ashley book,
check out some of her other titles
currently available from Zebra . . .

NIGHT'S TOUCH

One Kiss Can Seal Your Fate . . .

Cara DeLongpre wandered into the mysterious Nocturne club looking for a fleeting diversion from her sheltered life. Instead she found a dark, seductive stranger whose touch entices her beyond the safety she's always known and into a heady carnal bliss . . .

A year ago, Vincent Cordova believed that vampires existed only in bad movies and bogeyman stories. That was before a chance encounter left him with unimaginable powers, a hellish thirst, and an aching loneliness he's sure will never end . . . until the night he meets Cara DeLongpre. Cara's beauty and bewitching innocence call to his mind, his heart . . . his blood. For Vincent senses the Dark Gift shared by Cara's parents, and the lurking threat from an ancient and powerful foe. And he knows that the only thing more dangerous than the enemy waiting to seek its vengeance is the secret carried by those Cara trusts the most . . .

NIGHT'S KISS

He Has Found His Soul's Desire . . .

The Dark Gift has brought Roshan DeLongpre a lifetime of bitter loneliness—until, by chance, he comes across a picture of Brenna Flanagan. There is something hauntingly familiar about her, something that compels him to travel into the past, save the beautiful witch from the stake, and bring her safely to his own time. Now, in the modern world, Brenna's seductive innocence and sense of wonder are utterly bewitching the once-weary vampire, blinding him to a growing danger. For there is one whose dark magick is strong . . . one who knows who they both are and won't stop till their powers are his . . . and they are nothing more than shadows through time . . .

NIGHT'S MASTER

Passion Has A Darker Side . . .

Kathy McKenna was sure that the little Midwestern town of Oak Hollow would be isolated enough for safety, but the moment the black-clad stranger walked into her bookstore, she knew she was wrong. Raphael Cordova exudes smoldering power, and his sensual touch draws Kathy into a world of limitless pleasure and unimaginable dangers . . .

Oak Hollow was supposed to be neutral territory for supernatural beings. Instead it has become home to an evil force determined to destroy them—and kill any mortal who gets in the way. As leader of the North American vampires, Raphael has always put duty first, but then, no woman ever enthralled him the way Kathy does. And as the enemy's terrifying plan is revealed, Raphael's desire could be a fatal distraction for all his kind, and for the woman he has sworn to love forever . . .

NIGHT'S PLEASURE

Desire Casts A Dark Spell . . .

Savanah Gentry's life was so much simpler when she was a reporter for the local newspaper. That was before her father's sudden death drew her into a mysterious new world she was just beginning to understand. A vampire hunter by birth, Savanah has been entrusted with a legacy that puts everyone she cares for in danger—including the seductive, sensual vampire who unleashes her most primal desires . . .

Rane Cordova has always been alone, half hating himself for his dark gift even as he relishes its extraordinary power. But one look at Savanah fills him with the need to take everything she has to give and carry her to heights of unimagined ecstasy. And though he never intended their relationship to go this far, now Savanah is in more danger than she knows—and facing a relentless enemy determined to eliminate Rane and all his kind . . .

IMMORTAL SINS

Desire Is The Darkest Magic Of All . . .

Three centuries ago, vampire Jason Rourke succumbed to temptation with a wizard's lovely daughter—and that brief taste of pleasure earned him a powerful curse. Trapped within a painting, unable to quench the hellish thirst that torments him, Jason has given up hope of escape until Karinna Adams purchases the painting and unwittingly frees him . . .

At first, Jason plans only to enlist Kari's help in navigating this strange new world so he can find and punish the wizard who entrapped him. But Kari's enticing sensuality and innocence incite a growing need in Jason to touch and taste her, to possess her utterly. For the gulf between them—and the danger that awaits—is nothing compared to a potent, primal hunger that will last for all eternity . . .

And here's a sneak peek
at the latest from Amanda,
coming in October 2010!

Megan was ringing up a sale for the lead guitarist in a popular rock band when she felt an odd sensation skitter down her spine. Looking up, she felt a nervous flurry in the pit of her stomach when she saw the young man who had come into the shop late last night. Rhys Costain.

Her smile was forced as she bid good night to her customer, then quickly turned away, pretending to check something on the computer, all the while hoping Mr. Parker would come forward to assist their customer.

But Mr. Parker remained in his office, with the door closed.

Megan didn't hear Costain's footsteps come up behind her, but she knew he was there. She could sense his presence, feel the intensity of his gaze on her back as he waited for her to acknowledge him.

Megan took a deep breath, counted to three, and turned around. "Good evening, Mr. Costain," she said coolly. "How may I help you?"

"How, indeed?" he murmured.

His voice was smooth and soft, yet she detected a sharp edge underneath, like satin over steel. "Excuse me?"

"I'm looking for a black leather jacket."

"What length?"

He shrugged, a graceful, unhurried movement. "Mid-thigh?"

"We have a few back here you might like." Without waiting to see if he followed, she walked toward the back of the store. Pulling their most expensive coat from the rack, she held it up. "How about this one?"

He ran his hand lightly over the supple leather.

Watching him, Megan couldn't help imagining that pale, graceful hand stroking her bare skin.

"Do you like it?" he asked.

"Y-yes, very much."

"Do you mind if I try it on?"

"Of course not."

His hand brushed hers as he took the coat from the hanger. His skin was cool, yet a rush of heat flowed through her at his touch.

The coat fit as if it had been made for him, emphasizing his fair hair and broad shoulders.

"What do you think?" he asked.

Not trusting herself to speak, she nodded. What was there about this man that made her feel like a tongue-tied teenager?

She felt her cheeks grow hot when he looked at her and smiled, as if he knew exactly what she was thinking.

"So, you like it?"

Striving for calm, she said, "It looks very nice. There's a mirror over there. See for yourself."

"No need." Still smiling, he turned away, heading for the other side of the store.

Megan felt her blush deepen when he picked up several pairs of silk briefs, all black. Why was she acting so foolish? Men came in here and bought underwear six days a week.

Frowning, she watched him pick up a dozen wife-beater T-shirts before moving to the check-out counter.

Regaining her senses, Megan stepped up to the register. "Are you going to wear the coat?"

With a nod, he removed the price tag and handed it to her.

She quickly rang up the sale, dropped his briefs and T-shirts in a bag, and offered it to him, careful, once again, to avoid his touch.

Again, his lips curved in that knowing smile.

"Good night, Mr. Costain," she said, her voice tight.

"Good night, Miss DeLacey."

The way he said her name made her insides curl with pleasure.

And then she frowned. "How did you know my name?"

He shrugged. "You must have mentioned it."

She stared after him as he left the store. She was certain she hadn't told him her name. The fact that he knew it without being told left her feeling violated somehow.

He returned to the store every night just after midnight for the next week, and he always bought something: a dark pin-striped suit; a dozen dress shirts—black, brown, navy, and dark gray—all silk. He bought four pairs of Armani slacks in varying shades of brown, as well as three pairs of black slacks, two belts, three ties, a pair of black slippers, a black silk dressing gown.

Tonight he picked out a Trafalgar American Alligator wallet priced at five hundred and fifty dollars.

He gave her a long, lingering look that made her insides curl with pleasure before he left the store.

"He's a big spender, that one," Parker said, coming up behind Megan. "I wonder what he does for a living."

"I have no idea."

"Well, I hope he sticks around. We haven't had a week like this since Bono came in to do his Christmas shopping."

Megan nodded, though secretly she hoped that Mr. Rhys Costain would go back to wherever he had come from. His mere presence flustered her, and she didn't like it. She was far past the age to come unglued in the presence of a handsome man, especially when that man was at least ten years younger than she was.

It was close to three A.M. when Megan arrived at the small, two-story house she shared with her best friend, Shirley Mansfield. Shirl was a fashion model, which sounded a lot more glamorous than it was. Being a model involved dedication and self-denial, especially for Shirl, who was older than most of the popular models and had to work harder to keep fit. Of course, as far as anyone in the business knew, she was seven years younger than her actual twenty-eight years. Shirl rose every weekday at six and headed to the gym for a thirty-minute workout. Then she came home, took a shower, and ate a calorie-controlled breakfast. Then she was off to casting appointments and fittings, and because she was extremely popular, more often than not she had a fashion shoot in the afternoon. She didn't usually make it home before five. Of course, the pay was excellent.

Megan didn't see much of Shirl during the week, since Shirl was usually in bed long before Megan got home from work.

After taking a quick shower, she slipped into a pair of comfy pj's and curled up in her favorite chair, determined to read for a few minutes before she went to bed. But she couldn't seem to concentrate on the words. Instead, Rhys Costain's image drifted through her mind. She told herself to forget him. For one thing, he was much too young for her; for another, there was an air of danger about him that scared her on some deep inner level she didn't understand.

With a sigh of resignation, Megan closed the book and set it aside. Tomorrow was Saturday. She didn't have to work Sunday or Monday. If Shirl didn't have anything scheduled for Sunday night, maybe they could get together for dinner and a movie.

Later, lying in bed waiting for sleep to find her, Megan was irritated to find her thoughts again turning toward Rhys Costain. How did he spend his weekends? Was he buying all those new clothes to impress a new girlfriend? Or a new wife?

The thought of him with another woman was oddly disconcerting and she shook it away. She didn't like him. Didn't like the way he made her feel, or the dark thoughts that flitted through her mind whenever he was near.

Flopping over onto her stomach, she pounded her fist against the pillow. She had been spending far too much time thinking about the man.

Yet even as she tried to convince herself that she didn't care if she ever saw him again, a little voice in the back of her mind whispered that she was a liar.

Thrilling Suspense from
Beverly Barton

Available Wherever Books Are Sold!

Visit our website at **www.kensingtonbooks.com**

Romantic Suspense from
Lisa Jackson

See How She Dies	0-8217-7605-3	$6.99US/$9.99CAN
Final Scream	0-8217-7712-2	$7.99US/$10.99CAN
Wishes	0-8217-6309-1	$5.99US/$7.99CAN
Whispers	0-8217-7603-7	$6.99US/$9.99CAN
Twice Kissed	0-8217-6038-6	$5.99US/$7.99CAN
Unspoken	0-8217-6402-0	$6.50US/$8.50CAN
If She Only Knew	0-8217-6708-9	$6.50US/$8.50CAN
Hot Blooded	0-8217-6841-7	$6.99US/$9.99CAN
Cold Blooded	0-8217-6934-0	$6.99US/$9.99CAN
The Night Before	0-8217-6936-7	$6.99US/$9.99CAN
The Morning After	0-8217-7295-3	$6.99US/$9.99CAN
Deep Freeze	0-8217-7296-1	$7.99US/$10.99CAN
Fatal Burn	0-8217-7577-4	$7.99US/$10.99CAN
Shiver	0-8217-7578-2	$7.99US/$10.99CAN
Most Likely to Die	0-8217-7576-6	$7.99US/$10.99CAN
Absolute Fear	0-8217-7936-2	$7.99US/$9.49CAN
Almost Dead	0-8217-7579-0	$7.99US/$10.99CAN
Lost Souls	0-8217-7938-9	$7.99US/$10.99CAN
Left to Die	1-4201-0276-1	$7.99US/$10.99CAN
Wicked Game	1-4201-0338-5	$7.99US/$9.99CAN
Malice	0-8217-7940-0	$7.99US/$9.49CAN

Available Wherever Books Are Sold!
Visit our website at **www.kensingtonbooks.com**